The Midwife's Confession

DIANE CHAMBERLAIN

The Midwife's Confession

MIRA®

Recycling programs
for this product may
not exist in your area.

ISBN-13: 978-0-7783-2986-2

THE MIDWIFE'S CONFESSION

For questions and comments about the quality of this book please contact us
at Customer_eCare@Harlequin.ca.

www.MIRABooks.com

Printed in U.S.A.

First Printing: May 2011
10 9 8 7 6 5 4 3 2 1

In memory of Kay Eleanor Howe
2000–2010

PART ONE

NOELLE

I

Noelle

She sat on the top step of the front porch of her Sunset Park bungalow, leaning against the post, her eyes on the full moon. She would miss all this. The night sky. Spanish moss hanging from the live oaks. September air that felt like satin against her skin. She resisted the pull of her bedroom. The pills. Not yet. She had time. She could sit here all night if she wanted.

Lifting her arm, she outlined the circle of the moon with her fingertip. Felt her eyes burn. *"I love you, world,"* she whispered.

The weight of the secret pressed down on her suddenly, and she dropped her hand to her lap, heavy as a stone. When she'd awakened this morning, she'd had no idea that this would be the day she could no longer carry that weight. As recently as this evening, she'd hummed as she chopped celery and cucumbers and tomatoes for her salad, thinking of the fair-haired preemie born the day before—a fragile little life who needed her help. But when she sat down with her salad in front of the computer, it was as though two beefy, muscular arms reached out from her monitor and pressed their hands down hard on her head, her shoulders, compressing her lungs so that she couldn't pull in a full breath.

The very shape of the letters on her screen clawed at her brain and she knew it was time. She felt no fear—certainly no panic—as she turned off the computer. She left the salad, barely touched, on her desk. No need for it now. No desire for it. She got everything ready; it wasn't difficult. She'd been preparing for this night for a long time. Once all was in order, she came out to the porch to watch the moon and feel the satin air and fill her eyes and lungs and ears with the world one last time. She had no expectation of a change of heart. The relief in her decision was too great, so great that by the time she finally got to her feet, just as the moon slipped behind the trees across the street, she was very nearly smiling.

2

Tara

Going upstairs to call Grace for dinner was becoming a habit. I knew I'd find her sitting at her computer, earbuds in her ears so she couldn't hear me when I tried to call her from the kitchen. Did she do that on purpose? I knocked on her door, then pushed it open a few inches when she didn't answer. She was typing, her attention glued to her monitor. "Dinner's almost ready, Grace," I said. "Please come set the table."

Twitter, our goldendoodle, had been stretched out beneath Grace's bare feet, but at the mention of "dinner" he was instantly at my side. Not so my daughter.

"In a minute," she said. "I have to finish this."

I couldn't see the screen from where I stood, but I was quite sure she was typing an email rather than doing her homework. I knew she was still behind. That was what happened when you taught at your child's high school; you always knew what was going on academically. Grace had been an excellent student and one of the best writers at Hunter High, but that all changed when Sam died in March. Everyone cut her slack during the spring and I was hoping she'd pull it together this fall, but then Cleve broke up with her before he left for college, sending her into a tailspin. At least, I assumed it was the breakup that had pulled her deeper into her shell. How could I really know what was going on with her? She wouldn't talk to me. My daughter had become a mystery. A closed book. I was starting to think of her as the stranger who lived upstairs.

I leaned against the doorjamb and studied my daughter. We had the same light brown hair dusted with the same salon-manufactured blond highlights, but her long, thick mane had the smooth shiny glow that came with being sixteen years old. Somewhere along the way, my chin-length hair had lost its luster.

"I'm making pasta with pesto," I said. "It'll be done in two minutes."

"Is Ian still here?" She kept typing but glanced quickly out the window, where I supposed she could see Ian's Lexus parked on the street.

"He's staying for dinner," I said.

"He might as well move in," she said. "He's here all the time, anyway."

I was shocked. She'd never said a word about Ian's visits before, and he only came over once or twice a week now that Sam's estate was settled. "No, he's not," I said. "And he's been a huge help with all the paperwork, honey. Plus, he has to take over all Daddy's cases and some of his records are here in his home office, so—"

"Whatever." Grace hunched her shoulders up to her ears as she typed as if she could block out my voice that way. She stopped typing for a second, wrinkling her nose at her screen. Then she glanced up at me. "Can you tell Noelle to leave me alone?" she asked.

"Noelle? What do you mean?"

"She's always emailing me. She wants me and Jenny to—"

"Jenny and me."

She rolled her eyes and I cringed. *Stupid, stupid.* I wanted her to talk to me and then I critiqued what she said. "Never mind," I said. "What does she want you and Jenny to do?"

"Make things for her babies-in-need program." She waved her hand toward her monitor. "Now she's on this 'community work will look great on your college applications' kick."

"Well, it will."

"She's such a total whack job." She started typing again, fingers flying. "If you could compare her brain with a normal brain on an MRI, I'm sure they'd look completely different."

I had to smile. Grace might be right. "Well, she brought you into the world and I'll always be grateful for that," I said.

"She never lets me forget it, either."

I heard the timer ringing downstairs. "Dinner's ready," I said. "Come on."

"Two seconds." She got to her feet, bending over the desk, still typing furiously. Suddenly she let out a yelp, hands to her face. She took a step back from the keyboard. "Oh, no," she said. "Oh, *no!*"

"What's the matter?"

"Oh, no," she said again, whispering the words this time as she dropped back into her chair, eyes closed.

"What is it, sweetie?" I started toward her as if I might somehow be able to fix whatever was wrong, but she waved me away.

"It's nothing." She stared at her monitor. "And I'm not hungry."

"You have to eat," I said. "You hardly ever eat dinner with me anymore."

"I'll get some cereal later," she said. "Just…right now, I have to fix something. Okay?" She gave me a look that said our conversation was over, and I backed away, nodding.

"Okay," I said, then added helplessly, "Let me know if there's anything I can do."

"She's having a meltdown," I said to Ian as I walked into the kitchen. "And she's not hungry."

Ian was chopping tomatoes for the salad but he turned to look at me. "Maybe I should go," he said.

"No way." I spooned the pesto-coated rigatoni into my big white pasta bowls. "Someone needs to help me eat all this food. Anyway, it's not you that's keeping her away. It's me. She avoids me all she can." I didn't want Ian to leave. There was comfort in his company. He'd been Sam's law partner and close friend for more than fifteen years and I wanted to be with someone who'd known my husband well and had loved him. Ian had been my rock since Sam's death, handling everything from the cremation to the living trust to managing our investments. How did people survive a devastating loss without an Ian in their lives?

Ian set the bowls of pasta on the kitchen table, then poured himself a glass of wine. "I think she worries I'm trying to take Sam's place," he said. He ran a hand over his thinning blond hair. He was one of those men who would look good bald, but I knew he wasn't happy about that prospect.

"Oh, I don't think so," I said, but I remembered Grace mentioning that he might as well move in. Should I have asked her why she said that? Not that she would have answered me.

I sat down across the table from Ian and slipped the tines of my fork into a tube of rigatoni I didn't really feel like eating. I'd lost twenty pounds since Sam died. "I miss my little Gracie." I bit my lip, looking into Ian's dark eyes behind his glasses. "When she was younger, she'd follow me everywhere around the house. She'd crawl into my lap to cuddle and I'd sing to her and read to her and…" I shrugged. I'd known how to be a good mother to that little girl, but she was long gone.

"I imagine everyone feels that way when their kids become teenagers," Ian said. He had no kids of his own. Forty-five and he'd never even been married, which would be suspect in another man but we'd all just accepted it in Ian. He'd come close long ago—with Noelle—and I didn't think he'd ever quite recovered from the sudden ending of that relationship.

"Sam would have known what to say to her." I heard the frustration in my voice. "I love her so much, but she was Sam's daughter. He was our…our translator. Our intermediary." It was true. Sam and Grace had been two quiet souls with no need to speak to each other to communicate. "You could feel the connection between them when you'd walk into a room where they were sitting, even if one of them was on the computer and the other reading. You could *feel* it."

"You're such a perfectionist, Tara," Ian said. "You have this expectation of yourself that you can be a perfect parent, but there's no such thing."

"You know what they loved to do?" I smiled to myself, stuck in my memory, which was where I was spending a lot of my time lately. "Sometimes I'd have a late meeting and I'd come home and find them sitting in the family room, watching a movie together, drinking some coffee concoction they'd invented."

"Sam and his coffee." Ian laughed. "All day long. He had a cast-iron gut."

"He turned Grace into a caffeine addict by the time she was fourteen." I nibbled a piece of pasta. "She misses him like crazy."

"Me, too," Ian said. He poked at his rigatoni.

"And then to have Cleve break up with her so soon after..." I shook my head. My baby girl was hurting. "I wish she were a little more like me," I said, and then realized that was unfair. "Or that I was a little more like her. I just wish we had something more in common. Some activity we could share, but we're so different. Everyone at school talks about it. The other teachers, I mean. I think they expected her to be into theater, like me."

"I think there's a law there can only be one drama queen in a family," Ian said, and I kicked him beneath the table.

"I'm not a drama queen," I said. "But I've always thought the theater could be so good for her, don't you think? It would get her out of her shell."

"She's just quiet. It's not a crime to be an introvert."

Not a crime, no, but as someone whose need to be with other people bordered on the pathological, I had trouble understanding my daughter's shyness. Grace loathed any social event that involved more than one or two people, while, as my father used to say, "Tara can talk the ears off a stalk of corn."

"Has she mentioned getting her driver's license yet?"

I shook my head. Grace was afraid of driving since Sam died. Even when I drove her someplace, I could feel her tension in the car. "I suggested it a couple of times, but she doesn't want to talk about it," I said. "She would have talked to Sam, though." I slipped my fork into another piece of pasta. Sitting there with Ian, I was suddenly slammed by the reality that could catch me unawares at any moment—in the middle of my classroom, while casting the junior play, while doing the laundry: Sam was never coming back. He and I would never make love again. I'd never again be able to talk to him in bed at night. I'd never again feel his arms around me when I woke up in the morning. He'd not only been my husband but my dearest and oldest friend, and how many women could say that about the man they married?

We were loading the dishwasher when my phone rang, the electronic tones of "All That Jazz" filling the kitchen. I dried my hands and glanced at the caller ID. "It's Emerson," I said to Ian. "Do you mind if I take it?"

"Of course not." Ian was even more addicted to his BlackBerry than I was. He had no room to complain.

"Hey, Em," I said into the phone. "What's up?"

"Have you spoken to Noelle?" Emerson asked. It sounded like she was in her car.

"Are you driving? Do you have your headset on?" I pictured her holding her cell phone to her ear, her long curly brown hair spilling over her hand. "Otherwise, I'm not talking to—"

"Yes, I have it on. Don't worry."

"Good." I'd become überconscientious about using a cell phone in the car since Sam's accident.

"So have you spoken to her in the past couple of days?" Emerson asked.

"Um..." I thought back. "Three days ago, maybe? Why?"

"I'm on my way over there. I haven't been able to reach her. Do you remember her talking about going away or anything?"

I tried to remember my last conversation with Noelle. We'd talked about the big birthday bash she, Emerson and I were planning for Suzanne Johnson, one of the volunteers for Noelle's babies program...and Cleve's mother. The party had been Noelle's idea, but I was overjoyed to have something to keep me busy. "I don't remember her saying anything about a trip," I said.

Ian glanced at me. I was sure he knew who we were talking about.

"Not in a long time," Emerson said.

"You sound worried."

Ian touched my arm, mouthed, "Noelle?" and I nodded.

"I thought she was coming over last night," Emerson said, "but she didn't show. I must have— Hey!" She interrupted herself. "Son of a bitch! Sorry. The car in front of me just stopped for no reason whatsoever."

"Please be careful," I said. "Let's get off."

"No, no. It's fine." I heard her let out her breath. "Anyway, we must have gotten our wires crossed, but now I can't reach her so I thought I'd stop in on my way home from *Hot!*" *Hot!* was the new café Emerson had recently opened down by the waterfront.

"She's probably out collecting baby donations."

"Probably."

It was like Emerson to worry. She was good-hearted and caring, and no one ever described her without using the word *nice*. Jenny was the same way, and I loved that my daughter and the daughter of my best friend were also best friends.

"I'm in Sunset Park now and about to turn onto Noelle's street," Emerson said. "We'll talk later?"

"Tell Noelle I said hi."

"Will do."

I hung up the phone and looked at Ian. "Noelle was supposed to go over Emerson's last night and never showed up, so Em's stopping by her house to make sure everything's okay."

"Ah," he said. "I'm sure she's fine." He looked at his watch. "I'd better go and let you take some food up to Grace." He leaned over to kiss my cheek. "Thanks for dinner, and I'll pick up the rest of Sam's files in a couple of days, all right?"

I watched him leave. I thought about heating up a bowl of the pasta for Grace, but I doubted she'd appreciate it and I frankly didn't want to feel her coolness toward me again that evening. Instead, I started cleaning the granite countertops—a task that I found soothing until I found myself face-to-face with the magnetized picture on the refrigerator of Sam, Grace and myself. We were standing on the Riverwalk on a late-summer evening a little more than a year ago. I leaned back against the island and stared at my little family and wished I could turn back time.

Stop it, I told myself, and I started cleaning the counters again.

I pictured Emerson arriving at Noelle's, giving her my greeting. I talked to Noelle a couple of times a week, but I hadn't seen her in person in a while. Not since she'd shown up at my door on a Saturday evening in late July, when Grace was out with Jenny and Cleve, and I was sorting through Sam's desk in our den. I'd found combing through his desk agonizing. Touching all those things he'd so recently touched himself. I had piles of papers on the floor, neatly stacked. I would give them to Ian, because I couldn't tell if the documents and letters were related to any cases Sam might have been working on. Ian was still having trouble making sense of Sam's files. Sam was sloppy. His desk was a rolltop and we'd had an agreement: he could keep the desk as disorganized as he liked as long as I didn't need to see the mess. I'd give anything to see that mess right now.

I realized only later why Noelle had come that night. She'd known from Emerson that Grace was out with Jenny. She'd known I would be alone, on a Saturday night, when it felt as though everyone in the world was part of a couple except me. The summer was hard, since I didn't have my teaching job to throw myself into and I wasn't involved in any production at the community playhouse. Noelle had known she would find me sad or frustrated or angry—some emotion that made me too vulnerable to be around other people but safe with her. We were all safe with her, and she was always there for us.

I'd slumped in Sam's desk chair while she sat on the love seat and asked me how I was doing. Whenever people asked me that question, I'd answer, "Fine," but it seemed pointless to pretend with Noelle. She would never believe me.

"Everyone's tiptoeing around me like I'm going to fall apart any second," I said.

Noelle had been wearing a long blue-and-green paisley skirt and big hoop earrings and she looked like an auburn-haired Gypsy. She was beautiful in an unconventional way. Pale, nearly translucent skin. Eyes a jarring, electric blue. A quick, wide smile that displayed straight white teeth and a hint of an overbite. She was a few years older than me, and her long curly hair was just beginning to glimmer with the random strand of gray. Emerson and I had known her since our college days, and although she was beautiful in her own pale way, it was the sort of look that most men wouldn't notice. But there were other men—sensitive souls, poets and artists, computer nerds—who would be so mesmerized by her as they passed her on the street that they'd trip over their own feet. I'd seen it happen more than once. Ian had been one of those men, long ago.

That night in my den, Noelle had kicked off her sandals and folded her legs beneath her on the love seat. "Are you?" she asked me. "Are you going to fall apart?"

"Maybe."

She talked to me for a long time, guiding me through the maze of my emotions like a skilled counselor. I talked about my sadness and my loss. About my irrational anger at Sam for leaving me, for putting new lines across my forehead. For turning my future into a question mark.

"Have you thought of finding a widows' support group?" she asked after a while.

I shook my head. The thought of a widows' support group made me shudder. I didn't want to be surrounded by women who felt as bad as I did. I would sink down and never be able to climb up again. There was a floodgate inside me I was afraid of opening.

"Forget the support group idea," Noelle corrected herself. "It's not for you. You're outgoing, but not open." She'd said that to me once before and I was bothered by the description.

"I was open with Sam," I said defensively.

"Yes," she said. "It was easy to be open with Sam." She looked out the window into the darkness as if she was lost in thought and I remembered the eulogy she'd given at Sam's memorial service. *Sam was a champion listener,* she'd said.

Oh, yes.

"I miss talking to him." I looked at the stack of papers on the floor. The battery-operated stapler on his desk. His checkbook. Four pads of Post-it notes. I shrugged. "I just miss *him,*" I said.

Noelle nodded. "You and Sam... I hesitate to use the

term *soul mates* because it's trite and I don't think I believe in it. But you had an exceptional marriage. He was devoted to you."

I touched his computer keyboard. The *E* and *D* keys were worn and shiny, the letters faint. I ran my fingertips over the smooth plastic.

"You can still talk to Sam, you know," Noelle said.

"Pardon?" I laughed.

"Don't tell me you don't. When you're alone, I bet you do. It would be so natural to say, 'Damn it, Sam! Why did you have to leave me?'"

I looked at the keyboard again, afraid of the floodgates. "I honestly don't," I lied.

"You could, though. You could tell him what you're feeling."

"Why?" I felt annoyed. Noelle loved to push her agenda. "What possible purpose could it serve?"

"Well, you never know if he can get your communication on some level."

"Actually, I do know that he can't." I folded my arms across my chest and swiveled the chair in her direction. "Scientifically, he can't."

"Science is making new discoveries all the time."

I couldn't tell her how, when I ate breakfast or drove to school, I'd sometimes hear his voice as clearly as if he were sitting next to me and wonder if he was trying to contact me. I'd have long, out-loud conversations with him when no one else was around. I loved the feeling of him being nearby. I didn't believe people could reach out from the other side, but what if they could and he was trying and I ignored him? Yet I felt crazy when I talked to him, and I was so afraid of feeling crazy.

"You've always been afraid of having psychiatric problems

like your mother," Noelle said, as if she'd read my mind. She could spook me that way. "I think it's your biggest fear, but you're one of the sanest people I know." She got to her feet, taking in a deep breath as she stretched her arms high over her head. "Your mother had a chemical thing," she said, letting her long, slender arms fall to her sides again. "You don't. You won't, ever."

"The floodgates..." I looked up at her from the desk chair. I didn't want her to leave. "I'm afraid of opening them."

"You won't drown," she said. "Drowning isn't part of your makeup." She bent low to hug me. "I love you," she said, "and I'm a phone call away."

I'd polished the granite countertop until the ceiling lights glowed on its surface. Then I dared to look at the photograph of Sam, Grace and me on the refrigerator again. Noelle had helped me sort through so much on that hot, miserable July night, yet one emotion still remained unchecked inside me: fear that I was failing my daughter.

Grace stood between Sam and me in the picture, smiling, and only someone very observant might notice how she leaned toward Sam and away from me. He'd left me alone with a child I didn't know how to mother. A child I longed to know, but who wouldn't let me in. A child who blamed me for everything.

He left me alone with the stranger upstairs.

3

Emerson

Noelle's junker of a car sat in her driveway and I pulled in behind it. The light was fading, but I could still read all of her bumper stickers: Coexist, No Wetlands=No Seafood, Cape Fear River Watch, Got Tofu?, Bring Back My Midwives! Noelle's passions—and she had plenty—were spelled out across the dented rear of her car for all the world to see. Good ol' boys would pull up next to her at stoplights and pretend to shoot her with their cocked fingers, and she'd give them her one-fingered salute in return. That was Noelle for you.

She'd given up midwifery a year or so ago when she decided to focus on the babies program, even though it meant she'd have to live on her savings. At the same time, the ob-gyn offices in the area were making noise about letting their midwives go, so Noelle figured it was time to get out, though it must have felt like she was hacking off her right arm. Noelle needed ten lives to do all the things she wanted to do. She would never be able to fix the world to her liking with just one.

Ted and I had stopped charging her rent for the house

even though between the teetering economy and the start-up costs of *Hot!* we weren't exactly ready to put a kid through college. Ted had bought the dilapidated 1940s Craftsman bungalow shortly before we were married. I'd thought it was a lamebrain idea, even though the seller was practically giving it away. It looked like no one had taken care of the place since 1940, except to fill the front yard with a broken grill, a couple of bicycle tires, a toilet and a few other odds and ends. Ted was a Realtor, though, and his crystal ball told him that Sunset Park was on the brink of a renaissance. The ball had been right...eventually. The area was finally turning around, although Noelle's bungalow was still a pretty sorry sight. The grill and toilet were gone, but the shrubs were near death's door. We'd have to do a major overhaul on the place if she ever moved out, but we'd make a good profit at that point, so letting her live there for the cost of her utilities wasn't that much of a hardship.

Ted wasn't thrilled about the "no-rent for Noelle" idea in the beginning. He was feeding money into my café at the time and we were both biting our nails over that. I'd wanted to open a café for years. I fantasized about people lining up for my cooking and baking the way some women fantasized about finding Matthew McConaughey in their beds. The good news was that *Hot!* was already holding its own. I had a following among the locals downtown and even had to hire extra help during the tourist season. So Ted had come around, both about the café and Noelle's rent-free existence on our property.

From Noelle's weedy driveway, I could see the left-hand corner of the backyard where she'd planted her garden. She wasn't much for fixing up the house and the rest of the landscaping was in ruins, but years ago she'd surprised us by planting a small masterpiece of a garden in that one corner. It became one of her many obsessions. She researched the plants so that something was blooming nearly year-round. A sculptor friend of hers made the birdbath that stood in the center of the garden and it was like something out of a museum. It was your typical stone birdbath, but next to it, a little barefoot girl in bronze stood on her tiptoes to reach over the lip and touch the water. Her dress and hair fanned out behind her as if she'd been caught in a breeze. People knew about the birdbath. A couple of reporters wanted to take pictures of it and write articles about the sculptor, but Noelle never let them. She was afraid someone would try to steal it. Noelle would give away everything she owned to help someone else, but she didn't want anyone messing with her garden. She watered and mulched and pruned and loved that little piece of land. She took care of it the way other women took care of their kids and husbands.

The bungalow was a peeling, faded blue, like the knees of your oldest pair of jeans, and the color looked a little sick in the red glow of the sunset. As I walked up the crumbling sidewalk to the front porch, I saw a couple of envelopes sticking out of the mailbox next to the door, and even though the air was warm, a chill ran up my spine. Something wasn't right. Noelle was supposed to come over for dinner the night before and bring fabric for Jenny, who was actually sewing blankets for the babies program, much to my shock. That wasn't the sort of thing Noelle would forget to do. It bothered me that she hadn't answered my messages. I'd left her one the night before saying, "We're going to go ahead and eat. I'll keep a plate warm for you." I left the next one around ten: "Just checking on you. I thought you were coming over but I must have misunderstood. Let me know you're okay." And finally, one more this morning: "Noelle?

I haven't heard back from you. Is everything all right? Love you." She hadn't gotten back to me, and as I climbed the steps to the porch, I couldn't shake a sense of dread.

I rang the bell and heard the sound of it coming through the thin glass of the windowpanes. I knocked, then tried the door, but it was locked. I had a key for the house somewhere at home but hadn't thought to bring it with me.

I walked down the steps and followed the walkway through the skinny side yard to the back door. Her back porch light was on and I tried the door. Also locked. Through the window next to the door, I saw Noelle's purse on the battered old kitchen table. She was never without that purse. It was enormous, one of those shapeless reddish-brown leather shoulder bags you could cram half your life into. I remembered Noelle pulling toys from it for Jenny back when she was still a toddler—that's how long she'd had it. Noelle and that bag were always together. Auburn hair, auburn bag. If the purse was here, Noelle was here.

I knocked hard on the window. "Noelle!"

"Miss Emerson?"

I turned to see a girl, maybe ten years old, walking across the yard toward me. We were losing daylight fast, and it took me a minute to see the cat in her arms.

"Are you...?" I glanced at the house next door. An African-American family lived there with three or four kids. I'd met them all but I was terrible with names.

"I'm Libby," the girl said. "Are you lookin' for Miss Noelle, 'cause she had to go away all of a sudden last night."

I smiled with relief. She'd gone away. It made no sense that her purse and car were there, but I'd figure that out eventually. Libby had put one foot on the porch step and the light fell on the calico cat in her arms. I leaned closer. "Is that Patches?" I asked.

"Yes, ma'am. Miss Noelle asked me to take care of her at my house this time."

"Where did she go?"

"She didn't say. Mama says it was wrong for her not to tell me." She scratched the top of Patches' head. "I take care of Patches sometimes but always in Miss Noelle's house. So Mama thinks this time Miss Noelle meant she was going away for a long time like she does sometimes, but it was wrong she didn't say when she was coming back and she ain't answering her cell phone."

What the hell was going on?

"Do you have a key to the house, Libby?" I asked.

"I ain't got one, ma'am, but I know where she keeps it. I'm the only one that knows."

"Show me, please."

Libby led me across the lawn toward the little garden, our shadows stretching long and skinny in front of us. She walked straight to the birdbath and bent down to pick up a rock near the little bronze girl's feet.

"She keeps it under this rock," Libby whispered, handing me the key.

"Thanks," I said, and we headed back to the door. At the steps, I stopped. Inside, I'd find a clue to where Noelle had gone. Something that would tell me why she hadn't taken her giant bag with her. Or her car. That ominous feeling I'd had earlier was filling me up again and I turned to the girl. "You go home, honey," I said. "Take Patches back to your house, please. I'll try to figure out what's going on and come tell you, all right?"

"Okay." She turned on her heel, slowly, as though she

wasn't sure she should trust me with the key. I watched her walk across the yard to her own house.

The key was caked with dirt and I wiped it off on my T-shirt, a sure sign I didn't care about a thing except finding out what was going on with Noelle. I unlocked the door and walked into the kitchen. "Noelle?" I shut the door behind me, turning the lock because I was starting to feel paranoid. Her purse lay like a floppy pile of leather on the table and her car keys were on the counter between the sink and the stove. Patches' food and water bowls were upside down on the counter on top of a dish towel. The sink was clean and empty. The kitchen was way too neat. Noelle could mess up a room just by passing through it.

I walked into the postage stamp of a living room, past the crammed bookshelves and the old TV Tara and Sam had given her a few years ago when they bought their big screen. Past the threadbare brown sofa. A couple of strollers sat on the floor in front of the TV and three car seats were piled on top of some cartons, which were most likely filled with baby things. More boxes teetered on top of an armchair. I was definitely in Noelle's world. On the wall above the sofa were framed pictures of Jenny and Grace, along with an old black-and-white photo of Noelle's mother standing in front of a garden gate. Seeing the photographs of the children next to the one of her mother always touched me, knowing that Noelle considered Tara's and my girls her family.

I walked past the first of the two bedrooms, the one she used as her office. Like the living room, it was bursting with boxes and bags and her desk was littered with papers and books...and a big salad bowl filled with lettuce and tomatoes.

"Noelle?" The silence in the house was creeping me out. *A slip in the shower?* But why would she have told Libby to take care of Patches? I reached her bedroom and through the open door, I saw her. She lay on her back, her hands folded across her rib cage, still and quiet as though she were meditating, but her waxen face and the line of pill bottles on the night table told me something different. My breath caught somewhere behind my breastbone and I couldn't move. I wasn't getting it. I refused to get it. *Impossible,* I thought. *This is impossible.*

"Noelle?" I took one tiny step into the room as if I were testing the temperature of water in a pool. Then reality hit me all at once and I rushed forward. I grabbed her shoulder and shook her hard. Her hair spilled over my hand like it was alive, but it was the only living thing about her. "No, no, no!" I shouted. "Noelle! No! Don't do this! Please!"

I grabbed one of the empty pill bottles but none of the words on the label registered in my mind. I wanted to *kill* that bottle. I threw it across the room, then dropped to my knees at the side of the bed. I pressed Noelle's cold hand between mine.

"Noelle," I whispered. *"Why?"*

It's amazing what you can miss when you're an emotional wreck. The note was right next to me on her night table. I'd had to reach past it to use her cell phone to call for help. The phone had been inches from her hands. She could have called me or Tara. Could have said, "I just did something stupid. Come and save me." But she didn't. She hadn't wanted to be saved.

The police and emergency team poured into the room, taking up all the air and space and blurring into a sea of blue and gray in front of me. I sat on the straight-backed chair someone had brought in from the kitchen, still holding Noelle's hand as the EMTs pronounced her dead and we waited for the medical examiner to arrive. I answered the questions volleyed at me by the police. I knew Officer Whittaker personally. He came into *Hot!* early every morning. He was the raspberry-cream-cheese croissant and banana-walnut muffin, heated. I'd fill his mug with my strongest coffee, then watch him dump five packets of sugar into it.

"Did you call your husband, ma'am?" he asked. He always called me *ma'am,* no matter how many times I asked him to call me Emerson. He moved around Noelle's claustrophobic bedroom, gazing at another framed photograph of her mother on the wall, touching the spine of a book on the small bookcase beneath the window and studying the pincushion on her dresser as though it might give him an answer to what had happened here.

"I did." I'd called Ted before everyone had arrived. He was showing a property and I had to leave a message. He hadn't received it yet. If he had, he would have called the second he heard me stumbling over my words as if I were having a stroke.

"Who's her next of kin?" Officer Whittaker asked.

Oh, no. I thought of Noelle's mother. Ted would have to call her for me. I couldn't do it. I just couldn't and neither could Tara. "Her mother," I whispered. "She's in her eighties and...frail. She lives in an assisted-living community in Charlotte."

"Did you see this?" Officer Whittaker picked up the small piece of paper from Noelle's night table with gloved fingers. He held it out for me to read.

Emerson and Tara, I'm sorry. Please look after my garden for me and make sure my mother is cared for. I love all of you.

"Oh." I squeezed my eyes shut. *"Oh, no."* The note made it real. Until that second, I'd managed to avoid thinking the word *suicide*. Now there it was, the letters a mile high inside my head.

"Is it her handwriting?" Officer Whittaker asked.

I opened my eyes to slits as if I couldn't stand to see the entire note again, all at once. The sloppy slope of the letters would be nearly illegible to someone else, but I knew it well. I nodded.

"Was she depressed, ma'am? Did you have any idea?"

I shook my head. "No. Not at *all*." I looked up at him. "She loved her work. She would never have… Could she have been sick and not told us? Or could someone have killed her and made it look like suicide?" I looked at the note again. At all the pill bottles. I could see Noelle's name on the labels. One of the EMTs noticed that some of the prescriptions had been filled the month before, but others dated back many years. Had she been stockpiling them?

"Did she talk about her health lately?" Officer Whittaker asked. "Doctors' appointments?"

I rubbed my forehead, trying to wake up my memory. "She injured her back in a car accident a long time ago, but she hasn't complained about pain from it in years," I said. We'd worried about all the medication she was taking back then, but that had been so long ago. "She would have told us if something was wrong." I sounded sure of myself, and Officer Whittaker rested a gentle hand on my shoulder.

"Sometimes people keep things bottled inside them, ma'am," he said. "Even the people we're closest to. We can never really know them."

I looked at Noelle's face. So beautiful, but an empty shell. Noelle was no longer there and I felt as though I'd already forgotten her smile. *This makes no sense,* I thought. She'd had so much she still wanted to do.

I needed to call Tara. I couldn't handle this alone. Tara and I would figure out what to do. We'd piece together what had happened. Between us, we knew everything there was to know about Noelle.

Yet in front of me lay the evidence—our gone-forever friend—that we really knew nothing at all.

4

Noelle

Robeson County, North Carolina
1979

She was a night person. It was as if she were unable to let go of the day, and she'd stay up into the early hours of the morning, reading or—her mother didn't know this—walking around outside, sometimes lying in the old hammock, trying to peer through the lacy network of tree branches to find the stars beyond. She'd been a night person all thirteen years of her life. Her mother said it was because she'd been born exactly at the stroke of midnight, which caused her to confuse day and night. Noelle liked to think it was because she was one-eighth Lumbee Indian. She imagined the Lumbees had had to stay alert at night to fend off their enemies. She was also part Dutch and one-eighth Jewish, according to her mother, and she liked shocking her classmates with that element of her heritage, which struck them as exotic for rural North Carolina. But her mother sometimes made things up, and Noelle had learned to pick and choose the parts of the story she wanted to believe.

She was reading *The Lord of the Rings* in bed late one summer night when she heard the rapid-fire crunch of footsteps on the gravel driveway. Someone was running toward the house and she turned out her light to peer through the open window. The full moon illuminated a bicycle lying in the driveway, its tires and handlebars askew as though some nor'easter had tossed it there.

"Midwife?" a male voice yelled, and Noelle heard pounding on the front door. *"Midwife?"*

Noelle pulled on her shorts and tucked her tank top into the waistband as she rushed into the pine-paneled living room.

"Mama?" she shouted toward her mother's room as she headed for the door. "Mama! Get up!"

She flipped on the porch light and pulled opened the door. A black boy stood there, his eyes huge and frightened. His fist was in the air as he readied it to pound the door again. Noelle recognized him. James somebody. He was a few years older than her—maybe fifteen?—and he used to go to her school, though she hadn't seen him this past year. He'd been a quiet, shy boy and she once overheard a teacher say there was hope for him, that he might end up graduating. Maybe even going to college. You couldn't say that about too many of the kids in her school, black or white or Lumbee. But then he'd disappeared and Noelle hadn't given him another thought. Not until right now.

"Get your mama!" He was all wired up and looked like he might try to rush past her into the house. "She a midwife, right?"

"Maybe," Noelle hedged. People weren't supposed to know about her mother. Everybody did, of course, but Noelle wasn't supposed to say it straight out like that.

"What you mean, 'maybe'?" James pushed her shoulder,

nearly knocking her off balance, but she didn't feel afraid. *He* was the one who was scared. Scared and panicky enough to give her a shove.

"Get your hands off her!" Her mother swept into the living room, pulling a robe around her shoulders. "What do you think you're doing? Shut the door, Noelle!" She grabbed the door and tried to push it closed but Noelle hung on tight to the knob.

"He says he needs a midwife," she said, and her mother stopped pushing the door and looked at the boy.

"You do?" She sounded as if she didn't quite believe him.

"Yes, ma'am." He looked contrite now, and Noelle could see his body shaking with the effort of being polite when what he really wanted to do was shout and beg. "My sister. She havin' a baby and we ain't got—"

"You live in that house on the creek?" Her mother squinted past him as though she could see his house through the dark woods.

"Yes'm," he said. "Can you come now?"

"Our car's not running," her mother said. "Did you call the rescue squad?"

"We ain't got no phone," he said.

"Is your mother with her?"

"*Nobody's* with her!" He stomped his foot like an impatient little kid. "Please, ma'am. Please come!"

Her mother turned to Noelle. "You call the rescue squad while I get some clothes on. And you come with me tonight. I might need you."

She'd never invited Noelle to go out on a call with her before, but this whole situation was different than the usual. This was the first time a neighbor had come knocking at two in the morning. Sometimes there'd be a phone call in the middle of the night. Noelle would hear her mother leave the house and she'd know she'd be on her own for making breakfast and getting ready for school. Her mother would probably be back by the time she got home in the afternoon, but she'd be quiet about whatever had gone on. Noelle didn't really care. She was more interested in reading than she was in how her mother spent her time.

Her mother was ancient—fifty-two years old—and her mousy brown hair was streaked with gray. She had wrinkles around her eyes and on her throat. She was much older than the mothers of Noelle's classmates and people often thought she was her grandmother. Her friends' mothers painted their carefully shaped fingernails. They wore lipstick and went to the beauty parlor in Lumberton to get their hair done. Noelle was embarrassed by her mother's age and unconventional demeanor. But as she dialed the rescue squad and did her best to explain to the dispatcher where James lived, she had the strangest feeling that her perception of her mother was about to change.

She hadn't known her mother could run. They jogged down the dirt road behind James's bike. Even carrying her blue canvas bag of supplies, her mother was outpacing her. The air was heavy with the smell of the river, and Spanish moss hung from the cypress trees lining the road. They turned onto the lane that bordered the creek and some of the moss brushed Noelle's shoulders. When she was little, her mother told her that a Lumbee Indian chief's wife had disobeyed him, so he chopped off her hair and tossed it over the branch of a tree, where it grew and multiplied and soon began covering the branches of all the neighboring trees. What that had to do with Spain, Noelle didn't know, but she loved imagining that the Indian chief's wife might have been one of her long-lost ancestors.

Noelle and her mother followed James around the last bend in the lane. Moonlight flickered on the peeling white paint of the tiny shack, but they heard the screams even before the house came into view. The voice sounded more animal than human, and it cut through the dank air like a sword. The screams made her mother run even faster while Noelle slowed her own pace, a little unnerved. Birth wasn't completely foreign to her—she'd seen their cat give birth to kittens—but she'd never heard anything like those screams.

"Where *are* your parents?" her mother asked as James tossed his bike to the ground.

"Ma's up to Lumberton," he said over his shoulder. He grabbed the knob of the beat-up front door and turned it. "Her sister took sick."

He didn't mention his father and Noelle's mother didn't ask. They raced into the house, which was no more than two squat little rooms. The first was kind of a kitchen and living room together, with a couch at one end and a sink and stove and half-size refrigerator at the other. Noelle's mother didn't seem to notice the room, though. She followed the wailing to the second room, where a girl, slim as a reed except for the giant globe of her belly, lay on her back in a double bed. She could only have been a couple of years older than Noelle, and she was naked from the waist down, her green T-shirt hiked up to her breasts. Her knees were bent and the place between her legs bulged with something huge and dark.

"Oh, my stars, you're crowning already!" her mother said. She turned to James. "Fill every pot and pan in the house with water and set it to boil!" she commanded.

"Yes, ma'am!" James disappeared from the room, but Noelle stood frozen, mesmerized by what was happening to the girl's body. It couldn't be normal, could it? It looked and sounded like she was being torn apart.

"All right, darling." Her mother began pulling things out of her bag as she spoke to the girl. "Do *not* push. I know you feel like pushing, but don't push yet, all right? I'm going to help you and everything's going to be fine."

"Not...fine!" the girl yelled. "I don't want no baby!"

"Well, you're going to have one in just a few minutes, regardless." Noelle's mother turned to her. "Find me every clean towel and piece of linen that's in this house," she said as she wrapped her blood pressure cuff around the girl's thin arm. "Then wet a cloth with some of that water the boy's heating up and bring it to me."

Noelle nodded and began searching in the narrow bedroom closet, grabbing the neatly folded towels and sheets and pillowcases from the shelves. In the other room, she found James trembling over water-filled pots on the stove.

"I need to dip one of these in warm water." Noelle pointed to the pots. "Which one's warmest?"

"This one, maybe." He nodded toward the one closest to her and she dipped the washcloth into the water, then wrung it out in the sink and carried it back to the bedroom.

Her mother partly unfolded one of the sheets and slid it under the girl's bottom. Then she took the warm washcloth and held it to the bizarrely stretched skin that circled the baby's head. Noelle leaned down to whisper in her mother's ear, "Is this normal?" She pointed between the girl's legs and her mother brushed her hand away.

"Completely normal," her mother said out loud, and Noelle knew she was trying to reassure the girl at the same time she answered the question. "Why don't you go help the boy?" she suggested.

Noelle shook her head. "I want to stay here."

"Then get a chair." She nodded toward the girl. "Let her hold your hand."

Noelle dragged a straight-backed chair from the living room to the side of the bed. The girl was gripping the edge of the mattress with her fist, and Noelle awkwardly pried her fingers loose and then pressed them around her own hand. The girl squeezed her fingers hard. Tears ran down the sides of her face and tiny dots of perspiration covered her forehead. Her skin was lighter than James's, and even with her face contorted with pain, Noelle could see how pretty she was. And how scared.

She reached forward, wiping the girl's tears away with her fingertips. "What's your name?" she asked.

"Bea," the girl whispered. "I'm dyin', ain't I? This baby goin' kill me?"

Noelle shook her head. "No," she said. "My mother—"

Bea interrupted her with another scream. "I'm splittin' apart!" she yelled.

"No woman's ever split apart, darlin'," Noelle's mother said, "and you're stretching just like you're meant to do."

"My thing's burnin' up!" Bea said. She let go of Noelle's hand to reach between her legs. Her eyes widened as she touched whatever was down there out of Noelle's line of sight. "Lord Jesus!" Bea said. "Lord Jesus, save me!"

"Yes, Lord Jesus," Noelle's Jewish-Lumbee-Dutch mother said with a laugh, probably using those words together for the first time in her life. "Your Lord Jesus is right here with you, darlin', if you need him to be." She lifted her head. "Noelle, you want to see this baby come into the world?"

Noelle stood and walked to the end of the bed. The dark circle had grown even larger and she held her breath, wondering how her mother was going to get that baby out of skinny little Bea. All of a sudden, Bea let out a yelp and the dark haired, dusky-skinned head popped from her body.

Noelle gasped with amazement.

"Beautiful!" her mother said. "You're doing beautifully." She held her hands above and below the baby's head, not touching it, not touching Bea, just holding her hands there as if supporting the head in midair by magic. The baby's head turned to the side and Noelle could see its tiny face, all scrunched up as if this being-born business was as much work for him or her as it was for Bea. Suddenly, the little squinty eyes and blood-streaked lips blurred in front of Noelle's face and she realized that for no reason she could name she was crying.

All at once, the baby slipped from Bea's body into her mother's hands.

"A precious boy!" Her mother wrapped the squawking infant in a towel and rested him on Bea's belly, the movement so quick and easy that Noelle knew she'd done it hundreds of times before.

"I don't want this baby," Bea moaned, but she was lifting the corner of the towel, touching the damp hair of her son.

"We'll see about that," her mother said. "Right now we have a little more work to do down here."

Noelle watched as her mother cut the cord and delivered the placenta, answering her questions and explaining everything she was doing. Her mother was not the same woman who made their dinner each night, who cleaned their house and fed the chickens and grew tomatoes and mowed their scrawny lawn. In that room filled with animal cries and sweat and blood and air too thick to breathe, her mother became someone else—someone mysterious, part sage, part magician. She was beautiful. Every line in her face. Every gray thread in her hair. Every swollen knuckle in the hands that had brought the baby into the world with such ease and grace. Noelle knew in that moment that she wanted to be like her. She wanted to be *exactly* like her.

The rescue squad came way too late to be of much use, and the atmosphere suddenly shifted in the little house. There were pointed questions. Shiny medical equipment. Sharp needles and bags of liquid hanging from poles. A stretcher on wheels.

Bea was afraid. "Don't be." Noelle's mother squeezed her hand as two of the men in uniforms moved her from the bed to the stretcher. "You did a perfect job. You'll be fine."

"You deliver the baby?" one of the men asked her mother.

"She a midwife," James said, and the rescuer raised his eyebrows.

"Just a neighbor, helping out," Noelle's mother said quickly. A few years earlier, she'd spent several days in jail for midwifing and Noelle knew she didn't plan to go again. Daddy's girlfriend, Doreen, had stayed over while her mother was gone. Doreen was a maid, her father had explained to her. Noelle might have been only nine years old but she wasn't stupid. Her father eventually divorced her mother and married Doreen. Noelle hated that woman. Doreen had stolen her father. Stolen her mother's husband. "Don't ever hurt another woman the way Doreen hurt me," her mother said to her later. "Just don't ever." And Noelle swore up and down that she never would and she thought for sure that she was telling the truth.

★ ★ ★

It was nearly dawn by the time they walked home. Their pace was slow and easy, and for a while neither of them spoke. The buzz of the cicadas had given way to a peaceful quiet that enveloped them in the darkness. Every once in a while, Noelle could hear the call of a bird from deep in the woods. She loved that sound. She'd hear that same bird sometimes when she wandered outside in the middle of the night.

They turned from the lane onto the dirt road that led to their house. "How did you know how to do all that?" Noelle asked.

"My mama," her mother said. "And she learned it all from her mama. There's no big mystery to it, Noelle. Doctors today would like you to think that there is. They make you think you need drugs and C-sections—that's surgery that cuts the baby out of you—and all sorts of sophisticated interventions to have a baby. And sometimes you do. A good midwife needs to know when it's safe for a woman to have a baby at home and when it's not. But it's not rocket science."

"I want to do it."

"Do what? Have a baby?"

"Be a midwife. Like you."

Her mother put her arm around Noelle's shoulders and hugged her close. "Then I want you to do it the right way," she said. "The legal way, so you don't have to hide your light under a bushel like I do."

"What's the legal way?"

"You become a nurse first," she said. "I never took that step. I don't think it's necessary. Harmful even, because they indoctrinate you with the idea that more is better when it comes to having babies. But North Carolina's got its laws and you need to do it legally. I'm not having a daughter of mine spending time in jail."

Noelle thought back to Bea's steamy little room where her mother had done nothing but good. "That Bea girl," Noelle said. "She's only a couple of years older than me. If I had a baby, I'd want it. I don't understand not wanting your own baby."

Her mother didn't say anything right away. "Sometimes not keeping a baby is the loving choice," she said. "Sometimes you know you don't have the money or the support to give a baby a good chance in life and then letting the baby go to a good family is the right thing. That girl—" her mother drew in a long breath "—she'll have to decide for herself. The baby being black makes it harder to find adoptive parents for it, so I do hope she decides to keep it and maybe her mama can help out with it. But fifteen is just plain too young. So do me a favor and don't get pregnant until you're a lot older than that."

"Don't worry. I don't even want to kiss a boy, much less make a baby with one."

"That'll change." Her mother was smiling. Noelle could hear it in her voice.

The sky was beginning to pink up with the sunrise. The dirt road was visible now beneath their feet, and ahead of them Noelle could make out the corner of their house beyond the woods.

"There's something I need to tell you, Noelle," her mother said suddenly, her voice so different it might have been another woman speaking. "It's something I should have told you long ago, but with your father leaving and everything…it just seemed like too much of a burden to give you."

Noelle felt the muscles tighten in her chest.

"What, Mama?" she asked.

"Let's sit out in the yard while the sun comes up," her mother said. "I'll make some tea and we'll have a good talk."

Noelle slowed her footsteps as they turned into the gravel driveway, not sure she wanted to hear whatever it was that made her mother sound so strange and different. She couldn't shake the feeling that she'd left the house that night as one person, but would be returning to it as another.

She was right.

5

Tara

Wilmington, North Carolina
2010

It seemed like only a few weeks since I'd sat in this same church for Sam's memorial service, and I'd had to force myself to come today. Emerson and I had planned the service in a daze. Em had asked me if I wanted to sing, which I did occasionally at weddings or receptions, but I'd said absolutely not. As I listened to one of my fellow choir members sing Fauré's *Pie Jesu* in her beautiful soprano, I was glad I'd passed. My voice would never have made it past the lump in my throat. Not here, where the memories of Sam's service still hung in the air of the church. And not now, when I still couldn't believe our Noelle was gone.

Noelle's mother sat to my left. I hadn't seen her in about a year, and at eighty-four she was showing the early signs of dementia. She'd forgotten my name, although she remembered Emerson's and even Jenny's, and she certainly understood that Noelle was gone. Sitting next to me, she pressed one crippled fist to her lips and shook her head over and over again as if she couldn't believe what was happening. I understood the feeling.

Grace sat on my right next to Jenny, Emerson and Ted, twirling a strand of her long hair around her index finger the way she did when she was anxious. She'd pleaded to stay home. "I know it's hard," I'd said to her that morning. I'd sat on the edge of her bed where she had cocooned herself beneath her sheet. Her blue-and-green polka-dotted comforter lay in a heap on the floor and I had to stop myself from picking it up and folding it neatly on the end of the bed. "I know it reminds you of going to Daddy's memorial service, but we need to be there to honor Noelle's memory," I said. "She loved you and she's been so good to you. We need to be there for her mother. Remember how important it was to have people come to Daddy's service?"

She didn't respond and the hillock her head formed beneath the sheet didn't move. At least she was listening. I *hoped* she was listening. "It wasn't for *Daddy* that people came," I continued. "It was for *us,* so that we'd feel their love and support and for people to be able to share memories about—"

"All *right!*" She snapped the sheet from her head and pushed past me out of the bed, her hair a tangled mane down her back. "Do you ever stop talking?" she said over her shoulder. I didn't criticize her for her rudeness. I was too afraid of pushing her even further away.

I noticed now that Grace was clasping Jenny's hand between them on the pew and I was glad to see her comfort her best friend that way. Jenny looked even paler than usual. She'd already lost the little bit of tan she'd gotten over the summer, while Grace's skin still had a caramel glow. Jenny had inherited Emerson's too-fair skin and Ted's thin dark hair, which she wore in a sweep across her forehead that nearly covered her left eye. She was cute and I loved her to pieces, but to my biased eyes, she nearly disappeared next to Grace. When I saw them together at school, I couldn't help but notice the way the boys reacted to them. They would approach Grace and Jenny with their eyes glued to my daughter…until they all started talking. Then it was as though a magnet pulled them toward Jenny and my quiet child became invisible.

But Cleve had chosen Grace, not Jenny. Cleve was a handsome boy, the son of a white mother—Suzanne— and a black father, with killer blue eyes and a smile that could nearly make *me* weak in the knees, and I knew Grace thought she'd found The One. Now Jenny was seeing a boy named Devon, and Grace had to be feeling very alone. Father gone. Boyfriend gone. One inadequate mother remaining.

Ian sat in the pew behind us. He'd been the one to tell Emerson and me about Noelle's will. He'd known of its existence for months because he found it while going through Sam's files, but of course he'd said nothing to me about it and I'm sure he never expected it would be needed so soon. The will was fairly recent, written only a couple of months before Sam's death. I was frankly surprised that Noelle had drawn up a will at all; she was never the most organized person. But I was even more surprised that she'd turned to Sam for it. True, she'd known Sam as long as she'd known me and they'd always been good friends despite a rough patch now and then. But the contents of the will were such that she'd had to have been uncomfortable talking to him about it, and I'm sure he felt a little awkward hearing her wishes.

In her will, Noelle had named Emerson her executor. I felt hurt when Ian told me. I couldn't help it. Emerson,

Noelle and I had always been very close. A threesome. I'd
sometimes felt a little left out but I'd convinced myself it
was my imagination. Noelle's choice of executor told me
I'd been right all along. Not that anyone would *want* the
work involved in being an executor, yet I couldn't help but
wonder why Noelle didn't have us share the job. Did Sam
even think to suggest that to her?

More telling, though, was the division of her assets. She'd
lived simply, but she'd managed to save a little more than
fifty thousand dollars over the years. She wanted Emerson to be sure her mother's needs were met first. If there
was money left over, it was to be put in trusts for Jenny
and Grace in a seventy-five/twenty-five percent split, with
Jenny getting the larger sum. How did Sam feel as Noelle
made it clear that she favored Ted and Emerson's daughter
over his own? I knew the division was fair. It was right.
Jenny had helped Noelle with the babies program and she
seemed to appreciate Noelle in a way that Grace did not.
The money itself didn't matter. It was the jolt to my solar
plexus, the realization that the friendship between Emerson, Noelle and myself had been more lopsided than I'd
imagined.

Also in her will, Noelle had requested that Suzanne take
over the babies program if she was willing, which she was.
Suzanne sat in the pew behind us next to Ian. Her big fiftieth birthday party was right around the corner and now
I wondered if we should cancel it. Long ago, she'd worked
as a doula with Noelle and they'd been friends ever since,
through Suzanne's divorce and two bouts with cancer. After
this last time, her hair grew in curly and full and snow-
white. When I greeted her before the service, I noticed how
healthy she looked. Her huge round blue eyes always made
me think of an awestruck little girl and it was hard to look

at her without smiling, even in the days when she was sick and bald from chemo. Those eyes would hold you captive.

I'd imagined that all the women who had been Noelle's patients would have turned out for this service, but when I glanced over my shoulder I saw that the small church was less than half-full. I put my arm around Noelle's mother, willing her not to look behind us. I didn't want her to see that the people Noelle had touched had not cared enough to come.

The mayor was giving the eulogy and I tried to pay attention. He was talking about how they'd tried to give Noelle the Governor's Award for Voluntary Service for her babies program and she'd refused to accept it. So like Noelle, I thought. None of us had really been surprised. Noelle didn't think helping others should be treated as anything special.

I felt a tremor run through her mother's body as we listened to the mayor and I tightened my arm around her shoulders. At Sam's funeral, I'd sat with my arm around Grace. We'd been like two blocks of wood that day. Her shoulders had felt stiff and hard and my arm had simply gone numb—so numb that I'd had to pry it from her shoulders with my other hand. I remembered sitting so close to her that day, the length of our bodies touching. Now there was nearly a foot of space between us on the pew, nearly two inches of distance for every month Sam had been gone. Too much space for me to reach across. I couldn't put my arm around her now if I tried.

I wondered if, like me, Grace thought about the what-ifs. What if Sam had left the house five seconds later? The three of us had been rushing around the kitchen as we always did in the morning, not talking much, Sam pouring coffee into the hideous striped purple travel mug Grace had given him for his birthday years ago, Grace scrambling to find a book she'd mislaid, me straightening up behind them both. Sam forgot the mug when he raced out the door. I'd glanced at it on the counter, but figured he'd already pulled out of the driveway by then. What if I'd run out the front door with it? Would he have seen me? Then he would never have stopped at Port City Java for his coffee. He never would have been crossing the Monkey Junction intersection at exactly the wrong moment. Would he be sitting next to me right now if I'd tried to catch him?

If, if, if.

To my right, Emerson was sniffling, and the tissue wadded up in my hand was damp with my own tears. Emerson glanced at me and tried to smile, and I wished Grace and Jenny had not been between us so I could touch her arm. Emerson and I were a mess. When it came to Noelle's suicide, the what-ifs that tormented us were huge and haunting. Maybe there really *had* been something we could have done to change the course of things for Noelle. Noelle had killed herself. Much different than the freakish collision of two cars at an intersection. Much more preventable if one of us had only seen the symptoms. Yet what symptoms had there been? Noelle committing suicide made no sense. She'd always been so life *embracing*. Had we missed an emptiness in her? I wondered. She'd never married after breaking off her engagement to Ian years ago and she'd delivered baby after baby with no babies of her own. She'd seemed content in her choices, but maybe she'd put on a game face for all of us. I remembered Noelle comforting me as I grieved for Sam that Saturday night in July. I'd thought only of myself. What small, telltale ache had I missed in her that night?

I'd known Noelle since my freshman year in college and

I had thousands upon thousands of memories of her since that time. Yet the one that would always stand out in my mind was the night she helped me give birth to Grace. Sam had agreed to a home birth only reluctantly, and frankly, if the midwife had been anyone other than Noelle, I wouldn't have felt comfortable about it myself. I had total confidence in her, but Sam was afraid we were taking unnecessary risks, and the truth was, things did not go smoothly.

Noelle had been coolheaded, though. There are people whose presence alone can lower your blood pressure. Slow your breathing. Keep you centered. That was Noelle. *I'll take care of you,* she told me that night, and I believed her. How many women had heard those words from her over the years? I'd known they were the truth. The lamp she'd aimed between my legs lit up her electric-blue eyes, and her wild hair had been pulled back from her face, damp tendrils of it clinging to her forehead. In the lamplight, her hair glowed nearly red. She'd walked me around the moonlit room. She gave me brandy and strange teas that tasted like earth. She turned me in odd positions that, given my big belly and shivering legs, made me feel like a contortionist. She had me stand with one foot on the kitchen stool she'd dragged into the bedroom and told me to rock my hips this way and that. I'd cried and moaned and leaned against her and my worried husband. My teeth had chattered even though the room was very warm. I'd hated feeling so out of control, but I'd had no choice but to turn myself over to Noelle. I would do anything she said, drink any brew she gave me. I trusted her more than I trusted myself, and when she finally said something about calling an ambulance, I thought, *If Noelle says we should, then I guess we should.*

But she never did call for help and the rest of the night became a blur of pain to me. I woke up in the darkness to find Sam sitting next to our bed, a fuzzy silhouette against the lamplight. For a moment I didn't know where I was. My body ached and I felt raw and empty.

"You're a mom, Tara." He smoothed his fingers over my cheek. "You're an amazing, brave and beautiful mom." I couldn't see his face, but his voice held a smile.

"Am I in the hospital?" All that I could force from my throat was a whisper. I had no voice. My mouth felt dry and scratchy.

"No, Tara. You're here. You're home. Noelle pulled it off. She thought for a while she might need to take you to the hospital, but she was able to turn the baby." He smoothed my hair, held his hand against my cheek. I smelled soap.

"My mouth." I licked my dry lips. "Feels like sand."

Sam chuckled. "Cinders." He held a glass toward me, guided the straw to my lips, and I felt the scratchiness ease as I sipped.

"Cinders?" Had I misunderstood him?

"You passed out after the baby was born. Noelle cut off some of my hair—" he touched the dark hair above his forehead "—and burned it and put the cinders beneath your tongue to bring you back."

My head spun a little. "Did it work?" I asked.

He nodded. "I'm sorry everything was so hard on you, but our baby's beautiful, Tara. You held her. Do you remember?"

All at once, I recalled the mewing cry of my daughter as I reached for her. I remembered the soft flannel-wrapped weight of her in my arms. The tug at my nipple. The memories were dreamlike and I wished I could recapture every minute detail.

"Where is she? I want to see her." I looked past him toward the bassinet near the window.

"Noelle has her in the kitchen doing some midwifey thing to her. I told her I thought you were waking up and she said she'd bring her in." Suddenly, he leaned toward me, resting his cheek against mine. "I thought I was going to lose you," he said. "Lose both of you. I was so scared. I thought we'd made a terrible mistake, trying to have the baby here at home. But Noelle...no obstetrician could have done a better job. We owe her everything. She was so good, Tara."

I felt the heat of his cheek, the stickiness of his damp skin against my own, and I rested my hand on the side of his face. "The baby's name..." I whispered. We'd felt so certain the baby would be a boy, another Samuel Vincent, that we'd never settled on a girl's name. Grace, Sara, Hannah had all risen to the top, but we hadn't made a firm decision. "Noelle?" I suggested now.

He lifted his cheek from mine. For a moment, I thought I saw a flash of doubt cross his face, but then he smiled. Nodded.

"Here she is." Noelle walked into the room carrying the tiny bundle. "Your mama's waiting for you, darlin'." She leaned her head close to the bundle and I felt a hunger unlike anything I'd ever known. If I could have leaped out of the bed to grab my child I would have, but I held out my arms and let Noelle settle the baby into them.

Sam tipped his forehead to mine and we stared into the face of our daughter. I slipped the tiny yellow hat from her head to reveal light brown hair. Her cheeks were round and rosy, her eyebrows smudged pale crescents. She blinked her eyes open and looked at us blindly but with interest, as though she'd been waiting to see us as anxiously as we'd been waiting to see her, and I felt my own eyes fill at the miracle in my arms. I couldn't tear my gaze from her, but

Sam lifted his head to look at Noelle. She sat, a small smile on her lips, at the foot of the bed.

"We're going to name her Noelle," he said.

I looked up in time to see the smile leave her face. "Oh, no, you're not." She made it sound like a warning.

"Yes," I said. "We want to."

Even without my contacts, I could see the sudden rise of color in Noelle's cheeks.

"Please don't," she said. "Promise me you won't saddle this child with my name."

"Okay," Sam and I said together, quickly, because clearly we'd caused her distress. I didn't understand. Did she hate her name? I'd always thought it was a pretty name, lyrical and strong. For whatever reason, though, the thought upset her. It didn't matter. We'd pick another name, a beautiful name for our beautiful little daughter.

Now, sitting in the church next to the daughter born that night, I remembered my closeness with that daughter. Physical. Emotional. Spiritual. It had blossomed between us so easily in those early years. How did that closeness turn into this unbearable distance? Was there any hope of ever getting it back?

6

Emerson

God, I felt like a zombie. The reception after the service was in my own house, but I could hardly find my way around the rooms. Faces and voices blended together into a jumble of sight and sound. Nearly everyone was wearing black except me. I had on my favorite green blouse and the green-and-tan floral skirt that was getting too tight in the waist. Just plucked them out of the closet that morning without thinking. Noelle would have hated all the black, anyway.

I was only vaguely aware of what was happening: Jenny and Grace going upstairs to escape the adults; the caterer Tara'd hired floating through the rooms with trays of bruschetta and shrimp; Ted keeping an eye on me from wherever he was. He knew I was a wreck. I was glad that Noelle's mother had left with her aide after the service. I didn't think I could bear to see any more of her sorrow.

Tara was doing her social-butterfly thing, but for the most part she stayed close to my side. Ted and Ian were holding their little plates and talking in the corner of the living room, probably about sports. I still hadn't adjusted to seeing the guys together without Sam. Now Noelle was gone, too. Not only that, but my grandfather's nursing home had called that morning to tell me they were moving my beloved grandpa into hospice. I was losing everyone. Nothing was going to feel right again for a long time.

A few volunteers from Noelle's babies program had come over. I knew most of them, though not well. I tried to make small talk with everyone, nodding, smiling, shaking hands. People said nice things about Noelle. Nobody said, "Why did she do it?" At least, not to me. They asked me how the café was doing and I answered with my usual "Great! Stop in sometime!" But I heard their voices and my own through a thick fog. I kept searching the room for the one person who was missing: Noelle. When I'd catch myself looking for her, my body would suddenly jerk back to reality. I was losing my mind.

An hour into the reception—an hour that felt more like three—Tara finally pulled me away from a woman who was going on and on about knitting baby clothes. "Break time," she said in my ear.

I let her guide me through the living room and out to the sunroom we'd added on the year before. Tara took me by the shoulders and lowered me to the sofa, then plunked down on an ottoman in front of me. The voices from the living room were a hum through the closed sunroom door. They sounded wonderfully far away. I looked at Tara. "Thank you," I said. "I was drowning out there."

Tara nodded. "I know. It's hard."

I scrunched up my face. "I keep looking for Noelle," I admitted. "That's insane, isn't it? I mean, seriously, I'm not joking. I keep expecting her to walk through the door."

"Me, too," Tara said. "I *still* think I see Sam sometimes. I thought I saw him in the grocery store the other day. And there was a guy driving down Water Street and I almost turned the car around to follow him."

"I don't get why there weren't more people at the service," I said. The turnout—or lack of turnout—hurt me. "I honestly thought there'd be...that every mother whose baby she delivered..." I shook my head. "You know the kind of relationship she had with her moms. That closeness. I thought they'd all come."

"I know." Tara rubbed my hand where it rested on my thigh. "I thought the same thing, but maybe they didn't see the article in the paper." She'd written the piece about Noelle and she'd done a great job with it. A bit of melodrama in her description of Noelle, but that was Tara.

"Word would have gotten around, though, article or not," I said.

"They're probably so busy with their families," Tara said.

I suddenly pounded my fist on my thigh. "I just don't understand why she did it!" I sounded like a broken record. "What did we miss? What did *I* miss? How did we fail her?"

Tara shook her head. "I wish I knew." She massaged her forehead. "It wasn't financial trouble, right? She had that money socked away, so that couldn't have been it."

"She didn't give a damn about money, anyway," I said. "You know that."

"I keep thinking maybe she was sick and didn't tell us," Tara said. "She didn't have insurance and maybe suicide seemed like her only way out. Has the final autopsy report come back yet?"

"Not yet. I don't think she was sick, Tara, I really don't. I'm sure the report's going to show a massive dose of tranquilizers and narcotics and that's it."

Tara leaned back on the ottoman. "She was terrible at asking for help," she said.

"Or showing weakness," I added. "She always had to be the strong one."

The sunroom door opened a few inches and a woman poked her head into the room. "Is one of you Emerson?" she asked.

"I am." I wanted to get to my feet, but my body had other ideas and I stayed rooted to the sofa.

The woman crossed the room like a drill sergeant, all sharp edges and quick movements, jutting her hand toward me for a shake. I actually recoiled. I felt like a balloon she could pop if I let her get too close. "I'm Gloria Massey," she said. She was in her mid-sixties, with short, no-nonsense gray hair. Khaki pants. Navy blue blazer.

Tara stood from the ottoman and offered it to her and the woman sat down in front of me, her knees pointy knobs beneath her pants. *Gloria Massey.* Her name was familiar, but God only knew why. I glanced at Tara, frowning, and I could tell she was trying to place her, too. Both our minds were mush. She seemed to figure that out.

"I'm an obstetrician with Forest Glen Birth Center," she said. "Noelle used to be a midwife in our practice."

"Oh, right." I gestured toward Tara. "This is Tara Vincent. We were Noelle's closest friends."

"Yes, I remember," Gloria said. "You went to UNCW with her, right?"

Tara nodded. "She was a few years ahead of us, but yes, we did."

"Well, I'm sorry to get here so late," Gloria said. "I had a delivery this morning so I missed the service, but I wanted to be sure to see you two and tell you how sorry I was to hear about Noelle. She was one of a kind."

"Thank you," I said.

"I hadn't seen her in…oh, it must be ten years now, but she's the sort of person you never forget."

Ten years? "Maybe I have you mixed up with someone else," I said. "I thought she left your practice just a little over a year ago."

Gloria Massey raised her eyebrows in surprise. "No," she said. "I was actually confused by the article in the paper. It said she left us a couple of years ago, but it's really been at least ten. Probably more like twelve. I'd have to think. It was around the time she started that babies-in-need program."

I frowned, trying to remember. "I thought she'd worked with you all these years." I looked at Tara. "Am I that out of it? Wasn't she affiliated with Forest Glen right up until her retirement?"

Tara nodded. "I referred someone to her there just a couple of years ago," she said.

"Well, we always had requests for her, that's true," Gloria said, "but we referred them on to the other midwife working with us."

"So where was Noelle working, then?" I asked. "I'm confused."

"I…" Gloria looked from me to Tara. "I'm quite sure she quit midwifery altogether when she left us," she said. "I would have known if she'd gone to another practice."

Both of us stared at her. I felt like I was slipping into a long dark tunnel. I didn't think I could handle learning one more thing that didn't fit with what I knew about Noelle. My brain hurt. I wanted to shout to the universe, "Noelle was not a big mystery! Stop trying to make her into one!"

"I think," I said to Gloria, "for some reason, she didn't want you to know she'd gone someplace else."

With her sharp little machinelike gestures, Gloria pulled her cell phone from the purse slung over her shoulder. "Hold on." She quickly dialed a number. "Laurie, it's me," she said. "Do you recall when Noelle Downie left us?" She nodded, looked at me and repeated what she was hearing, "Twelve years as of December 1," she said. "This is my office manager on the phone and she says she remembers the date because it was the day her husband asked for a divorce. Which he didn't get and it's all patched up now, right, Laurie?" She smiled into the phone, while my mind scrambled to take in this bizarre information.

"Where did she go?" Tara asked.

"Did she go somewhere else?" Gloria asked her office manager. She nodded again. "Uh-huh. That's what I thought. Okay, thanks. I'll be in a little later." She dropped her phone back in her purse. "Noelle let her certification lapse after she left us," she said.

"What?" I said. "No way!"

"That doesn't make any sense at all." Tara dropped down next to me on the sofa.

"Maybe this Laurie person has her mixed up with one of your other midwives," I suggested.

Gloria shook her head. "I don't think so." She looked straight at me and I could practically *hear* her thinking what a shitty friend I was for not knowing what Noelle was up to. "I remember there being talk about it and everyone saying she just wanted to focus on the babies program," Gloria said. "I know she was having a lot of back pain. I remember that. One of the other practices tried to get her to join them when they realized she'd left us, but she told them she was out of the business."

"But she's been delivering babies all this time!" I said.

"That's true," Tara agreed. "She's been practicing as a midwife."

"Are you sure?" Gloria tipped her head to one side. "Under whose supervision?"

I looked at Tara, who shook her head. "I don't know," she said.

"She'd tell me she was with a patient sometimes," I said, but I spoke slowly, suddenly unsure about what I was saying. Unsure about everything. Did she tell me that? I pressed my fingers to my temples. "Twelve *years?* This is ludicrous!" As far as I knew, Noelle had had three passions for the past twelve years: her local midwifery practice, the babies program and what she called her "rural work." Every couple of years she'd spend a few months in an impoverished rural area volunteering her skills as a midwife. She grew up in an area like that and it was her way of giving back. Could twelve years of Noelle's life have slipped past without us knowing what was really going on with her?

"I *know* I heard her mention her patients," Tara said. If I was crazy, Tara was, too.

"I'm so sorry." Gloria stood. "I've upset you both and that was the last thing I meant to do when I came here." She leaned down to give me a quick, soulless hug, then another one to Tara. "I need to run," she said. "Again, please accept my condolences. This is such a loss to the whole community."

She left the room and Tara and I sat in quiet confusion for a moment. My gaze blurred on the sunroom door.

Tara rubbed my back. "There's an explanation for this," she said.

"Oh, there's an explanation, all right," I said. "And I know exactly what it is. I hate it, but we have to accept it."

"What are you talking about?" she asked.

"The explanation is that we never really knew Noelle." I looked at Tara, determination suddenly taking the place of my confusion. "We have to figure out why she died, Tara," I said. "One way or another, we need to get to know her now."

7

Noelle

Robeson County, North Carolina
1984

Her mother stood in the middle of their living room, look-ing around with a worried sigh. "I hate to leave you with this mess," she said. "The timing of this is all wrong."

"You're making too much out of it, Mama," Noelle said as she ushered her mother toward the door. "Everything's going to be fine."

Her mother looked through the open doorway to the two cars in the gravel drive. Her old Ford stood next to Noelle's "new" car—a dented, faded Chevy she'd picked up for six hundred dollars. The weather was threatening to storm and a hot wind blew through the treetops.

"Everything's changing so fast," her mother said.

"For the better." Noelle gave her a little shove toward the door. "It's not like you ever loved living here."

Her mother laughed. "That's the truth." She touched her daughter's cheek. "It's being apart from you. That's the change I can't stand."

"I'll miss you, too," Noelle said. She would. But she had her future spread out in front of her and that would make up for any sense of loss she felt over being apart from her mother and leaving the house she'd grown up in. "I'm going to see you in a couple of days," she added. "It's not like this is goodbye."

Her mother's car was packed to the gills for the short trip to New Bern but not everything would fit, so Noelle had promised to bring the rest of her things to her in a few days. Then she'd have to turn around and come home to pick up her own belongings and head to UNC Wilmington.

"Remember, Miss Wilson has a spare room you can stay in on vacations."

"I'll remember," Noelle said, not sure she'd ever want to stay in the house of a stranger, even if her mother would be there. Miss Wilson was the elderly sister of one of her mother's friends. She'd broken her hip and needed a live-in aide and was hiring Noelle's mother for the job. With Noelle going off to college on a full scholarship, the timing was right to sell the house. They'd sold it nearly overnight to a young couple from Raleigh who were looking for a place in the country. It had all happened fast. They'd donated their old furniture, but there was so much left to do.

"I love you, honey." Her mother pulled her into a hug, then stood back and tried to smooth Noelle's unsmoothable hair.

"I love you, too." She gave her mother a gentle shove through the doorway. "Drive safely."

"You, too."

Arms folded tightly across her chest, Noelle watched her mother's car crunch down the gravel drive to the dirt road. She felt so much love for her mother that her eyes filled as the car disappeared around the bend. Fifty-eight years old now, her mother was. She was active, vibrant, full of life. Yet fifty-eight seemed so old to Noelle and it worried her. Her father had died two years earlier at fifty-seven. She'd learned about it in a stilted letter from Doreen. The letter arrived nearly a month after his death with a check for four hundred dollars, made out to Noelle. "He didn't have a will," Doreen wrote, "but I thought Noelle should get something from his estate." His estate. The word made Noelle and her mother laugh for hours, the sort of laughter that was borne of hurt and pain. But the four hundred dollars had helped her buy the car, which she named Pops, and she hoped it would treat her better than her father ever had.

Aside from Noelle's trimmed-down belongings and the boxes she had to transport to Miss Wilson's, the only other thing left in the house was an old recliner. James was borrowing a truck to take it to his house. After the night that Bea's baby was born, James became a fixture around their house, mowing their lawn at first out of gratitude but later for the few dollars Noelle's mother insisted on paying him. That family had been full of surprises. As it turned out, James wasn't Bea's brother, but her boyfriend and the father of the baby she had that night. That baby was now five years old and he already had two younger brothers, both "caught" by Noelle's mother, as she would say, with Noelle as her assistant. Noelle's mother had tried to persuade Bea and James to practice birth control, but her pleas had fallen on deaf ears. Bea, it turned out, liked being a mother and she doted on her kids.

Noelle was carting boxes to her car when James showed up with his truck.

"Hey, Miss Noelle," he said as he hopped out of the cab, "did I miss your mama?"

"She took off an hour ago." Noelle heaved a box into the cramped trunk of her car.

"What we gonna do without her?" he asked.

"You and Bea better stop having babies, that's what."

James grinned. He'd grown into a handsome man and he had the sort of grin that made you grin back. "Too late for that," he said.

Noelle put her hands on her hips and stared at him. "Again? What are you going to do with all these kids?"

James shrugged. "Love 'em up," he said.

People have a right to make their own choices, Noelle, her mother had told her when Noelle complained the last time Bea announced she was pregnant.

"Well," Noelle said now, "let me help you carry that recliner out to your truck."

It took them nearly half an hour to carry the recliner through the tight doorway of the house, across the windy yard and into the truck. Then James helped her with the rest of her mother's cartons.

She was walking from the car toward the house to pick up another box, when she saw James suddenly drop one of the cartons to the grass, his arms flung out in the air.

"Girl!" He nudged the box with the toe of his shoe. "Where these boxes been? They got spider shit all over 'em."

Noelle hadn't noticed, but he was right. Round egg sacs hung from the corners and cottony webs crisscrossed the untaped flaps.

"Leave it there, James," she said. "Nothing's alive, I don't think, but I don't want to drag these filthy things into that Miss Wilson's house. Let me get a rag and I'll clean them up."

"You got some tape?" James squatted down next to the

box. "I'll check inside a couple to make sure they ain't no infestation or nothin'."

Finding a rag in the cleaned-out kitchen was easier said than done, and Noelle finally resorted to pulling one of her washcloths from her suitcase. She dampened it under the tap and headed back to the front yard.

By the time she reached James and the box, he was on his feet, a manila folder in his hands. He looked at her from behind a frown.

"Was you adopted?" he asked.

She froze. How would he know that? She'd only found out herself the night Bea's first baby was born, when her mother finally told her the truth. They'd sat together on the hammock in the backyard while her mother apologized for not telling her sooner. "You had a right to know way before now," she'd said, "but I didn't want you to think that you being adopted had anything to do with Daddy leaving."

Noelle had felt stunned, like a huge void opened up inside her. "My mother?" she'd asked. "Who were my real mother and father?"

"Your father and I are your real parents," her mother said sharply. "But your *biological* mother was a fifteen-year-old girl like that one we just left. Like Bea. Your father..." She'd shrugged. "I don't think anybody knew who your father was."

"I'm not yours," Noelle said, trying on the fit of the words.

"Oh, you're mine, honey. Please don't ever say that again."

"I'm not part Lumbee?" She felt the magic drain out of her. The Spanish moss hanging above the hammock suddenly looked like nothing more than Spanish moss, not the hair of an Indian chief's wife.

"I believe you're a mishmash. A little of this and a little of that." Her mother had taken her hand and held it on her lap. "What you are," she said, "is the best thing that ever happened to me."

Now, Noelle looked at James. "Yes, I'm adopted," she said, as though the fact meant nothing to her. "But how did you know?"

He handed the folder to her. "Some papers fell out of this thing in the wind," he said. "Ain't nothin' to me," he said. "But maybe mean somethin' to you."

His soft brown eyes told her he'd seen something he shouldn't have seen. Something she'd never been meant to see, either. And when he gave it to her, he touched her hand. Not like a man would touch a woman. It was the touch of a friend who knew that the papers in that folder just might change her world forever.

8

Tara

Wilmington, North Carolina
2010

Oh, God, this felt strange.

I sat across the table from Ian at the Pilot House, wondering if I was on a date. It had seemed casual enough yesterday when he said he had two tickets for a film at Thalian Hall. Then he suggested we grab something to eat first, and when you put dinner on the waterfront together with a film at a place as nice as the renovated Thalian Hall, what else could it be but a date? I liked Ian. I'd known him for so long and in some ways I could honestly say I adored him, but I didn't want to date him. I didn't want to date anyone. The thought of kissing or even holding hands with someone other than Sam made me shudder—and not with desire. It was actually repellent. I felt a deep, deep loneliness in my bed at night, but it wasn't for just any man. It was for my husband.

"This isn't a date, is it?" I asked Ian after the waiter had poured my second glass of wine.

Ian laughed. "Not if you don't want it to be," he said.

"Were you thinking it was? Is?" I was smiling. I liked that I could talk easily to Ian. I needed a male friend much more than I needed a lover.

"I was just thinking it would be good to see you smile," Ian said, "like you are right now."

The moment he said that, I felt my smile disappear. There was something I needed to tell him. I'd planned to wait until tomorrow so that tonight we could both relax and unwind. Suddenly, though, I knew I wasn't going to be able to keep my mouth shut.

After school that afternoon, I'd driven to Noelle's to help Emerson start cleaning out the house. Emerson had been waiting for me on the porch, and as soon as I'd reached the top step she grabbed my hand and sat down with me on the glider. Her face was red and gleamed with perspiration, and I knew she'd already been hard at work inside the house. But the stress in her face was from more than physical labor.

"You're not going to believe the autopsy report," she said.

"She was sick," I said. I wanted that to be the case. A terminal illness that Noelle could see no escape from. I could envision her making the choice to end her life then, not wanting to put any of us through a long drawn-out illness with her.

But that wasn't it at all.

Now I looked across the table at Ian. "Noelle had a baby," I said.

He stared at me, then laughed. "What are you talking about?"

"Emerson got the autopsy report today. Cause of death was the overdose, as we'd expected. But the autopsy showed that, sometime in her life, she'd been pregnant and given birth."

All signs of levity left Ian's face. *"When?"*

"I don't know." I hesitated for just a moment, then asked, "Could it have been yours, Ian?"

He looked jarred by the thought. I was certain we were both remembering back to the abrupt end to his and Noelle's engagement. Was there a connection?

"I don't see how," he said. "I—*all* of us—would have noticed if she'd been pregnant. Especially pregnant enough to actually give birth."

"It must have happened when she was a teenager, then," I said. "Before any of us knew her. Emerson and I figure that she relinquished the baby for adoption. Maybe she's been dealing with sadness from that experience all these years and none of us knew."

"Well," Ian said, "maybe you're right or maybe the baby died or... I guess we'll never know. I just...I thought I knew her so well back when we were together. Why didn't she tell me?"

"Why didn't she tell Emerson or me?" I added. "Her best friends?" I looked down at my plate where a few bites of flounder remained. I wasn't sure I could finish it. "Anyhow, it probably has nothing to do with why she killed herself," I said.

"Unless it's something she never got over." He looked miserable.

"I'm sorry I brought this up tonight. I should have kept my mouth shut."

"No, I'm glad you told me," he said.

I ate another bite of flounder without really tasting it. I was tired. Emerson and I had packed up everything in Noelle's kitchen, filling boxes with items Ted would take to the women's shelter. There wasn't much. Noelle had pared down her life. She'd never been a pack rat, but I'd been surprised at how empty her kitchen cabinets had been. A few plates. A few glasses and cups and bowls. Nothing extraneous. Her dresser and closet had been the same way, stripped down to the necessities. It had been hard to see her familiar old long skirts and loose cotton blouses, knowing we'd never see Noelle in them again. Then there were the black garbage bags filled with baby items that had been all over the house. Ted and Emerson piled the bags into their car to take home with them, where Grace and Jenny promised to organize the mess and turn it over to Suzanne.

I'd been shocked when Grace told me she planned to help out with the babies program as Noelle had requested. Emerson had given her Noelle's old sewing machine and shown her how to hem the little blankets that were part of the layettes donated to sick or needy infants. When Grace told me what she was up to, I put my hand on her forehead as if checking for fever. "Are you all right?" I'd smiled. Wrong move.

She'd jerked her head away from my hand. "I'm fine," she said. "Don't make a big production out of it."

I doubted she'd be one of the volunteers who delivered the layettes to the hospital. Ever since Sam's accident, she'd been nearly phobic of hospitals. She'd told me that if I ever needed hospitalization, she wouldn't visit me. She wouldn't even visit *Cleve* in the hospital, she'd said. I blamed myself. When we reached the emergency room after Sam's accident, I plowed through the treatment room doors in a panic with Grace close on my heels. Even I couldn't bear to remember what we saw in that room—Sam's beautiful face, bloodied and torn apart. Grace had fainted, dropping to the floor behind me like a stone.

"So," Ian said, "did you find anything at Noelle's that seemed...out of the ordinary?"

I shook my head. "Emerson had to examine everything she touched for clues," I said. "She thinks something in that house is going to tell us why she killed herself or what happened to her child or why she lied to us about being a midwife."

Noelle and *midwife*. The words went together like *milk* and *cookies*. "Midwife" defined who she was in my mind. In *all* of our minds. Hadn't at least one of us introduced her as a midwife over the past decade and hadn't she said nothing to correct us? It was bizarre.

Ian tapped his fingertip against the base of his empty wineglass. "Noelle..." He shook his head. "It was impossible to know what was going on with her sometimes."

I felt sorry for him. I knew how much he'd once loved her. "It must have been so hard on you when she broke off the engagement."

"Oh, God, Tara." He brushed the comment aside. "It was so long ago. Another lifetime ago."

"I don't remember you getting angry. I think most men would have been furious."

"I was more worried about her than angry," he said. Then he shifted in his chair and smiled again. "Let's lighten up, okay. Let's not talk about Noelle or Sam or anything sad for the rest of the night."

"Perfect," I agreed.

"So—" he cut a plump scallop in half on his plate "—when's the last time you actually went *out* to a movie instead of watching a rental at home?"

I thought back through the recent months, then wrinkled my nose. "Not since Sam," I said.

He laughed. "Okay, let me try that again." He looked up

at the ceiling as if searching there for a safe topic. His eyes suddenly brightened behind his glasses. "I'm thinking of getting a dog," he said.

"You're kidding!" I knew he loved our dog, Twitter, but I couldn't picture him with one of his own. "A puppy? Or an older rescue, or—"

"Puppy," he said. "I haven't had one since I was a kid. I'd have to do more of my work at home for a while, I guess."

"I think it's a great idea," I said. "Maybe you could get two so they could entertain each other while—"

"Tara?" I looked up to see an older woman walking toward our table. I was so caught up in the idea of Ian with a puppy that it took me a moment to recognize her.

"Barbara!" I rose to my feet and gave her a hug. "It's good to see you." I hadn't seen Barbara Read since her retirement party a couple of years ago. Ian was getting to his feet, as well. "Ian, this is Barbara Read," I said. "She used to teach math at Hunter."

"Sit down now, both of you." Barbara smiled. She looked great, her coppery hair cut very short and her skin satin-smooth. Retirement definitely agreed with her. "Oh, honey," she said to me once I took my seat again, "I'm glad to see you looking so well. I was just devastated to hear about Sam. And poor Grace. I know this must be a terrible time for both of you."

"Thank you." I nodded toward Ian. "Ian was Sam's law partner," I said. I felt the need to explain why I was sitting in a restaurant, sipping wine with another man a mere six months after Sam's death. I saw a smile play on Ian's lips. He was on to me and my guilt.

Barbara barely seemed to hear me, though. "And I just heard about Noelle Downie," she said. "Oh, my Lord, what a tragedy."

I nodded. "It's very sad," I said.

"I know you were close to her," Barbara said. "She had a big heart. I saw her and Sam at the South Beach Grill a couple of times last year and it's hard to believe they're both gone. Did he mention seeing me? I told him to tell you hello."

I thought I'd misunderstood her. "You saw Sam and Noelle at the South Beach Grill? In Wrightsville Beach?"

"I love that restaurant, don't you? I often go over there for lunch. Off season, of course. I don't go near the beach during the summer."

"When was this?" I didn't want to sound upset—or worse, jealous—but this was very strange. Noelle and Sam were friends, but certainly not the meet-for-lunch sort of friends.

"Oh, let me think." Barbara tapped her chin as she looked out the window toward the river. "Well, it must have been the spring. April, maybe?"

"Sam died in early March." I felt impatient with her. I glanced at Ian and saw the crease between his eyebrows.

"Hmm, then maybe late winter, or it might even have been last fall." Barbara laughed. "Retirement messes with the calendar in your head, just you wait and see! It was twice, I remember that. I talked to Sam both times. I didn't know Noelle personally, but everyone knows who she is. Was. I figured he was probably the lawyer for that baby program she ran."

"Probably right," Ian said. He was looking at me and his eyes told me to get rid of her.

"Barbara, it's been so good seeing you," I said, "but Ian and I'd better finish up here or we're going to miss our movie."

"Oh, same here." She looked over her shoulder in the

direction she'd come from. "My husband probably thinks I got lost in the ladies' room." She leaned over to pat my wrist. "Wonderful seeing you, honey. And nice meeting you, Ian. Y'all have a good evening."

Ian and I stared at each other until we were sure she was out of earshot. "The babies program needs a lawyer?" I asked.

He shook his head. "I'm sure that's not it," he said, "but I just wanted her to leave. I could see she was upsetting you."

"I'm not upset. I'm confused."

"Look." Ian licked his lips and studied his plate for a moment. "I think it was probably the will." He raised his eyes to mine. "It was written in February, and I'm sure Sam and Noelle had to have a couple of meetings to talk about it. There were papers having to do with her mother's care that Sam had to draw up, and…he probably helped her think through how she wanted to divide her assets."

"Why at a restaurant and not his office?"

"Because they were friends, so they decided to be comfortable while they worked. I do it, and Sam took his clients out all the time." He reached across the table and rested his hand on mine. "Hey," he said, "you're not thinking…?"

I shook my head. "Noelle and Sam? No way. Sam always liked her but he also thought she was wacky. It's just weird to hear something like that out of the blue, when I had no idea…" My voice trailed off.

"You had no idea about it because Sam was ethical," Ian said. "He didn't tell you about her will for the same reason I didn't tell you about it when I came across it in his files. Until she died, it was frankly none of your business."

"Right." I nodded. It wasn't the first time I'd discovered that Sam had handled the legal affairs of someone I knew without telling me. I'd learned early in our married life not to ask questions.

Our waiter delivered our bill and Ian leaned back in his chair to pull out his wallet. "Well—" he laughed as he set his credit card on the table "—we didn't have much success not talking about Noelle or Sam, did we?"

"Not much." I set my napkin on the table. "Let's go lose ourselves in a movie."

"Deal," he said, and it wasn't until we were walking from his car into the theater that I realized I'd let him pay for my dinner.

I guessed it was a date, after all.

9

Emerson

The human race lost something when digital photography was invented. I sat cross-legged on the floor of Noelle's small living room, my back against the sofa, as I paged through one of her old photo albums. Like my own albums, hers had few recent pictures. They were all on her computer. Generations to come—my grandkids, for example—would never get to look through my photo album and wonder, *Who is this guy and why was he important to Grandma?* Honestly, it made me sad. The handful of recent pictures in Noelle's album were Jenny's and Grace's not-very-flattering school pictures and some photographs taken at fundraising events, like the big baby shower Noelle held each year on the grounds of our church.

I wasn't sure what I was looking for in the album, anyway. A picture of her with a stranger, maybe? A grown son or daughter whom she'd hidden away from us? Someone who had the answers we needed? As I dug through the pages, it was the pictures of Noelle herself that I lingered over, each one giving me a bittersweet twist of pain in my chest. I was mad at her for leaving the way she did with no explanation and mad at her for the lies, but I hated being angry with her. The only way to get rid of the anger was to make sense of what she'd done.

"I love this picture of her," I said to Ted, who was pulling books from the shelves on either side of the fireplace and stacking them in boxes. He was working like a dog while I played detective. I knew he thought I was merely brooding and he felt sorry for me. He hadn't gotten on my case at all. Yet.

"Uh-huh," he said as he dropped another couple of books into the box. I'd mentioned to him my need to find answers to Noelle's mystery life, but he thought I should just let it go, so now I was keeping my sleuthing to myself. I'd never had the sort of close—quite honestly, *passionate*— relationship with Ted that Tara had with Sam, but he was a good provider, a faithful husband and a caring dad. They were my three main requirements and he met them handily, so I was keeping him.

In the photograph, Noelle stood in front of a decorative wall hanging. The picture was overexposed with far too much light on her face. It made her fair skin look like alabaster. Simple silver hoops hung from her ears. The intense light brightened the already neon-blue of her eyes and nearly erased her eyebrows. She was very slender and always had been, even before her Spartan vegan diet. I envied her skinniness, but I loved food too much—my TV was always set to the food channel. I'd carry a few extra pounds around with me for the rest of my life and that was just the way it was going to be. She and I both had thick and annoying hair. In the picture, Noelle's wild, unruly hair was pulled back from her face, which was the way she always wore it. The unruliness was there, but under control. That's how I would have described her to someone who didn't know her:

unruly, but under control. I guessed the description still fit. She'd played her cards exactly the way she'd wanted, right down to the bitter end.

Ted straightened up from the box he was filling, his hands on the small of his back. "Em," he said, "we're never going to get out of here if you pore over everything you find."

I laughed. "I know," I said. Enough. I closed the album and leaned forward to add it to the box of stuff we were keeping. I'd sort through her personal things later. Right now, we needed to get everything out of the house. Ted and I had decided we'd renovate before putting it up for rent. We'd redo the kitchen and the scratched hardwood floors and paint inside and out. And we'd tend the garden, as Noelle had asked. Tara was more into gardening than I was, so she said she'd be responsible for it. It wouldn't take much work until the spring and by then the house would have a tenant. Suzanne Johnson was interested. She'd been renting ever since her divorce years ago, and with Cleve at college in Chapel Hill, she was ready to downsize. Plus she loved Sunset Park. I'd need to make sure she also loved gardening. My anger at Noelle didn't erase even a molecule of the love I felt for her. She wanted her special little garden cared for, so I'd make sure that happened.

Patches was now part of my household and she didn't seem thrilled at finding herself living with two dogs. She'd adjust. It struck me as strange that Noelle had asked us to take care of the garden in her note, but not her cat. Maybe she'd figured her neighbors would keep Patches once they found out what happened, but Noelle had loved that cat and I didn't want her with strangers.

I opened a fresh packing carton and started in on the bookcase to the left of the fireplace while Ted continued with the shelves on the right. Tara and I had taken care of the kitchen and bedroom that morning, but the living room and Noelle's office were the bigger challenge. The office closet and file cabinets still needed to be emptied out and I'd put them off because they were overflowing with papers and who knew what. I was itching to get at those papers, though. I knew Ted would want to toss them all, but I planned to scrutinize every receipt, every bill, *everything,* looking for answers. I also wanted to check out her computer. I didn't think it was password protected and if I could get into her email, maybe I'd find The Answer. And maybe not.

I looked at the title of one of the books in my hands. *The Midwife's Challenge,* it was called. I opened it and glanced at the copyright date: 1992. Old. I sighed. I kept looking for a clue that she'd left midwifery only a couple of years ago. I was still in denial even after calling the certification board and learning that Noelle had let her certification lapse eleven years earlier. Eleven years! "I still don't get it," I said to Ted now. "Why would she lie to us?"

Ted let out a sigh. He was tired of the whole subject. "Did she actually *lie* or did she just leave out information?" he asked.

"She *lied*. Up until a couple of years ago, she was always telling me she had a delivery scheduled or she'd mention something going on with a patient." I couldn't think of any specific examples, but I was sure she'd talked to me about her patients. "Then there were those trips she was always making to the country or the backwoods or...wherever. You know, her so-called 'rural work.' She'd stay there for months, delivering babies. That's what she always told us."

"Could she have been practicing under the radar?" Ted asked.

"I can't imagine it." As unorthodox as Noelle could be, she wasn't the sort to skirt the law. She'd been professional and cautious. She'd always dissuade her high-risk patients from considering a home birth. I knew, because I'd been one of them. Tara and I had been due three weeks apart, and we'd both wanted home births. But I'd had two miscarriages before getting pregnant with Jenny as well as some complications during my pregnancy with her, so Noelle vetoed a home birth for me and referred me to her favorite obstetrician. She'd wanted to assist at the hospital delivery, but nothing went according to plan. Ted was out of town when I went into labor three weeks early—the same night as Tara—and I ended up with a C-section. So Noelle was with Tara when Jenny made her happy, healthy way into the world, and I don't think I'd ever felt quite so alone. "I can't picture her practicing without her certification," I said now to Ted. Yet, I couldn't picture her killing herself, either. "We should have known what was going on with her." I reached for another book on the shelf.

"Hon, please stop blaming yourself." Ted sat down on the sagging sofa, rubbing his lower back. "Look," he said, "Noelle was great, but she wasn't the most stable person in the world. You know that."

"She was perfectly stable. Different? For sure. Unstable? No."

"What stable person keeps a secret life from the people who love her? What stable person happens to have...what was it? Twelve? Twelve bottles of drugs lying around, stockpiled for the day she killed herself? What stable person kills herself, for that matter?"

"I think she had those pills from after the car accident, when she hurt her back." Noelle had been driving back from a middle-of-the-night delivery when she was rear-ended at a stoplight, and I remembered that dark period long ago when she'd been so often in pain. Then she organized the babies program and came back to life.

"What are these?" Ted was back on his feet, leaning over to lift one of several fat, leather-bound books from the bottom shelf of the bookcase. He blew the dust off the cover and leafed through the pages. "Handwriting," he said. "Is this a journal or something?" He handed the book to me.

"No." I recognized it as I took it from his hand. "They're her logs." I opened the book and looked at the first entry: January 22, 1991. The patient's name was Patty Robinson and Noelle had detailed her labor and delivery over four and a half pages. I smiled as I read her words. "She was such a strange mix, Ted," I said. "She has all these really technical notes and then she says, 'I left Patty and her new little angel at 10:00 a.m., when birdsong poured through the open window and the scent of coffee filled the air.'" I looked at the other leather-bound logs lined up on the bottom shelf of the bookcase. "Oh, give me the one with Gracie in it!" I said. "This one ends in 1992, so Grace is probably in the third one, maybe."

Ted handed the third book to me and I sat down on the floor and flipped through the musty-smelling pages until I reached Grace's delivery in September. I scanned Noelle's notes. I knew that Tara's labor had been long and harrowing compared to mine, which had been cut short by the C-section.

I skimmed Noelle's notes until I came to this one: "'Baby girl came into the world at 1:34 a.m., nineteen inches long, six pounds two ounces,'" I read aloud to Ted. "'She's a beauty! They're naming her Grace.'"

Ted bent over to plant a kiss on the top of my head, though I didn't think he'd heard a word I'd read. "You want to finish up the shelves while I tackle the closet in Noelle's office?" he asked. "Can't put it off any longer."

"Okay," I said, but I held on to the book as if I were holding on to Grace. "I'll come help you in a sec. Don't throw anything away."

I was sitting at the small desk in Noelle's office a couple of hours later, looking through months of email on her monitor. There were some exchanges with Tara, myself, Jenny and Grace, but most of them were with Suzanne and other volunteers. There was nothing out of the ordinary. There was just plain *nothing*.

Ted dragged a huge cardboard box from the closet into the middle of the room. "Can we just toss this stuff?" he asked.

He'd opened the top of the box and I could see envelopes, cards, handwritten letters, photographs. "What is it?" I asked, reaching in for a handful. I set them on the desk and opened one of the cards.

Dear Noelle,
It's hard to put into words what you've meant to us over the past nine months. I only wish that I'd had a home birth with all my kids now. It was extraordinary. Your warmth and gentleness and the way you were always there for me was incredible. (Even that night I called you at 3:00 a.m. and you came right over even though you guessed correctly it was just Braxton Hicks. Thank you!) Gina is nursing well and growing like crazy. We are so grateful to you, Noelle, and hope you will always be a part of our lives.
Fondly, Zoe

"They're thank-you cards and letters from patients," I said. I plucked a picture of a baby from the box. "And pictures of babies she delivered." *And clues,* I thought, although by now I was doubtful. I'd gone through stacks and stacks of memos and receipts and all sorts of junk and had to admit that most of it could be trashed.

"Toss them?" Ted asked hopefully.

I opened another card and read the words inside.

I couldn't belive it when the lady brung the cute baby clothes to the shelter for me and my baby. Thank you, Miss Noelle!

I looked at Ted. "I can't," I said. "Not yet. I'll take the box home with me. I'd like to look through it when I have time."

Ted laughed. "When do you ever have time? You've got *Hot!* to manage and you're trying to visit your grandfather a couple of times a week. And are you still planning to have Suzanne's party at our house?"

I nearly choked on my breath. *Suzanne's party.* I put my hands on my head. "I forgot all about it," I said to Ted. I'd agreed to have the party at our house, since Noelle wanted to invite half the world and we had the space.

"Cancel it," Ted said.

I shook my head. "We can't. The invitations have all gone out and—"

"I'm sure Suzanne would understand, given the circumstances."

Suzanne hadn't said a word to me about it, probably not knowing how to bring it up. She was a single mother who'd fought cancer twice and never expected to see fifty. Noelle would want the party to go on. "No," I said. "We're having the party. It's three weeks away and Tara's going to help." If there was anything that needed to be planned or managed or organized, Tara was the person to do it.

"Are you sure?" Ted asked. "I think you're taking on too much."

He was probably right and I wanted more time, not less, with my dying grandfather. I could hardly think about him without crying. Jenny and I'd visited him in Jacksonville the day before and he'd looked so emaciated in that big bed at the hospice that I'd barely recognized him. He'd been alert and happy to see us, though. My childhood was filled with memories of him. My father was always traveling and it was Grandpa who taught me to ride a bike and fish and even to cook. Making time to visit him was a priority.

Nevertheless, I wasn't giving up this box.

"I want to keep the box for now," I said to Ted. "I just want to see what all these women had to say to her."

"I wish you'd dump it," he said. "We don't have room for all her stuff."

"I'm taking it," I said, feeling stubborn as I folded the top of the carton into place. Maybe, just maybe, something in the box would lead me to her son or her daughter and, in that small way, I could help Noelle live on.

10

Noelle

UNC Wilmington
1988

She sat in the lounge of the Galloway dormitory with the other Resident Assistants on the last day of their training. The freshmen would arrive the following day and then the lazy calm that had enveloped the Wilmington campus would give way to mayhem. Noelle was looking forward to it. She loved this school.

Empty pizza boxes and soda cans littered the tables of the lounge. Noelle hadn't touched the artery-clogging pizza. She'd kicked off her sandals and sat cross-legged on one of the sofas, her long blue skirt pooling around her like the sea, and she ate carrot sticks and almonds from the Baggie she carried with her everywhere. She offered the bag to one of the other trainees, Luanne, who sat next to her on the couch and who helped herself to one of the carrot sticks. Of all the RA trainees in the lounge, Noelle was closest to Luanne, but that wasn't saying much. Her fellow UNC students liked Noelle and respected her, but she was just a little too different to fit in. It had been that way all her life, and she didn't really mind. She was used to holding herself a bit apart from her peers. The other girls treated her warmly and even turned to her with their problems, yet there was always a distance, and she never formed those intense, heart-to-heart connections that most women had with other women.

As for the guys…well, the jocks and frat boys had no idea how to relate to someone like Noelle. There was something weird about her, they'd say dismissively, not sure how to handle the discomfort they felt around her. She was the quirky woman you could see wandering alone around campus after midnight. She was pretty in an unconventional way, but she was too hard to get to know and not worth the effort. It was as if she were covered by a veil that couldn't be pierced or lifted. She was simply out of their league, and deep down, they knew it.

Yet she had no dearth of lovers. There were certain guys on campus who were intrigued rather than intimidated by her. They were the cerebral or artsy types who were too shy to talk to the typical coeds, but who recognized in Noelle a kindred spirit. So although she'd had no real boyfriend during her first three years at UNC, she did have relationships that went deeper than friendship, even if those relationships would never lead to anything permanent. That was fine with her. She had one single goal and that was to become a midwife. The rest of her life could sort itself out later.

This would be her senior year as a nursing student and she was already researching midwifery programs for next year. She'd have no problem getting in wherever she wanted to go; she was at the top of her class. No one ever said as much, but they didn't need to. She was a hard worker and her professors adored her. She had issues with some of the ridiculous rules she was required to follow in the hospital setting during her clinicals, but she did everything she was told. When she grew frustrated, she called her mother, who was still working for Miss Wilson and who could always calm her down. "Just do what they say and get your degree," she'd tell her. "Then you'll be freer to make your *own* rules. You have to find a way to work with the system, Noelle."

Now, sitting with the other RA trainees in the lounge, Noelle focused her attention on the young man leaning against the back of one of the sofas. He was a grad student in psychology and he'd been their trainer for the past couple of days. "So tomorrow's going to be chaos," he said. "People will be complaining about their rooms and their roommates within an hour of their arrival. Just expect it and it won't overwhelm you. If you have any problems, you know how to reach me, right?"

Everyone murmured a weary response. They were all tired of being cooped up in the lounge, and Noelle was no exception. The day was gorgeous, not too hot for the end of August, and she wanted to be outside. But the trainer was going to hand out their dorm assignments and she couldn't leave until she'd received hers.

She'd requested the Galloway dorm, where she was sitting right that moment. It was where she'd spent her freshman year and she remembered the kindness of the RA she'd had back then. She wanted to be that helpful, nonjudgmental sort of RA for a new, green group of students.

The grad student was sifting through sheets of paper and Noelle knew they were the lists of students on each floor of the various dormitories.

"Noelle?" he said, holding one of the sheets toward her. "You've got Galloway. Third floor."

"Excellent." She stood to take the paper from him, then sat down next to Luanne again.

The grad student handed Luanne her list.

"I have Galloway, too," Luanne said, studying the sheet of paper. "Cool."

"What floor?" Noelle asked.

"Fourth."

Noelle bit her lip, surprised when she felt a little seed of longing forming in her chest. "That's where I lived my freshman year," she said.

"Are you sentimental about it?" Luanne smiled at her. "I don't have any big preference if you want to switch."

She realized that she *did* want to switch. She couldn't have said why. That year had been so good for her. She'd come into her own—away from home, living in a city for the first time in her life and loving every minute of it. The floors of the Galloway dorm were nearly identical, so it seemed silly to switch, and yet...

"You wouldn't mind?" she asked.

"Uh-uh." Luanne started to hand her the list of fourth-floor students, but as Noelle reached toward her with her own list, she noticed one of the names near the bottom of the paper and stopped. She looked hard at the name, her eyes narrowed as she tried to make sense of what she was reading. She drew the sheet of paper back.

"I'll keep the third floor." She heard the tremor in her voice. "I was just being silly. They've got our floors re-corded and we'll mess everything up if we trade."

Luanne frowned at her. "I doubt it would be any big deal," she said.

"No, this is fine," Noelle said, and she pressed the list to her chest as if it were a long-buried treasure.

11

Tara

Wilmington, North Carolina
2010

I knocked on Grace's door and heard her scramble a little, as though she might be doing something she didn't want me to know about.

"Come in," she said after a moment.

I opened the door and saw her sitting at her desk, a textbook open in her lap. She'd probably been on Facebook or answering email but was trying to convince me she was actually working. I didn't care. I really didn't. I just wanted her to be happy and okay. She looked up at me as she sipped from her favorite black mug. High-test coffee, no doubt. I couldn't even drink the stuff she and Sam would make.

"Just wanted to see if you need any help with the sewing machine," I asked.

"I don't have time to do it *now*, Mom," she said. "I'm studying."

"Well, whenever." I sat down on the edge of her bed, longing for a real conversation with her. Longing for contact. Twitter rested his big head on my knee and I ran my hand over his back. "Noelle would be so pleased you're helping with the babies program."

"Uh-huh." She lifted her backpack from the floor and dug around inside it, pulling out a notebook. She looked everywhere in the room except at me. I hated the strain I felt between us. Just hated it.

I smiled at her mug. "I don't know how you can drink coffee this late in the day," I said.

She flipped open her notebook with an exasperated sigh. "You say that every single time you see me with a cup of coffee in the afternoon," she said.

Did I? "It reminds me of your dad," I said. "You two were so much alike that way."

"Speaking of Dad," she said, now looking directly at me, "how was your big date with Ian?"

I frowned, surprised by the question. Sarcasm wasn't her style at all, and she'd caught me off guard. "It was *not* a date, Grace," I said.

She looked out the window, her cheeks reddening, and I thought she'd blurted out the question before she'd been able to stop herself. "I think of Daddy being *dead* while you're out having fun," she said. "I don't know how you can do that to him."

"It wasn't a date," I said again. "Not the way you're implying, anyway. It'll be a long time before I'm interested in a man other than Daddy, but I need to be able to go out to dinner or a movie with a friend sometimes, the way you go out with Jenny. We *both* need to get out." I leaned forward and lowered my head, trying to get her to look at me again. "Can you understand that?" I asked.

"It's fine." She didn't sound convincing.

"I know you miss Cleve," I said, straightening up again.

She looked down at her notebook and I had the feeling I'd touched an exposed nerve.

"It's no big deal," she said.

I'd never been certain how far things had gone between Grace and Cleve. Had they had sex? They'd gone out together for eight months and although I couldn't picture it—I didn't *want* to picture it—I suppose they had. The one thing I knew for sure was that she'd loved him. Even now, his pictures dotted her dresser and desk and the bulletin board behind the computer. She *still* loved him. I wished I could make the hurt go away.

"I remember what it was like when your father and I were separated," I said.

"Separated? What are you talking about?"

"Oh, I don't mean while we were married," I said. "I mean when he went away to college while I was still in high school."

"Well, the big difference with you and Daddy being separated was that Daddy didn't break up with you before he left." She looked surprised at herself for giving me a glimpse into her emotions. I needed to capitalize on that glimpse.

"I know, honey," I said. "I know how hard it must be."

"No, you don't," she muttered.

"I know it's different than it was with your dad and me, but the way I dealt with being apart from him was to get busy. Get involved with things. Take *action*." I leaned toward her. "I wish you could see how that would help you, Grace."

"I am totally involved with things!" she snapped. "I'm working at the Animal House and going to school and now doing the stupid babies program. What more do you want?"

"All that's good," I said, "but it's all work and no play,

isn't it? You could branch out a little, honey. I know you love Jenny, but you should do things with other friends, too. When your dad and I were apart, I made friends with Emerson and Noelle. I got into my studies and acted in plays."

"Yeah, you were Miss Perfect, like always," she said.

"I'm not saying that," I said. "I'm just trying to tell you some possible ways to cope." I twisted my wedding ring on my finger. I was doing that a lot lately whenever I felt tense. Whenever I felt as though I needed Sam by my side.

"You just stay busy so you don't have to think about anything," Grace said. "So you can forget about how messed up your life has gotten."

"Oh, Grace." I shook my head. "It has nothing to do with that. Being involved in things is just healthy." I stopped twisting my ring and laid my hands flat on my thighs. "You know," I said, "we haven't talked about this in a while, but I wish you'd seriously consider joining the drama club. You don't have to *act*. You're such a good writer. You could write plays. I know you're afraid it would seem weird, since I'm the—"

"You don't know me at all!" She slapped her notebook down on her desk. "I'm not you, okay? I don't deal with stuff the same way you do."

"No. I know you don't." I slumped a little on her bed. I was failing with her again. "And that's okay. It was just a thought."

"I really need to study." She lifted her biology book an inch or two off her lap to show me how I was interrupting her.

"All right." I pushed myself off her bed, walked over to her chair and leaned down to give her a hug. She was stiff as a board beneath my arms. "I'll call you when dinner's ready," I said.

I left her room, shutting her door behind me, and stood in the hallway feeling frustrated and a little lost. This chilly girl who treated me with such impatience and disdain was not the Grace I'd known and loved for sixteen years. This was a girl who was angry with me. I wasn't sure exactly why. For going back to work only two weeks after Sam died? She'd been horrified by that, but I'd needed to stay as busy as possible to survive. Was she still angry I'd gotten rid of Sam's things? Did she think I was betraying him by seeing Ian?

One thing I knew for certain was that, rightly or wrongly, she blamed me for Sam's death.

There were moments when I even blamed myself.

12

Emerson

It was Friday afternoon, and I thought I would finally have some time to myself to look through the box of Noelle's cards and letters. Jenny was still at school, Ted was showing a property to a client and I'd closed up the café after the lunch crowd. People were telling me I should start serving dinner, but lunch and breakfast were all I could manage. Right now I could hardly keep up with that.

When I got home, I was surprised to find Jenny and Grace in the bonus room above the garage, sorting through the stuff for the babies program.

"What are you two doing home?" I asked, surveying the neat piles they were making of clothing and blankets.

"Half day today," Jenny said. She gave me a hug. Jenny was a hugger and always had been. She got it from me. She sure didn't get it from Ted.

"How are you doing, Grace?" I asked, picking up a tiny yellow hand-knit sweater from one of the piles. "God, this stuff is cute."

"I'm good," Grace said. "I totally suck at sewing, though." She held one of the little blankets toward me and

I had to laugh at the puckered hem. "The rest I did are better," she said. "It was the tension on the machine. Mom had to fix it for me."

I could picture Grace sewing. Maybe even enjoying it. She'd always loved things she could do alone. Writing. Reading. Drawing.

"Listen," I said. "Suzanne's party is in a couple of weeks and Tara and I can really use some help with the decorations. Would you two have the time to—"

"Suzanne's having a party?" Grace looked up from the blanket she was folding.

I nodded. "Her fiftieth birthday party," I said. "We're going to have it here at the house and—"

"Will Cleve come home for it?" she asked. Her face was so hopeful, so filled with longing, that I could hardly bear to look at her.

"I'm not sure, honey," I said. "Maybe." A light had gone out of Grace's eyes when Cleve broke up with her.

Grace dropped the blanket she'd been holding and pulled her phone from her pocket. I watched as she texted a message—to Cleve, no doubt. Jenny watched, too, and I didn't miss the worry in my daughter's face.

Jenny looked up at me. "We can help, Mom," she said.

"Great," I said. "And one other thing. When I spoke to Suzanne this morning, she said a couple of preemies were born overnight and asked if one—or both—of you could take a couple of layettes over to the hospital this afternoon."

"Sure," Jenny said. She loved any excuse to drive now that she had her license.

Grace looked up from her phone. "Can you drop me off home first?" she asked Jenny.

"Don't you want to see the babies?" Jenny asked.

Grace shook her head, but I knew it wasn't the babies she didn't want to see. It was the hospital. Tara had told me that Grace couldn't even look at the road sign for the hospital these days without going pale.

"They need to go over this afternoon sometime," I said, "so I'll let you two work it out."

"Okay," Jenny answered.

I headed for the stairs and was halfway down them when I heard Jenny ask Grace, "What does he say?"

I stopped walking and stood still, snooping.

"Can't miss it or she'd disown me," Grace said. I pictured her reading the text message from her phone display. I could hear the smile in her voice. The hope.

Oh, Gracie, I thought. *He's eighteen and in college, honey. There's no place for this to go.*

Downstairs, I headed for our home office where the box of Noelle's cards was waiting for me. The box was beginning to feel like another person in my house, a person with too much power for the space she took up. It was our last hope, that box. Nothing in Noelle's house had given us answers. Tara and I had spoken with the staff at every single obstetrical office in a twenty-mile radius, and they all knew what we hadn't known: Noelle gave up midwifery years ago. Few of them had seen her recently, so we didn't bother asking if they knew she was depressed. Suzanne and the other volunteers were all coming to *us* with that question. Whatever had been bugging Noelle, she'd kept it to herself. I suspected that the box wasn't going to give us the answer, either, but if I ignored it, at least it gave me hope.

No more excuses. I had time now. I was going to start digging.

Ted and I shared our home office. It was a big low-ceilinged room that the previous owners had added on as an in-law suite…for in-laws they must not have liked too much. The low ceiling was oppressive, but the space worked for us. Ted's desk and office equipment were on one side, while my smaller desk was on the other. We'd had bookcases built into one windowless wall, and two long tables were set up in front of the windows where Ted could spread out his area maps. At that moment, Shadow and Blue were snoring beneath the tables. Before I'd opened *Hot!* I'd used my part of the office for household records. Now, I had my own filing cabinet devoted to the café. It was so wonderful how things had fallen together for me, and I'd started to feel as though my life was charmed. Now Sam and Noelle were dead and I was about to lose my grandpa, and I knew I would never have that everything's-right-in-my-world feeling again.

I sat down in the armchair by the window and lifted a fistful of cards and letters from the box, but I quickly realized that a leisurely approach wasn't going to do. In my hands I had a letter dated a month ago and another dated eight years ago. There was a copy of an email exchange between Noelle and another midwife. Two pictures of babies. A picture of a teenage boy. A birthday card from Jenny that I remembered picking out for her to send Noelle years earlier. It was as though Noelle had taken a giant Mixmaster to the box and scrambled the contents. I wished Tara had the time to help me. In thirty minutes, she could have this mess alphabetized and arranged by date.

I stood, cleared off one of the tables by the windows and began sorting the cards and letters and pictures and a few newspaper clippings. Ted still thought I should just toss the whole mess, but Noelle had kept these things. They'd been important to her. I wanted to try to feel whatever she'd felt as she dropped each of them into the box. Why did she keep them? Ted thought I was becoming maudlin, grieving over Noelle and worrying about my grandfather. He said I was obsessed, and maybe I was, but the box felt like my last link to one of my two best friends. These were the things she'd cared about enough to save.

If I approached the items chronologically, maybe I'd be able to follow what had gone on in her mind over the years. Maybe I could even write a minibiography of her. If we ever found her now-adult child, maybe he'd appreciate having that remembrance of his—or her—birth mother.

"Like you have time to write," I said to myself as I neatened the stack of cards. Shadow lifted his head to look at me on the off chance I was talking about food.

I spotted the card I'd sent Noelle for her last birthday. Her *very* last birthday. I touched the card, heavyhearted, then pulled another handful from the box. There was a newspaper clipping from the year before about the obstetrical practices in the area getting rid of their midwives. I shook my head. That was why we thought she'd quit. She told us that, didn't she? That she was getting out while the getting was good, when the truth was, she'd gotten out long ago. "Why didn't you tell us?" I asked out loud.

My plan to organize the items chronologically quickly fell apart because so many of the cards and letters had no dates. So I stacked them according to type: cards in one pile, letters in another, printouts of emails in a third pile and newspaper articles in a fourth. Tucked in the bottom of the carton, caught halfway beneath the flap, was a valentine Grace had made for Noelle when she couldn't have been more than four. I pictured Noelle holding the card above her trash can, then deciding to add it to this box of keepsakes instead.

I heard the girls leave the house and used that interruption to take a break. In the kitchen, I made a cup of tea and unwrapped one of the scones I'd brought home from the café, breaking off the corners to give to the dogs. Then I carried the scone and tea back to the office.

When I walked into the room, a little blue-and-white-checked note card on the top of a pile jumped out at me. I rested my mug and plate on my desk and picked up the card. When I opened it, I had to sit down in the armchair as it hit me: the card was from *me,* and it was ancient. Seventeen years old, to be exact.

> *Noelle,*
> *Thank you for taking care of me. You seem to under-*
> *stand exactly how painful this has been for me and*
> *know just the right things to do and say to help. I don't*
> *know what I'd do without you.*
> *Love, Em*

I remembered writing the words a few weeks after my second miscarriage. My second baby lost. Ted and I had lived near the campus then, and Noelle moved in with us for a couple of weeks to take over everything. She cooked and cleaned and, most important of all, listened to me grieve. Ted had run out of words to comfort me by then; he had his own grief to deal with. Noelle knew how badly I'd wanted those babies. Little more than a year later, I'd be holding Jenny in my arms. She couldn't make up for the loss I felt—the loss I *still* felt when I thought of those babies I never got to know—but Jenny brought me back to life.

I held the card in my hand for a while. What was the point of keeping it? Of keeping any of the notes written to

Noelle? Yet I put it back on the pile. I didn't need to make any decisions right now.

I sipped my tea as I read through some of the letters. They were filled with happy words of gratitude, the sort of sentiments you wrote when you were bursting with joy, and I needed to read them after being broadsided by my own sad old card. I held the stack of letters on my lap, scanning most of them, reading every word of others, turning each of them upside down on the arm of the chair as I finished with it.

I came to a nearly blank sheet of notepaper and it took me a moment to recognize it as Noelle's stationery. There was a familiar, faint peach-basket-weave pattern to the paper. I hadn't seen her stationery in years—did anyone still write letters by hand?—but I remembered getting the occasional note from her on this paper. There was only one line on the sheet.

> *Dear Anna,*
> *I've started this letter so many times and here I am,*
> *starting it again with no idea how to tell you*

That was it. Just that line. Tell her what? Who was Anna? I sifted through the letters and cards looking for anything from an Anna. There was a card signed by an Ana. All she wrote was, "Noelle, Our family adores you! Ana." Spelled differently from the Anna in Noelle's letter. No surname. No date. There was a picture of a little boy attached to the card with tape, and when I pulled it off I saw a name written on the back: Paul Delaney.

No idea how to tell you.

The letter was old. The peach-colored paper was soft with age. What could it possibly matter now?

I shrugged off the unfinished letter and continued making my way through the pile, nibbling my scone and sipping my Earl Grey. It wasn't until I reached the bottom of the stack that I found another partial letter Noelle had written, this one typed. It was a bit crumpled. I remembered needing to flatten it when I first stacked the letters. I read it, sucking in my breath and forgetting to let it out again, and I stood so quickly, so violently, that I knocked my cup of tea to the floor.

13

Noelle

UNC Wilmington
1988

The second day after the freshmen filled the Galloway dormitory, Noelle made her rounds, saving Room 305 for last the way she saved the blueberries for last in her fruit salad each morning because they were her favorite. She never felt anxious about those blueberries, though, and she was definitely feeling anxious about Room 305.

In the hallway, she heard laughter coming from the room even before she neared the open doorway. They were bonding, the two girls. Emerson McGarrity and Tara Locke. She knocked on the doorjamb, peering inside. The girls were sitting on the bed closest to the window, culling through a stack of record albums. They looked up at her and she knew immediately which one was Tara—the brown-eyed blonde—and which one was Emerson. Her hair was long, dark and curly. Noelle knew exactly how hard it would be to pull a comb through that hair.

"Hi." She smiled. "I'm Noelle Downie, your Resident

Assistant. I'm making the rounds to get to know every-one."

The blonde hopped to her bare feet and held out a hand. "I'm Tara," she said.

Noelle shook the girl's hand, then turned her attention to Emerson, who had a stack of records in her lap and didn't bother to get up. Noelle had to lean forward to shake her hand. "Emerson?" she asked.

"Right." She had a nice smile, warm and encouraging, and Noelle had a hard time letting go of her hand.

"You want to sit?" Tara motioned to the desk chair and Noelle was surprised at her need to drop into it, her knees suddenly too soft to hold her upright.

"I could hear you two laughing like you've been friends for a long time," she said. "Did you know each other before you got here?"

They laughed again and looked at each other. "It only feels that way," Tara said. Of the two of them, she was clearly the more outgoing. You could see it in her bright eyes, hear it in the self-assured volume of her voice.

"We clicked right away," Emerson said. "I mean, we talked on the phone once over the summer about what we were bringing and everything, but we didn't know each other at all, really."

"And then when we met yesterday it was like we'd known each other forever," Tara said. "We stayed up all night talking."

"That's super," Noelle said. "Doesn't always work out that way." *Doesn't always last, either,* she thought. She hoped it *did* work out for these two. Already, she wanted every-thing good for Emerson. Her feelings scared her; they were so visceral, so deep. She had to watch what she said and did. She could lose herself too easily here in this room. She had to treat Emerson no differently than she did the other students.

She glanced at the dressers. Framed photographs stood on each of them. Testing her legs, she got to her feet and picked up one of a young man with dark hair so long it brushed his shoulders. He looked familiar. He had a symmetrically shaped face and that combination of blue eyes and black hair that was hard to forget. "Who's this guy?" she looked from Emerson to Tara.

"Sam," Tara said. "My boyfriend. He's here. Prelaw." She sounded proud of him. "He lives off campus."

"Ah," Noelle said. "I think I've seen him around. Will it be good to be closer to him?"

"Hell, yes." Tara laughed as though it had been a stupid question and Noelle supposed it had been, but she was not thinking as clearly as she usually did.

"He cut his hair over the summer so he looks totally different now," Tara said.

Noelle picked up the photograph from the second dresser. It was the one she was really after. The blueberries in her fruit salad. A family shot. Emerson with a man and woman. The woman's hair was short, auburn, frizzy. She had a wide, wide smile and she looked young. Mid- to late thirties, maybe. Noelle looked at Emerson. "Your parents?" she asked.

"Uh-huh. No boyfriend, yet." She laughed. "Gotta get me one of them."

"Where do they live?" She was having trouble taking her eyes off the face of the woman.

"California."

"California!" Could she be wrong? "So...Wilmington is... You haven't lived here before?" It was a weird question to ask and she knew it as soon as it left her mouth, but Emerson didn't seem to notice.

"Actually, I lived here until my sophomore year of high school and then my dad got transferred to Greensboro, so I finished high school there. Then in July, he got transferred to L.A., but I wanted to stay in North Carolina. I love Wilmington."

"And I'm from Wake Forest," Tara volunteered.

Noelle forced herself to put the photograph back on Emerson's dresser. "Where did you get your name?" she asked Emerson.

"My mother's maiden name," Emerson said.

Yes, Noelle thought. *Yes.* "Well, tell me more about your families," she said, sitting down again. She hadn't asked that question of any of the other students. With them, she'd talked about their schedules, their majors, their interests. But she would make this conversation sound like her usual getting-to-know-you drill.

Tara went first, as she'd expected her to. Her father was an accountant, her mother a homemaker, and she was an only child.

"Me, too," Emerson piped in.

No, you're not, Noelle thought to herself.

Tara could talk a blue streak. She was a theater major, which didn't surprise Noelle a bit. In any other circumstance, Noelle would have found her intriguing—her energy, her extroversion—but right now, she was desperate for Emerson to have her turn.

"So you're an only child, too," she said, when she was finally able to shift the focus back to Emerson.

"Yeah. My mom's a nurse and my dad's in sales for this big furniture company."

A nurse! "I'm a nursing major," she blurted out. *This is not about you,* she reminded herself. Yet this conversation was entirely about her and she knew it. She glanced at the photograph of Emerson's parents again, drawn to the woman and her wide smile. "Will they visit you here sometime, do you think, or will you be going to California to see them instead?"

"Right now they're gaga over California," Emerson said, "but my grandparents live in Jacksonville, so they'll have to come back to North Carolina sometime."

Noelle's heart gave a thud. *Grandparents.* She thought of the manila folder she had in her room down the hall—one thing of her mother's that she had kept for herself. "Your mother's parents or your father's?" Was she sounding like a nutcase? She hadn't asked any other student about her grandparents. Why would she?

"My mother's," Emerson said. "My father's parents are both dead."

"I've got all of mine," Tara said. "But they all live in Asheville where my parents grew up, so I hardly ever see them."

"That's a shame," Noelle said. "You'll have to try to visit them sometime soon." She swept her attention back to Emerson, hoping she didn't seem as rude as she felt. "Any other interesting names in your family?" she asked. "What's your father's name?"

"Plain old Frank," Emerson said.

Tara was frowning. Noelle could see her expression out of the corner of her eye. Tara wasn't exactly on to her—who could possibly figure out what she was up to? But Noelle was afraid Tara was beginning to think the Resident Assistant was not all there. Yet she had the answer she needed. She had all the answers now, and she couldn't stay in the room another second. Something was going to burst inside her if she did.

She looked at her watch. "Whoa," she said, "I've been here way too long! I need to move on but wanted to get to know you two. We'll have a hall meeting tomorrow night with cake and games, so make sure you're around." She stood, holding on to the back of the desk chair because she felt wobbly. "Meantime, if you have any questions or problems, you know where my room is, right?"

"Right," Tara said.

"Thanks for stopping by," Emerson added.

Noelle made it out the door before she had to lean against the wall to hold herself up. From Room 305, she could hear giggling, then Tara whispering to Emerson, "I think she's totally in love with you."

She was not far off.

Back in her room, she dialed Miss Wilson's house and was relieved when her mother answered. "I need to talk to you, Mama," she said. "Seriously talk."

"Are you all right?" Her mother sounded breathless as if she'd run to answer the phone.

"I'm fine." Noelle sat down on her bed, not fine at all. "Do you have time?"

"Hold on." Her mother left the phone and Noelle could hear the clank of dishes. Then she was on the line again. "I'm back. What's wrong?"

She'd thought about this conversation a hundred times in the past few years but had never honestly expected to have it. She hadn't expected Emerson. She hadn't even known that Emerson existed. Meeting her changed everything.

Noelle drew in a breath. "When I helped you move out of our house before my freshman year, I saw one of your files. Not on purpose. It was windy that day and… It doesn't matter. I saw it. The file on me."

"On you?"

"On my birth. My adoption. I took it. The file."

Her mother was quiet and Noelle imagined she was trying to remember exactly what had been in that file.

"It had the social worker's notes about my birth mother and…everything."

Her mother was quiet once again. "Why are you bringing this up now?" she asked finally.

Noelle remembered the conversation on the way back from the birth of Bea's first baby, when her mother told her about the girl who had given birth to her and relinquished her for adoption. "You said you didn't know who she was. Just that she was fifteen."

"I didn't see any purpose in telling you her identity. Her identity was unimportant."

Noelle shut her eyes. "Mama," she said, "there's a girl here. She's on my floor. She's a freshman. Her name is Emerson McGarrity."

Her mother sighed. "Emerson was the surname of your biological mother, but I don't see why that would make you think anything—"

"McGarrity, Mama. Her father's Frank McGarrity. Isn't that name familiar to you?"

"Should it be?"

"It was in the social worker's notes." She wondered if, after all this time, her mother had simply forgotten the story. "Susan Emerson got pregnant at a party. She didn't even know the boy's last name. But she had a boyfriend, Frank McGarrity, and she didn't want him to know what she'd done. Her parents didn't want anyone to know, either, and they sent her to live with her—"

"Her aunt." Her mother sighed again. "Yes, I know all this, Noelle. I know it all very well, although I'd forgotten the boyfriend's name. He wasn't really in the picture. I don't understand…" She suddenly gasped. *"My God,"* she said. "You think this girl in your dorm is her daughter? Susan Emerson's daughter?"

"She's my half sister, Mama. You should see her."

"You can't tell her," her mother said quickly. "The adoption record is sealed. Her mother never wanted anyone to know."

"Well, the social worker's records *weren't* sealed, were they? You had them."

Her mother hesitated. "I was the midwife at your birth, Noelle," she said finally. "I knew the aunt Susan stayed with. The family wanted everything kept quiet. You were placed in foster care for a couple of months while your father and I worked out the adoption. I was privy to the social-work notes. To the whole…to everything. But I never should have had them somewhere where you could stumble across them. You *cannot* do anything with this information, Noelle. Do you understand?"

"She's my *sister.*"

"It was something that family needed to pretend never happened. Especially since it sounds like she wound up marrying the boyfriend—the McGarrity boy—who had no idea she had a child. It's not your place to tamper. I know this is hard, Noelle. I *know* it," she said. "When you feel a longing for a mother, call *me.* Please, darling. Call me. And ask to switch to another dorm. You shouldn't be around that girl."

"She's my sister," Noelle said again.

"You shouldn't be around her."

"I *want* to be around her."

"Don't hurt her with this, honey," her mother said. "And don't hurt that family. And most of all, Noelle, don't hurt yourself. Nothing good can come from opening up the past. All right?"

Noelle thought of the girl in Room 305 and the picture of the woman who was her mother. She thought of what she probably represented to that woman. A huge mistake. Something she needed to pretend never happened, her mother had said. Something she'd wanted to go away. She thought of the love in Emerson's face when she talked about her family. Her mother. Her grandparents.

"All right," she said, tears burning her eyes, and she knew she would only be able to love her sister from afar.

14

Tara

Wilmington, North Carolina
2010

I had a quick break between my last class of the day and the play rehearsal with the juniors. Sitting at the desk in my classroom, I slipped my day planner into my purse and noticed the message light on my phone was blinking. I only had about thirty seconds until I had to head to the auditorium, but I hit a couple of keys on the phone and listened.

Emerson sounded frantic. "Call me right now!" she said, then added, as if an afterthought, "Nobody died. Just call me." I frowned as I slipped the phone back into my purse. What had our lives come to that we had to add "nobody died" to our phone messages?

I headed for the auditorium. I could put one of the students in charge for a few minutes while I returned Emerson's call to make sure everything was okay.

The kids were all there ahead of me when I walked into the auditorium.

"Mrs. V!" a couple of them called out when they spotted me.

"Hey, guys!" I called in response.

They were hanging out in the front seats, a few of them sitting on the edge of the stage, and they were smiling at me. Grinning. These kids liked me. I wished I could say as much for my own daughter.

Hunter had a fabulous auditorium with rows of deep purple seats that sloped in a graceful bowl toward the stage. The acoustics were to die for. But I didn't walk toward the stage. Instead, I called one of the boys, Tyler, to join me where I stood inside the auditorium door.

"I need to make a quick phone call," I told him. Tyler was a nice kid, new to the school, very artistic. He'd be one of our set designers. "Would you be in charge for a few minutes?"

"Me?" He looked surprised.

"Yes," I said. Then I called to the rest of the students. "Everyone! I have to make a quick phone call, so Tyler's going to talk to you about the set. Give him your input and I'll be back in a minute."

They were quiet as I left the auditorium and I knew bedlam would likely break out the second the door shut behind me, but they'd survive for a few minutes. I'd be fast.

I walked down the hall toward the teachers' lounge, hoping I hadn't set Tyler up for failure. I could have picked a different student; I knew many of the other kids better than I did him and there were some real stars among the junior actors. I was careful always to pick a different student for any special task, though. I didn't want anyone to accuse me of having a pet. Never again.

I'd always hated that expression "teacher's pet." When I

was in high school, people used it to describe *me* because Mr. Starkey, the head of the drama club, doted on me. He saw talent and passion in me and thought he'd found a student who could help him raise the drama club above the mundane. It was probably his belief in me that fed my arrogance about my talent and led me to think that I could somehow get into Yale, which had been my dream school, without paying much attention to the rest of my studies. In retrospect, I was angry at him for making me into his prodigy. It cut me off from the other students who resented the attention he paid me and it gave me an unrealistic sense of my own ability. Just because I was the best actor in my small high school did not mean I was a good actor. I was only the cream of a lackluster crop.

When I became a teacher myself, I vowed never to have a pet. I knew I'd have favorites, gravitating to the students who made my life easier with their dedication and who made me feel like a success through their achievements. But I promised never to treat any of them with favoritism, and I honestly thought I'd succeeded in reaching that goal. Somehow, though, even as I worked to hide the fact that Mattie Cafferty amazed me every time she took the stage, people knew. I didn't even realize it until after the accident, when people would say how ironic it was that my favorite student had been driving the car that killed Sam. Worse, Grace knew. "And you thought she was so perfect!" she said to me when we'd learned it had been Mattie behind the wheel of that car. Mattie texting her boyfriend. I would have put Mattie in charge of the group in the auditorium in a heartbeat. I knew I could count on her.

My cheeks grew hot, thinking about Mattie, and when I walked into the teachers' lounge, one of the science teachers was just leaving and she gave me a worried look. "Are you all right?" she asked.

"Fine." I smiled. "Just rushing, as usual."

Grace had been right. I *had* thought Mattie was perfect.

I'd been teaching my Improv class when the police officer showed up in the doorway of the classroom. My first thought was that something had happened to Grace and my heart started to skitter.

"It's your husband," the officer said as he walked with me toward the principal's office, only a few doors down from my classroom. "He's been in a very serious accident."

"Is he alive?" I asked. That was all that mattered. That he was alive.

"Let's talk in here," he said, opening the door to the principal's office. The two administrative assistants looked at me with white, flat expressions on their faces, and I knew that they knew something I hadn't yet been told.

One of them stepped forward, gripping my forearm. "Shall I get Grace out of class?" she asked.

I nodded, then let the officer usher me into one of the counselor's offices, which we had to ourselves.

"Is he alive?" I asked again. My body was shaking.

He pulled out a chair for me and nearly had to fold me into it, my body was so frozen in place. "They don't think he's going to make it," he said. "I'm sorry. As soon as your daughter gets here, I can—"

I stood again. "No!" I shouted. "No. *Please!*" I pictured the office staff looking toward the door. They could no doubt hear me, but I didn't care. "I need to get to him!" I said.

"As soon as your daughter gets here, we'll go," he said.

The door opened and Grace stood there, her eyes full of fear. "Mom," she said. "What's going on?"

I pulled her into my arms. "It's Daddy, honey." I tried to sound calm, but my voice splintered apart. I was squeezing her so hard in my arms that neither of us could breathe. I knew I was frightening her. I was frightening myself.

In the back of the police car, I held Grace's hand in a death grip as the officer filled us in on the details. Sam had been crossing the Monkey Junction intersection when his new Prius was broadsided by a girl sending a text message. He didn't tell us the girl was Mattie. He would have had no idea the significance her identity would have for either of us.

A month or so ago, I was looking through the school's online newspapers trying to find a particular review from a play we'd put on last year, when I stumbled across a photograph that had appeared in one of the winter issues. There we were, Mattie Cafferty and me. The caption read *Mrs. Vincent Directs Mattie Cafferty in* South Pacific. Grace had seen this picture, of course. She worked on the newspaper. She may even have written the caption. In the picture, I stood next to Mattie, my hand on her shoulder, her dark hair spilling over my wrist. I remembered how I felt, working with her during that play. I'd had the feeling I'd discovered the next Meryl Streep. I wondered how Grace must feel now when she'd stumble across a picture of Mattie as she worked on the paper. I wished I could delete all of Mattie's pictures from the school files—or at least delete the moment captured in that particular photograph, when my attachment to Mattie was so evident, even to me.

Mattie's parents pulled her out of Hunter immediately after the accident. They moved to Florida, and a month later, I received a heartfelt letter from her filled with grief and regret. "I can't ask you to forgive me," she'd written. "I just want you to know I think of you and Mr. Vincent and Grace every single day."

I *had* forgiven her. She'd been irresponsible and stupid, but it could have been Grace. It could have been *me* at her age. Grace would never forgive her, and I had the feeling she would never forgive me for once caring about Mattie. For connecting to Mattie in a way I couldn't seem to connect to her.

I found a quiet corner of the lounge and reached into my purse for my phone. "Tara!" Emerson answered.

"What's up?" I asked.

"I need to talk to you," she said. "Meet me for dinner tonight?"

"Did you find out something about Noelle? Something about her baby?"

"I don't want to get into it over the phone. I just…oh, my God, Tara."

"What?"

"Henry's at six, okay? I really… This will have to stay between the two of us."

She didn't sound at all like herself and she was starting to scare me. "Are you sick?" I felt panicky at the thought of losing someone else I loved.

"No, I'm fine," she said. "Is six okay?"

"Fine," I said. I hung up the phone, worried. *She isn't sick and nobody died,* I told myself as I flipped my phone shut and returned it to my purse. Whatever it was, then, I could handle it.

15

Emerson

Henry's was as familiar to me as my own living room. It always had this sort of amber glow inside. Something to do with the woodwork and the lighting and the mocha-colored leather seats in the booths. It usually comforted me, that space, but it would take a lot more than that to comfort me tonight.

I spotted Tara sitting near the window in the booth we always claimed as ours. "It should have a plaque with the Galloway Girls on it," Tara said once, back when we were really good about getting together every week. Before life got in the way.

Tara stood to give me an unsmiling hug. She knew something serious was up.

Our waitress took our drink orders and since we knew the menu by heart, we ordered our meals at the same time. Tara wanted steak and a baked potato, and I ordered a house salad. I hadn't been able to eat much of anything since discovering the letter and I doubted I'd be able to get through the salad, either. I was sure, though, that I could make quick work of a glass of white wine.

"That's all you're having?" Tara asked.

"Don't have much of an appetite," I said. "I'm glad to see yours is back to normal, though." I tried to smile. Tara had always been one of those women who could eat whatever she wanted and not gain an ounce. After Sam's death, though, she became almost skeletal. Noelle and I had worried about her.

"There *is* no normal for me anymore," Tara said, and I thought about the bombshell I had in my purse. In a few minutes, there would be no normal for either of us. I felt my eyes begin to tear and even in the low amber light, Tara noticed.

"Sweetie." She reached across the table to squeeze my hand. "What is it? Is it your grandfather?"

"No." I pulled in a long breath. *Well,* I thought, *this is it.* "I found something at Noelle's house."

The waitress set a glass of white wine in front of me and a red in front of Tara. I took a huge gulp while Tara waited for me to continue. My head already felt light.

"There was a box of letters...mostly thank-you cards and that sort of thing from patients and...just miscellaneous things." I tapped my fingertips on the table. My hand was shaking. "I read through them all," I said. "I just had to. I wanted to feel close to her, you know?"

"I know," Tara said. Of course she understood. She told me that after Sam died she read some boring legal briefs he'd written just to feel connected to him.

"Anyway, I found these two letters." My palms were damp as I reached into my purse. I'd folded the two sheets in half. Now I unfolded them, the peach-colored stationery with its brief handwritten message on top. "They're *from* Noelle, not to her. This one's just one line." I smoothed my fingers over the paper and leaned closer to Tara. "'Dear Anna,'" I read, "'I've started this letter so many times and here I am, starting it again with no idea how to tell you...'"

"Who is Anna?" Tara asked. We were both leaning so far across the table that our heads were nearly touching.

"I don't know." I took another swallow of wine. "But I do know what Noelle wanted to say, though I still can't believe it." I slipped the sheet of peach stationery beneath the white sheet. "Here's the second letter," I said. "She obviously wrote this one on her computer and printed it, but it's unfinished and I just have no idea—"

"Read it," Tara interrupted me.

"It's dated July 8, 2003," I said. Then I began reading, my voice close to a whisper.

"Dear Anna,

"I read an article mentioning you in the paper and knew I had to write to you. What I have to tell you is difficult to write, but I know it will be far more difficult for you to hear, and I'm so sorry. I'm a midwife, or at least I used to be.

"Years ago, I was taking painkillers for a back injury, which must have affected my balance as well as my judgment. I accidentally dropped a newborn baby, who died instantly. I panicked and wasn't thinking straight. I took a similar-looking infant from the hospital where I had privileges to substitute for the baby I killed. I hate to use that word. It was a horrible accident.

"I realize now the baby I took was your baby. I'm terribly sorry for what I put you through. I

want you to know, though, that your daughter has
extraordinary parents and is loved and…"

I looked up at Tara, whose eyes were wide. "That's it," I said. "That's all she wrote."

PART TWO

ANNA

16

Anna

Alexandria, Virginia

I could kiss my daughter goodbye in the morning, and it could be the last kiss I ever gave her. So every time I left for work, every time I sent her off with friends, I embraced Haley as if it might be the last time. She never balked, although I knew that day was coming. She was twelve, rapidly pushing thirteen, and someday soon she would say, "Mom, just *go*." That would be okay. I wanted Haley to live long enough to rebel and say, *"I hate you!"* in the healthy, normal war dance of mothers and daughters all over the planet. So when she left the house with Bryan, slipping on her helmet and forgetting to say goodbye to me as they wheeled the bikes out of the garage, I stopped myself from calling her back for a hug. For a "Be careful." I just bit my lip and let her go.

Although Bryan had been back in our lives for nearly two months now, I wasn't exactly relaxed when I sent Haley out the door with him. Today, he was taking her for a bike ride along the Potomac River. I knew there was plenty to celebrate in that fact. First, Haley felt well enough to go for a ride. This was week eight in her treatment. A rest week away from the hospital and chemotherapy when she could act and feel like a normal kid. That alone was worth celebrating. Except for the puffy face from the steroids and the occasional bitchy little outbursts (which I secretly applauded because I loved that feisty toughness in her), she seemed like her old self this week. Second, Bryan was playing Good Dad with her. I wasn't used to it yet. Two months of playing Daddy didn't make up for ten years of desertion and part of my heart was still hardened with anger toward him. Oh, he'd sent child support checks every month from the day he'd crapped out on us, cut by his bank in sunny California. He'd sent gifts on Haley's birthdays—gifts that showed he had no idea what her interests were. Barbie dolls and jewelry? Not hardly. *Get a grip,* I told myself now as I watched them pedal toward the Mount Vernon Bike Trail. *He's here now. He's trying hard and Haley's loving it. Loving* him.

I walked upstairs to my desk—my office away from the office. My desk overlooked the river, and even after living in the town house for seven years, it still took me a few minutes to tear my eyes away from the water and the distant tree-lined shore of Maryland. I was behind in my work, though, and I finally began answering the stack of email that had piled up in the past few hours. That was how I'd let Bryan know about Haley's relapse: by email. I'd written to him three days after I got the news, when I was finally able to stop crying long enough to clearly see the screen. I'd thought we were safe, damn it! Ten years of remission should count for something. She was my kick-butt kid, active and smart and so much fun that I'd choose hanging out with her over my friends any day. You'd never know she'd been so sick as a little girl and she had only the vaguest memories of that eighteen-month nightmare herself. But the new bruises, the fevers and uncharacteristic malaise scared the shit out of me. I resisted taking her to the doctor, afraid of what he'd say. When I finally did, and he told me the ALL was back, I couldn't say I was surprised. Devastated, yes. Surprised, no.

I *was* surprised, though, by Bryan's response to my email. It had been Haley's first bout with leukemia that had sent him packing. Well, it had been more than that, but the leukemia had been the final straw. He'd moved from Virginia to California, as far from his sick kid and terrified wife as he could get, so I'd expected the news of Haley's relapse to make him disappear from our lives altogether. Instead, he called me. He'd just been laid off, he said. I couldn't remember exactly what kind of work he did. Something to do with software for a company in the Silicon Valley? Anyway, he said he was coming to Virginia. He wanted to help.

For days after that call, my mood jumped all over the place. Haley'd started her massive doses of steroids and it was hard to say which of us was acting crazier. I was angry at how late Bryan's help was in coming. We could have used him during the past ten years. Now, though, Haley and I had become a team. Our favorite saying when she was helping me fix the plumbing in our town house or raking leaves with me in the yard was "We don't need no stinkin' man!" so I was worried how he'd fit in. Would he suddenly decide he wanted a say in her care? Forget that! And how would Haley react to him? She didn't remember him and never seemed to care much about the cards and gifts he sent. Living in Old Town Alexandria, Haley had friends from single-parent families, blended families, gay families, black families, Hispanic families, Muslim families. You name it.

So I didn't think she ever felt as though she stood out by not having a dad.

I guess I'd convinced myself that she didn't care about Bryan, but she surprised me. When I asked her if she wanted him to come, she said, "Hell, yes! It's about time." I'd laughed. She had a mouth on her for a twelve-year-old. I knew where she'd gotten it from, so what could I say?

Bryan showed up two weeks after we spoke on the phone, and it shocked me how easily Haley welcomed him into her life. It made me proud of myself—I'd done a better job than I'd thought of not turning her against him, which had been a challenge. I told her she got her computer skills from him. She sure didn't get them from me. She'd created a website for siblings of missing kids practically by herself. I'd made excuses for his complete absence from our lives. "He loved you so much that he couldn't bear to watch you suffer," I'd said, when I explained about the divorce. "And then he got a job in California and it's hard for him to travel across the country." I was sure that she'd figured out that was B.S., but it didn't seem to matter to her. She wanted her father.

She didn't remember him at all. It was a stranger who showed up in her hospital room during her third week of chemo. He'd held the basin for her while she got sick. He sat frowning at her bedside, his hands knotted beneath his chin, as she slept fitfully after an aspiration of her bone marrow. He brought her lemon drops when she complained about the nasty taste in her mouth from the chemo. He bought her bandannas in a rainbow of colors because she hated her baldness. But he didn't recognize Fred, the tattered stuffed bear who was her constant companion, as the gift he'd given her on her first birthday.

She seemed comfortable with him from the start. More

comfortable than I was, that was for sure. She looked nothing like him. Her resemblance to me had been strong from the day she was born. She had my light brown hair and green eyes, while Bryan was very dark haired—or at least he used to be. He showed up now with George Clooney–like salt-and-pepper hair. He still had those long-lashed brown eyes behind rectangular-framed glasses and a nose that looked like it came out of the Roman Empire even though he was of English and German descent. He'd been thirty-five when I last saw him and he'd been a good-looking guy back then. Now at forty-five, he looked a little softer all over and the skin around his eyes was beginning to wrinkle—like my own—and I had to admit to myself if to no one else that the anger I'd felt toward him had done nothing to dull the attraction I'd once had for him.

He rented an apartment not far from Old Town and began looking for work, but he hadn't yet found a job and I thought all three of us were glad. The truth was, he was a help. An enormous one. I'd been up for the directorship of the Missing Children's Bureau when Haley relapsed, and I'd really wanted that job. I'd worked for MCB for years, frustrated by the organizational structure that needed changing. I wanted to be at the helm. When Haley got sick, I thought I'd have to let someone else take the appointment, but with Bryan's help, I'd been able to accept the job. Haley was spending most weekdays at Children's Hospital in D.C. and most weekends at home. I could bring work with me to Children's, but when I needed to attend a meeting or whatever, Bryan took my place at her bedside. He'd brought her to the doctor twice this week, both times for routine blood work. Taking her out for something fun, like he was doing today, though, was the biggest help of all. He was treating Haley like a normal, healthy kid. Like his daughter. Yet

I didn't completely trust him. I kept waiting for him to get his fill. To pack his bags and escape to the West Coast again. I'd kill him if he hurt Haley that way. Just slaughter him.

Haley had forgiven him for the way he'd treated her in the past, obviously. Maybe she'd never even been angry with him. He'd caught her in time. She didn't yet have that pissy teenager's attitude toward her parents, although the steroids could sometimes make her seem like it. I caught the brunt of her irritable moods. Not Bryan. She was sweet as sugar around him, and I knew she was afraid of losing him again.

I'd been working online for over an hour when I heard Haley and Bryan walk into the kitchen from the garage. I went downstairs and found them laughing. Haley was tying her blue bandanna back onto her head. She'd lost her hair over the course of a single day and she'd cried from sunup to sundown. As far as I knew, she hadn't cried since.

"Have fun?" I asked.

"She's like a machine on a bike." Bryan touched her shoulder proudly, as though he had something to do with how she'd turned out. I honestly wasn't sure how much I had to do with the person Haley had become, either. She'd been born smart and self-confident and independent. The independence was a problem, since I wanted to keep her chained to my side. I'd lost one child and I had no intention of losing this one.

"Dad hasn't ridden a bike in a long time," Haley said, "but he only crashed three times."

"Twice," Bryan corrected her, grinning.

I could tell how much Haley liked saying that word. *Dad*. She used it a lot, as though she was making up for all the years she'd never been able to say it.

"Stay for dinner?" I asked, but Bryan shook his head.

"Gonna give you two some girl time." He drew Haley into a hug. "Want to do this again tomorrow?" he asked.

"Sure," she said.

"You have homework?" I asked.

"Not much." She was keeping up with her schoolwork even during the weeks in the hospital. I didn't think I'd have her motivation if I were in her place. She didn't want to fall behind her friends.

"Go do it and I'll finish up my work and then we can eat."

"Okay," she said, heading for the stairs. She looked over her shoulder at us. "Bye, Dad," she said.

"See you tomorrow." Bryan waved.

We listened to her clomp up the stairs. "Thanks for your help today," I said.

"It's my pleasure. Believe me."

"She's enjoying getting to know you."

"Not half as much as I'm enjoying getting to know *her*."

I felt angry all of a sudden and I turned away from him to take two plates from the cabinet above the dishwasher. We'd had long conversations about Haley's condition and treatment. Long talks about *Haley*. I'd shown him videos of her in ballet class and playing T-ball and beating the crap out of another swim team with her phenomenal breaststroke. But we hadn't talked about the way he left. His cowardice. The sheer *meanness* of it. "I can't handle the possibility of losing another child," he'd said before he left us the first time Haley got sick. Well, neither could I, but that didn't give me the right to walk out the door.

Neither of us had uttered a word about Lily. When I told him I'd been named the director of the Missing Children's Bureau, I'd watched his face for a sign that he got it, but he acted like I'd said I was the director of a publishing company or a preschool, something that had nothing at all to do with our lives.

I'd have to talk to him about it at some point, because I'd burst if I didn't and it was really pissing me off that he acted as though he could waltz back into our lives without consequence. Right now, though, I didn't dare do anything that would hurt the relationship he was forming with Haley.

I set the plates on the counter, then walked to the garage door. "So we'll see you again tomorrow?" I asked, pulling the door open.

"Right." He walked to the door, then turned to face me, smiling. "She's going to grow up to be just like you," he said. "She already reminds me of you."

"What do you mean?"

"You know," he said with a shrug. "Just...pretty incredible." His smile was sort of rueful. I could see the regret in his eyes. "See you tomorrow," he said.

He left and I watched him walk through the open garage door to his car where he'd parked it on the street. *Don't you fall for him, too,* I told myself. I wouldn't. Too much water under that ol' bridge.

I had salmon baking in the oven when the phone rang an hour later. I picked up the receiver from its cradle near the fridge. I *always* answered the phone, never bothering to look at the caller ID. That came from years of wanting the phone to ring. Of wanting answers. I always answered the phone with hope in my voice.

"Hello?" I turned the heat down under the rice.

"It's Jeff Jackson."

Oh, shit. Haley's oncologist, calling at six o'clock. Not a good sign. I tensed.

"What's wrong?" I asked. *She's doing so well,* I wanted to say. *Please, please let her have this week in peace.*

"Just got the lab reports," he said. "Her blood count's low."

"Oh, crap." I ran a hand through my hair. "Jeff, she looks great. She went for a long bike ride today and—"

"She needs a transfusion."

I shut my eyes. "Now?"

"I'm afraid so."

"Damn it!"

"I'll call Children's and have them get a room ready for her," he said, then added softly, "Sorry."

It took me a few minutes to pull myself together before I went upstairs. I stood quietly in the open doorway of Haley's room. She had no clue I was there and she was Skyping with one of her cousins. I could see one of the twins—Madison or Mandy, I could never tell them apart—on her monitor. Madison or Mandy was laughing and talking. She held a boxy little Westland terrier in her arms and was making the dog wave at the camera with its paw. Bryan's sister, Marilyn Collier, lived an hour away in Fredericksburg and she and her four girls had remained a big part of our lives in spite of Bryan's absence. Haley loved her cousins and they loved her. Tears burned my eyes as I listened to her talking a mile a minute to Madison/Mandy. I hated spoiling the moment.

I knocked lightly on her open door.

"Whoops!" Haley quickly turned off the screen. She swiveled her chair to face me, all innocent green eyes. "I finished my math, Mom, so I was just Skyping for a minute with Mandy."

I couldn't have cared less if she was lying. Let her Skype. Let her do whatever she wanted.

"That's okay," I said, then sighed. "Dr. Jackson just called, honey. He said your blood count's low."

"*Shit.*"

"Don't say *shit.*"

"You say it all the time."

"Yeah, well, I shouldn't."

"I don't want to go in, Mom." Her eyes pleaded with me to let her stay home and my heart cracked in two.

"You've got to, honey. I'm sorry."

She dragged herself to her feet. "This totally sucks."

"I couldn't agree more."

"Does this mean I won't be able to get chemo next week?"

I couldn't tell if she was hoping she wouldn't have to have chemo or if she was worried the weeks of chemo would have to be drawn out that much longer.

"It depends on how your blood work looks by then," I said. "Get what you need and we'll hit the road."

She frowned at me, her hand gripping the arm of her chair. "Mom?" she said. "Don't tell Dad, okay?"

Maybe another mother wouldn't have understood, but I did. She was scared. It was her illness that had caused Bryan to turn tail years ago. Now they'd spent a healthy, happy few days together, and she was afraid of appearing sick to him again.

"He won't leave, honey," I said, and I walked out of her room, hoping against hope that I hadn't just told her a lie.

17

Emerson

Wilmington, North Carolina

"My God," Tara breathed. She grabbed the letter and read it through in silence.

I felt my heart beating in my ears. I touched the paper in her hands. "I don't know what to do with this," I said.

Tara looked up from the letter. "I can't believe Noelle would do something like that," she said.

I shook my head. "Neither can I. It seems impossible."

"Here we go!" The waitress appeared at our table again, this time with my salad and Tara's steak. "I wasn't sure if you wanted your dressing on the side or on the salad," she said as she set the plate in front of me.

"This is fine," I said, looking at the little cup of dressing. I wasn't going to eat the salad either way, so it didn't matter. I just wanted her to put the food on the table and leave.

"Is there anything else I can get you right now?" she asked.

"No," Tara said. "Thank you. We're fine."

The waitress walked away and Tara pushed her plate to

the side of the table, her appetite apparently gone, as well. "Maybe this is why she stopped being a midwife," she said.

Of course. I couldn't believe I hadn't thought of that.

"I feel like I didn't know her," I said. "I know I've said that a lot lately, but now I really, *really* feel that way. I don't know whether to hate her for this or feel sorry for her that she was holding on to this hideous secret all these years."

"Is there a chance this is…just not true?" Tara asked. "I mean, maybe she was writing a novel or…a short story or something and this was just a literary experiment."

"I love that idea, Tara," I said. "But do you really believe it?"

Tara gave a small shake of her head. "She killed a baby," she said slowly, quietly, as if trying the words on for size. "Some poor woman didn't even know that her baby died."

"And that she was raising another woman's child."

"And *this* woman's baby was kidnapped." Tara held the letter in the air. "Do you think she might have written *another* email or letter to Anna?" she asked. "One that actually made it to her?"

"I've wondered that myself," I said. "But wouldn't we know? Wouldn't it have come out? Wouldn't there have been a monumental lawsuit?" I reached for my wineglass, but the room was beginning to spin and I lowered my hand to my lap.

"Did you find any documents in her house that might be related to a suit?" Tara asked.

"No, nothing like that," I said.

"Maybe she did actually mail a letter, but made it anonymous so Anna couldn't figure out who she was."

I nodded. "It sounds like she was planning to make *this* letter anonymous," I said. "She just talks about the 'extraordinary parents' to reassure her—Anna—that her daughter was being taken care of, not that she planned to reveal who they were. So I don't think she was going to reveal who *she* is...who she *was*...either."

"What did she mean about the article in the paper?" Tara asked.

"No idea," I said.

"What does Ted say?"

"I haven't told him." Maybe I never would. I'd thought of telling no one at all, trying to forget what I knew, but I couldn't live with the secret. I couldn't live with it *alone,* anyway. "What do we do with this, Tara? Do we ignore it?"

"I don't think we can," Tara said.

"Oh, Tara, this is horrible! Ted didn't even want me to bring the box of cards home, and I wish now that I'd listened to him. If I'd just thrown it away, I wouldn't know any of this."

"But you do know. *We* know."

"I hate this," I said. "If we go to the police...I don't want a media frenzy. And Noelle...her legacy. All the good she's done. She'll be dragged through the mud."

"Look." Tara leaned back in the booth. "We have very, very slim evidence here. And maybe she *was* writing a short story, for all we know. I think the first thing we should do is try to figure out who Anna is. If we discover there really is an Anna and this looks like something that really happened, then we can figure out the next step."

I felt both relief and guilt that I'd dragged her into this. "I'm sorry I told you, Tara. It's the last thing you need right now, but I didn't want to be alone with it."

"You're not alone with it, sweetie."

"So—" I turned the letter to face me again, the words blurring a bit in my vision "—how do we try to figure out who Anna is? Noelle said she read an article about her in the paper, so we could…I don't know. Check old newspapers, I guess?"

"Maybe the baby that died—" Tara shuddered as she said the word "—maybe that was the last baby Noelle delivered."

I felt a chill. "I have her record books," I said. Could I be that close to knowing whose baby Noelle had dropped?

The waitress neared our table and I could see her checking out the uneaten food. "How are you doing over here?" she asked.

"We're fine," I said, and Tara made a little whisking motion with her hand that said, *Please leave us alone,* as clearly as if she'd spoken the words.

"I can read the last entry in her record books," I said once the waitress was gone. "If it was a girl, well…" I looked at Tara and shrugged.

"If it's a girl," Tara said, "then we'll figure out what to do next."

18

Noelle

Noelle was happier than she'd ever been in her life. Her classes and clinicals were going well and she loved her work as a Resident Assistant. The girls on her floor turned to her easily with their concerns, and it wasn't unusual to find her sitting with a group of them on the floor at the end of the hall, chatting about their boyfriends or their professors or their relationships with one another. The gathering had the feel of a mini support group, a relaxed get-together with meat at its heart. Noelle made sure everyone felt welcome, though. She didn't want her end-of-the-hall group to turn into a clique.

The other RAs thought she was overly involved with the students. "You should just be there in case they need something," they said, but Noelle felt protective of her charges. She wanted to be their safe harbor. The night one of them nearly died of alcohol poisoning, she wept because she should have seen it coming. But she did recognize another student's bulimia, intervening before it was too late, and she counseled yet another girl as she decided what to do about an unwanted pregnancy—even though she was privately heartbroken when the girl decided to have an abortion.

All in all, she loved her girls. The fact that she loved one of them more than the others was something she was learning to hide.

She'd gotten her emotions at least somewhat under control when it came to Emerson McGarrity, doing her best to treat her like all the other girls on her floor. If anyone noticed that she paid a little more attention to Emerson, that she lit up each time she saw her, that she questioned her more than the other girls about her adjustment to campus life, her classes, her family, no one said a word about it, at least not to her. She no longer needed Emerson to know their relationship. Being close to her, being a part of her life, was enough. It was clear that Emerson knew nothing about her mother's teenage pregnancy, and clear that Noelle's existence had been swept under the rug. Noelle made a conscious decision to leave it there forever. She wouldn't hurt Emerson or her family, but one way or another, she would always be a part of her sister's life. She wouldn't lose her now that she'd found her.

She was coming to like Tara, too. Tara's exuberance was a good counterbalance to Emerson's gentle, calm nature and she was far deeper than Noelle had originally guessed. For most of Tara's life, her mother had spent her time in and out of psychiatric hospitals. It was not something she talked about easily, and Noelle felt touched when she finally revealed that part of herself to her. Noelle came to see Tara's love of theater as her escape from a childhood and adolescence that had been difficult to endure.

There was, however, one small, niggling problem in Noelle's life: Sam Vincent.

Plenty of guys on campus were intrigued by Noelle, but Noelle herself had been drawn—*seriously* drawn—to only two men in her life. Sam was number three.

She met him the second week of school when she stopped by Tara and Emerson's room to offer them a couple of granola bars. He was there alone because Tara and Emerson were baking cookies in the dorm kitchen, and he was stretched out on Tara's neatly made bed, writing something in a notebook. He looked up and gave her a quick, easy smile and that was all it took. The smile slayed her. She felt her internal organs melt and her heart thumped as hard as it had the first time she'd walked into this same room and laid eyes on Emerson.

"You're Sam," she said, glancing at the long-haired guy in the picture on Tara's dresser. This Sam looked different. The guy in the picture was a boy. The short-haired guy on the bed, a man. He was slender. Not overtly masculine; macho had never appealed to her. Thick, jet-black lashes framed his blue eyes, and his lips were full and a little pouty. It was only the broad cut of his chin that saved him from being too pretty.

"Yeah," he said. "I'm waiting for Tara. You live in the dorm?"

"I'm the RA. Noelle."

"Oh, yeah." He sat up a little straighter, his back against the wall. Setting his notebook on the bed beside him, he folded his arms across his chest. "Tara told me about you. She thinks you're cool."

Noelle smiled and sat down in Emerson's desk chair. "I'm glad she thinks so. I like her, too." She nodded toward the notebook. "What are you working on?"

"Journal." He grinned with the tiniest hint of embarrassment as he lifted the notebook from the bed and set it on his thigh. His arms were very tan and dusted with dark hair. "Thought I'd give it a try," he said. "You know, writing down my deepest, darkest thoughts."

She loved the answer. What guy journaled? If she hadn't already pinned him as a rarity, she did now.

They talked for a while about UNC and his plans for law school. He told her he'd known Tara since they were kids, although Noelle already knew that. Actually, nothing he told her was new; Tara talked about him all the time. Words passed between them, but they could have been any words at all. They could have been talking about the weather or what they'd had for dinner the night before. It wasn't the words that were being communicated. Something deeper was going on. Noelle felt it and she knew in all those melting, hungry organs of her body that he felt it, too. The way he held her gaze. The way he couldn't stop smiling at her no matter what he was saying.

She offered him one of the granola bars and watched his tanned, perfect fingers slit open the wrapper. He took a bite, then licked a crumb from his lips, his blue eyes back on her. She pictured him in her bed, both of them nude. He was between her legs, slipping inside her. She didn't even try to erase the image from her mind. If he had not been Tara's, she would have asked him flat out, "Do you want to make love?" because that was her style. Why mince words? And if he were not Tara's he would say yes.

But he *was* Tara's and, deep in her heart, she knew he always would be.

19

Anna

Washington, D.C.
2010

There were few things I hated as much as having Haley under general anesthesia. For an hour or two or three, it was as though she was gone. I always tried to reassure myself that at least she was in no pain during the time she was out. Yet the goneness, the unreachableness, still scared me.

She'd received the transfusion a couple of days before and her red blood count had bounced back nicely, but now the surgeon was moving her port from one side of her sore chest to the other and aspirating her bone marrow at the same time. It was never ending, the torture they put her through. Haley'd been stoic when the surgeon told her his plans for today, but I had the feeling she would have chewed him out if Bryan hadn't been present. She was on her good behavior around Bryan. I actually preferred her feisty side. I liked when she cussed out her doctors. Holding in her anger and frustration wasn't a good thing. She wanted her Daddy to think she was a sweet girl, though—which she was most of the time, when she wasn't loaded up on steroids and fighting for her life.

I didn't think Haley totally grasped the implications of this bone marrow aspiration. They'd be looking at her MRD level. Minimum Residual Disease. If it was too high, it would mean the chemo was not doing the job and she'd need a bone marrow transplant. Going down that road terrified me. It would mean more grueling chemotherapy plus full-body radiation to destroy her immune system and all that simply to prepare her for the transplant itself. And of course a donor would have to be found. So if I'd been the praying type, I would have been praying for a very low MRD. Very, very low. Although it had required nearly two full years of treatment, chemo alone had taken care of the cancer when she was a toddler. I was hoping for the same outcome this time.

I made sure the staff had my cell number, then walked down to the cafeteria for a cup of coffee and to check in with my office. Bryan was on a job interview in Bethesda. He'd offered to cancel it when I told him about the surgery, but I encouraged him to go. *I'm used to dealing with her alone,* I nearly said, but caught myself. Now wasn't the time to guilt-trip him.

I didn't go straight back to the East Wing, but walked instead to the neonatal intensive care unit. It wasn't the first time since Haley's relapse that I'd found myself wandering through the halls of the NICU, even though they now had the babies safely tucked away in private rooms and I wasn't able to see them as I could years ago. I was actually glad. I wanted those babies to be out of sight.

My work occasionally took me to hospitals, and I always wound up trying to see the babies. The tiniest babies got to me. All those wires and tubes. Those little rib cages pumping air in and out, every breath looking like an effort. They were so vulnerable. Their dependence on others to protect them always cut into me.

Why did I do that to myself? Why did I look? Why did I search the features of the babies, looking for one who resembled Lily? I sometimes felt as though I couldn't leave. I needed to stand guard. The nurses couldn't watch every baby every minute. Even here in the remodeled NICU at Children's, I searched for evil intentions in the face of each person I saw. That's when I knew it was time to walk away. I became the director of the Missing Children's Bureau in part because of my own pain and my passion, but also because I'd been able to hold on to my sanity. That sanity allowed me to distance myself from my own ordeal so that I could be rational as I kept the bureau functioning. That's why I had to walk away when I began to imagine someone—one of the nurses? A total stranger?—coming into the nursery, detaching one of those fragile, helpless infants from her tubes and wires and slipping out the door with her.

I'd opted for a home birth with Haley for that reason alone. I'd never been the home-birth type. I wasn't one of those women who distrusted the medical system or worried about having an unnecessary C-section because my obstetrician wanted to get out on the golf course. But I knew I wanted to give birth to Haley surrounded by trusted friends, by a midwife whose references I'd grilled for hours and a doula I'd known forever.

My phone rang as I walked toward the oncology unit and I checked the caller ID. Haley's surgeon. I stopped walking and pressed the button on my Bluetooth. "How is she?" I asked.

"She's in recovery," he said. "She did great."

"I'll be right there."

I called Bryan as I started walking again. "She's in recovery," I said. I could hear a woman's voice in the background. Laughter. Was he at a job interview or what? For a moment, I felt a profound stab of distrust. Then I reminded myself once more that he was back in the area for Haley, not for me. I had to remember that.

"How'd she do?" he asked.

"They said great."

"I'll be there in a couple of hours," he said. "Is that okay?"

"That's fine." I heard the coldness in my voice.

"Can I bring you anything?"

"No, I'm good." I walked faster as I neared the recovery room. "I just want to see her."

In the recovery room, I slipped my hand into Haley's. Her puffy little face was at peace for the moment. I sat down next to the bed and watched for the flutter of eyelids. The twitch of her flaky lips. Any sign that she was coming back to me. She'd had to have general anesthesia three times in the past couple of months and each time I worried she would not come back the same girl, that somehow the anesthesia would alter her. But Haley opened her eyes and I saw my brave daughter in her tired smile.

"Ta da," she said.

I touched her cheek. "It went perfectly," I said. "Just great."

A nurse lowered the blue hospital gown a few inches to check the pink skin around the new port in Haley's chest. "How's your pain on a scale of one to—"

"Three," Haley said before the nurse could finish the question.

"Three in Haley world is about a six in typical people

world," the nurse said. She knew my daughter. Everyone at the hospital knew her. They called her a "frequent flier," one of those kids who returned to Children's again and again.

"Whatever," Haley said. She raised her eyes to mine. "Where's Dad?"

"On his way."

"Good," she said, and the corners of her mouth curled up ever so slightly as she drifted back to sleep.

I was still sitting with her in her lime-green hospital room an hour later. She'd been awake off and on in the recovery room, but now she slept deeply and I let her. I sat on the sofa that converted to a double bed, doing a little work on my laptop. It was admin stuff, boring but necessary. Every few minutes, I'd stop and look at Haley's face, her too-pale, too-rounded cheeks and the remnants of a rash on her neck from one of her medications. I'd tucked Fred into her arms, and his big brown plastic eyes stared into space. After a while, a nurse walked into the room. He was African-American, skinny as a toothpick and bespectacled, and I recognized him right away.

"Tom!"

"Hey, Ms. Knightly," he said. "You remember me?"

"I do!" I stood and gave him a hug. Ten years earlier, Tom had been one of Haley's nurses, a favorite of both of ours. He looked exactly the same. "I don't believe you're still here!" I said.

"Where am I going to go?" He laughed. "I've actually been out for the past few months taking care of some family business—" he rolled his eyes "—and when I came in this morning and saw Haley Hope Knightly on the board..."

He shook his head. "I'm sorry she has to go through this again."

"Me, too," I said. I remembered him slipping one time long ago, talking about how he often saw kids come back to the oncology unit years after remission. Strange, the things you remembered. The things that could haunt you. He'd caught himself; I remembered that, too. He'd backpedaled, telling me that most kids did just fine and that he was sure Haley would be one of them.

I watched as he took Haley's vital signs and adjusted one of the bags hanging from the IV pole. Then his gaze lit on the framed photograph of Haley and my nieces where it sat on the nightstand. He let out a whoop and picked it up.

"The cousins!" he said. "Look at them! All grown up."

"You remember them?" I asked, surprised.

"How could I forget them? They'd come barrelin' into the room like a flock of geese, chattering up a storm, looking more like quintuplets than sisters."

"Quadruplets," I corrected. "There were only four of them. Just seemed like more than that. One set of twins and another two just a couple of years apart."

"I have to tell you, I hated the days they visited." He laughed. "They'd come in all chaotic with their little-girl germs."

"Haley loved it, though," I said.

Tom pointed to the girl in the center of the photograph. "And this here in the middle is our Miss Haley." The picture had been taken in the Outer Banks last summer. The redbrick Corolla lighthouse stood in the distance behind the girls who were posing like little vamps in their bathing suits. Madison and Mandy stood on the left. Megan and Melanie on the right. Each of them wore her hair in a dark ponytail slung over her shoulder. Haley stood out from her cousins with her lighter brown hair. Her lighter eyes. She'd been giggling so hard it had been a challenge to get her to hold still long enough for me to take the picture. Haley looked so incredibly healthy in the picture. No sign of the disease that had been planting its seeds in her body at that very moment. She'd insisted on bringing the picture to the hospital with her each time she came. I hadn't wanted her to. What was it like for her to see that vibrant former version of herself every day?

"I hear her daddy's with y'all this time," Tom said. He'd set down the picture and was writing something in Haley's chart.

All sorts of responses ran through my mind, but I decided to be charitable. "He is," I said. "He was living in California, but he moved back here as soon as I told him Haley'd relapsed."

"I remember the last time, how it was just you and her." He finished writing and looked across Haley's bed at me. "I don't remember every single patient but I remember you and Haley real well, because even though she was just a kid, she was like a little adult. She took care of you as much as you took care of her."

It might have seemed a weird thing to say except that it was so true. Haley always seemed to sense that there was something broken inside of me, even when I hid that brokenness from the rest of the world. She knew. When she got older and I told her about Lily, she finally understood. She seemed to feel the loss herself.

"You were a drug rep back then, right?" Tom asked.

"Uh-huh." I closed my laptop. "I quit when Haley got sick." My job had already been on the skids because I refused to travel once Haley was born and travel had been a major part of my work. All those trips to Wilmington. I'd once liked that city. Now I loathed it. "Bryan had just gotten out of the military and was working for IBM."

"I don't remember him at all," Tom said.

"Well, he left right after she got sick. He couldn't handle Haley's illness." On top of everything else, I thought.

"How long were you married?" Tom asked. I saw the ring on his finger. I couldn't remember if he'd been married the last time or not.

"Six years." In my mind I divided those years into three segments. There'd been two wonderful years when it was just the two of us. We lived on base at Fort Belvoir and I'd loved my job doing pharmacology sales. We'd been young, so much younger than we were now. Our relationship had an energy and a heat I could barely remember.

Then everything went south. Bryan was stationed in Somalia where he'd nearly gotten killed, Lily was born and I had a stroke and nearly died myself. A complete and utter nightmare. Bryan and I settled into a tense, suddenly love-less marriage and he went overseas again, happily I thought. I got pregnant with Haley unintentionally and against doctor's orders on one of Bryan's leaves, proof that birth control pills were not one hundred percent effective. Proof you could still make love when you felt dead inside. My pregnancy had all my health care workers in a tizzy, but my blood pressure behaved itself and I felt good and full of hope. For a year after Haley was born, there was a cautious joy in our house. Bryan left the military and took the job with IBM so he could stay closer to home. I remembered thinking he was guarding us, making up for not protect-ing us well enough the first time around. Our happiness was fragile and we were only beginning to trust it when

Haley's fevers began. Bryan's retreat was so fast I didn't see it coming. One minute he was there, the next he was gone. How he could leave Haley and me, cutting himself off from his child, was as unbelievable to me as it was unforgivable.

"He's back now, though," Tom said, "just when she needs him."

I nodded. "You're right," I said, swallowing my anger. I would have to find a way to put the past aside.

I was back on my laptop twenty minutes later when Bryan walked into the room. He barely looked at me before heading straight to Haley's bed. "How's she doing?" He lightly touched her arm as he peered down at her face.

"She was asking for you when she first woke up," I said.

"Really?" His glasses caught the sunlight from the big windows near Haley's bed.

I couldn't help it. I was touched by the emotion his voice carried in that one word. "Yeah," I said. "So how did the interview go?"

He shrugged. "All right, I guess. Time will tell."

I remembered the laughter in the background. I didn't know why that bugged me so much. I'd been sitting with our unconscious daughter while he was laughing with some woman. So? I wasn't sure exactly what I wanted from him.

"When will they know her MRD level?" he asked.

"Probably not for a day or so."

"You want to take a break? I can stay with her for a while?"

I looked at my sleeping daughter. If she'd been awake, I might have taken him up on the offer, but I couldn't leave her when she looked so drained and weak. I'd let another defenseless child of mine out of my sight. I would never do it again.

★ ★ ★

The following evening, Jeff Jackson called with the results from Haley's bone marrow aspiration. "The chemo's not doing the job," he said. "I'm sorry."

"Shit." I was in the cafeteria at Children's catching up on email while Bryan stayed with Haley in her room. They'd been playing Bananagrams when I left them. I hadn't expected the news so soon, and it was news I didn't want to hear. "So we have to go forward with a transplant now?" I asked.

"We'll start her on a maintenance level of chemo to hold her steady while we look for a donor. Her MRD's higher than I'd like to see and we'll have to move quickly to find a good match. I'll have you meet with Doug Davis tomorrow. He's head of the transplant team. He'll fill you in on what it entails."

"Will he test Bryan and me to see if we're matches?" I asked. "Can we be tested right away?"

"I'll let Doug go over all of that with you."

"So—" I looked at my laptop screen without really seeing it "—is this ultimately good news or bad?"

"Neither," he said. "It just is what it is."

I loathed that expression. Imagine if I said it to the family of a missing child. *Well, it just is what it is.*

"I want a better answer than that," I said.

He hesitated. "I wish it were more positive news," he said finally. It was the best he could do. The most I could ask of him.

"All right." I let him off the hook. I was alone in this. Then I thought of Bryan in the oncology unit, sitting with Haley. I thought of Haley's new fondness for him. The affection in her voice when she talked about him. How attached she'd become to the very word *Dad.* I remembered

Bryan from the day before when he'd shown up in Haley's room after the surgery, how he walked directly to her bed. Touched her arm. And I thought maybe, just maybe, I wasn't alone, after all.

20

Tara

Wilmington, North Carolina

I thought I was screaming. I woke up abruptly and bolted out of bed and only then did I realize it wasn't my voice I was hearing but Grace's. I raced down the hall to her room, imagining someone hurting her. I was ready to tear out the intruder's eyes with my bare hands.

But she was alone. Sitting in her bed in the half-light from the moon, she was doubled over, her hands covering her ears, and by the time I reached her, her voice had grown so tiny and strangled sounding that I could barely hear it.

"Help, help," she whimpered.

"Grace!" I wrapped my arms around her like a cocoon. "Sweetheart. It's okay." I rocked her and she settled against me. "A bad dream," I said. "Just a bad dream." I remembered this. I remembered her letting me hold her this way when she was little, and while I hated that she was frightened, I loved the feeling of holding her without her pushing me away. "What was it, honey?" I asked. "Do you want to tell me about it?" She always used to tell Sam her dreams.

She'd pour them out to him and he'd listen so carefully, as if he'd treasure every detail forever.

I felt her shake her head beneath my chin. She clutched my arm, let go, clutched, let go, reminding me of the way she'd open and close her fist against my breast when she nursed as a baby.

"Was it about Daddy?" I asked, then bit my lip. She hated my probing.

"My fault Noelle died." Her voice was so soft and muffled that I thought I'd heard her wrong.

"Your fault?" I asked. "Gracie, no! How could it possibly be your fault?"

She shook her head again.

"Tell me," I said. "Why would you think that?"

She drew away from me, but only a little so that our bodies still touched. When I reached out to stroke her back she didn't withdraw.

"The day she died, she sent me an email," she said. "It was the kind she always sent, trying to guilt me into volunteering."

"Uh-huh," I said.

"And Cleve sent an email, too. I was writing back to him, telling him how annoying Noelle could be…saying all kinds of negative things about her. About her being a whack job and everything. And right after I hit send, I realized I'd sent it to her, not Cleve."

"Oh, no." I was glad it was dark enough that she couldn't see my smile. I'd done that myself more than once. Who hadn't? But I felt for Grace and I felt for Noelle being on the receiving end of an email like that from a girl she adored. "We all make that mistake at least—"

"Then she killed herself." Grace cut me off. "Like a couple of hours—maybe a couple of *minutes*—after she got my email. She read these horrible things I said about her and then she killed herself."

"No, Grace," I said. "You can't pin her suicide on yourself. Maybe she never even read your email, but even if she did, that's not enough to send someone over the edge. Whatever was bothering Noelle was deep and had been going on for a long, long time."

I'd had my own problems sleeping in the two days since Emerson showed me the letter she'd found. I could think of little else. I kept picturing a baby slipping out of Noelle's grasp. When? Where? How horrible she must have felt! I kept trying unsuccessfully to wipe the image from my head. I wished I could tell Grace about it to ease her mind, but the secret needed to stay between Emerson and me for now. Maybe forever.

As usual, though, I couldn't bear the silence and distance that began to open up between us again as she recovered from her dream.

"There are some things I know about Noelle," I said, needing to fill the silence and keep her engaged with me. "There were some reasons for her depression that explain her suicide, honey, and trust me, they have nothing at all to do with you. This would have happened whether you'd sent that email or not."

"What kind of things?" She looked at me almost suspiciously, her eyes glistening in the moonlight.

"I can't talk about them yet. Emerson and I are trying to figure out the reasons Noelle was so down. We think something happened to...with Noelle a long time ago that—"

"Like she was molested or something?"

"No. Nothing like that." I shouldn't have said a word. There was a good possibility I would never be able to reveal what I knew about Noelle to Grace. "*I* don't even know all the details, but I'm just telling you this to put your mind at ease. All you need to know is that you had absolutely nothing to do with what happened to Noelle. Okay?"

She gave a small nod as she lay down.

"You going to be able to go back to sleep?"

"I'm fine." She settled down under the covers and turned on her side, facing the wall. My body felt chilled where she'd been close to me. I didn't want to leave. I touched her shoulder. Rubbed it.

"You don't work this afternoon, do you?" I asked.

"No. Tomorrow."

"I can drive you home today, then."

"Jenny'll give me a ride."

I hesitated. "I can tell you're still upset," I said. "You're so much like your daddy, honey. You ruminate on things and it's not good. Maybe tonight we could—"

"Mom!" She rolled onto her back, and although I couldn't see her face well, I knew she was staring daggers at me. "I want to *sleep!*"

"Okay." I smiled ruefully to myself. She'd given me an inch and I'd tried for a mile. I leaned over, kissed her cheek. "I love you," I said. "Sleep tight."

I had to fight the urge to check on Grace the next day to be sure she was okay after her rough night. That was both the benefit and the curse of teaching at your child's school: access to her was way too easy. She wouldn't appreciate my interference, though, and I actually went out of my way to avoid seeing her during the day.

When I walked into the house after school that afternoon, the message light was blinking on the kitchen phone. I punched in the pass code and lifted the receiver to my ear.

"Hi, Tara," Ian said. Then he chuckled. "I have to tell you, I get a jolt every time I hear Sam's outgoing message on your voice mail. It's nice, though. Nice to hear his voice. So I'm just checking on you. Hope you and Grace are doing okay."

I set down the phone.

Well.

I had honestly, completely, forgotten that Sam had recorded our outgoing message. Emerson mentioned it in the first few weeks after he died, but someone could have told me my house was purple back then and it would have sailed clear over my head. I guessed no one had had the nerve to mention it to me since. Except Ian, and he did it in a nice way.

I pulled my cell phone from my purse and dialed our home number. The phone on the counter rang four times while I bit my lip, waiting. Then the voice mail picked up.

"Hey, there!" Sam sounded like he was in the next room. "You've reached Sam, Tara and Grace and we hope you'll leave us a message. Bye!"

I stared at the phone in my hand for a moment, then started to cry, hugging the phone to my heart. I sat on the stool next to the kitchen island and sobbed so hard my tears pooled on the granite. I'd thought I was done with this part of the grief—this sucking-down, soul-searing pain—but apparently not.

It took me twenty minutes to pull myself together. Then I looked at the phone again, with determination this time. I needed to change the message. The thing was, I had no idea how to do it.

I wondered, too, what Grace would say. I remembered her reaction when she walked into our bedroom to see that I'd packed all of Sam's clothing in black trash bags marked for Goodwill. He'd been gone two weeks by then, and I'd felt an extraordinary need to get rid of the clothes he would never be able to wear again. I'd heard that some women hung on to their deceased husband's clothing for years, but another piece of my heart chipped off when I saw those suits and shirts and khakis and tracksuits in the closet each morning.

"You're erasing him!" Grace had screamed at me when she saw the bags. I'd tried to hold her—I'd wanted us to cry *together*—but she'd pushed me away and run to her room. I'd thought, *Tomorrow she'll talk to me,* but now two hundred tomorrows had passed and she was as cut off from me as ever. Why *had* I gotten rid of Sam's things so quickly? Was it normal? I'd thought it would help, not seeing his clothes in the closet each morning. I hadn't thought about how hard it would be to see the emptiness in their place.

I picked up the phone and pushed a few buttons, trying to figure out how to change the message. Grace would probably not even notice, anyway. She never used the house line.

I was listening to the instructions when Grace walked into the kitchen. I jumped. I hadn't realized that she'd beaten me home from school, and I hoped she hadn't heard my breakdown. From the start, I'd felt the need to be strong for her. Now I turned the phone off quickly, not wanting to change the message in front of her.

"What are you doing?" She stood on the other side of the island, eyeing the phone with suspicion.

"I thought it was time I changed the outgoing message," I admitted, "but I can't remember how."

"To take Dad's voice off it, you mean."

I tried to determine if there was an accusation in her words. "Yes," I said. "I thought it was time."

She looked at the phone in my hand instead of at me. "I guess." She reached for the receiver. "I can do it if you want."

"I'd appreciate it."

She deftly hit a few buttons, then said, "Hi, this is Grace." She held the phone out to me and I stared at it, not certain what she wanted me to do. She gave me a look that said, *You are a dork,* and pressed a button. "I'll say, 'This is Grace,' and you just add, 'And Tara,' and then I'll finish it. All right?"

"Yes. Good." I moved closer to her, our heads touching. I could smell her shampoo. I was so lonely for that scent. It put a lump in my throat.

"Hi, this is Grace."

"And Tara."

"Leave us a message," she said, and then she hung up. "There."

"Thank you." I smiled.

"Anytime." She picked up an apple from the fruit bowl on the counter and turned toward the hallway. I wanted to grab her. Keep her in the kitchen with me. *Were you able to get back to sleep after your nightmare last night?* I wanted to ask her. *Tell me about your day! Who's your favorite teacher this quarter? Have you spoken to Cleve lately?* But I forced myself to keep my mouth shut, because what just happened between us, insignificant though it seemed, felt like magic to me and I didn't want to ruin it.

21

Anna

Washington, D.C.

Bryan and I sat across the desk from Doug Davis, the transplant specialist at Children's, as he leafed through Haley's thick file. He pulled out one of the sheets of paper, set it on the desk and tapped it with his finger. "I have the report on Haley's bone marrow," he said, "and unfortunately she has a cell type that's a bit more challenging to match but certainly not impossible, so there's no reason to be pessimistic." He was looking directly at me. Did I look pessimistic? I was scared out of my wits. Was that the same thing?

It felt strange to be at Children's without Haley. She was with Marilyn and the kids for a long weekend and I couldn't wait to hear all about it tonight. I was glad she was having a getaway, but three days without her and I was in withdrawal. I missed my daughter. I hated that I'd have to bring her back to Children's tomorrow for another dose of the maintenance chemo.

She'd called me that morning and I could tell she was having a blast with her cousins. They'd skated at an indoor rink, cheered at Megan's soccer game, camped out in the backyard, went to the movies and hung out for hours at the mall. I wasn't crazy about kids hanging out in malls, but I felt like cramming as much fun into Haley's life right now as possible. If she wanted to hang out at the mall and she was safely with her herd of Collier cousins, well, then, damn it, let her.

"Can you test us today?" Bryan asked Dr. Davis. "I don't understand why this isn't being rushed. Why no one's running in here right this second to swab our cheeks."

Dr. Davis smiled. He was so young. I woke up one morning and all the doctors I dealt with were suddenly younger than me. "We'll see if you're compatible," he said, "but parents are usually the last resort. They're rarely a good match. Best, of course, is a sibling. Does Haley have any brothers or sisters?"

I opened my mouth to speak, but Bryan beat me to it. "We had another child." He cleared his throat. Adjusted his glasses. "A girl," he said. "She disappeared shortly after she was born. We don't even know if she's alive."

His words rocked me. They were *my* words. The ones *I* usually said. The ones that made my throat tighten up every time I said them out loud. He hadn't mentioned Lily once since his sudden appearance in Haley's hospital room two months ago. Had I thought he'd forgotten our lost child? There was real sorrow in his voice. There was agony. I'd thought I was alone with that sorrow all these years.

"How tragic." Dr. Davis took off his own glasses. "Both for that little girl and for Haley," he said. "There's a one in four chance that a sibling will match. When we get into the general population, it's closer to one in twenty-five thousand."

The sudden anger I felt at Bryan—at the *world*—surprised

me, and I struggled to keep it in. If we hadn't lost Lily, we'd have a one in four chance of saving Haley. It was that simple.

"She has cousins," I said, wondering how cousins would fit into the confusing picture of who would be a compatible donor and who wouldn't. "Four girls. They're Bryan's sister's children."

"We'll test all of them," he said. "But most likely we'll be turning to the global donor database. If any of them are a possible match, they'll be asked to give a blood sample. Donors are almost always found—" he nodded encouragingly "—it's just a question of how quickly."

I thought of all the stories I'd heard of people who died while waiting for a transplant. I remembered a little boy who'd been receiving treatment here at Children's when Haley was a toddler and how they'd been unable to find a donor for him in time. I began to shiver as if I were freezing.

"We'll keep Haley on the maintenance regimen until we find the donor," Dr. Davis said. "The good news is that she'll probably get some hair back." He smiled. "At least for a while."

"Why just for a while?" Bryan asked, and I realized he hadn't seen her hair since she was a year old. Back then, it had been downy and nearly blond. As a twelve-year-old, she wore it in a messy ponytail, long tendrils of it coming out of the elastic band and falling around her face. She didn't care what it looked like. I wanted her to reach the age of caring. I'd never really reached that age myself—I was still a low maintenance sort of woman, not even wearing makeup unless I had a speaking engagement. I didn't care if she was like me or not. I just wanted her to have the chance to figure out what kind of woman she wanted to be.

"When we find a donor, we'll begin preparing her for the transplant. She'll have a couple of weeks of intense chemotherapy and radiation, and she'll lose her hair again. After the transplant, she'll have at least another month or longer in the hospital and about four months' recovery at home." He told us about the isolation area and the extreme hygiene measures we'd have to take in caring for Haley.

"Whew." Bryan sounded as overwhelmed as I felt. Nothing the doctor was telling us was a surprise to me. I'd done my research. I'd seen other kids and their families on the unit go through this ordeal. But the reality of the situation was only now hitting home for me. Now it was *Haley* I pictured enduring the ordeal ahead of us.

Bryan and I were pretty quiet in the car on the drive back to Alexandria. We stopped in Old Town for lattes, carrying our cups to a bench on the waterfront. The day was spectacular. One of the white riverboats was docked to our left. It positively glowed in the sunlight and the Potomac River was a sheet of silver in front of us. Everything I experienced in that moment, I wanted for Haley. I wanted her to be able to see that riverboat. To take a ride in it. To sit on the bench and marvel at the silvery water. To taste a caramel latte. I couldn't seem to see or smell or touch anything without desperately wanting her to be able to do the same.

Bryan and I sat in silence for a few minutes, taking in the view as we tried to digest everything we'd heard from Dr. Davis.

"I'm scared," I admitted finally. "Even if they find a match, it seems like there are so many things that could go wrong."

He didn't say anything right away. He sipped his coffee

and stared out at the water. I was about to prod him when he finally spoke.

"Listen," he said, "I want you to know I'm not going anywhere. I'm not going to take off again."

I supposed he was trying to reassure me, but instead his words pissed me off. "You'd better not," I said. "Not after you've let Haley care about you again."

"I won't."

I looked out at the water, getting my nerve up for what I was going to say next. "I was surprised when you mentioned Lily," I said.

"Why? Did you think I could ever forget about her?"

"I frankly wondered."

"Oh, Anna. Seriously?"

I turned on the bench to face him. "You ran off, Bryan," I said. "You started a new life. You never talked about her. I mean, you talked to the police and the authorities back when it happened, but all these years, you've never talked to *me* about her."

"It was such a difficult time."

"'Difficult' doesn't begin to describe it."

He took off his sunglasses and rubbed the bridge of his nose. "I have regrets," he said.

And damn well you should, I thought. "Tell me your regrets." I wanted an accounting. I wanted to make sure he didn't miss any.

He looked at me as if deciding whether to take the bait.

"First and foremost, I regret not being a father to Haley," he said. "There is no excuse for it other than cowardice. I wasn't a good father to her from the start. I never let myself get close to her. I was afraid of getting close and then having her disappear the way Lily did. I know that was irrational, but it's how I felt."

I remembered how little he'd had to do with Haley during her first year. I'd thought it was normal. Babies and mothers were so attached to one another that I figured fathers didn't quite know how to fit into the picture. I never realized it was fear that kept him from bonding with her.

"When she got sick—" he shook his head "—that was it. I had to escape. Gutless. I know."

"You're taking the risk of losing her now," I said. "How come?"

"I think this is my personal brand of midlife crisis." He smiled. "Some guys see life passing them by, going too quickly, and they fill the void with a hot car or a hot girlfriend. I saw life passing me by and felt the void, but I knew it wasn't a car or a woman I needed. I knew what I was missing. My daughter." He slipped his sunglasses back on. "I was trying to figure out how to gracefully come back into her life when you called. Then I knew it wouldn't be graceful, but I had to do it. To be here for her. For you, too. Though it scared the shit out of me, Anna." He looked at me. "It still does. But if anything happened to her and I didn't make the effort to get to know her, I'd never forgive myself. There was already so much I couldn't forgive myself for. I earned a medal for bravery in the army, but I was a coward when it came to my own family. I wanted to give that medal back."

I was softening toward him. I believed him. "I'm glad you're telling me all this," I said. "It's kind of late, but I'm still glad."

"There's something else," he said. "I have a friend here. He and his wife own a car dealership in Maryland. When I told you I had a job interview last week, I was really over there talking to them."

I remembered his call from the interview. The woman's

laughter in the background. I frowned, waiting, wondering where this was going.

"They had a child who died of leukemia many years ago. I told them about Haley before I came out here and they told me if she ended up needing a transplant, they wanted to sponsor a bone marrow drive for her. So that's what I was talking to them about. Just in case she ended up needing it. And she does. So—"

"Wow." I felt guilty for having doubted him. "Wow."

"As I understand it, the possibility of finding a donor from the drive is slim," he said, "but the point is, it puts more people into the pool. They told me if you and Haley are willing to go public with, you know, Haley's story, it helps pull people in. But you don't have to."

I'd have to think about that. We—all three of us—had a pretty damn poignant story, given Lily's disappearance and Haley's first bout with leukemia. But I wasn't sure I wanted to put my daughter on display.

"I'll talk to her about it," I said. "*We* can talk to her about it. Either way, thank you for thinking of this. For doing this."

I watched a group of tourists line up to get on the riverboat. I was still amazed by the fact that Bryan had this whole donor drive up his sleeve. That he'd been thinking ahead.

"You know," he said now, "the whole Lily thing... It took me a long time to figure it out for myself. I still...it's still hard for me to talk about her. I know you were angry with me for not going to Wilmington to check on her back then. Believe me, I wish I had, but I couldn't leave you. I thought Lily was safe, but that I could lose you at any minute. You were hanging between life and death."

"I know," I said. "I know what you did seemed to make

sense at the time." I still wished he had tried harder. Called the hospital in Wilmington sooner than he did. Pressed them harder for more information. *Something.* Yet he couldn't have known that Lily had vanished. How could anyone have known?

"I felt like it was my fault she disappeared," he said.

"I made you feel that way." I had wanted him to apologize to me for everything, but I could suddenly see my own culpability. I'd blamed him because I didn't know who else to blame. I'd been in a coma at Duke University Hospital when he'd been called back from Somalia and of course I'd been his main concern. Yet when I came out of the coma and we learned that Lily had somehow disappeared from the Wilmington hospital, I was furious with him for not going there to check on her. I froze him out. "We were screwed up, both of us," I said. "We should have been getting some serious marriage counseling."

"No kidding." He smiled. "We should have had a counselor move in with us." He took a sip of his coffee. "Have you ever…did you ever get any leads on what happened to her?" he asked.

I shook my head. "The investigators thought she died, as you know," I said. "Maybe a medical mistake someone was trying to cover up, but I've never been able to accept that theory." I didn't *want* to accept that theory. "Then there were all sorts of dead ends. They called me one time when Haley was about three. A woman had contacted them from South Carolina to say she thought her cousin's little girl was actually Lily. She said the cousin just appeared with a baby one day around the same time Lily was taken and this woman thought it was weird. The investigators asked why she'd waited so many years to call and she said she'd been afraid to get her cousin in trouble, but now she thought the cousin was abusing the girl so she was making the call. It turned out the cousin *had* kidnapped someone's baby, just not mine. Not ours." I could still feel the letdown when the investigator called me with the DNA results.

"I really got my hopes up, Bryan," I said. "After Haley went into remission when she was nearly four and I could finally think about something other than getting her well, she and I went to Wilmington for a week. We just walked the streets, while I looked for a seven-year-old girl who might be Lily. I hung out around the schools. It was a little crazy of me, especially since the hospital she'd been in covered such a huge geographical area. Lily could have been anywhere. I've always clung to the hope that someone who desperately wanted a child saw the most beautiful baby in the hospital and took her. At least that way, she would have been wanted and cared for."

"I never got to see her." Bryan's face was slack with sadness.

"I know," I said. "At least I had her for a few hours."

"Does Haley know about her?"

"Of course." He was not used to openness. To hard truths. It had taken him two months to get up the courage to mention Lily. "I told her very early," I said. "She couldn't have been more than five or six. Bryan, she's an unusual girl."

"I know that," he said with a smile. "She's fantastic."

"Maybe it was because she had to go through all the medical stuff when she was so small, I don't know, but she's always been different from other kids her age. She even helps me look for Lily."

He looked startled. "What do you mean?"

"She knows the sort of work the Missing Children's Bureau does. She goes through the leads we get, looking for anything that might be related to Lily. She hangs out at the office with me sometimes. She and I have gone back to Wilmington twice, looking for Lily. She and I share that gigantic hole in our hearts. She even has a website she made herself called 'Sibs of the Missing.'"

"You're kidding. She made it herself?"

I nodded. "She's a computer geek, just like her father."

He leaned his head back, looking up at the sky. "I love her," he said. "All these years, I sent money and Christmas presents and all that, but I didn't love her. I didn't feel anything except guilt for being a shitty father. Now I love her and…I can honestly say I've never felt like this before. This kind of emotion. The moment I first saw her in the hospital room, bald and puking—" he looked at me, his smile both confused and tender "—I wanted to take her place," he said. "Give her my health. Let me be the one sick in that bed."

"Oh, yeah," I said. "I know that feeling."

"I'm so pissed at myself."

I didn't want to hear any more regrets. The need to hear them, years in the making, had evaporated. "Let's put the past behind us," I said. "You're here now. Now you're earning that medal for bravery."

22

Emerson

Wilmington, North Carolina

Hot!'s kitchen was far cleaner than the one I had at home. That was because the health department never showed up at my house, but they could sashay into the café at any moment. We had a ninety-nine rating and I was aiming for a hundred, which was why I was making Jenny clean the ice machine and scour every inch of the countertop before I'd let her go for the evening.

"I'm going to the library straight from here, Jenny," I said, checking the refrigerator to make sure we had enough half-and-half for the morning, "so there's a container of leftover butternut squash chili in here for dinner tonight. Will you take it home and heat it up for you and Dad?"

Jenny looked up from the counter. "You're not coming home for dinner?" She acted like I'd said I planned to fly to the moon, but I couldn't blame her. Except for the occasional girls' night out with Tara, I was always home for dinner. Tonight, though, I had other plans. Unfortunately, I needed to lie about them.

"I need to do some research on heirloom recipes I want to add to the lunch menu," I said. "I can't get to them on Google, but the library has access." My vagueness paid off. Jenny's eyes glazed over at the word *research*. It had worked with Ted, too, when I gave him the same story. I'd lost Ted with *heirloom*. I had the feeling this wouldn't be the last lie I told my family for a while. Not until I had things figured out. "So is that okay with you?" I took off my apron and hung it from the hook near the rear door. "You'll take care of dinner?"

"I guess." She pumped the spray bottle in an arc across the counter and began rubbing. "But I wanted to talk to you about my job. I'd like to work fewer hours." .

I laughed. "Wouldn't we all," I said.

She didn't look at me and I wondered if she expected me to give her grief about it. I honestly didn't need her that much right now. My manager, Sandra, and my other waitress and one cook could take care of things most of the time. Jenny needed the money, though, and she was a big help on the days she worked.

"I'm serious." She moved the toaster to clean behind it. I tried to remember the last time I'd moved our toaster at home. "I'm doing more of the babies stuff because of Noelle being—" she shrugged "—you know."

"And you want more time with Devon."

Jenny smiled down at the counter, red-cheeked and busted. "I don't have much free time right now," she said.

She was smitten by this guy. I was so caught up in my own life, I'd barely noticed what was going on in hers.

"Less hours means less money in your pocket," I said, putting away the bowls that had been air-drying in the dish rack.

"I know."

"You work out a new schedule with Sandra and we'll see how it looks," I said. Jenny was a good kid. She was so much like me. Easygoing, with plenty of friends. Maybe not the most ambitious person in the world, but frankly, I thought it was more important to be liked than to be successful. I knew you could find experts who would argue with that, but I didn't care. I wanted to be liked. So sue me. Jenny seemed to be well-liked by every person—child or adult—who knew her. I'd rather raise a child like that than one who'd stab another person in the back to get ahead.

The few boys she'd dated all seemed like nice kids, too. She hadn't been serious with any of them—at least, not as far as I knew—and that had been fine. Maybe Devon was different. I liked when they went out as a foursome with Grace and Cleve over the summer. Safety in numbers, though maybe I was kidding myself about that.

"How's Grace holding up?" I asked as I closed the cabinet door.

"You mean about Cleve?"

"It's got to be hard for her since you're still with Devon."

"She's…" Jenny shrugged. "She's bummed. And Cleve is being a cretin."

"Well, I can understand his feelings." I took the chili out of the refrigerator, afraid she might forget it. "He probably wants to experience college and being away from home without being tied down."

"It's not that," Jenny said. "I get that. It's how he's acting now. He constantly texts her and emails her and that keeps her hopes up that he'll get back together with her."

"Oh," I said. Not good.

"I mean, she does it first," Jenny said. "Texts him or

whatever. But he always gets back to her and then she thinks he still cares."

"I'm sure he *does* still care."

"Not the way she wants him to." She put the spray bottle in the cabinet beneath the sink and tossed the paper towels in the trash. "I think he's being mean," she said.

"It's a double whammy for her." I slipped the chili into a plastic grocery bag. "First her dad and then Cleve." Poor Grace. She'd been so close to Sam. I'd envied that. Ted and Jenny didn't connect the way Sam and Grace had. "I feel bad for her," I said.

"Me, too." Jenny washed her hands at the sink, then leaned back against the counter as she dried them with a paper towel. "I can't imagine Daddy dying, Mom," she said. "It's hard enough having Noelle die and Great-Grandpa at hospice."

"I know, baby." One of the hospice nurses had called me that morning to tell me my grandfather wanted to see me alone the next time, without Jenny or Ted. I had no idea why, but I'd honor his wish, of course. I'd do anything for him.

I stepped closer to Jenny, brushed aside the hair that nearly covered her left eye and planted a kiss on her temple. "Love you," I said.

"You, too." She shook her head to let the curtain of hair fall across her forehead again. Then she looked at the bag on the counter. "Ready to lock up?"

"Uh-huh." I put my arm around her as we headed for the back door. I'd miss spending so much time with her if she cut back her hours in the café. "So how serious is it getting with Devon?" I asked.

"Not serious," she said.

I felt the invisible wall go up between us and knew our

mother/daughter bonding moment had passed. There'd be no getting it back this evening. That was all right. I'd remember these few minutes with Jenny as I tried to track down Anna, the woman who'd never had the chance to know her daughter because of what Noelle had done.

I sat down at one of the computers in the library, pulled up the NC Live website and typed in the password they'd given me at the desk. At home, I'd checked Google for *Anna* and *baby* and *Wilmington* and *hospital* and received plenty of useless hits. I was hoping NC Live would give me something more to go on.

According to Noelle's record books, the last baby she delivered had been a boy, so our guess that she'd given up practicing after the "accident" was wrong. Unless, of course, she'd written nothing at all about that botched delivery in her records. I wanted to find the newspaper article Noelle had mentioned in the letter she'd started to write on July 8, 2003. Maybe an impossible task, but I needed to try.

It took me a while and some help from one of the librarians, but I finally found the search page for the *Wilmington Star*. Noelle's letter didn't say exactly *when* she saw the article mentioning Anna. NC Live only had issues of the *Star* back to April 2003, so I hoped the article was later than that. Maybe it actually appeared on the eighth and that was what prompted Noelle to write to her.

Optimistically, I decided to search June and July 2003 for any *Wilmington Star* articles containing the name Anna. How many could there be? Fifty-seven, as it turned out. I was swamped by Annas. I began sifting through the articles—obituaries, track team results, a crooked sheriff, a couple of births. I narrowed the results down to women who might have been of childbearing age during the years

Noelle was a midwife. There was an Anna who won a Yard of the Month award, a twenty-seven-year-old Special Olympics athlete and a woman who stole beer from an IGA store. I jotted down the surname of the Yard of the Month winner—Fischelle—who seemed the only real possibility. She lived in midtown. I pictured her putting all her energy into her yard to try to fill the empty place her missing child had left behind.

I searched online for her. There was only one Anna Fischelle, and she did indeed live in Wilmington, but as close as I could figure from the White Pages website, she was about sixty-eight years old.

I tried another search of the Wilmington paper using the words *hospital* and *baby* and *missing,* but none of the results seemed promising. I sat back and frowned at the computer.

Time to get serious. Noelle had been a news junkie. At one time, she'd even had the *New York Times* delivered to her door in Wilmington each morning, but that had been long ago, before she started reading it online. I knew she'd read the *Washington Post* online, too, because she was always complaining about how conservative it had become. She read it, anyway. She loved any excuse to rail against pundits who annoyed her.

I tried the *Post* first, searching for an Anna between June 1 and July 8, 2003, and quickly had ten pages of two hundred and two results. I stared up at the library ceiling. This was a losing battle. It seemed silly to look at the *Post* and would be sillier still to look at the *New York Times.* The baby was taken from a *Wilmington* hospital. The article had almost certainly been in the Wilmington paper. I was about to switch back to the *Star* when my eye fell on a headline halfway down the first page of results: Police Defend Actions in Case of Missing Three-year-old Girl. I stared at the headline, caught by the word *missing*. But that couldn't be the right article. The child Noelle had taken had been an infant. Maybe it was because I felt lost in a sea of search results and didn't know what else to do that I clicked on the headline and began scanning the article for the name *Anna*.

On June 3, 2003, a little Maryland girl had disappeared from a campground in the Shenandoah Valley while vacationing with her family. Apparently, there'd been some controversy over the way the police had dealt with her disappearance, and that's where Anna came in. I found her in the very last sentence.

Anna Knightly, spokesperson for the Missing Children's Bureau, defended police handling of the case. "Issuing an Amber Alert with only a physical description of the child would have been inappropriate," she stated.

This couldn't be our Anna, but I checked Google for her name, anyway. The name Anna Knightly was more common that I could have guessed. Anna Knightlys were breeding dogs, blogging about counted cross-stitch and teaching school. I added the word *missing* to my search and up popped an article I hadn't even known I'd been looking for. It appeared in the *Washington Post* on September 14, 2010—the day Noelle killed herself—and the headline read New Director Named for Missing Children's Bureau. The article was brief and to the point.

Anna Knightly has been named director of the Missing Children's Bureau. Ms. Knightly has worked with the bureau in various capacities since 2001, inspired by the disappearance of her own infant daughter from

a North Carolina hospital. She has been committed
to the cause of reuniting missing children and their
parents since that time.

I sat back in my chair, an icy sweat breaking out all over
my body. I didn't really believe Noelle's half-written letter
until that moment. I couldn't picture her stealing a pack of
gum, much less an infant. I couldn't imagine her living a
life of lies. Yet here it was. Here was the proof.

Now, what was I supposed to do with it?

23

Noelle

Wrightsville Beach, North Carolina
1989

"Hey, Galloway Girls," Sam said from the back door of the little oceanfront cottage, "here's my contribution to dinner tonight."

Flanked by Emerson and Tara, Noelle walked across the musty-smelling living room and peered into the bucket Sam was holding. Four sad-looking, silver-scaled fish lay one on top of the other in the bottom of the bucket.

"Wow, excellent!" Tara said.

"What are they?" Emerson asked.

"Fish." Sam grinned proudly.

Emerson swatted his arm. "I meant what kind."

"Who cares." He laughed. The four of them had been at the beach for two days and his skin was already a rich caramel, his eyes the color of the sky behind his head.

Noelle could see that at least one of the fish was still alive and laboring to breathe. She shuddered and raised her eyes from the bucket to Sam's face.

"You're a brute, Sam," she said.

Sam looked in the bucket himself. "I don't think they suffered too much," he said, but now he actually looked a little worried and that touched her. Sam was a softie.

He leaned over to peck Tara on the cheek. "I'll clean them out here," he said. "I just wanted to show them off first."

The oceanfront house on Wrightsville Beach was small and funky and perfect. Tara and Sam had the largest bedroom, while Emerson had the nicest of the smaller ones. She'd suggested that she and Noelle draw straws for it, but Noelle told her to take it. She would do anything for Emerson. She said it didn't matter which room she had and that was the truth. She was happy just to be at the beach with friends she'd come to love over the past ten months. She would never have the tight, freshman roommate bond that existed between Tara and Emerson, since she was three years older and had spent the year as their RA, but both of the younger women had become the closest friends she'd ever had. Early on, she'd worried that they'd think she was insinuating herself into their lives, but she gradually felt their genuine affection for her. They accepted her, quirks and all, the way few people had.

In some ways, though, she was even closer to Sam.

It turned out he'd been a teaching assistant in her Medicine and the Law course early in the semester and she discovered he was far more than just a pretty face. While her professor focused on how medical personnel could protect themselves from lawsuits, Sam seemed more concerned about the patients and Noelle loved that about him. He became a part of her world both in the classroom and out. They'd fallen into a pattern of meeting at the restaurant in the student union during their break after class, and she'd tell him about patients she was working with in her clinicals and he was always fascinated. Always concerned. She'd thought of lawyers as calculating hustlers who twisted the truth to suit their clients' needs, but Sam would never be that sort of lawyer. She hoped law school wouldn't jade him. He'd be going in the fall and she warned him at least once a week to hang on to his values the way she'd hung on to hers during nursing school.

Their conversations in the student union would occasionally stray from the professional to the personal, and she'd share with him things she usually kept to herself. Her father's desertion. Her mother's midwifery. She'd point out the handful of men she'd slept with, as well as the men who wanted her whom she'd turned away, disinterested.

"You like the kooks," he said to her.

"What do you mean?"

"The guys you've slept with." He nodded toward one of them who was sitting at a nearby table, hunched over a book, his waist-long braid over his shoulder. "They're outside the norm."

They were. So was Sam, in his own way, and if he had not already been taken she would have hoped for something more with him. She knew he was attracted to her, yet his commitment to Tara was as strong as if they'd been promised to each other at birth.

Things would be so different in the fall, and that's what made this summer and her time with her friends so precious. In the fall, Sam would be in law school at Wake Forest and she'd be heading to midwifery school in Greenville. While she was excited about getting closer to her goal, she felt a profound sadness at the thought of being apart from Emerson, Tara and Sam.

Especially, of course, Emerson.

Although her mother knew she'd befriended Emerson, she thought Noelle had made a sort of peace with the whole situation and could leave it alone. She would leave it alone, yes. She had no desire to hurt anyone. But peace? Peace was impossible.

All during the year, she'd hoped that Emerson's parents might visit her from California and Noelle would finally get to meet her birth mother. That never happened. Once, Emerson's grandparents visited unexpectedly from Jacksonville, but Noelle arrived back in the dorm mere minutes after they'd left. Ironically, she'd felt relieved. She was afraid that a surprise meeting with her grandparents might have caused her to blurt out something she'd later regret. She wanted to meet them, but she needed to be prepared.

The fourth night in the cottage at Wrightsville Beach, Noelle woke up with a start. She lay quietly in the darkness trying to figure out what had jolted her awake. Voices? The phone? Everything was so still.

Suddenly, though, her bedroom door flew open.

"Noelle, wake up!" Sam moved toward her bed. He shook her shoulder, and she sat up, brushing her hair back from her face with her hands.

"What's going on?" she asked.

"Emerson's mother's dead!" he said. "She—"

"What?"

"Her father just called. They were riding bikes and she was hit by a car. Emerson is—"

"Oh, no." She swung her legs over the side of her bed and pulled on her shorts, her hands shaking. This couldn't be happening. "Where's Emerson?"

"She ran out to the beach." Sam headed for the living

room. "She's hysterical. Tara's gone after her and I'm on my way out there."

"I'm right behind you," she said.

They ran through the living room and onto the porch. Sam pushed open the screen door and Noelle followed him out to the beach. She couldn't absorb this. Her mother dead? *No, no, no.*

The air was like tar, thick and black, and the sea was so calm that they could hear Emerson before they saw her. The keening tore at Noelle's heart. They found her sitting in a crumpled heap in the sand, Tara cradling her in her arms like a child.

"I can't believe it!" Emerson wailed. "I can't believe it!"

Noelle and Sam dropped to the sand next to them, wrapping their arms around both Emerson and Tara. Sam and Tara murmured words of comfort, but Noelle had no voice. It was caught fast in her throat and she was glad of the darkness so she could shed her own tears for the mother she would never have the chance to know.

None of them slept that night. There were a dozen more phone calls, arrangements being made, flights being booked. Tara decided she would fly to California with Emerson. Noelle somehow missed the information about Emerson's grandparents picking them up for the drive to the airport, so she was the one who opened the cottage door and came face-to-face with a man whose vivid blue eyes were very much like her own. She knew instantly who he was and she stood frozen in the living room, her hand locked on the doorknob.

"I'm Emerson's grandpa," he said. "Are they ready?" He had starbursts of laugh lines at the corners of each eye as though he laughed often and hard. He wasn't laughing now, though.

Noelle's mouth was dry as sand. She knew she should say something—*I'm sorry for your loss*—but the words wouldn't form. "I'll get her," she finally managed to say. She turned around and saw Sam walking toward the door. "Tell Emerson her grandfather's here," she said, heading for the bathroom. "I don't feel well."

She'd wanted to hug Emerson and Tara goodbye. Instead, she stayed in the small bathroom, sitting fully dressed on the toilet, waiting for them to leave. She heard muffled voices through the door. Voices belonging to her sister. Her grandfather. She sat there alone as the sound of slamming car doors sifted through the screen of the bathroom window.

Still, she didn't budge from the bathroom. She stayed there so long that Sam finally knocked on the door. "Noelle? You okay?" he asked.

She splashed water on her face and walked out of the room into the hallway. "I'm all right." She didn't look at him. She wasn't sure what was written in her face, but she didn't want him to read it.

"Tara and Emerson wanted to say goodbye."

"I just...I was nauseous for a minute."

Sam looked at his watch. "I can't believe it's only two," he said. "It feels like days since that call came this morning."

"I know." She felt him staring at her. "I'm going to read in my room for a while," she said.

"Sure you're okay?" he asked.

"Are any of us okay right now?"

He shook his head. "I guess not," he said, but he was looking at her with a mixture of worry and curiosity, and she had to turn away.

★ ★ ★

She wanted to call her mother to tell her what had happened and yet she wasn't ready. She would cry too hard and her mother would worry about her, but Noelle knew she would not be able to sympathize. Not the way she needed her to. Her mother already had such mixed feelings about Noelle's secret closeness to her biological family.

She picked up the phone a few times and started to dial the number at Miss Wilson's, but each time she put the receiver down again. Finally, she walked out to the beach where Sam was sitting in a beach chair, an open book resting on his bare thighs. She knelt in the sand next to his chair as if she were about to pray. She wrapped her hands around his arm, warm beneath her palms.

"Can I talk to you?" she asked.

He set down his book, and although she couldn't see his eyes behind his sunglasses she saw the concern in his face. "Of course you can talk to me," he said.

She reached forward to lift his sunglasses to his forehead. "I can't see your eyes," she said. "I need to see them."

He squinted, studying her for a moment. "Are you all right?"

She shook her head.

"Let's go inside." He handed her his book, then stood and folded his chair. He carried the chair in one hand and put his other arm around her shoulders as they walked back to the cottage.

Noelle's throat felt tight and achy. Could she do this? Could she tell someone? Would she be able to get the words out? *Should* she?

Sam motioned to the rockers on the screened porch and they sat down. "Talk to me," he said.

She opened her mouth, but her throat locked tight

around her voice and she lowered her face to her hands. Sam pulled his rocker right in front of hers and she felt his hands on either side of her head, his lips against her temple. It was exactly what she needed. The comfort of a friend. The comfort of a friend she knew loved her.

She lifted her head, wiping her tears with her fingers, and Sam sat back in his rocker, unsmiling. He rested his fingertips on her bare knee as he waited for her to get her emotions under control.

"What I say now..." She shook her head. Tried again. "If I tell you something, Sam, can you promise me you'll never tell anyone? Not even Tara. Not ever."

He hesitated, a line of worry between his eyebrows. "Yes," he said. "I promise."

Noelle licked her lips. "Emerson is my half sister," she said.

The line in his forehead deepened. "She's..." He cocked his head to the side as though he must have misunderstood her. "What are you talking about?"

"Her mother was my mother."

"But I've met your mother," he said.

"You've met my adoptive mother."

Her meaning was slowly sinking in. He rocked back in his chair. "Holy shit," he said.

"No one knows," she said. "Only my adoptive mother and me. And now you."

She explained everything. The file she'd found. How she'd felt when she saw Emerson's name on the list of students at Galloway. How her mother made her swear she would never tell any of this to a soul.

"Was it legal?" Sam asked. "Your adoption?"

"Yes, although there might have been some...I think my parents got some preferential treatment because my mother was involved in my birth. I don't know. At this point, it really doesn't matter."

"So you... *Shit*." His eyes widened. "You lost your biological mother this morning and you can't tell anyone."

She felt her lower lip tremble. "Except you."

"Your father," he asked. "Do you know who...?"

She looked down at her knees where his tan fingers still rested against her fair skin and shook her head. "Some boy she met at a party," she said. "I don't even have a name for him." She pounded her own knee with her fist. "That was my grandfather at the door earlier!" she said. "*My* grandfather. And I just stood there staring at him."

"I'm so sorry, Noelle," Sam said.

"I don't exist for that family. I couldn't say anything."

"Maybe..." Sam looked through the screens toward the beach. "You know how sometimes women who relinquish their kids for adoption later agree to have the records unsealed if both parties want to—"

"She didn't," Noelle said. "I've checked. I'm just a giant hideous reminder of a mistake she made. That's all right. I have a great mother, so I lucked out. But I thought I'd..." Her voice broke and she struggled to go on. "I thought I'd get to meet my birth mother someday," she said. "I thought there was time."

Sam stood and held out his hand. "Come here," he said, and when she stood, he closed his arms around, holding her while she cried. There were men who would be afraid of what she'd told him, she thought. Men who'd fear that level of intimacy or who'd crumble under the weight of such a monumental secret. But Sam felt like a pillar beneath her arms. Someone she could lean on. Someone she could talk to about anything. Her biggest wishes. Her worst secrets. Someone she'd be able to talk to. Always.

★ ★ ★

They spent the next three days together in the cottage. Tara would return on the evening of the third day, though Emerson would stay with her relatives in California another week. Noelle would always treasure those three days with Sam—days of a friendship that deepened by the hour. The only difficult thing was that she knew there was only one Sam and he was not hers. She'd always thought she could live without a man, easily. This man, though, she was not so sure she could live without.

By the morning of the third day, she'd found her smile again. She and Sam had cooked together, gone out to eat one night, rubbed sunscreen on each other's backs, swam in the sea and talked and talked and talked. The words felt like an aphrodisiac to Noelle, but she fought back the desire. He was not hers. *Don't ever hurt another woman the way Doreen hurt me,* her mother had told her. *Never,* she thought, lying in her bed at night, wishing Sam could be beside her. *Never.*

"I want you to know something," he said to her the night before Tara returned. They'd built a small illegal fire on the beach and were toasting marshmallows on bamboo skewers they'd found in the cottage.

"What's that?" Noelle nibbled the gooey white candy from the skewer.

"That I love you." Sam had his eyes on his skewer instead of on her. "But Tara is it for me. I think you know that." He glanced at her.

She felt dizzy from the heat of the night as well as from his admission.

"I love you, too," she said.

He nodded. That was no surprise to him. "You understand how it is with Tara and me, don't you? Our history. And how we've always just known we'd be together."

She nodded. "I love Tara, too," she said honestly. "If I can't have you, I'd want her to have you."

"The sort of life I want, I can have with her." He seemed lost in his own thoughts. "A normal, settled-down kind of life."

She felt the slightest sliver of pain. "What am I?" She smiled. "A freak?"

He laughed. "You're different, Noelle. Wonderfully different. You're never going to want the big house and the white picket fence and the two kids and a dog."

She wondered if that was really what *he* wanted. There was a very large part of Sam Vincent that was not a white-picket-fence sort of guy. But she didn't want to hurt him or Tara, and debating the merits of a settled-down life with him could only lead down that path.

"Just be my forever friend, okay?" she asked.

He held his skewer in front of her, offering her the perfect golden marshmallow. "You've got it," he said.

She slipped the marshmallow from the skewer with her fingertips and popped it into her mouth, feeling proud of herself for not asking more of Sam, proud of herself for not hurting Tara, not daring to think that forever was a long, long time.

24

Tara

Noelle's house looked sad to me as I pulled into the drive-way. The painters had scraped much of the blue from the front of the cottage and the siding was mottled and ugly. The sun had just risen, glowing pink in the windows. It was Saturday and I didn't know if the painters were working today. I hoped not. I was here to work on the garden and I wanted the time to think.

Emerson had found Anna. She was the head of a missing children's organization, which made her into a real human being to me, a woman who'd lived through an unimagin-able horror and come out of it strong and determined. I'd felt sick to my stomach when Emerson called to tell me what she'd learned. With each new piece of information, this woman's story was going to feel more real and our need to do something about it more inescapable. Emerson was coming over to my house that afternoon and we'd figure out what to do next. I knew she regretted ever opening that box of letters.

I got out of my van and surveyed Noelle's front yard. It was a mess, overgrown and weedy. Noelle'd had no interest in yard work with the exception of the garden. Although I was in charge of that garden until the house was rented, I'd only had time to water it and pull a few weeds. Now, nearly three weeks after Noelle's death, it needed some major attention. I pictured people driving by the decrepit house and yard, whispering to one another, *Something terrible must have happened here.* They wouldn't know the half of it.

Emerson had left Noelle's gardening tools in a large bucket on the back steps, but I'd brought my own. I sat on the steps, slipping on my kneepads and gloves as I looked out over the yard. It was small, the grass tired, the one tree stunted and scraggly. Someone had cut the grass recently; I could see the lines left by the mower. The yards on either side of Noelle's bled into hers. It was a sorry sight. Except for the garden. The rising sun seemed to settle on that corner of the yard, lighting it up like a jewel.

Behind me, Noelle's house felt so haunted that I shivered and got to my feet, walking away from it and toward the garden. If you have a friend, I pondered, a good friend, a woman you love, and you learn she's done something abominable, do you stop loving her? In spite of everything we were learning about Noelle, I refused to forget what she'd meant to us. To *me.* I was haunted by the note she'd left behind in which her one request was to take care of her garden. I would do that for the Noelle I knew and loved. The Noelle who lied and deceived had not been well, and I blamed all of us for not recognizing that fact and taking better care of her.

The garden was laid out in a triangle, the sides about

seven feet long, and it was bursting with color in spite of the fact that we were now into October. Containers of all shapes and sizes were filled with chrysanthemums that she must have planted right before she died. I got to work, cutting back the coneflowers and black-eyed Susans and Shasta daisies. I weeded around the impatiens. I'd brought a flat of pansies with me and I carried it from the van and planted them around the birdbath. I felt as though I wasn't alone— the little bronze girl on her tiptoes was so real that I started talking to her.

"Look at these herbs," I said to her as I weeded around the parsley. Noelle had tricolor sage and pineapple sage and rosemary. She had gorgeous Thai basil. I cut some of every herb to give to Emerson that afternoon.

I was deadheading the mums when I remembered a conversation I'd had with Sam not long before he died.

"What's with Noelle's garden?" he'd asked me in bed one night.

"What do you mean?" The question seemed so out of the blue.

"She was telling me about it." Sam rarely had a reason to go to Noelle's house. He'd probably never even seen her garden.

"Well, it's tiny but beautiful," I said. "She loves it and she has a real green thumb, though you'd never know it from the front yard."

"She said she has a special birdbath."

I described the birdbath to him and told him about the reporters who'd wanted to write about it and how she wouldn't let them. It hadn't struck me as strange that Sam asked me about the garden at the time. I figured Noelle had collared him at a party and talked his ear off. Now, though, I wondered if that conversation had taken place over lunch

in Wrightsville Beach. Something about them getting together like that still upset me. Not that I thought they were
having an affair—I couldn't picture that at all—but I was
bothered that neither of them had ever mentioned it to me.
Ian was probably right that it had to do with Noelle's will,
in which case I suppose it made sense that Sam never mentioned it. Either way, I would never be able to know the
answer. Maybe that's what bothered me the most.

A few hours later, I was in my kitchen with the coffee
brewing as I waited for Emerson. I'd made a fruit salad
the night before, some of which I'd tried to push on Grace
before driving her to the Animal House that morning, but
she'd wanted a Pop-Tart and that was it.

Emerson was bringing over some of her zucchini and
Gruyère cheese quiche and homemade coffee cake. How she
could cook with everything that was going on was beyond
me, but baking and eating had always been the way she
coped with stress. I coped by straightening up, which was
why I'd cleaned the windows in the kitchen before I made
the mimosas. Now I opened the cabinet above the coffeemaker to get out my blue-and-white floral cups. Tucked
behind them, sticking up like sore thumb, was the ugly
old purple-striped travel mug Sam had used every day. It
stopped my heart every time I saw it and I wasn't sure why
I hadn't gotten rid of it when I'd donated his clothes and
cleaned out his desk. I took out two of the blue-and-white
cups and set them on the counter. Then I carefully reached
behind the rest of the cups for the travel mug. I carried it to
the mudroom and tossed it in the box I'd take to Goodwill
sometime this week. The box was now full, ready to go.
For some reason, getting rid of the mug seemed even more
final than taking Sam's name off the voice mail and I felt

sad as I folded the cardboard flaps down tight. Back in the kitchen, I pictured him with that mug heading out the door each morning—except that last morning. If the doorbell hadn't rung at that moment, I might have pulled the mug out of the box again.

Emerson and I carried platefuls of quiche and cups of coffee into my living room and sat on the sofa. On the coffee table, Emerson had stacked Noelle's record books along with a copy of the newspaper article she'd found about Anna Knightly. I'd read it already—several times—but I read it again now. The few lines made me shudder.

"Well, I think it's clear this is our woman," I said. "Our Anna." I didn't know why I'd started thinking of her as "our Anna." It was as though she'd become our responsibility.

"Now we have to figure out who has her baby," Emerson said.

"We'll have to involve the authorities if we get that far," I said.

Emerson sighed. "I know. I just… This is such a mess. I haven't been able to find anything to pinpoint exactly when her baby was taken. The article makes it sound like it was around 2000, but Noelle says 'years ago' in the letter she wrote, which makes it sound like more time had passed."

"Although Noelle wrote that letter in 2003," I pointed out.

"True," Emerson said. "Still 'years ago' sounds like a long time."

"Which is the last record book?" I asked, and Emerson handed the top volume to me.

"We know the 'last baby' theory doesn't hold water, since it was a boy," she said, "but I have to say the last six months or so of her records are not as...I don't know, as complete and orderly as they used to be."

I looked at the last record. "Nineteen ninety-eight." I shook my head. "Still hard to believe that's when she stopped practicing and we never knew it."

"And if you look, you'll see she really slowed down before then. There are weeks between each delivery toward the end. The only other possibility is if there were records she kept someplace else. I went through every sheet of paper in her house, though. Ted and I have emptied the whole place out now. I didn't find anything else."

"Maybe she destroyed some records before she died," I suggested as I flipped through the pages. "She never would have wanted us to know about this." I came to a page that was completely obliterated by a black marker. "This might be it, don't you think?" I asked. "Why else would she black it out?"

"That's my guess, too," Emerson said. "And look." She reached for the book and I stood to hand it to her. Emerson flattened it open on the coffee table, spreading the pages apart. Leaning over, I could see that a page had been torn out.

"Is that right next to the blacked-out page?" I asked.

"Uh-huh," Emerson said.

"That must be it." I ran my finger down the torn sheet. "Have you tried to read what's under the black?"

"It's impossible to make out," Emerson said.

"What year is it?" I asked.

"The babies born before and after this record are both in '97," Emerson said.

"Why didn't she just tear that page out, too?"

"I think because there are notes about another case on the back of it."

"Maybe that boy baby *wasn't* actually her last delivery," I said. "Maybe she tore out the pages on the last one, too."

"She didn't," Emerson said. "No torn pages after that baby was born."

"Can I tear this page out?" I pointed to the page that had been blacked out by the marker. "We could hold it up to the light and maybe be able to read the writing behind the marker."

"Okay."

"Let me get a knife." I hopped to my feet. In the kitchen, I pulled the paring knife from the knife block and carried it back to the living room. Emerson took it from me. She ran the blade carefully along the inner edge of the page, then tore the sheet of paper cleanly from the book as though she did that sort of surgery every day.

"Here." I reached for the page since I was already on my feet. I carried it to the window and pressed it against the glass. It was hard to see the letters behind the black marker and they bled into the writing on the back of the page. "I think it's an R-a-b-a-e-e-a...oh, those first two *a*'s are *e*'s. Rebecca?"

Emerson stood behind me now, so close I could feel her breath on my neck. "Can you see the last name?" she asked.

My eyes were already tearing from trying to make out the letters. "Is the first letter a *B*?" I stepped aside to let Emerson take my place at the window.

"Baker?" she said. "Rebecca Baker."

"Good job!" I said. "Of course, now we have to figure out what we *do* with the name."

"I can't make out the address at all." Emerson was still scrutinizing the sheet of paper against the windowpane.

"We can check online for her." I was looking at the

record book again. "I still think Noelle would have stopped after it happened," I said. "Don't you, Em? I mean, there are a bunch of babies born after this one. After Rebecca's. Have you read the entry for the last girl born."

"Yes," Emerson said. "The last baby was a boy, but the baby before him was a girl. And the records look fine, just a little...sloppy."

I read the name of Noelle's second to last patient. "Denise Abernathy. That's the girl's mother," I said. "I think we should check her out in addition to Rebecca."

Emerson sat down on the sofa again, the blacked-out sheet of paper in her hand. She tapped her fingers to her lips. "How exactly are we going to do this?" she asked. "Try to meet these women and see if their daughters look like them or what?"

I gnawed my lip. What *would* we do with these names? "Well," I said, "I guess we need to make up a reason to talk to them. I know it's...creepy, but how else can we do it?"

She nodded. "I'll try to find the Denise woman and you try to find Rebecca?" She sounded very unsure of herself, but in spite of the somber nature of what we were doing, I felt my usual thrill at taking on a new project. But then I remembered Grace's words. *You just stay busy so you don't have to think about anything,* she'd said. *So you can forget about how messed up your life has gotten.*

Well, I thought, what's so wrong with that?

25

Anna

Alexandria, Virginia

Haley sat at the kitchen table doing her homework Sunday morning while Bryan and I straightened up after a late breakfast. She had on her blue-and-yellow-dotted bandanna today, her favorite. She'd been home all weekend, riding bikes with Bryan, helping me play catch-up in the office and watching movies with a friend in our basement den. Today, the Collier cousins were coming, as they did every year for Alexandria's fall festival, and Haley was excited. The streets of Old Town Alexandria would be roped off and booths set up with food and artwork and handcrafted things. My town house was only a couple of blocks from the heart of Old Town and the girls could walk there easily while Marilyn, Bryan and I hung out at the house. In years past, it had been just Marilyn and me and I wondered how Bryan would fit in. Marilyn was divorced, too, and she and I had always gotten along well, talking mostly about the kids. In the early years, we commiserated about Bryan and what an asshole he was to walk out on Haley and me, but after a while he no longer figured into our conversation or our lives. She'd been as shocked as I was when he suddenly showed up two months ago. She still nursed some anger at him, but I'd told her I was done with it now. Life's too short, I wrote her in an email last week. He's back now and he's wonderful with Haley. That's what matters.

The first week's search for a donor had come up empty, but Dr. Davis told us that wasn't uncommon and not to panic. I'd only panicked—truly panicked—once in my life, and that was when I realized that Lily had vanished into thin air as though she'd never been born. I didn't panic when Haley had her first bout with leukemia or even when she was diagnosed this second time. It was as though I'd worn out my ability to reach that level of anxiety with Lily's disappearance. I was scared now, yes, but we had to take things one day at a time and the fact that Haley was doing well made that easier.

Her blood work looked good. *She* looked good. I sometimes wondered if her diagnosis could possibly be wrong. I knew that was crazy, but when she looked and acted so healthy, it was hard to believe she was actually so sick.

"Check out the cardinals," Bryan said from where he stood at the kitchen sink. Haley and I looked out the sliding glass doors to see the male and female cardinals on the bird feeder.

"Cool," said Haley. She got up from the table to move closer to the glass. "The cardinals never come to the feeder," she said. "It's that new seed we got, Mom."

"Could be," I agreed, but I wasn't watching the cardinals. I was watching Bryan, who was leaning closer to the window, absorbed in the birds. Since his return, I'd barely noticed how he looked except to see that he had a few lines in his face now and that his hair was slowly on its way to gray. But the sun filled his eyes as he stood at the sink, and for the first time since before Lily was born and my world collapsed I felt a physical yearning for a man. For *him*. It had been so long since I'd experienced anything approaching desire that I barely recognized the feeling.

My life since Bryan had been all about children—taking care of Haley and looking for missing kids as a way to deal with my own lost child. It hadn't been about men. I had women friends, both married and unmarried, and they were always talking about guys. They'd shake their heads at my total lack of interest. All I wanted was to get Haley safely grown up and to make the Missing Children's Bureau more effective at performing miracles for frightened families.

I hadn't completely withered away as a woman, though. There were certain celebrities who could still make me weak in the knees. I just wasn't up to dating real-life, complicated and—too often—untrustworthy guys.

Suddenly, though, Bryan was back. In these past few weeks since I felt myself softening toward him, I realized that I liked him as a person. He was no longer the handsome young guy I'd fallen in love with when I was twenty-one, and he was no longer the man who'd deserted me when Haley got sick. He was someone new. Older, wiser, braver, contrite. He cared deeply about Haley and her sense of security with him was growing. Now I wondered if there could be something more between us. Not what we once had, but something different. Something better.

He was serious about not leaving. He'd had a job interview in D.C. a few days ago and now the company had asked him to fly to San Francisco for an interview at their headquarters. He'd told them yes, as long as the job itself would be in D.C. He wasn't leaving.

"What time is it?" Haley took her seat at the table again.

"Nearly eleven," I said. "They should be here any minute."

"I wish they'd hurry up!" She closed her history book and got to her feet. She was antsy this morning. She had to return to Children's tomorrow for more of the maintenance chemo and I knew that had to be on her mind.

"It's got to be hard to think about going back to the hospital tomorrow," I said as I poured water into the coffeemaker.

She screwed up her face at me. "That's why I *don't* think about it, Mom," she said. "Why'd you even have to bring it up?"

"Sorry," I said, and Bryan gave me a sympathetic smile. Haley's steroid-induced irritability was in full force, but I didn't blame her for snapping at me. She did a better job of living in the moment than I did. Today, she had no nasty poison pumping into her veins and I needed to let her savor every second of that freedom.

I was pushing the start button on the coffeemaker when we heard a car door slam out front.

"They're here!" Haley yelled, and ran toward the living room. I followed her into the room and saw her pull the door open, then freeze. "Holy shit!" she shouted loud enough for people on the other side of Alexandria to hear. "Mom, look!"

I walked to her side and saw Marilyn getting out of her car as four bald-headed girls ran up the front walk.

"Oh, my God." I laughed, stunned and moved. Haley ran out the front door and down the walk and I watched the four bald heads and one blue-and-yellow-dotted bandanna bouncing up and down as the girls hugged one another. "Bryan!" I called toward the kitchen. "Bring your camera."

He came to the door. "Look at that," he said with a smile as he snapped a picture. Then he put his arm around me and it felt right. He gave my shoulder a squeeze before dropping his hand to his side again.

Marilyn skirted the clot of girls on the walk and smiled at me as she climbed the front steps. "It was their idea." She gave me a big hug, then a shorter, more anemic one to her brother.

"That's the sweetest thing," I said, pointing to the girls. I watched as one of the twins—I had no idea which one— handed out turquoise baseball caps to each of her sisters and Haley. The cousins had all had their cheeks swabbed during the past week. Everyone I knew had had his or her cheek swabbed, and not one of them was a match for Haley. Not even close.

Haley whipped off her bandanna and all five girls put on their hats, giggling and pointing at one another as they headed toward us.

"Girls," I said to my nieces, "you've blown my mind."

"That's a beautiful thing you did," Bryan said to them.

It had been hard enough to tell my four nieces apart when they had hair. Now, it was impossible. Twelve-year-old Melanie was the only one I could pick out with certainty. She was thinner, slighter and smaller breasted than her sisters, but she still shared their round brown eyes, their small chins and the smattering of freckles across their noses.

"We had to drive like ten blocks out of our way to get here because the streets are blocked off for the festival," one of the girls said.

"Can we have money, Mom?" Melanie asked Marilyn. "I know I'm going to want to buy a ton of stuff."

Marilyn doled out a twenty to each of her daughters and I reached for my purse where it hung from the banister, but Bryan beat me to it, pressing a bill into Haley's hand.

"Thanks, Dad." Haley grinned. Then the girls were gone as quickly as they'd arrived, a whirlwind spinning down the sidewalk, this time with Haley at its center.

"God, she looks so good!" Marilyn said as we followed Bryan toward the kitchen. "If it weren't for the round face and the hair—the *lack* of hair—I'd have no idea anything was wrong."

"I know," I said. "She's tough as nails."

"And how about you? How are you holding up?" She stopped walking, turning me toward her and holding me by the shoulders to study my face. She leaned close to whisper, "Is it a help or a hindrance having Bryan around?"

It's wonderful, I thought. "He's been a huge help," I said. "The bone marrow drive is set for next week and he's taken care of all the arrangements himself."

"I'm so glad he's coming through for you," Marilyn said.

"What are you two talking about?" Bryan asked when we reached the kitchen.

"You." Marilyn put her arm around him. "Tell me all about the bone marrow drive. How can I help?"

"How about some coffee first?" I asked, and she nodded and sat on one of the bar stools at the island.

"Well—" Bryan pulled out another of the stools and sat down facing his sister "—we're going to get some press going. The *Post* will be sending someone to Children's this week to interview Haley and Anna. Then closer to the drive, one of the TV stations will do a piece on them, too."

"Really?" Marilyn looked a little worried. "That's okay with Haley?" she asked me.

I nodded. "She understands why we're doing it. We might not find a donor for her through the drive, but if we can get a few hundred more people to register in the global data bank, it might help someone else." I *did* have misgivings about going public. I'd never been quiet about my own story—how Lily's disappearance led to my passion for finding missing children. But I wasn't entirely comfortable trotting Haley's story out for all the world to see. Yet I knew Bryan was right. From everything I'd heard, personalizing the need for a bone marrow donor was the best way to encourage people to show up for the drive.

We drank coffee and talked a while longer, then Marilyn looked out the window. "It's the most beautiful day," she said. "What do you say we go to the festival, too? It'll be fun."

So that's what we did. We strolled among the throng of visitors and vendors along King Street with what seemed like every other citizen of northern Virginia. Occasionally we'd catch a glimpse of five turquoise baseball caps in the crowd and we'd head in the opposite direction to let them enjoy their independence. It choked me up a little every time I saw them. I knew it would be Haley's last day of feeling well for a while. One of her last days to act like just another kid. For today, she was one of five giggling bald girls in a turquoise baseball cap.

I tried to adopt my daughter's living-in-the-moment perspective as I walked through the crowd. I tried not to think about our return to Children's the next day. Instead, I breathed in the scent of hot dogs and popcorn and the river.

I reveled in the friendship of my sister-in-law and the new and unexpected friendship with my ex-husband, and in that moment, the world felt right and full of hope.

26

Tara

Wilmington, North Carolina

Now that I was sitting in my van in front of Rebecca Baker's house, I was having second thoughts about the plan we'd come up with. Emerson and I must have exchanged a dozen emails trying to figure out what to say to the two women we'd agreed to contact.

I thought we should come as close to the truth as we could without revealing what we knew. We would tell the women that we were Noelle's closest friends and that we were devastated by her suicide. We knew she'd had some personal problems around the time their children were born, and since they'd had intimate contact with her, maybe they could help us figure out what had been going on with her. We'd say that we just wanted to understand Noelle better. That was certainly the truth. Hopefully, we'd each be able to see photographs of the women's daughters and, like magic, some utter lack of resemblance would give them away.

That hadn't happened in Denise Abernathy's case, though.

Emerson said it had taken all her courage to walk up to the Abernathy's front door, but when she told Denise why she'd come, Denise invited her in and talked her ear off, raving about Noelle.

I don't think she's it, Emerson emailed me after her visit. There are four kids and they're all green-eyed blonds, like their mother. Denise said Noelle had been wonderful and made it a great experience. Noelle also delivered her older daughter and she said she was upset when she found out Noelle was no longer practicing when she had her last two kids. I bet it's going to be your Rebecca.

My Rebecca.

I could have used Sam's guidance as an attorney. Was what we were doing legal? It was certainly unethical, but what choice did we have? Even if Sam were alive, I wouldn't have been able to talk to him about it and I certainly couldn't ask Ian. Emerson and I were on our own with this burden.

So now I sat in front of Rebecca Baker's house, reminding myself I was an *actress*. I could do this.

I'd dawdled as much as I could since leaving school a few hours ago. Suzanne's birthday party was only three days away and I'd met with the caterer to iron out a few last-minute details and stopped at the party store to order several dozen helium balloons. I had no more excuses to get in the way of seeing this woman. I stepped out of my van and started walking up the long driveway, hoping no one was home.

I'd had a bigger challenge finding Rebecca Baker than Emerson had had finding Denise, who still lived at the address Noelle had for her in her record book. Rebecca's address had been blacked out along with her name. Emerson finally found her for me on the LinkedIn professional website. Rebecca Baker was an accountant. There was nothing about a husband or children in her profile, but her age and location fit the woman we were looking for.

On the front porch, I pressed the doorbell and heard a protracted chime from inside the house. Someone was home. I could hear a dog barking. Footsteps. In a moment, a girl a few years younger than Grace opened the door.

"Hey," she said. She was pixyish, athletic, dark-haired. Her eyebrows were raised in a question. *And you are?* they asked.

"Hey," I said back. "I'm Tara Vincent. I'm looking for Rebecca Baker."

"Hold on." She pivoted on her heel and headed down the central hall toward a kitchen. I could hear the clang of pots and pans. "Mom!" she called. "It's someone for you."

A woman walked toward me dressed in sweats. She raised her eyebrows in the same motion as her daughter, yet she looked nothing like her. Her hair was white-blond. Her eyes a vibrant blue. Nothing like her daughter at all.

"I'm so sorry to interrupt your evening," I said. "And I know this will sound kind of strange and intrusive, but my name is Tara Vincent and I was a close friend of Noelle Downie."

She frowned as if trying to follow me. I couldn't blame her. "I heard Noelle killed herself," she said.

"Yes," I said. "And I...I'd like to talk with you for a few minutes if you have time. I could come back on a different day if—"

"What about?" she asked.

"Do you have some time now?"

She looked over her shoulder. "Well, you'll be taking me away from cleaning the kitchen and I don't mind that sort of interruption." She pointed to the rockers on the porch. "Have a seat."

"Thanks." We moved to the rockers. They were dusty. A little grimy. My cardigan was white and I had to fight the urge to clean the chair with a tissue before I sat down.

"I have to say, I wasn't surprised to hear that Noelle killed herself," Rebecca said as she lowered herself into the rocker. "I mean, you were her friend and I'm sorry for your loss, but I'm not surprised."

Her words jarred me. Those of us close to Noelle had been surprised. What did this stranger know that we didn't? "Really?" I asked. "How come?"

"She was such a mess the last time I saw her."

"When was that?"

"Oh, a long time ago. She was my midwife for my first two kids. My son and the girl you met at the door. Petra. Though she didn't actually deliver Petra. Long story. So what did you want to talk about?"

My mind spun. Noelle didn't deliver Petra? How did that fit the puzzle we were trying to put together?

"My friends and I *were* shocked that Noelle killed herself," I said. "It sounds like you knew her better than we did in a way. We're really trying to understand why Noelle did what she did. She stopped being a midwife more than ten years ago and we wondered if something happened around then to start her downfall." The downfall we hadn't recognized. "So we're trying to talk to some of Noelle's last patients to see if we can understand why she became so depressed." The explanation sounded ridiculously hokey to me, but Rebecca was nodding as though it made perfect sense.

"Well, first I have to tell you that she was great when she delivered my son. I loved her. I couldn't wait for a repeat performance with Petra. But when she showed up when I went into labor with Petra, she was a mess, like I said. So was I at the time." She smiled. "I'd been having back labor for days and was not in a good place. So I wouldn't have realized it if she'd shown up with two heads, but my husband did."

"What do you mean, 'she was a mess'?"

"Spaced out."

"Spaced out?" I repeated. My head felt thick and stupid.

"She was on something and she was very, very loopy. With my son, she was totally in charge and calm and I knew I was in good hands with her."

I nodded.

"Well, that was not the woman who showed up when I went into labor with Petra," she said. "She was stumbling over her own feet. Her eyes were glassy. If I hadn't been so worried about myself, I would have been worried about her. I honestly wasn't sure what to do. It was about 3:00 a.m. and I thought maybe she was still groggy from waking up suddenly, so I just rolled with it for an hour or so, but she didn't get any better. Finally, my husband said she had to go. I knew he was right, but I was terrified. I figured I'd have to go to the hospital and give birth with a doctor I didn't know. I heard my husband talking to her in the hall outside my room. He was totally frank, saying that she seemed drugged and he wasn't comfortable with her taking care of me and he was going to take me to the hospital."

"What did Noelle say?" I asked.

"Her voice was really quiet and I couldn't hear, but my husband said she didn't put up a fight. Almost like she agreed with him. She apologized and said she was having back pain and had probably taken too many pills. She was really upset and apologetic and my husband ended up comforting *her*. Noelle called this other midwife, Jane Rogers, and said she was sick and could Jane take over. Jane came right away and she was great."

"She sometimes did need to take pain medication," I said. "I'm sorry it had such an impact on you."

"My husband thought maybe she was an addict."

"I don't think she was an addict," I said, though what did I know? Our theory about the blacked-out name belonging to the woman whose baby had been replaced was crumbling. She was blacked out because Noelle didn't deliver her baby at all. Still, Petra didn't look like she came out of the body of this svelte blonde. Might something have happened when *Jane* delivered the baby and Noelle helped cover it up? I wanted to ask her what she remembered of the delivery. Was the baby out of her sight for a while? Could Noelle have come back? But the questions would make no sense in light of what I'd given as my reason for coming.

"At least Noelle had the good sense to let someone else take over," I said.

"That's true," Rebecca said. "I was angry at the time. My husband thought we should file a complaint against her, but she did the right thing by bringing in someone else and we had a beautiful healthy little girl and that's what we focused on."

"She's adorable," I said. "I have a teenage daughter, too."

Rebecca smiled. "You know the challenge, then."

I felt so comforted by those words. I was not the only mother trying to cope with a teenager. Emerson had so few problems with Jenny that we couldn't really commiserate.

"Definitely," I said. I got to my feet. "Thanks so much for taking the time to speak with me."

"Did I help?" she asked.

"Yes, I think you did. We all missed something going on with her that you picked up on. I feel bad about it."

"I know," she said. "One of Petra's friends killed herself last year and she's been feeling guilty about it ever since, but everybody missed the signs. You can't help someone who doesn't want to be helped."

As I drove away, it was no longer Noelle I was thinking about, but Rebecca's comment about Petra's friend. Teenagers killed themselves. I thought of Grace's moodiness. Her nightmares. I'd been spending all this time trying to figure out what had been going on with Noelle while my daughter was the greater and more immediate mystery. I felt suddenly frightened. Could I be missing something going on with her, right under my nose? How would I ever know?

Let me in, Gracie, I thought as I drove. *Please, honey, let me in.*

27

Emerson

Jacksonville, North Carolina

Grandpa looked better when I walked into his room at hospice. Either that, or I was simply getting used to the emaciated, drawn features of his face.

"Hello, honey." He smiled when he saw me, reaching a frail arm out to draw me into a hug as I leaned over his bedside.

"You look good," I said, pulling a chair close.

"I let them shave me." He ran a tremulous hand over his chin. "Just in your honor."

"I brought you pumpkin bread," I said. "I left it with your aide and she's going to bring it to you with dinner."

"Always loved your pumpkin bread," he said.

"That's because you're the one who taught me how to make it."

"Oh, hogwash." He shook his head with a smile. "You outpaced me in the baking department by the time you were ten." He looked directly at me then, and we both sobered. The nurse had said he wanted to see me alone, without Jenny or Ted, and I knew Grandpa must be seeing this visit as some sort of farewell. Just the thought put tears in my eyes.

"Now don't cry," he said. "I haven't even said anything yet."

"You wanted to see me alone." I reached over the bar of the bed to hold his hand.

He nodded. "I need to talk to you," he said, "and I'm afraid this will shock you a little, honey."

I pressed my lips together, unable to imagine where this was going. He looked worried about me. "I'm fine," I said. "You can tell me anything."

"You have a good friend," he said. "Noelle Downie."

He'd met Noelle a few times over the years, but I couldn't imagine why he'd be talking about her now. I hadn't mentioned her death to him. There'd seemed no reason to mention it, and something in his voice told me not to bring it up now.

"Yes." I nodded.

"Noelle is your half sister."

I leaned toward him, frowning. A few times in recent weeks he'd said things that made no sense. *There are butterflies in the bathroom* or *They always give me spaghetti for breakfast here.* The staff told me it was the medications talking. Was that what was happening now?

"What do you mean, Grandpa?" I asked.

"Just what I said. She's your half sister and my granddaughter. You were never supposed to know."

"I... Would you explain—"

"Yes." He turned away from me, looking out the window at the manicured landscape. "I can't die without telling you the truth about Noelle." A tear slipped from each of his blue eyes and I reached for a tissue and blotted his cheeks. My mind scrambled to take in what he was telling me.

"Your mother had a baby when she was fifteen years old," he said.

I sucked in my breath and sat back. "Oh, no." I tried to picture my mother as a teenager. Discovering she was pregnant. Grappling with a decision. "You're saying...that was Noelle?"

He licked his parched lips. "Susan was going with Frank at the time, but another boy got her pregnant. We didn't know until she was pretty far along. Frank didn't know. No one knew, and Susan wanted it that way. We sent her to your great-aunt Leta's in Robeson County. She told Frank... well, I don't remember exactly what she told Frank. That Leta was sick, I think, and she had to help out. Leta found this midwife to take care of your mother and...make the problem go away, so to speak."

A midwife? Noelle? I felt suddenly, thoroughly confused. I rubbed my forehead. "I don't understand how—"

"The midwife wanted a child," he said. "She and her husband adopted the baby."

"But...how do you know it was Noelle?" I asked. I felt a crushing pain starting low in my rib cage as the loss of one of my closest friends began to grow into a greater loss than I ever could have imagined.

"Around the time your parents moved to California, your mother began toying with the idea of finding her daughter," he said. "She held off, though. She was afraid to tell your father the truth, even after all that time. Afraid he'd be angry she'd lied to him. But, anyway, your mother knew the midwife had the last name Downie and she knew where she lived and I guess it wasn't that difficult to find out Noelle's name. She found all that out right around the time she died, but we never realized you were friends with her…with Noelle…until a while after her death. We were shocked, your grandma and me, the first time you mentioned her name to us. It wasn't such a coincidence that you both went to UNCW, but to end up friends was just…" He shook his head, then gave me a long look. "Do you think somehow she knew?" he asked.

I thought of Noelle's will. Naming me executor. I thought of the surprise split of her money with seventy-five percent of her assets going to Jenny. I remembered the first time Tara and I met her in our dorm room. Even years later, we joked about how weird Noelle had been that day, questioning me about my family, my name, my grandparents.

"She knew." I could barely speak. "I don't know how she figured it out, but she knew."

"Your grandma and I decided we'd best keep it to ourselves, since your father never knew about her. We didn't want to do any harm to his memory of Susan. But now your father's gone, and I'm about to leave this good earth myself, so it's time." He looked at me with hope in his blue eyes. I'd always loved those eyes and suddenly I saw Noelle in them. "I want to ask you a big favor, Emerson," he said. "Only if you're comfortable with it, okay? I know it's a lot to ask."

I nodded. "Anything," I said.

"I'd like her to know the truth. I want to spend some time with her. My granddaughter." His lips trembled in a way I couldn't bear. "Would that be all right?"

"Oh, Grandpa." I took his hand again, holding it between both of mine, and then I told him the part of Noelle's story that *I* knew. The ending.

28

Tara

Emerson and I sat side by side on the back steps of Noelle's house, our arms around each other's shoulders as we looked out toward the garden. We were waiting for Suzanne to stop over to see the house in the hope that she'd become the new tenant. Her current lease wouldn't be up until the spring, but that was fine with Emerson and Ted, who needed time to renovate.

Suzanne had been in the house many times over the years, but it had been such a mess that when Emerson asked if she was interested in renting, she'd made a face before saying, "Maybe." She would have to look past the scarred floors and dirty walls and the empty places in the kitchen where new appliances would go. Hopefully, she'd be able to see the potential, because we wanted someone who'd loved Noelle to have her house.

We also wanted to pick Suzanne's brain a little to see if she knew any more than we did about the waning years of Noelle's practice. We doubted it since Suzanne herself had been stunned to learn Noelle was no longer a midwife, but it was worth a few questions.

Most of all, though, Emerson and I were grieving all over again, this time for the Noelle we now knew had been Emerson's sister. We'd been sitting there more than thirty minutes, remembering back to our days in the Galloway dorm when Noelle had befriended us. We'd felt pretty smug back then that this older girl—this *woman,* really—became *our* friend over all the other girls on the floor. Why didn't she ever tell Emerson what she knew? If only she had. If only she and Emerson could have enjoyed their sisterhood out in the open. The truth explained so much. No wonder I'd always had the feeling of being a little on the outside of the two of them. No wonder Noelle seemed to love Emerson just a little bit more than she did me. I wished that Sam were alive so I could tell him. It would blow his mind.

We'd decided not to tell Jenny or Grace yet. Life was too chaotic right now, and besides, Emerson needed some time to absorb the news herself. She'd told Ted, of course, and with her permission, I'd told Ian. He'd come over for dinner last night while Grace went to the movies with Jenny. I felt as though I needed to sneak around with Ian these days. There was nothing between us other than a good and growing friendship, but Grace was so disapproving that I felt uncomfortable even mentioning his name around her.

He'd been astonished when I told him about Noelle and Emerson. He stood in middle of the kitchen, shaking his head in disbelief. "I was engaged to a woman I didn't know at all," he said. Then he ran his hand over his thinning blond hair. "I wonder if *anybody* knew her. It must have been so lonely, being Noelle." For the first time, I realized he still loved her. Maybe only a little bit, but the love was still there in his eyes and in the sadness of his voice.

"Hello!"

Emerson and I heard Suzanne's voice coming from inside the house. We'd left the front door open for her.

"We're out here, Suzanne!" Emerson called, getting to her feet. She looked at me, motioning toward the garden. "We might as well show her the best thing first," she said.

Suzanne pushed open the screened door and joined us on the porch, her blue eyes round with wonder, as usual. "Hi!" She gave us each a hug, then put on a scolding look. "Listen, you two. You have to let me do *something* to help with the party."

"It's all under control," I said. Mostly the truth.

"We just want you to have a good time," Emerson said. Her eyes were a little bloodshot and I hoped Suzanne didn't notice.

"The house looks so different without Noelle's things in it," she said. "Can I help choose the paint colors?"

"Absolutely," Emerson said. "As well as the stain on the hardwood floors and the tile in the kitchen."

"Look at Noelle's garden!" Suzanne started down the porch steps and we followed. "I remember how spectacular it is in the spring."

"It was Noelle's pride and joy," Emerson said.

"Her birdbath." Suzanne pointed at the little girl on tiptoe. "Isn't that the sweetest thing? And the herbs!" She bent over to touch the Thai basil. "She'd always give me some. Now I can be the one giving them away."

Behind her back, Emerson gave me a thumbs-up. "We were hoping you liked gardening," she said.

"I do, and I've had no room to do any of it in the dinky little yard I have now." Suzanne tore her gaze away from the garden. "Are you sure you can wait till March to rent it? I know that's a long time."

"Not a problem," Emerson said.

"Will Cleve be living with you over the summer?" I asked. The house was fine for one low-maintenance person. Add a teenage boy and I wasn't so sure.

"He'll be doing his Habitat for Humanity thing and I know he wants to spend time with his father in Pennsylvania and who knows what else," she said. "I can fit a daybed in that second bedroom for him, and I'll probably set up my desk in the living room. Besides, Cleve's not going to be living with me for the rest of his life, I hope." She looked at me. "How's Grace doing?" she asked. There was sympathy in her voice.

"She's doing well," I said. I felt protective of Grace. I'd never let Suzanne know how much my daughter missed her son.

"She's a beautiful girl with beautiful manners," Suzanne said.

"Thanks." I smiled. Grace was definitely a beautiful girl, and I was happy to hear that her manners passed muster, at least away from home.

"Suzanne, I wanted to ask you if you knew Jane Rogers," Emerson said. "She was a midwife who worked with—"

"Oh, sure," Suzanne said. "She used to work at the Birth Center. She retired years ago and moved to Australia."

"Australia!" Emerson said.

"You wanted to let her know about Noelle?" Suzanne asked.

I glanced at Emerson, wondering how much to say. "Actually, we were talking to an old patient of Noelle's who said that when she went into labor, Noelle wasn't feeling well and called Jane in to take over for her. So we were just wondering who Jane was."

Suzanne nodded. "That would make sense. They covered for each other. I was really out of the business by then, though. After Cleve was born, I just wanted to play mommy for a while." She bent down and plucked a leaf from the sage and lifted it to her nose. "Here's something I've been wondering about," she said. "If Noelle hasn't been a midwife all these years, why did she still do that rural work every year or so? Some years, she'd be there a few months." She looked from me to Emerson. Emerson's eyes were as startled as mine and I knew she was wondering the same thing I was. Were the patients Noelle saw during those months documented in her record books?

"I don't know, Suzanne," I said slowly. "There are so many questions and I don't think we're ever going to get the answers."

"Do you know exactly where she'd go?" Emerson asked her.

"I always thought she was going back to where she grew up. She said it was a poor area. A lot of Native Americans."

"The Lumbee," I said. "She grew up in Robeson County." Was that where she went? Had she told us that or did we all just assume it? She'd always stayed in touch with us by email or cell phone, but I didn't think we'd ever had an actual street address for her.

"Well, listen." Suzanne sniffed the sage again. "I'm going to walk through the house and think about how my furniture will fit, all right?"

"Absolutely," Emerson said. "Holler if you have a question."

We watched her walk back to the house, then turned to each other.

"We're idiots," I said. "Are the months when she was away in her record books?"

"I don't think so. I think I would have noticed addresses outside this area. I bet that's when it happened."

"You're right." But then I remembered the article about Anna Knightly and shook my head. "Maybe not, though. Anna Knightly's baby was taken from a Wilmington hospital," I reminded her. "Robeson County's, what—an hour and a half away?"

Emerson put her hands on the sides of her head and looked like she wanted to scream. "I'm going to figure this out if it's the last thing I do," she said.

My cell phone rang, electronic strains of "All That Jazz" filling Noelle's backyard. I dug the phone from the purse slung over my shoulder and glanced at the caller ID. Ian.

"Hey, Ian," I said.

"Where are you?" He sounded almost curt, and I frowned.

"Emerson and I are at Noelle's. Suzanne is here looking at the—"

"Can the two of you come to my office right now?" he asked.

"Right now?" I looked at Emerson. "We've got things we need to do for the party tomorrow."

"It's important," Ian said. "I figured out when Noelle had a baby."

29

Noelle

Wrightsville Beach, North Carolina
September 1992

This is the most despicable, most insane thing you've ever done,
she told herself as she walked through the quiet, dimly lit
hallway of the Blockade Runner. It was two in the morning
and Wrightsville Beach had been sleeping when she pulled
into the parking lot of the massive oceanfront hotel. She
wanted privacy. She wanted everyone to be sleeping. There
was only one other person she wanted to be awake.

She walked into the empty foyer. A huge sign greeted
her. Welcome LSAS! She had no idea what the letters stood
for. The *L* was either *legal* or *law*. It didn't matter. She didn't
care about the conference. She turned left and started walking down the hall.

Her life was very full these days, and she was grateful.
She was finally doing what she'd longed to do since she
was twelve years old—practicing midwifery. She lived ten
minutes from Emerson and her new husband, Ted, renting
the little Sunset Park house Ted had lived in before he and

Emerson were married. Sunset Park was exactly the type of neighborhood Noelle loved: diverse, utterly unpretentious, with a growing sense of community. Emerson was already pregnant and very happy, and when Emerson was happy Noelle was happy.

It seemed ironic that Ted and Emerson, who'd known each other less than a year, were already married while Tara and Sam still were not—although that was about to change. Their wedding was only two weeks away. Tara would have been delighted to get married the day after she graduated from UNC, if not before, but Sam had taken things at a slower pace. He wanted everything in place before he got married, he'd said. He wanted the bar exam behind him and his law practice set up before he took on a wife and family. Now, things were as in place as they were going to get. Tara was in her first year of teaching and Sam had sailed through the bar exam and joined an already established attorney, Ian Cutler, in his practice. Sam could stall no longer. That was the way Noelle had come to view his reluctance to plan the wedding. He was having his doubts, and although he never said as much, she felt certain she was the cause. How could he marry one woman when he had feelings for another? She couldn't let him. Not without a fight. As full as her life felt, there was one thing missing and that was Sam. His wedding date now loomed on her calendar like a death.

She found his room easily. First floor, oceanfront. They could leave the sliding glass doors open and listen to the sea. She'd gotten the number from Tara, telling her she needed to talk to him about a midwifery case. She hated lying to Tara about why she wanted Sam's room number. Somehow the lie felt even worse than what she was doing now. But Tara, ever trusting, bought her excuse. It wouldn't be the first time Noelle had consulted with Sam about one of her patients. He was focusing on health law, which pleased her, and she liked to think she had something to do with his choice since she was always bending his ear with her concerns about child and maternal health. When the five of them got together, she and Sam often wound up talking shop while everyone else discussed wedding plans or the real-estate market. She felt closer to him than ever. He was the only person who knew that she was Emerson's sister, the only person she could ever talk to about how that relation-ship gave her both joy and pain.

She knocked on the door to his room, then waited in the silence. Nothing. She knocked again, harder.

Sam pulled the door open and she knew she'd awakened him. His dark hair was tousled, his jeans unsnapped, his chest bare. His eyes widened when he saw her, his lashes so long that they cast shadows on his cheeks from the hallway lights.

"What's wrong?" he said. "Is Tara all right?"

"Everyone's fine," she said. "I just wanted to see you."

He hesitated a moment, and she knew he was trying to make sense of what she'd said. What she was doing here at two in the morning, two weeks before his wedding.

Reaching for her wrist, he drew her into the room. She walked straight to the unmade side of his bed and sat down on the edge. She felt the light from the night table pool over her and wondered what he saw in her face.

He looked at her, hands on his hips, and for the briefest of moments, neither of them spoke.

"Ah, Noelle," he said, finally. The words sounded tired. They sounded a little bit like surrender. "What are you doing?"

"Trying to keep you from making a mistake," she said. "A mistake for both you and Tara. And for me." She swallowed. For the first time since making the decision to come here, she felt nervous.

He looked toward the curtained sliding glass doors. "I don't want to have this conversation in here." He nodded toward the bed as if it could overhear them. He switched off the lamp, then began opening the curtains. Beyond the glass, she could see the white ripple of waves as they rushed toward the shore. Sam snapped his jeans, then slid open one of the doors. "Let's go for a walk," he said.

She slipped off her sandals and dangled them from her fingertips as she followed him out to the patio. They climbed over the iron railing and crossed the grass to the beach where the air was dark and balmy, filled with salt and the rush and fall of the waves. A crescent moon bisected the ocean with a sliver of light. He took her hand. *Yes.* She'd needed that. Needed to know he wasn't angry that she'd come.

"No babies tonight?" he asked.

"None. Last night, I delivered my doula's first." It had been a peaceful birth in the small candlelit bedroom Suzanne shared with her husband, Zeke, who had been by her side every minute. The infant with the big name, Cleveland Ezekiel Johnson, had slipped into Noelle's hands with such ease for a first baby. "It went very well." Now Emerson was talking about a home delivery. Being the midwife of a relative was frowned upon, but the thought of delivering her own niece or nephew made Noelle smile. No one—except Sam—would be any the wiser.

"You'll be there for Tara and me when we're ready," Sam said, like a test. "Right?"

She focused on the way his hand felt in hers. "Sam," she said, "you can change your mind. People do it. People realize they're making mistakes that will impact so many people for the rest of their lives. You can—"

"Shh." He squeezed her hand hard. "Please, just...don't mess with my head, all right? I've thought about it inside out and backward these past couple of years, Noelle. You know that. You know I've wrestled with this and I've made a choice. Please respect it."

"You love me," she said.

He didn't deny it. "There's more to consider than love," he said.

"I don't think so."

"I love Tara, too, and we're better matched than you and I are. You know that. I *want* a house in the burbs. I want—"

"The white picket fence. The dog. The kids. I know you say that, but—"

"You're one of the best people I know." He interrupted her. "On the scale of incredible women, you're up there with Tara. In some ways, you even top her. But she wants the same life I want, Noelle. Admit it to me. You don't want to entertain a roomful of lawyers, do you? You don't want to do the Wilmington social scene, the things I'll need to do—my *wife* will need to do—for my career."

She didn't answer. It was all true. She didn't want any of that, but she believed with all her heart that, deep down, Sam didn't want it, either.

He stopped walking, turning to face her. She saw the moon—two little silver crescents—reflected in his eyes. "You're a fantasy," he said, "and Tara's my reality. With you...I always feel as though if I touch you, my hand will pass right through you. Like you're an apparition."

She lifted his hand, slid it beneath her shirt to her bare breast. "Does this feel like an apparition?" she asked. She

let go of his hand but he didn't lower it. She felt his thumb
graze her nipple and knew he was making a decision. She
knew in her heart, though, it wasn't a decision that would
erase the wedding coming up in two weeks. He was making
a decision for tonight. For right now.

He leaned forward, pressing his lips against hers. She felt
his erection through his jeans, through her skirt. *Right now*
was not what she'd come here for. She wanted forever. Yet
as her nipple tightened beneath the touch of his fingers and
her heartbeat thrummed between her legs, she forgot about
forever. She would take whatever he would give her tonight. It would have to last all their lives, through his world
of picket fences and expensive haircuts and clean, pressed
suits and her world of patchwork furniture and middle-
of-the-night runs filled with blood and birth. If tonight
was all she could have of him, she would make it worth
remembering.

They lay on their backs in the sand afterward, staring
at the bowl of stars above them. They'd rolled her skirt up
to form a pillow beneath her head and Sam rested his own
head on his jeans. She could feel spray from the waves on
her bare skin as she rolled toward him, running her hand
across his chest. "Are you all right?" she asked.

He didn't answer, but he sank his fingers gently into her
hair. "I should feel worse than I do," he said finally.

"You feel guilty for not feeling guilty?" She smiled.

"I don't think it's sunk in yet. You know, I've never
cheated on Tara. In the seven years we've been together.
Never."

"Don't use that word. *Cheat.* Please."

"This...you understand this doesn't change anything?"
His chin brushed her temple as he spoke.

"It changes something for me," she said. "It gives me a memory to hold on to."

He curled a strand of her hair around his finger. "You could have any of a hundred men who want you," he said. "Ian, for example."

She ignored the comment. She knew Sam's new law partner had a thing for her, but the attraction was one-sided. Ian was nice enough, good-looking in a clean-cut sort of way and smart as a whip. She'd considered sleeping with him, but thought that might be a mistake. He was the type who'd want more, and the truth was, if she was going to be with a man for anything long term, he would need to be a Sam clone, and Ian wasn't.

"I don't want you to worry about this," she said. "About tonight. I'm not going to ask anything of you like this, ever again. If you feel sure you're doing the right thing by marrying Tara, I'll support that one hundred percent because I love you both." She heard the crack in her voice, completely unexpected. Sam rubbed her shoulder. "I'll go out with Ian a few times and give him a chance, okay?"

"Good," he said. "You'll make him a happy man."

She sat up with a sigh and reached for her clothes. "I should go," she said, pulling her blouse over her head. She stood and dusted the sand from her thighs as Sam began to dress. It was good she had done this, she thought. Yes, she'd betrayed one of her closest friends and she knew that would haunt her, but she'd needed to do it to let Sam go. Otherwise, she'd be mooning over him for years. Decades. And that could only have been more harmful to her friendship with Tara in the long run. Now she was finished, she told herself as she slipped into her skirt. This chapter of longing was closed.

She pointed toward the parking lot behind the Blockade Runner. "My car's on this end of the lot," she said.

He put his arm around her as they walked across the sand. His silence worried her, but once they reached her car he hugged her, holding her for a long time, and she pressed her hands flat against his bare back. "No regrets, Sam," she said. "Please."

He pulled away from her slowly, running his palm down the length of her arm before opening her car door for her. "Be well," he said.

"You, too." She sat down behind the wheel and, without looking back at him, drove away.

Her tears surprised her with how quickly they came. Her body convulsed with them as she drove and she could barely see the road in front of her. The night was inky black as she crossed the bridge to the mainland, and when she stopped at a red light she could see no other cars on the road at all. She pressed her hands to her face, wishing she could escape from her body.

Suddenly, the squeal of brakes filled her head and she opened her eyes to see headlights swerving toward her. Letting out a scream, she turned her wheel sharply to the left and stepped on the gas. The oncoming car caught her right bumper, spinning her car around and tossing her, unbelted, against the dashboard. She pressed hard on the brake and felt as though every muscle in her back snapped in two as her car jerked to a stop.

A man jumped out of the other car and began running toward her, shouting, waving his arms wildly in the air. She locked her car doors. Was he crazy? Furious? It took her a moment to understand what he was saying.

"You don't have your lights on, asshole!" he shouted. "Where the fuck are your lights?"

No lights? God! What was wrong with her? Her hands shook as she flicked the knob for her headlights. She saw the man pull a phone from his pocket. *The police.* Jumbled thoughts raced through her mind, one of them rising quickly to the top: she didn't want to have to explain to anyone what she was doing in Wrightsville Beach in the middle of the night.

She stepped on the gas pedal and took off across the intersection, speeding away from the man and his shouting, hoping she was disappearing into the darkness too quickly for him to be able to read her license plate number. When she was a few blocks away, she pulled into a deserted parking lot, turned off her car and sat very still, waiting for her heart to settle down. But as the beat slowed and steadied, the muscles in her back contracted into a knot that was tight and sharp and savage, and she knew that her betrayal of Tara was not all that would haunt her about this night.

30

Tara

Wilmington, North Carolina
2010

I hadn't been in Sam's office since before he died. Ian had brought two boxes of personal items to me a few weeks after his death and I wished he hadn't bothered. The spare pair of sunglasses, a couple of business awards, framed photographs of Grace and me and other odds and ends—I would have just as soon not seen them. Now Emerson and I sat on the sofa in front of the windows in Sam's old office waiting for Ian. Sam's desk still had a monitor and keyboard on it, but nothing else. The only other things in the room besides the furniture were the floor-to-ceiling bookcases filled with law books and three gleaming wooden antique file cabinets. They were the file cabinets Ian had slowly been making his way through as he tried to determine which of Sam's old cases needed his attention.

"You want something cold to drink?" he asked as he walked into the office. "Water? Soda?" He had a legal-size manila folder in his hands. It was neither thick nor thin.

The edges were worn as though it had been beaten up a little over time.

"We're good," I said. I knew we both just wanted him to get to the point.

Ian sat down in one of the leather chairs in front of Sam's desk. "Well." He looked at me—apologetically, I thought. "Noelle continues to surprise us."

"Ian," Emerson said impatiently. "What did you find?"

He held up the folder. "This was with Sam's old cases. The name on the file is Sharon Byerton. It's a made-up name, I'm sure."

"Why a made-up name?" I asked.

"I've done it myself," Ian said. "If I'm working with a client whose identity I want to protect from anyone who might stumble across the file, I'll give it a false name. When I opened the folder, though..." He shook his head. He wore an expression of disbelief, as if he still couldn't fathom what he'd found inside. He opened the file now and I could see a stack of the heavy, creamy sort of paper Sam used for legal documents. "Remember Noelle's so-called 'rural work'?" he asked.

We nodded.

"She wasn't practicing midwifery then," he said, "except maybe on herself."

"What are you talking about?" Emerson asked.

"These are contracts," he said, holding the papers in the air. "She was a gestational surrogate."

"A...?" The words wouldn't come out of my mouth.

"Five times. When she went away to do her rural work, she was actually in Asheville or Raleigh or Charlotte, finishing the last few months of a pregnancy and turning over a baby to that child's biological parents."

I couldn't speak and Emerson seemed to have lost her voice, as well. It was too much to take in. Way too much.

"How can this be?" Emerson looked at me. "How can this possibly *be*? Why would she do this?"

"Oh...my...God," I said slowly. "Are you sure?"

Ian leaned forward to hand us each a contract. I looked down at the pages of legalese. There were the names of strangers in the blanks marked *genetic father* and *genetic mother*. Noelle's name in the blank for *embryo carrier*. I looked up at Ian. "Who *are* these people?"

He shook his head. "I have no information other than what's in those contracts. The contracts are well drafted, but they're not your typical surrogacy contract, not that I've seen a lot of them. Usually surrogates are married and have children and the husband would sign the contract also. Of course, that's not the case here. She went into each contract prior to the in vitro fertilization, which I'm glad to see. She covered herself carefully. Or, I guess, Sam did. In each case, the parents paid all her expenses, of course, plus fifteen thousand dollars, which is low for this sort of thing, but I could see Noelle thinking that was just fine. She didn't have many personal expenses."

"We didn't charge her much rent." Emerson's voice was husky.

"There's the usual restrictions on the surrogate not interfering with the raising of the child or ever trying to assert parental rights. And there's—"

"When did she start doing this?" Emerson asked.

"The first contract was signed in April 1998." He cleared his throat and looked down at the contracts in his lap, and when he spoke again, his voice was thick. "Usually there's something in a surrogacy contract about a psychiatric evaluation of the surrogate, but there's no provision for that here, and I..." His voice trailed off and he lowered his head, his hand rubbing his chin, his eyes glistening behind his glasses. I felt so sad for him. I stood and crossed the room to lean over to hug him.

"She wasn't right, Ian," I said. "Something was off with her and none of us saw it."

"I want to talk to some of these parents," Emerson said. "At least the last couple. Can I do that?"

Ian lifted his head again and squeezed my arm in a little thank-you gesture as he regained his composure. "I'll contact them and see if they're willing," he said. I stood next to his chair, my hand still on his shoulder. My own eyes had misted over, not for Noelle but for him, and I realized that I cared about him more than I'd thought.

"We missed her being pregnant," Emerson said. "Five times!"

"The way she dressed, she could cover up a lot," I said.

"Could this be why she and Sam were meeting at the restaurant in Wrightsville Beach?" Emerson asked.

"Possibly," Ian said. "Although the last contract was from 2007 and she was forty-four when she died, so I think she was...finished. It would be very rare for someone to hire a surrogate her age."

"Well, they hired her unmarried and without children," I said as I sat down next to Emerson again. "How could Sam do this?" I asked. I was stunned by Sam's involvement and especially by the fact that he'd known something like this about Noelle when the rest of us were in the dark. "Wasn't this unethical of him? Shouldn't he have tried to stop her?"

"He probably did," Ian said. "I'm guessing he saw the contracts as the only thing he could do for her. It looks to me as though every *i* was dotted and *t* was crossed." He held up the folder in his hand. "It bothers me that she had psychological problems none of us knew about, but if she was determined to be a surrogate and she refused to get therapy, I have to trust that Sam was protecting her interests the best way he knew how. Through the contracts..." He opened the folder again. "He has no notes in the file about any meetings he had with her, but that's not uncommon," he said. "I often toss those notes myself, especially if it's about something sensitive. The only thing other than the contracts in here is this." He held up the folder itself, open to the inside back page. From where I sat, I could see something written in pencil, but I couldn't make it out.

"What does it say?" I asked.

"Just one word with a question mark," Ian answered. *"Penance?"*

31

Noelle

Wilmington, North Carolina
1993

She sat in the lounge of the women and newborn unit at the hospital, waiting for Tara. She was heartbroken, but trying to hold it together because the waiting area was full of anxious families and kids and she didn't want to cry in front of them.

She'd left Emerson and Ted in the recovery room, where Emerson was still blissfully groggy after the D and C. Her first pregnancy had ended just before the twelve-week mark, but she'd made it eighteen weeks this time and everything had seemed to be going so well. Noelle would not agree to be her midwife the next time. It was hard enough going through pregnancy loss with one of her patients. With Emerson, the sadness was too much for her.

Tara nearly burst into the lounge, all energy and worry. "I ran a red light," she said after giving Noelle a hug. "Where is she?"

"In recovery. Ted's with her."

Tara sank into the chair next to Noelle. Her dark blond hair was pulled up in a messy ponytail and she wore no makeup, a sure sign she'd rushed out of the house. "I can't believe she has to go through this again," she said. "It was so bad the last time, Noelle. This is going to be so much worse. I'm afraid for her."

She was right. After her first miscarriage, Emerson had sunk into a dark depression that lasted weeks. She'd been unable to work in Ted's real-estate office, which she'd been doing since before they were married. Unable to shop for groceries or straighten the house. Some days, she couldn't even get out of bed in the morning.

"It's the hormones," Noelle said. "Postpartum depression. She may need some medication to get through it this time. I asked Ted if I could move in for a while and he's all for it."

"Oh, fantastic!" Tara grabbed her hand. "That would be such a relief to know you're there. I can bring meals over."

"Good," Noelle said. "We'll take care of her together." She shifted her weight in the chair. Her back was seizing up as it did regularly ever since the accident. Sometimes it was impossible to find a position that didn't hurt.

Tara glanced toward the unit. "Do you think I can see her now?"

Noelle nodded and got to her feet. "Come on," she said. "I'll ask them to let you in."

They walked through the hallway toward the recovery room.

"Her miscarriages are scaring me," Tara said. "She takes such good care of herself and does everything right, and…I don't think I could handle it."

"Of course you could." Noelle rested a hand on her back. "You're tough. But let's hope you never have to."

She knew that Tara and Sam were already trying to

conceive and she wished them nothing but success. Their wedding day, nearly eight months earlier, had been one of the hardest days of her life. She'd felt sick that morning and wasn't sure she'd make it to the wedding at all, much less be able to be a bridesmaid. Her illness wasn't physical, though. She'd been sick with self-disgust. Why did people get so stupid when it came to sex? Why was it so hard to just say no? When she'd realized that night in Wrightsville Beach that Sam wouldn't give Tara up, why didn't she say, "I understand," and leave? Then she wouldn't have this unrelenting back pain or this unrelenting guilt.

Most of all, she wouldn't have destroyed one of the richest friendships she'd ever known. Now, Sam kept his distance. He went out of his way never to be alone with her. Even Tara had noticed that something was different. "Did you and Sam have a fight?" she'd asked her a few weeks after the wedding. She'd looked concerned, not wanting a rift between two people she loved. Tara was so guileless. So trusting when it came to Sam. Noelle had laughed off the question. "Of course not," she said. Then she'd hugged Tara hard, thinking as she held her in her arms, *I'm sorry. I'm so sorry.*

She let Tara into the recovery room but didn't go in herself. The nurses wouldn't appreciate a crowd around Emerson's gurney. Instead, she walked into the ladies' room and swallowed a few of the pills she had stashed in her pocket. She leaned back against the cool wall and closed her eyes, anxious for the relief to kick in.

She'd told everyone a drunk driver had run a red light, crashing into her as she was on her way home after a middle-of-the-night delivery in Wilmington. Ian, whom she'd been seeing ever since Sam and Tara's wedding, wanted her to sue, but she told him the incident had seemed

242   DIANE CHAMBERLAIN

so minor at the time that she hadn't bothered to get the other driver's name. She pleaded with him not to badger her about it. She wanted that night to go away.

A woman walked into the restroom and Noelle moved away from the wall. She washed her hands and left the room and walked straight through the corridor and the lounge and out to the parking lot. She needed to go home and throw some things in a suitcase so she could move into her sister's house.

In her car, she felt the Valium and Percocet start to kick in. *Thank God.* She was taking more medication these days, playing around with the cocktail of drugs. She was careful, though, trying to find a balance between keeping her back pain to a manageable level and being able to function. She didn't ever want to compromise her medical practice or put her patients at risk. She'd known drug-addled doctors and nurses and had vowed never to be one of them. She had more sympathy for them since her back injury, though. She'd tried acupuncture, Reiki, rest, heat, ice, but nothing worked as well as a nice healthy dose of narcotics. She tried to save them for those times she knew she wouldn't be called on to catch a baby or manage a patient's care. On those occasions, she worked through the pain. It was a pain she thought she deserved.

She took over the guest room at Ted and Emerson's, dragging some clothes, her medical supplies, her heating pad and drugs and her logbooks with her. For the first time since leaving home eight years earlier, she felt part of a family. She cooked and cleaned and shopped and nursed her sister slowly back to life. She listened to Emerson talk about the lost baby, the plans and hopes she'd had for him—it had been a boy—how she'd allowed herself to imagine him starting school, graduating, marrying, having kids of his own. In Emerson's imagination, he was musical and artistic, even though she and Ted were, to be honest, neither. He would have been kind and loving, though. Emerson was sure of that and Noelle didn't doubt it. She listened to it all, thinking, *My nephew,* and she felt the loss herself.

She was the only midwife she knew who had no children of her own, and her dream of having a child, of creating her own family, was growing with every baby she delivered. That longing made her look at Ian with fresh eyes.

"I admire you," he said to her in Emerson's guest room one night. They'd just made love in the double bed, quietly, not wanting to be overheard. "The way you stepped in and took over to help Emerson and Ted."

Ian not only admired her, he *worshipped* her, the same way a few other men had worshipped her over the years. Worship had never been much of a turn-on for her. Did she love him? Yes, the way she loved all her friends, and that would have to do. There were no Sam clones around and Ian would be a good father and a more faithful husband than she deserved.

"It's easy to help Emerson," she said, resting her head on his shoulder. "I love her. I just want to see her happy."

"She and Ted seem good together."

"Yeah," she said. "I think they are." Ted was one of those guys who never talked about his feelings, but every once in a while Noelle would catch him doing something that touched her. The way he'd tenderly stroke Emerson's cheek while they were watching TV, or the sad look in his eyes as he wrapped the unneeded car seat in plastic before storing it in the attic. Moments like that, she felt a hunger for something more than she had in her life.

"So, does living in this domestic harmony give you any ideas?" Ian teased her.

Usually, she would laugh him off. He'd already asked her to marry him a couple of times, but she'd told him it was ridiculously early to talk about marriage. Tonight, though, thinking about Ted and Emerson, how good they seemed together despite their very different personalities, she hesitated.

"Actually," she said, "it's nice."

"Wow," Ian said. "I didn't expect that answer. So will you marry me?"

Now she did laugh, but she raised herself up on an elbow to look at him. "Do me a favor, Ian?" she asked.

He brushed a strand of her hair over her shoulder. "What's that?"

"Keep asking me, all right?" She smiled. "One of these times, I just might surprise you."

32

Emerson

Wilmington, North Carolina
2010

The night after Ian told us about Noelle's surrogacy, I lay in bed, bone tired but unable to sleep. After leaving Ian's office, I'd driven to Jacksonville for a too-quick visit with my grandfather, who slept the entire time I was there. That was just as well. I knew he was upset that he'd never gotten to spend time with Noelle and it hurt me to see his sadness and regret.

By the time I got home, Ian had left a number for the last woman Noelle had served as a surrogate. I was glad Ted and Jenny weren't home yet. I sat at my kitchen table and dialed the number. The woman's name was Angela and she sounded weepy as I explained who I was and why I was calling.

"The lawyer told me she killed herself," Angela said. "I'm in total shock. We loved her so much. We wouldn't have our two children if it wasn't for her."

"Did Ian explain that we didn't know Noelle was a surrogate?" I asked.

"Yes. I guess that's not a huge surprise to me, because she was a very private person. Rob and I didn't know much about her life, either. We were nervous about using her in the beginning because she didn't have kids of her own. They always say the surrogate should have her own family. But we'd spoken with another couple she'd been a surrogate for and they recommended her so highly, we felt confident going ahead with her."

"So..." I was having trouble formulating my questions, even though I'd thought them through before dialing the phone, "where did she live when she was waiting to give birth?"

"When she was pregnant with our son, we put her up in a hotel. But by the time our daughter was conceived, we felt much more comfortable about the whole thing and she lived with us the last three months of her pregnancy. She was a huge help, actually."

"Did she say why she did it?"

"She said it was her calling. That was the word she used. Her calling."

"Did she ever seem like she was drugged to you?" I hadn't expected to ask the question, but there it was, popping out of my mouth, and Angela didn't answer right away.

"Why would you ask that?" she said finally. "It specifically said in the contract that she was to use no drugs without her doctor's—and our—approval."

"She had back problems and needed pain medication for a while and I wondered how she made out without it."

"I knew about her back," Angela said. "I knew she was in pain sometimes, but she just put up with it. Plus, she was with us 24/7 those last three months. We would have known if she was using something. I trusted her completely."

"Did you think she was mentally stable?"

Angela laughed. "I would say Noelle was crazy in a stable way, if you know what I mean. I mean, she was lovably crazy. Not a psych case. Just..." She sighed loudly. "She loved what she was doing," she said. "She was happy doing it. I'm absolutely certain about that. I'm so sorry you lost her. It's hard for me to imagine her taking her own life."

"Did she talk about her family?" I asked. "I know I'm badgering you with questions, but I—"

"No, that's fine. I'd feel the same way if I suddenly discovered someone in my family had led a secret life. And yes, she talked about her sister—about you—a lot. She raved about your cooking and baking."

"She called me her sister?"

"Yes. You are, aren't you?"

"Yes, but I only learned that recently."

"Wow. She always called you her sister. Unless she has some *other* sister."

"Just me," I said, but in the back of my mind I was thinking, *Who knows what else she was hiding?* "I have just one more question," I said. "Did she ever mention a woman named Anna Knightly to you?"

"Anna Knightly." Angela sounded as though she was mulling the name over. "I don't think so. Was she another parent Noelle helped?"

I shut my eyes. *Hardly,* I thought. "No," I said. "Just someone I'm trying to track down."

Now as I lay in bed, all I could think about was Noelle and her secrets and I stared at the moonlight reflected on the ceiling. Ted was finally asleep next to me, but it had taken him a long time to get there. As bizarre as Noelle's surrogacy seemed to me, it was a hundred times more so to Ted. He'd barely recovered from the realization that Noelle and I were sisters when I hit him with the *real* purpose of her "rural work." We'd stayed up late, talking about it, but I didn't think that either of us had fully accepted the truth by the time we went to bed. He didn't know the half of it. I wished I could tell him about Anna Knightly. At the same time, I felt protective of Noelle. Ted was starting to make a face every time he said her name. I could only imagine his reaction if I told him everything else I knew about her.

Tara and I thought we'd figured out Noelle's motivation: she'd stolen a child. Through surrogacy, she'd found a way to give one back. It was her penance. Yet, one child hadn't been enough to absolve her for what she'd done. She'd had to give and give and give. The baby she'd accidentally killed and the baby she'd stolen—they must have haunted her every day of her life until she found a way to permanently lay them to rest. It made me so sad. I knew she'd wanted children of her own. She loved kids. She must have felt undeserving of ever having them. If only she'd let me know we were sisters. If only she could have confided in me. Maybe I could have helped her.

I kept picturing those surrogacy contracts and imagining Sam being a party to the whole thing. He'd known about the surrogacy. What else had he known?

I pictured Noelle's record books, wondering if the identity of the woman whose baby had died was truly locked away somewhere in their pages or if we were way, way off in our search. I was beginning to think that the page she'd torn from the logbook held the answer we were looking for and that page no longer existed. We had no way of knowing who that patient might be. The Birth Center wasn't going to give us the information—if they had it to begin with. Only if we went the legal route would they turn over their old records and Tara and I weren't ready to go there. Part of me was slipping back into denial. I had to remind myself of the letter Noelle had written to Anna Knightly to remember that this whole mess was real.

I kept thinking about Denise Abernathy's green-eyed blond kids. Denise's daughter had been the last girl Noelle delivered. Lying next to Ted, wide-awake, I imagined Noelle desperately searching for a newborn baby whose eyes might turn green like her mother's and older sister's. Noelle had a sixth sense about eye color. She could always tell what no one else seemed able to—the color a baby's eyes would eventually turn. I pictured her wandering through the hospital in the dead of night, lifting the eyelids of babies, checking their eyes for their color. The whole idea was insane and very, very bizarre. As bizarre as being a secret surrogate mother, five times over.

If only we knew the date Anna Knightly's baby had been born, that would clinch it, right? We'd know then if Denise Abernathy's green-eyed blonde daughter was the one. At the very least, we'd be able to see if Noelle had recorded the birth that had gone so horribly wrong. I sat up in bed with a start. Were birth records online?

I got out of bed. I'd find out right now.

Downstairs, I snitched one of the stuffed mushrooms I'd made for Suzanne's party from the refrigerator and carried it to my office on a napkin. I nibbled the mushroom as my computer booted up. Then I dug around a little and found the birth records site for North Carolina, but I couldn't get any information without both a last *and* first name.

I stared at the screen, thinking about Anna Knightly. She

was the director for the Missing Children's Bureau. She'd turned her own loss into a way to help others. I liked the very little I knew of her and I felt intense sympathy for her. How had she felt when she discovered her baby had simply disappeared? How had she gone on? And how could Noelle have done this to her?

I didn't want to know too much about her personally; I only wanted to know when her baby disappeared. I wanted Anna herself to remain a faceless name. Once we knew who had her child, I'd let the authorities deal with her. I hoped I never had to meet her.

Yet without the help of the birth records, it seemed the only way to find a date for her baby's disappearance would be to find *her*. I surfed over to the Missing Children's Bureau. I'd briefly looked for her on that site before, thinking there'd be an in-depth bio of her someplace in its pages, but there wasn't. It was a cramped site so full of information I didn't know where to begin. There were resources for families and forms you could use to report the sighting of a child who might be missing and information on Amber Alerts. I dug around for a while and found some news reports in which Anna Knightly made statements related to specific cases, but nothing about Anna herself.

Then, finally, I got it.

How far back could I search for a missing child on the site? I opened the search form and entered the little bit of information I had: *North Carolina. Female. Knightly.* How many years missing? I picked *thirteen,* since Noelle had quit practicing twelve years ago and that was also the year she first became a surrogate. Then I clicked Go and quickly received the message *0 results found.* Maybe the baby had a different last name.

I sat back in my chair and stared at the screen again, and

that's when I noticed the tiny green letters at the bottom of the page: *site search.* I clicked on them and the search box appeared. Finally! I typed *Anna Knightly* into the box, and suddenly, there she was—her photograph and a short bio. I wanted to turn away from her picture, but it was too late. I stared at her. She had a round face. Not overweight, but soft and sweet. Her light brown hair was chin length and wavy. Her eyes were large and very green. Green, like Denise Abernathy's children. It was her smile that got to me, though. Not a broad smile, but the sort you'd wear for an executive portrait. Warm, confident, yet sober. *I am all about serious business,* her smile said. *I'm all about finding your children.*

I read the few lines of text below her picture.

Missing Children's Bureau director, Anna Chester Knightly, 44, has worked for MCB for ten years. Her infant daughter, Lily, disappeared from a Wilmington, North Carolina, hospital in 1994. She has one other daughter, Haley.

Oh! She had another daughter. I was so glad.

But 1994? That long ago? We'd definitely been off on our dates. I went back to the search form for missing children and changed my thirteen years to seventeen and up popped Lily Ann Knightly.

There was no picture—just one simple line.

Lily Ann Knightly was born August 29, 1994, and disappeared from a Wilmington, NC, hospital shortly after her birth.

My heart gave a sudden *thud* in my chest. *August 29, 1994.* I rolled my chair back from the computer and walked to the long table by the windows where I'd stacked Noelle's record books. I picked up the one labeled March 1994–November 1994. I opened it slowly, holding my breath as I turned the pages.

"No," I said out loud when I came to the page I'd been looking for, although I'd known perfectly well what would be written there. At the top of the page was the patient's name: Tara Vincent. The date was August 31, 1994—the date Jenny was born by C-section and Tara went into labor with Grace. For the first time, I thanked God that I hadn't been able to have a home birth and Noelle had been nowhere near my daughter. I reread Noelle's notes about Tara's long and terrifying labor, ending with the perilous delivery early in the morning of September 1. I flipped the pages quickly, hoping Noelle might have made another delivery close to that date, but the next record was for a child born September 15 and that had been a boy. I turned back to Tara's delivery and the pages upon pages of Noelle's notes. I read the last few lines, searching for the place where Noelle's handwriting would change from that of the careful, confident midwife to that of a frightened woman who'd accidentally dropped her friend's child. A woman about to race to the hospital to find a replacement. I studied her notes, but she'd covered her tracks well. I saw her final sentence again—"She's a beauty! They're naming her Grace"—and I wondered if at that point she was referring to the Grace Tara had given birth to, or the Grace I'd known and loved all these years.

The Grace who belonged to none of us.

PART THREE

GRACE

33

Grace

I woke up at six and didn't bother trying to go back to sleep. Cleve would be home for his mom's party in just a few hours! In his email last night, he said a friend was giving him a ride and he thought he'd be home in time for lunch, though he didn't say I should come over and have lunch with him. But he'd been emailing and texting me more over the past few days, like I was on his mind a lot now that he was coming home. He said, See you soon! in his text to me yesterday and I'd been dissecting those three words ever since. The exclamation point was my favorite part.

I had our day all planned out. If the weather was good we could go hang out by the Riverwalk and talk. *Really* talk for a change, like we used to. I was hoping, of course, that we'd get back together. It was a three-day weekend, so even if he wasn't convinced by the end of today that we belonged together, I had two more days to work on him.

I was on Facebook around eight when my mother poked her head in my door. "You're up?" She sounded surprised.

"I guess that's a rhetorical question," I said.

"Smarty pants." She smiled at me. She'd been weird the

past few days, and her smile wasn't a real one. "Want to help me run errands?" she asked. "I have a million things to do to get ready for the party tonight."

"I can't, sorry. I have to write a paper. And Cleve's coming home in a little while." Why did I add that? I just couldn't help myself. But now she was going to ask me all kinds of questions.

"You're going to see him?" She didn't think that was a great idea. I could tell. "Besides tonight at the party, I mean?" she added.

I shrugged like I didn't care. "I guess," I said.

"You can ask him about his classes and what he likes about Chapel Hill."

I looked at her like she'd just been dropped on the planet from outer space. "I know how to talk to him, Mom," I said.

"Well, what are you going to wear tonight?" She was in one of her twenty questions moods, and usually I'd just find a way to put an end to it, but I was so psyched about my dress that I decided to show it to her. Jenny and I went shopping Monday after school and I was in love with the dress I found. I pulled the hanger out of the closet and lifted the white plastic bag from the dress and she took in a breath, which was exactly what I did when I saw it in the store.

"Oh, Gracie, that's so cute!"

Cute was not what I was after. I wanted sexy and sophisticated, but I knew what she meant. The dress was red, short and strapless. It was made out of a satiny material and had a silver belt at the waist. It might have looked cute on the hanger, but it was hot on me. Jenny swore up and down that it was.

"Thanks," I said.

"What shoes will you wear?"

I pulled out the strappy red shoes. They'd just about killed my savings.

"Perfect," she said. "Not too high. You're smart. I haven't even thought about what I'm wearing." She glanced at her watch. "Have you eaten?"

"Not yet."

"Want me to make—"

"No, thanks. I'm good." I sat down at my computer again.

"You sure you don't want to come with me? I'll drop you off back here by noon."

"I really have to do this paper, Mom." I was glad she couldn't see the Facebook page on my monitor from where she stood.

"Okay," she said. "Have a good day."

I didn't write the paper, of course. I didn't even try. I did some math homework, ate a banana, washed my hair, looked at my phone a million times to make sure it was turned on and exchanged comments with a bunch of Facebook friends I'd never met in person. At noon, I couldn't take it any longer and I sent him a text message.

R u home yet?

In less than a minute, he wrote back. Got here hour ago. C u at party?

My heart dropped to my toes. Seriously. C u at party? Was he kidding? Why not now? We had all afternoon we could be together. We could be on the Riverwalk. Talking. Laughing.

I pounded the keys on my phone with my thumbs. Can u get together now? Im not working.

Helping Mom with something. Later.

I sat down on my bed and started to cry. I didn't *get* it. I felt almost as bad as when he broke up with me. I tried to call Jenny, but she wasn't picking up. Twitter started whimpering and I let him on the bed. He knew I was upset and he tried to squeeze his entire body onto my lap. I buried my face in his neck and sobbed.

Almost an hour later, I got up and looked at my reflection in the bathroom mirror. Everything was red—my nose, my eyes, my cheeks. I had to pull it together or my face would be the same color as my dress at the party tonight. I straightened up, wet a washcloth and pressed it over my eyes.

I wasn't hungry at all, but I was dying for coffee. I went downstairs to the kitchen and saw that there was still coffee in the pot, but of course it was cold. I'd nuke it. I opened the cupboard to look for a mug. Something was different. My favorite black mug was there and I took it out, but I knew that something was missing. Mom was always rearranging things and it was incredibly annoying. Then I got it. The purple travel mug I'd given my father! I loved that mug. I loved seeing that reminder of him every day. I opened the other cabinets one by one looking for it, but it was gone.

I would not cry. Would not. I'd just gotten my face to look okay again. Instead of crying, I grabbed the phone and dialed my mother's number.

34

Tara

My van was full of balloons. The overly pierced young girl in the store asked me what colors I wanted and I told her to surprise me. Usually I would care, but my mind was going a thousand miles a minute between the preparations for Suzanne's party and the discovery that Noelle had been a surrogate and that Sam had known about it all along—it was overwhelming. All those years, he'd known! My God. I knew he'd been dying to tell me. I was in awe of his ethics. I don't know if I could have kept it to myself if I'd been in his place. I was glad that Noelle had turned to Sam to help her, though. I was glad that she'd trusted him that much.

All I could see in my rearview mirror was a sea of balloons, and I drove slowly toward the bakery where I was to pick up Suzanne's birthday cake. Driving with a van full of balloons was no less dangerous than driving while texting, I thought to myself as I found a parking place a half block from the bakery. I put my van in Reverse and inched my way into the spot with only my side view mirrors to guide me.

My phone rang as I turned off the ignition and I figured

Emerson had thought of something she needed me to pick up. I didn't even glance at the caller ID.

"Hi, Em," I said.

"How could you do it?" Grace shouted so loudly that I jerked the phone away from my ear. I didn't know what I'd done, but I felt instant guilt, anyway.

"What are you talking about?" I asked.

"Couldn't you have left one single thing of Daddy's in the house?" There was so much rage in her voice that she sounded like someone I didn't know. What had I done now? I thought of Sam's side of our closet, still so empty it echoed. Where his night table drawer had once been full of his books and pens and reading light, it now contained only a flashlight and some spare batteries. I'd donated his file cabinet. His desk drawers now held my stationery and school supplies.

"What do you mean?" I asked.

"The mug," she said. "The purple travel mug I gave him."

I pictured the mug. I saw myself reaching for it, an unattractive, no longer needed item taking up space in my cupboard. Why keep something we'd never use? I saw myself tucking it into the box for Goodwill. "Oh," I said. "Oh, no. I...wasn't thinking, honey. I saw it and you know how I can't stand clutter and I forgot that—"

"It's always all about you, isn't it?" she shouted. "*You* can't stand clutter so the mug has to go. You don't even ask me what *I* think. If you hated it so much, you could have given it to me and I could have kept it in my room, because I don't have a fucking problem with clutter, Mom! I don't give a *shit* about clutter!"

She hung up and I sat there clutching the phone. She'd never spoken to me that way before, with that fury and certainly not with that language. I didn't know she was even capable of speaking that way. I looked past the sting of her words and saw that she was right. I'd been selfish. And stupid. She'd bought that cup for Sam. I saw a painful reminder of him each time I looked at it, but she saw a treasured connection to someone she'd loved. I felt my throat tighten as I called her back, but she didn't pick up. She'd said everything she had to say to me.

I pulled out of the parking lot. The cake would have to wait. I drove to Goodwill and got out of my helium-filled van and ran up to the front door. In the small drop-off room, a woman was handing a kitchen stool to the lanky, somber young guy who gave out the receipts.

"Excuse me," I said. "I brought something here the other day and I need to get it back. Is that possible?"

"No, ma'am," he said, taking the stool from the woman and setting it sideways on a pile of cartons. "No way."

I looked through the open doorway behind him to the huge room where women wearing gloves were sorting through bags and boxes and all sorts of detritus. I tried to spot my lone small carton but knew it was a lost cause. Needle in a haystack.

I walked to my van and drove slowly and carefully back to the bakery, thinking all the while about what it had been like for Grace to open that cupboard and see that her last physical link to her father was gone. I felt myself inside my daughter's skin. I could hardly stand how much it hurt.

I practically floated to Emerson's house from my van as I held on to the cloud of balloons above my head. Her door was unlocked and I let myself in, freeing the balloons in her spacious living room.

"Em?" I called.

"In the kitchen."

"I'm here. Just need to get some more stuff from the car."

I made another trip to the van for the cake, which I carried to the side door that led into the kitchen. Shadow and Blue sniffed the air around me as I set the box on the granite counter. Emerson was washing a mixing bowl in the sink. "Hey." She glanced up at me absently. "I made room in the fridge for the cake. Thanks for getting it."

I moved the cake to the empty bottom shelf of her refrigerator. The other shelves were crammed with who knew what. Emerson's refrigerator was never a pretty sight.

"I left the balloons in the living room," I said. "I'll spread them around a little later."

"We have one small problem." Emerson was scrubbing the daylights out of the mixing bowl and I knew she was stressing out. "Suzanne's sister sent us a bunch of pictures and Jenny was working on making a collage out of them but she's not feeling well and went up to bed. Do you have time to work on it? I had her put it in my office."

"Sure." I said. "Anything to keep my mind off…everything." I smiled at Emerson, but she was too frazzled to smile back. "What's wrong with Jenny?" I asked.

"She thinks she's getting a cold." She gave the bowl a final rinse and put it in the drainer. "She said she woke up with a sore throat. She helped me set out the plates and things on the table in the dining room and then crashed. I think she just doesn't feel like helping. She'll probably be fine for the party."

I saw there was still some coffee in the pot and reached for it. "Okay if I help myself?" I asked.

"If you don't mind heating it up." She dried her hands on

a dish towel, then walked past me to the pantry without so much as a glance in my direction.

"Are you all right?" I asked as I reached into the cupboard for a mug. I couldn't help picturing my own cupboard, nice and orderly now without the purple travel mug towering above the others.

"I'm fine," she said, pulling a package of napkins from the pantry. "I just—" she shook her head "—you know."

"Yeah." I put my arm around her shoulders. I knew about her conversation with the woman whose baby Noelle had carried. As strange as the revelations felt to me, they had to feel so much stranger to Emerson. We'd had little time to process everything and it was getting to both of us. Once the party was over, we'd be able to catch our breath. It was almost as though we needed to have another memorial service for Noelle. The first one was for a woman we didn't really know.

"Well," I said as I poured coffee into the mug, "I think I just screwed up big-time."

She'd reached into a drawer for scissors and now held them above the napkins' plastic wrapper. "What do you mean?" For the first time since my arrival, she was looking at me.

"I threw away Sam's travel mug." I put my cup into the microwave and hit the timer. "I forgot that Grace gave it to him. Or rather, I didn't think about the fact that Grace gave it to him. She called me while I was getting the cake and chewed me out royally. I've never heard her so angry at me."

Emerson cut the plastic film, then slipped the scissors back in the drawer. "It'll blow over," she said. "She'll be fine."

"Are *you* fine?" I asked. "You seem really upset."

"I just…" She pulled the plastic from the napkins and appeared to be counting them.

"There's twenty-four, I think," I said. It would say right on the plastic sleeve, but I didn't have the heart to tell her.

"I just want it to go well tonight," she said.

"It will, sweetie." The microwave dinged, and I took out my cup. "I'm a little worried about Grace and Cleve, though."

"Do you think you could work on the collage?" she asked as though I hadn't spoken.

"On my way," I said. She was acting more like me than herself, worrying about the details, wanting perfection. I'd take care of the collage and get that out of the way and then see what else needed to be done.

I found the huge white cardboard collage about half-finished on one of the tables in Emerson and Ted's shared office. I balanced the stack of pictures and the glue stick on top of the collage and carried the whole mess back into the kitchen so Emerson and I could talk while I worked on it.

She was taking wineglasses from a cabinet when I walked into the room and she looked surprised to see me.

"I thought I'd work in here," I said.

"There's so much more room to spread out in the office."

"Too lonely in there," I said as I rested the collage on the table and took a seat. I began looking through the photographs. There were a few pictures taken of Suzanne with Noelle over the years and I found them hard to look at. *Is Noelle pregnant in this picture?* I'd wonder. *How about in this one?*

There were tons of pictures of Cleve at different ages. Skin the color of pecans. His dad's jet-black hair and his mom's blue eyes. Handsome child. Even better-looking young man. "Cleve was the most adorable kid," I said to Emerson.

She was cleaning water spots off the wineglasses with a dish towel and she didn't seem to hear me. Grace once told me I didn't need another person to have a conversation with—that I was content to hold up both sides of it on my own—but that wasn't the case. I stood and carried a picture of Cleve over to the sink where Emerson stood, holding it in front of her so she didn't have to put down the glass in her hands. "He's about three here, don't you think? Isn't he precious?"

Emerson barely glanced at the picture. Instead, she suddenly set the glass and dish towel on the counter and pulled me into her arms, surprising me. She held me tight. Almost too tight.

"Hey," I said, patting her back. "What's wrong?"

"I love you," she said. "Sorry I'm so preoccupied."

I drew away from her. There were tears in her eyes and I took her hand. "Emerson, what's the matter?" I lowered my voice in case Jenny or Ted were around. "Is it all the stuff with Noelle?" I whispered, then it hit me. "Your grandfather! Is he—"

"He's okay," she said. "I think I just have major PMS or something."

"O-kay," I said slowly, not sure I believed her. She never complained about PMS. "Why don't you lie down? I can get everything ready."

"Do you mind?" She looked so relieved. "I didn't sleep well last night and I—"

"Go." I pushed her gently toward the hallway. "Everything's under control. Don't worry."

"All right," she said. "I'm going."

I watched her walk down the hall. She needed a good

nap, I thought, and she probably wouldn't be able to get one until tomorrow when the party would be behind us. She had too much going on. All the revelations about Noelle. Her grandfather in hospice. Suzanne's party. No wonder she was a wreck.

I sat down in front of the pictures again. I'd have to finish the collage, then make sure everything was ready for the caterer. And then I'd go home and get dressed. I wanted to take a picture of Grace in her new red dress, but I had the feeling she wouldn't let me. I could imagine the two of us in the van together as we drove back over here to Emerson's. Me blathering. Her quiet and still angry. We needed to finish that argument before the party, I thought as I glued a picture of Suzanne and Noelle in the lower corner of the collage. We needed to be done with it.

I reached in my purse for my phone and hit Redial again, but she didn't pick up. She wasn't going to make this easy.

35

Noelle

"I just want it to be simple," Noelle said. She and Ian were sitting in her Sunset Park living room with Tara and Emerson, whom she'd enlisted to help plan the November wedding. She had no experience and definitely no skill in that department.

"It can be simple in *style,*" Ian said, "but I'd really like to have all of our friends there."

Noelle knew she drove Ian batty with her desire for simplicity. She'd already nixed the idea of a church wedding—something he'd wanted—as well as renting a reception hall. The engagement ring he'd given her had weighed down her hand with its diamond and she'd insisted they exchange it for something far less ostentatious. He'd wanted to get married in August, but she'd put him off until November so Tara and Emerson would be completely recovered from having their babies. Tara was due in late August, nearly a month away, while Emerson was due in mid-September.

They would be her bridesmaids. No maid of honor. She was always careful to treat them equally.

"Maybe we need to define what *simple* means for each of you," Tara said. She sat on one end of Noelle's old sofa, a notepad on her lap and excitement in her eyes, thrilled to be planning a wedding. Emerson sat on the other end of the sofa, and Noelle thought they looked like counterweights—two very pregnant women holding down her couch. Emerson was going to make it this time. Her pregnancy had tested all of their nerves with one problem after another, and although she wanted a home birth there was no way Noelle would take that risk with her. She'd assist at her hospital delivery, but one of the OBs would be in charge and that was definitely the way she wanted it. As long as everything continued to look good for Tara, though, her baby would be born at home.

"Simple to me means getting married in something comfortable," Noelle said. "You know, just what I wear every day."

Ian let out a small groan. He looked at Tara and Emerson. "See what I have to put up with?" His voice was so full of love that Noelle leaned over to kiss his cheek. He was a sweet guy. They would have a good marriage. She was determined to make that happen.

"So let's get serious for a minute." Tara clicked her pen above the notepad on her lap. "November's too cold for an outside wedding, and since you don't want to go the church route, Noelle, how about having it at my house? We have the room. Everybody might not be able to sit down for the ceremony, but there's tons of space."

"And I can do some of the cooking," Emerson added, "and—"

"I don't want you two to go to any trouble," Noelle said.

Being married in Sam's house after all that had passed between them made her feel squeamish. "You'll both have new babies, and trust me, any spare minute you have, you'll want to sleep."

"Oh, let us do it." Tara brushed away the protest. "You know we'll love every second."

Ian looked at Noelle. "I like the idea of having it at Tara and Sam's," he said. "We can pay to have someone move furniture around and clean up before and after. And you can wear whatever you want."

"No, she can't," Tara said. "Em and I will take her shopping. If I see her walking down the aisle in one of her old skirts, I'll—"

"There'll be an aisle?" Noelle interrupted. "I don't want an aisle." She didn't. She didn't want all that attention focused on her.

"It's a figure of speech," Tara said. "You can be married in front of our fireplace."

It was a nice image, Ian and herself in front of the fireplace, their hands joined, their friends surrounding them. She was surprised when her eyes misted over at the thought. "Well," she said to Tara, "why don't you check with Sam about having it at your house," she said. "Make sure it's cool with him."

"Oh, it'll be fine with Sam," Tara said.

Noelle wasn't so sure. Her relationship with Tara had deepened during the months of prenatal care, and she'd discovered that the intimacy she always experienced with her patients was even more intense when that patient was a close friend. But things still felt a little strained between her and Sam. They were improving as he became more and more involved in the pregnancy, but she knew he had reservations about her being their midwife. Not that he didn't trust her skills—he did—but he seemed uncomfortable being around her in any sort of emotional situation. He never said as much, of course; they didn't talk that openly to each other anymore. It was that "not talking" that told her of his discomfort. She missed him and she blamed herself for the distance between them.

She was reminded of that night on the beach in every small twisting motion she made with her back and in the sleepless nights when her muscles tightened up and wouldn't let go. She needed more medication to get through the day and—as long as she had no possibility of a delivery—even more at night. Her mounting dependence on the drugs scared her. Right now, right as she was sitting in her living room planning the wedding, she had a welcome Percocet buzz going on and she didn't know how she would be able to function without it. How much of her pain was physical and how much emotional, she wondered, borne of a guilt and a longing that wouldn't go away?

It was time to *make* it go away.

"You know what?" she said now to Ian. "I don't care how we do it. Whatever you want is fine with me. I just want to be your wife."

"Yay!" Emerson clapped her hands together.

"That's the spirit!" Tara said, and jotted something down on her notepad.

Ian smiled at her, pink coins of surprise on his cheeks. "Would you consider the church, then?" he asked, pushing.

"Yes." She gave him an emphatic nod. "You want the church? We'll do the church."

What did it matter? She wanted to marry Ian. She loved him as much as she knew how and she would do everything she could to make him happy. With any luck, in a couple of years they'd start their own family. For now, though, as she sat there with a man who adored her, her two best friends and enough drugs in her system to ease the ache in her back, she felt something approaching contentment, and that was more than she could ask for.

36

Emerson

Wilmington, North Carolina
2010

What the hell was I going to do?

I'd wanted Suzanne's party to be special, but I was so wrapped up in what I now knew about Tara and Grace that as people arrived and began eating and drinking and laughing and talking, I felt as though I was experiencing the whole thing underwater. I saw faces, but they were blurry. I heard words but couldn't make them out. I wanted the night to be over, and more than anything, I didn't want to be alone any longer with what I knew. I moved through the rooms torn between heartache and indecision. What was I going to do?

People seemed to be having a good time. Everyone was gathering around Suzanne, making toasts and cracking jokes and celebrating her fifty hard-earned years, but even if my mind hadn't been full of Grace and Tara, I would have been miserable. The party, with so many of the babies-in-need volunteers present, reminded me too much of the gathering after Noelle's memorial service only three weeks earlier. Three weeks that felt like a lifetime. Things were moving too fast for me. I had the feeling that everything was spinning out of control.

Ted walked toward me where I stood between the living and dining rooms, a drink in his hand. He rubbed my shoulder. "Nice job, Em," he said. "You holding up okay? I know you didn't get much sleep last night."

"I'm fine." I smiled at him. At least, I hoped I was smiling. I had no idea *what* I was doing. I felt drugged by exhaustion and anxiety. I hadn't slept at all the night before, and when I'd told Tara that afternoon that I wanted a nap, it had been a lie. I'd only wanted to get away from her. I couldn't look at her. It was like knowing your best friend was going to die very soon and you could do nothing to stop it and nothing to warn her.

I was kicking myself for digging into Noelle's past. For not tossing out that carton of cards and letters like Ted had suggested. I could still do it. Throw away the letter, the articles, the record books. I could make this nightmare go away. All I had to do was keep my mouth shut. But I knew I could never live the rest of my life with this secret.

Grace and Tara had arrived early so that Tara could help me put the finishing touches on everything. There'd been a sheet of ice between the two of them and I sensed Tara's frustration over not being able to break it. Obviously, Grace hadn't forgiven her for… What had Tara done? Thrown away Sam's mug? Oh, that felt like such a small thing. Such a tiny, inconsequential thing. Yet Grace was still angry. She'd barely said hi to me before running upstairs to Jenny's room, while Tara met with the caterer and the bartender and I moved woodenly through the house, pretending to be busy.

Now the kids—Cleve, Jenny and Grace—were all upstairs. They'd put in just enough time with the adults to be polite before disappearing. Jenny was sniffling with the hint of a cold, but seemed otherwise fine, though I knew she was upset Devon wasn't there. He was traveling with his family for the long weekend. Cleve had grown even more handsome in his month and a half away from home, if that was possible. But it was Grace I'd had my eye on, of course, as I examined her features, searching for a trace of Tara or Sam in them. She looked beautiful. I'd never thought of that word with regard to Grace before. Adorable, yes. But beautiful? Yet her strapless red dress hugged her body perfectly. It wasn't provocative, but it exposed the gentle slope of her small breasts and Cleve's gaze kept darting in that direction. Her hair was a thick, sleek curtain of silk down her back, and she was wearing smoky eye makeup. Not too much, but enough to alter her features. Her eyes had always been unusual. They were brown like Tara's, but when you looked closely, you saw that they were filled with jewel-like splinters of jade. Whatever clever thing she'd done with her makeup tonight made her eyes seem greener than ever.

Suddenly, she didn't look like Grace at all and I was upset as I tried to find the girl I loved in this new young woman. I used to think I could see Sam in her, more in her mannerisms than in her facial features. She had that same shy smile that had seemed affable and warm on Sam but made Grace look unsure of herself. Seeing her insecurity as she tried to talk to the adults at the party, the ones she didn't know well, tore at my heart. This girl was part of us and we loved her. We'd raised her, all of us. There was no way we would let her go. No way I could allow Tara to lose her daughter right after losing her husband. She *wouldn't* lose her, would she? Certainly not physically. Grace couldn't be taken away from her mother at the age of sixteen. Although, what did I know about the legalities of such a bizarre situation? I *didn't* know, and that scared me. On top of that, I thought of how Tara would feel when she realized that the baby she'd given birth to had died. What had Noelle done with that baby? I didn't want to think about that baby girl, forgotten and unmourned.

I could keep it all to myself, I thought again. Reveal nothing. Grieve for Tara's baby alone. Keep the truth about Grace to myself. Yet even as I considered making that choice, I was searching the rooms for Ian. I needed to share this burden with someone who cared about Tara— and I knew Ian did. Someone who'd understand the legal implications.

I spotted him chatting with Tara and a few other people in the dining room and I kept my eye on him until he moved toward the makeshift bar, where I was able to corner him alone.

"There's something I need to talk to you about," I said.

He raised his eyebrows. "About your conversation with Angela?" he asked.

"Who?" For a moment, I couldn't even remember who Angela was. "Oh...no. It's something else, but I can't talk about it here. Could you stop over tomorrow sometime? Early afternoon?" Ted would be showing houses and Jenny would no doubt be out with Devon or Grace.

"Can it wait, Em?" he asked. "I'm going out of town tomorrow night and I'm a little swamped."

I shook my head, and he must have seen the tears beginning to well in my eyes.

He touched my arm. "All right," he said. "I'll be there."

"And please don't mention it to Tara." I glanced ner-

vously over my shoulder at the partyers in the room, hoping
I wasn't being overheard.

Ian was frowning. "What's going on?"

"I'll tell you tomorrow." I stepped away from him, letting myself be pulled back into the throng. *There,* I thought.
A decision. Finally.

Yet I felt no relief at all.

37

Grace

Cleve was different. How could somebody change so much in a month and a half? Seriously. He even looked different. When he walked into the party with Suzanne, I felt like I didn't know him. I was sure he was taller and his face was a different shape or something. He walked right over to me, though, and gave me a hug.

"You look great," he said, and the one thing that hadn't changed at all was the way he smelled. I wanted to hold on to him and just breathe.

After staying at the party for a while, Jenny, Cleve and I all went upstairs and hung out in the bonus room talking. It felt almost like it used to when we were all just friends, except that I was having trouble thinking of things to say. Jenny and I showed him the stuff for the babies program, including the layette bags I'd learned how to make, and he said it was cool we were doing that but I could tell he was bored. He talked about school a lot and he'd totally gotten into basketball and the Tar Heels.

"I want to go to UNC," Jenny said. "Chapel Hill would be so cool." She and I were sitting on the futon, our shoes off. My dress was fine for standing around in but definitely not fine for sitting and I kept having to tug the skirt down and the top up. Jenny's dress was loose and really cute, but she looked terrible. She was getting a cold and her voice croaked and she had a bunch of tissues wadded up in her hand.

"You can't get into Chapel Hill if you don't have a clue what you want to do with your life, Jen." Cleve was sprawled out on the beanbag chair. He'd picked up one of the pacifiers from the baby stuff and was tossing it from one hand to the other. "You're Miss Popularity, but your grades suck, am I right?" he asked.

"Go to hell." Jenny laughed. "I could get in if you could."

"I had a 5.2 GPA," he said.

"You're half-black," Jenny said. "That's why you got in."

I kicked her leg with my bare foot. "You're so rude," I said. It was practically the first words I'd said since we'd come upstairs. Why did I feel so stupidly shy around him all of a sudden?

Cleve grinned. "It probably didn't hurt," he admitted.

"I have time to figure it out," Jenny said. "All I know is I want to go into a helping profession."

"What the hell is a helping profession?" Cleve asked. "You mean like a nurse?"

"Or a doctor, you sexist asshole." Jenny laughed again. They'd always talked this way to each other. "Or a teacher or a counselor. Something that helps people, unlike architecture that only helps buildings."

"God, you are ignorant," Cleve said. "Who do you think lives and works in buildings?"

I was watching his hands as he tossed the pacifier from one to the other. I knew how it would feel to have him slide those hands up my thighs and under my skirt. Seriously, if Jenny hadn't been there I would have stood and unzipped my dress and been all over him. Well, maybe not. But that's what I wanted.

"At least Grace has some ambition." Cleve caught me totally off guard by mentioning my name. "How many people do you know who can write as well as she can?"

"Yeah, but it's hard to make money writing," Jenny said.

"Hard but not impossible. And she'd be doing something she loves and that's what matters." They were talking about me like I wasn't there, but I didn't care. He was smiling at me. A really good smile. *He's still into me,* I thought. I wanted Jenny to disappear. I could talk to him much more easily if it was just the two of us.

Cleve tossed the pacifier high in the air with one hand and caught it with the other. "Let's go to the park," he said, standing.

Yes, the park! We'd spent so many evenings there. We'd had sex there for the first time the night before he broke up with me. I'd always worried there'd been some connection between the two things: sex and the breakup.

"That'd be cool." Jenny got to her feet.

"I'll catch up," he said, heading for the hallway. I guessed he wanted to use the bathroom. I grabbed Jenny's arm before we started down the stairs.

"Could you stay here, Jen?" I asked. "Please? I'm sorry. I just need to talk to him alone."

She looked surprised, but only for a second. "No prob," she said. "I feel like crap, anyway. Tell him my mom asked me to help with something."

"You're the best," I said, hugging her.

"Just—" she wrinkled her nose "—don't get hurt, okay?"

I was already halfway down the stairs. "I won't," I said. The thought of getting hurt wasn't even on my radar.

I waited for him on the front lawn and saw him walking down the driveway. He'd come out the back door, probably to avoid all the people in the living room.

"Jenny's got to help Emerson," I said when he was close enough to hear.

"Cool," he said, but I could tell by the way he said it that he meant "okay," not "that's great." We headed toward the park, walking in and out of the pools of light from the streetlamps. "Jenny should probably be with us, though," he said after a minute.

"Why?"

"Just...not a good idea for you and me to be alone together."

I laughed. "You think we need a chaperone?"

"Actually, yeah. Especially with how hot you look tonight."

Oh, God. "Thanks," I said.

"Seriously. I was looking at you tonight thinking what an asshole I was for breaking up with you."

Did he want to get back together? I nearly asked him, but I was afraid of pushing my luck. "Yeah," I said. "You were."

"It was the right move, though, Grace," he said. "I mean, you look amazing tonight, but I'd only hurt you if we got back together. I'm three hours away and I want to be able to get to know people without feeling guilty about it."

"Other girls, you mean." We'd had this conversation before.

"Girls. Guys. New people." He shoved his hands in his pockets. "I just need to be free for now."

"I know all this," I said. "Let's not talk about it." Talking about it now only reminded me of how much it hurt when we discussed it the first time. "I get it. We don't need to go all over it again."

"Good," he said. Neither of us said anything for a couple of minutes. We'd gotten to the park entrance and headed toward the playground as if we were on autopilot. I was honestly having trouble thinking of things to say to him that had nothing to do with us getting back together. Before everything fell apart, I could talk to him pretty easily and now I couldn't think of a single thing to say to him that wouldn't end up with me crying.

He sat down on one of the swings, and I took off my shoes and sat on the swing closest to him. "I didn't care if we had to be long distance," I said before I could stop myself.

"Grace," he said, "don't start."

"You could even go out with other girls, as long as you didn't...you know. I know you need to make friends and stuff."

"Look," he said, "who knows what'll happen in the future? But for now, we really need to experience the rest of the world. Both of us. Until we get to know lots of other people, how can we ever know who's the right one for us?"

I was speed-reading between the lines. I heard him say, *You're the one I want, but I need to be able to say I've gone out with other girls so when I come back to you, I know for sure.*

Neither of us was swinging on the swings. We were just holding the chains, pushing ourselves around a little with our feet in the sandy pit beneath us. Suddenly, I couldn't stand the physical distance between us any longer. I stood and walked over to his swing. I knew how to do this. I knew how to change everything in less than a minute. I held on to the chains right above his hands and leaned forward to kiss him. He didn't resist at all. I knew he wouldn't, and when I finally lifted my lips from his, it was only to reach down and touch his hard penis through his pants. He caught my hand, more to hold it there than to pull it away. But I stepped back, hiked up my dress and slipped my thumbs under the top of my panties.

"Oh, Gracie, don't," he said, but he didn't mean it, and when I climbed onto the seat—onto *him*—he was every bit as lost as I was.

38

Grace

"I don't want to go to church today," I told my mother as we ate breakfast the morning after the party. At least, *she* was eating breakfast. Oatmeal and bananas. I was too wired to eat the toast on my plate.

"Oh, come with me, honey," she said. "I have a solo today." She was already in her church clothes—tan pants, white blouse, blue jacket with white-and-blue-checked scarf around her neck. I was still in my pajama bottoms and T-shirt.

"I'm really tired," I said. "I just want to stay home, okay?" She looked disappointed—maybe even hurt—but I never really liked going to church. I hated afterward when you were supposed to stand around and talk to people. Of course, that was Mom's favorite part. The only thing that made it okay was that Jenny was usually there. I was sure she'd be staying home today because she was sick, plus I needed to wait for Cleve to call. I wanted to get together with him before he left. Even though it was a three-day weekend, his friend needed to go back tonight and Cleve had no other ride, so he was stuck.

I'd called Jenny late last night to tell her how great things went with him.

"Are you back together?" she'd asked. Her voice was so hoarse I could hardly hear her.

"We didn't specifically get into that," I'd said. Last night had been about action, not conversation. I smiled now as I nibbled the corner of my toast, remembering my mother's words from a couple of weeks earlier: *you need to take action.* Well, Mom, I did and you were right.

Omigod, it had been so good! Cleve kept saying, "Holy shit!" after it was over. He was holding me and kissing my hair and it was just the most amazing night.

"How did it go with Cleve last night?" my mother asked, and I jerked my head up. It was like she was able to hear my thoughts. What did she know?

"What do you mean?" I asked.

"Just…seeing him." She sipped her coffee. "I worried it'd be hard for you."

"It was no big deal," I said. "We're good."

She was looking at me like she wasn't sure she believed me, and I stood to carry my plate to the counter and get away from her eyes.

"Well, I'm glad to hear that," she said. "What did you think of the party?"

"It was nice." I threw my toast in the trash beneath the sink.

"I still feel bad about the travel mug, Gracie," she said.

"I don't want to talk about it." I wasn't ready to let her off the hook on that one.

She stood and looked at her watch. I couldn't wait for her to leave. I was worried Cleve would call while she was still home. My phone was on the counter and I kept looking at the display, waiting for it to light up.

"I have a meeting with the choir committee late this afternoon," she said. "We're meeting at Port City Java to plan the music for the rest of the year. Do you want to come? You could do your homework there and then we could grab something to eat."

I didn't understand how she could even *look* at Port City Java when that was the last place my dad had ever been. "No, thanks," I said. "I'm probably just going to hang out with Jenny." I rinsed my hands and reached for a paper towel. I couldn't tell her I'd be hanging out with Cleve. That would start a whole new bunch of questions.

"Could you clean your bathroom, please?" she said as she headed for the door. "It's looking pretty bad."

"All right," I said. I just wanted her to go.

At ten-thirty, I carried my phone to the living room and laid down on the sofa. He should be up by now. I texted, U up yet?

A few seconds later, he replied. On my way to CH.

What? I sat up, staring at the words. U said tonite! I typed, then waited, my fingers gripping the phone.

Friend needed go back early. Sorry.

I stared at the display. Screw texting! I dialed his number.

"Hey," he said when he picked up.

"I can't believe you just left without letting me know!" I said.

"Listen, Grace," he said. "I'm sorry about last night."

"What do you mean, 'sorry'?"

"I really shouldn't have… I took advantage of you."

"No, you didn't! I wanted to do it."

"I know you did, and I took advantage of that fact."

"Cleve! I—"

"You wanted to do it because you want us to be together again, but that's not what I want."

"Yes, you do," I said.

"Nothing's changed, okay, Grace? Everything I said about us needing to see other people...about being free... It's still all true."

"Cleve!"

"Look, you know I care about you a lot, right?"

"Yes."

"I always will. No matter what happens, okay? But I screwed up by emailing and texting you after we broke up."

"What do you mean?"

"I thought it would be okay," he said. "I didn't want to, like, cut you off cold turkey, but I think all the contact made you feel like we're not really broken up. We need to chill on being in touch with each other, at least for a few months."

A few months? The thought of not being able to talk to him felt like one more death. I started to cry. I tried to hide it at first, but I couldn't speak and he knew. My life was totally empty. No Daddy. Jenny spending more and more time with Devon. Now no Cleve. He'd been my lifeline.

"Grace, don't," he said. "Come on. I'm sorry, but this is the right thing to do. I should have done it sooner. My buddy says it's like taking off a Band-Aid. I should have done it fast instead of bit by bit. It'll hurt like hell for a few minutes, but better than... I think I've been leading you on, staying in touch."

"And screwing me last night!"

"Don't talk about it like that."

"That's all it was to you, though. That's what you're saying."

I heard him let out a big, frustrated-sounding sigh. "This is pointless," he said. "I don't know how to end things with you. We have to just *stop*. Starting right now, as soon as we hang up, no more texting or anything. It's the best way for you to start living your life without me."

"Because you want to live your life without *me*," I said.

"Yes, I do," he said. "Right now, I need to."

I hung up, then speed-dialed him right back, but he didn't pick up.

I texted him. Sorry I hung up. I waited, staring at the black display on my phone. Nothing. He wasn't going to answer me.

I remembered how amazing it had been with him the night before. When he was *with* me, he wanted me. The second he was away from me, though, he was influenced by his stupid friends.

I had to see him.

I would take action.

39

Tara

Grace was in the kitchen when I got home from church. She sat at the table with a mug of coffee, her phone in front of her.

"How was your solo?" she asked.

I didn't even think she'd heard me when I mentioned the solo earlier. "It went well," I said. People had told me I sounded wonderful, and I'd forgotten how it felt to fill that beautiful space with my voice. But I'd felt empty inside and it wasn't until I was driving home that I realized why: Sam wasn't there. He always said my singing moved him. Not in so many words, but I knew how he was feeling by the way he'd hold my hand when I came back to the pew.

"When are you going out?" I asked. She was wearing cropped pants and a long-sleeved striped T-shirt and her hair was damp.

"In a little while," she said. "I cleaned my bathroom."

"Excellent!" I leaned over to give her a hug and her cool, damp hair stuck a little to my cheek. It was rare for me to only have to ask her once.

She folded her hands on the table, pressing them together so hard that her knuckles were white.

"Mom, listen." She looked up at me. "I know you're going to say no right away, so just listen to everything I say before you react, okay?"

It seemed like the longest sentence she'd said to me in months.

"Okay." I leaned back against the counter. This was good. I would *not* say no right away. I'd let her talk.

"I'm going to Chapel Hill this afternoon. For the night. I—"

"Chapel Hill? Today? *Why?*"

She gave me her frustrated look. "There's this girl," she said. "She's a graduate student and Jenny knows her and she—this girl—wants to see some friends in Chapel Hill, but she doesn't have a car, so she'll go with me and be my supervising driver and I'll come back tomorrow."

I was, for once in my life, speechless. Grace was terrified to get behind the wheel of a car and I was just as terrified to have her there. "Well, first of all," I said, "you can't go."

"Mom, I told you not to just react!" She pressed her hands together even harder and her eyes were wide, imploring me. "Listen to the whole explanation," she pleaded.

"Does this have to do with Cleve?" I asked, although that made no sense. Cleve was home for the weekend so why would she want to go to Chapel Hill?

"Yes," she admitted. "He had to go back today and I absolutely *have* to see him. Plus, I want to see UNC, too, because I'll probably be applying there."

I knew that was bullshit. She might be applying there, but this sudden need to see UNC was such a weak excuse that even she knew it, and she turned her head away, unable to look me in the eye.

"You know that doesn't make sense, Grace," I said. "If you want to see Cleve, at least be honest with me and don't make up some nonsense about wanting to see UNC all of a sudden."

She flattened her hands on the table. "Cleve didn't realize he had to go back early today and we didn't get to finish talking last night and he asked if I could come."

"Are you two back together?"

I could see her trying to decide how much to reveal to me. "He's mixed up about us," she said. "He thinks we should stay broken up, but we need to talk about it more and didn't get the chance." She frowned up at me. "I'm upset, Mom! I need to talk to him in *person*."

"And where exactly would you stay?" I asked.

"With Jenny's friend."

"What's her name?"

"Elena."

"How does Jenny have a friend who's a grad student?"

"She was... I don't know. A neighbor or something. Do you want to talk to her? I can—"

"No, because you're not going."

"What if I let Elena drive instead of me?"

"No, Grace. I'm sorry you and Cleve are still struggling, but you'll have to talk it out on the phone. If you want to go to UNC sometime in the future, we'll plan it ahead of time. You'll have to show me you're comfortable driving first and—"

"Elena can drive."

"This is too half-baked a plan, all right? You can't go. I'm sorry, but this is a nonnegotiable."

She sprang out of her chair. "You don't understand!" she said, and in an instant, tears had filled her eyes.

"Then help me understand." I caught her shoulders and

held on tight as she tried to squirm out of my grasp. "Why
can't you and Cleve resolve this on the phone?"

She pried my hands from her shoulders. "I just wanted to
go, that's all!" She turned and headed for the stairs.

"Grace!" I called after her. "Don't run off like that. Talk
to me!"

But her footsteps skittered up the stairs and I lowered
myself to a chair. I'd blown it again, yet I didn't know what
I could have said or done differently. *This is normal,* I told
myself. *Mothers and daughters fight.*

I touched my cheek where I'd pressed it against her hair.
I wanted to feel that sweet damp hair against my skin again.
It had reminded me of when she was little and I'd hold her
and rock her and she was so happy in my arms.

A long, long time ago.

40

Emerson

My plan was not going well so far. I hadn't counted on Jenny feeling too sick to go out that afternoon, so I was anxious as I stood by the living room window watching for Ian's car. The sky was gray and thick with clouds. We were going to get a downpour soon. In my hands I clutched Noelle's record book and the thin file folder with her letter to Anna and copies of the information I'd printed from the Missing Children's website.

I left the window for no more than a second to take the tray of leftover spanokopita out of the oven, and when I returned I saw his car out front but no sign of him, and I knew he was already heading up my driveway toward the side door.

People always just walked in my kitchen door without knocking, so I raced through the house to head him off, opening the door just as he was about to walk in. "Jenny's home," I whispered. "I was hoping she'd be out, but she's sick, so just...play along with whatever I say."

Ian frowned. "What's going on?" he asked.

I put a finger to my lips. "I'll tell you—"

"Hey," Jenny said from the doorway to the kitchen. She was still wearing her pajama shorts and a tank top and her hair stuck out on one side.

"Hi, Jenny," Ian said. "You're not feeling well?"

"Too much wild party for me last night," Jenny rasped, rubbing her throat. She gave me a confused *what's-Ian-doing-here?* sort of look.

"Ian and I have some issues to talk about related to Noelle's estate," I said. I thought she was looking at the book and file in my arms with suspicion, but that might have been my paranoia. "What can I get you, Jen?" I asked her. "Some tea with lemon and honey?"

"I'm just going to crash again," she said.

"Good idea. Want some juice to take up with you?"

"Yeah. Maybe." She headed for the refrigerator, but I beat her to it. I set the record book and file on the kitchen table and quickly poured a glass of orange juice. Ian stood quietly next to the island, and I knew he didn't know what was safe to do or say. I handed the glass to Jenny.

"Thanks," she said. "See you all later."

"She sounds miserable," Ian said as we watched her head for the stairs.

"I know." I moved the spanokopita from the baking pan to a plate. "We can nibble party leftovers," I said, setting the plate on the kitchen table.

"Your hands are shaking," Ian said, and then he lowered his voice. "Is this really about Noelle's will or the...other things we've been talking about with regard to her?"

"Neither." I rested my hands on the island and let myself simply breathe in and out for a moment. "I'll tell you in a minute," I said finally, glancing toward the hallway and the stairs. I'd really wanted no one home for this conversation. Especially not a sick kid who might need me. I motioned to the table. "Have a seat," I said. "I have coffee? Iced tea? I can brew decaf if you like. Or you might actually need a glass of wine when I tell you what I have to say."

"Coffee's good." He lowered himself to one of the kitchen chairs, his eyes never leaving my face.

I poured him a cup, then sat down at the end of the table, glancing toward the hallway again.

Ian looked at the book and file on the table, but didn't touch it. "What's this?" he asked.

I let out a long breath. "I've opened a gigantic can of worms and I don't know how to get them all back in the can," I said quietly. "I thought of just keeping it to myself, but I can't. I don't know who else to talk to." I pressed my fingers to my temples. "I need your help to know what to do."

"It's a legal matter?" he asked.

"Yes and no." I pulled out the typed letter Noelle had written to Anna and set it in front of him. The color drained from his face as he read it.

"Holy..." He looked up at me. Shook his head. "What's next? I mean, seriously. What the hell is Noelle going to dump in our laps next? And who is Anna?"

I explained how I'd stumbled across the letter and how Tara and I finally figured out Anna's identity. "But to answer your question about what's next, I can tell you exactly what's next."

He looked as though he wasn't sure he wanted to know.

I leaned toward him. "I believe the baby Noelle dropped was Tara's," I said quietly.

He jerked back as if I'd stung him. "What the... Why would you think that?"

"I found the date Anna Knightly's baby disappeared on the Missing Children's website," I said. "Or, at least, the date she was born. The only baby Noelle delivered during that time was Grace. Or the baby who...the *real* Grace." I pulled a sheet of paper from the file on the table. "This is from the Missing Children's website. It says that Lily Ann Knightly was born on August 29, 1994, and disappeared from a Wilmington, NC, hospital shortly after her birth."

He still wore his frown as he looked up from the paper. "Wasn't Jenny born around the same time?"

"Jenny was born on the thirty-first and Grace on September 1, but I had Jenny in the hospital and Noelle wasn't involved at all. Tara was in labor while I was having a C-section."

Ian looked up at the ceiling. "I distinctly remember the night Grace was born," he said. "Noelle and I were engaged back then, remember?"

I nodded.

"She called me a few times from Sam and Tara's, telling me how rough going it was. She was really worried. She'd talked about getting Tara to the hospital, but in the end, it worked out all right." He abruptly shook his head. "This doesn't make any sense, Emerson," he said. "Tara would have known if another baby was suddenly substituted for hers."

"I don't remember it all that well since I was busy having a baby myself, but I do remember Tara telling me she was so zonked after the delivery that she barely remembered even holding Grace until the next morning."

"But Sam was there," Ian said. "He would have been awake and alert and known if his baby was suddenly dead."

"Don't say it like that." I shivered.

"Well, that's what we're talking about, isn't it?" Ian sounded suddenly angry. I wished he would lower his voice. "Noelle killed a baby and somehow got rid of it and then she came up with this—" he waved at the letter "—this lamebrain plan and went to the hospital and found an appropriate substitute and brought it back and all that supposedly happened when? While Sam and Tara were sleeping on the most exciting night of their lives? It's hard to swallow."

"We know it happened, though," I said. "We have it in Noelle's own words."

"Maybe there were babies Noelle delivered that she never recorded in her logbook," Ian suggested.

"Then I think there would have been torn-out pages and there are none from 1994."

"You and Tara should have come to me right away with this," he said.

"We… Honestly, Ian. We had no idea how deep this was going to get. I think we were hoping we'd find out it was all a mistake somehow."

He took off his glasses and rubbed his eyes. "How much of this does Tara know?"

"She has no idea it could be Grace," I said. "Noelle quit practicing in 1998, so we naturally assumed the patient whose baby was…lost was from around that time."

Ian reached for the logbook. "Let me see her record of Grace's birth," he said.

I had the pages marked and I opened it for him. I watched as he scanned the account of Grace getting stuck during Tara's labor. "Posterior arrest," Noelle called it, and it was followed by hours of manipulation and excruciating pain that put me in awe of both Noelle and Tara. Reading the account, I'd thought Noelle had been a miracle worker to be able to deliver her at all.

"This sounds ghastly." Ian winced. "But there's nothing here about a dropped baby," he said.

"She didn't write that part, obviously," I said. "She falsified what happened. In case you haven't figured it out by now, my *sister* Noelle was pretty good at lying."

"Where's the baby?" Ian asked. "Tara's real...the baby she gave birth to?"

"I don't even want to think about that." I felt my eyes burn. Tara was more sister than friend to me, and I was haunted by what might have happened to her baby. Did she end up in a shallow grave? A Dumpster somewhere? What happened to the baby we should have been allowed to love and grieve? I put my hands to my face. "What do I *do,* Ian?" I asked.

"Well, first off, Tara needs to know," he said.

"Oh, God," I said, because of course she did. I knew that, but I'd needed to hear someone else say it. "It seems so cruel," I said.

I thought I heard the faintest creaking sound from the direction of the stairs and I glanced toward the hallway, but Ian didn't seem to notice.

"Let's say Tara and I knew that Jenny wasn't your biological child," he said, "would you want us to tell you?"

"Yes, of course, but I would...." I shut my eyes, trying to imagine getting that news. "It would kill me to know my own child had died and I'd known nothing about it. And that Jenny had been stolen from some other woman." I shook my head. "Oh, my God. It would just kill me."

"No, it wouldn't, because Tara would be there for you," Ian said. "You two have seen each other through thick and thin, and you'll be there for her, all right? And I will be, too."

"She just lost *Sam,* though, Ian," I nearly wailed. "How

can we take away her daughter?" I was upset, but felt relief that suddenly I could use the word *we* instead of *I*.

"We're not talking about taking away anyone's daughter," he said. "To be honest, I have to do a little research into this to figure out the best approach, but we'll take it one step at a time. It shouldn't be too difficult to track down the officers who investigated this case back in '94. I may even know some of them."

"I think we need to let Tara know before you talk to anyone else, though," I said. "I'm afraid she'll be angry that I told *you* before I told her. And I can tell her that maybe I'm wrong. When it comes right down to it, we don't have proof, do we? I can just tell her what I know. Maybe some-how I'm misinterpreting things."

"That's very true," he said. "There will have to be DNA tests and interviews, and as I said, we'll take it one step at a time."

"Should we tell her today?" My voice was so tentative. I was dreading what lay ahead of me.

Ian folded his arms across his chest. "Can you wait an-other couple of days?" he asked. "I'm leaving tonight for Charlotte and I'm in a golf tournament all day tomorrow." For the first time since his arrival, he smiled, then rested his hand flat on the logbook. "Not that I think my golf game is more important than this," he said, "but tomorrow's a holiday and this has held for sixteen years. I won't call the investigator until after we talk to Tara, so if you can handle waiting, we can talk to her Tuesday afternoon when she gets out of school."

I heard another creak coming from the direction of the stairs, and this time both Ian and I looked toward the hallway.

"Jenny?" I called, but there was no answer.

I turned back to Ian. Licked my dry lips. "Yes," I said, my voice very low now. "I can wait."

41

Grace

It was like having a giant ball of thorns in my chest, the pain was that bad. I felt like I was having some kind of breakdown. I'd gotten my hopes up that Cleve and I would get back together. They were *still* up and I wanted to try calling him again in the worst way. It made me realize how often I'd been calling and texting him. Had I been annoying him? I could call to apologize for calling him too much. I couldn't stop thinking of excuses to contact him. But I knew I couldn't or I'd drive him even further away.

Instead, I lay on my bed with my feet up on my headboard and texted Jenny all afternoon while my mother was out. I told her how I'd come up with the plan to drive to Chapel Hill and what a bitch my mother was. I told her I'd made up that Elena girl in case my mother ever asked about her. I hardly ever lied. Everyone else I knew lied all the time, but I really didn't and it had felt amazingly easy. My mother was so gullible. I had to admit the whole thing had been a really stupid idea, although I still wanted to do it. It was pouring rain out now, though, and I wouldn't be able to get there until dark and wouldn't know where I was

going. I had his dorm address, but…it was just a stupid idea.
I'd look like the pathetic girl he thought I was.

Jenny texted me that she needed to get some juice, so for
a few minutes it was just me and my phone. Dangerous. I
typed Sorry i annoyed u so much to Cleve, but I erased it
without sending.

Jenny was taking forever to get her juice. R u there yet?
I texted her, but she didn't text me back. Somehow I fell
asleep and when I woke up, my phone was ringing and her
cell number was on the display.

"I fell asleep," I said, instead of hello.

"I'm coming over there." She sounded terrible and I
knew it had to hurt for her to talk.

"You are? It's pouring out and you're sick."

"There's something I have to tell you. To show you. Is
your mom home yet?"

"No. What are you—"

"I'm coming right now, okay?"

I lowered my feet from the headboard and sat up. "Is it
about Cleve?" I asked, but she'd already hung up.

When I opened the front door a few minutes later, Jenny
stood there shivering and holding an umbrella over her
head. I grabbed her arm and pulled her inside.

"What's so important?" I asked.

"Your mom's not home yet, right?" Her voice was low
and hoarse and her nose was red. She was holding a plastic
grocery bag with a book or something inside it.

"No. This is about Cleve, isn't it?" What if he'd been in
an accident? Oh, God! I'd die.

She gave me a little shove toward the stairs. "It's not
about Cleve," she said. "Let's go to your room."

I let her push me across the hall. "You're seriously freaking me out," I said as we climbed the stairs.

"Just go," she said.

In my room, Jenny grabbed the box of tissues from one of the nightstands. She sat on the edge of my bed with the tissues on one side of her and the plastic bag on the other. She pulled a tissue from the box and blew her nose while I just stood there, twisting my hands together, waiting for her to get to the point.

"Look," Jenny said finally, "this timing sucks and I'm sorry about that, but I found out something you need to know. It has to do with you. Who you are."

"What do you mean, who I am?" Did she mean my personality? Did I have some trait so horrible that she had to rush over in the rain while she was sick as a dog to tell me about it? Maybe so. After all, Cleve wasn't crazy about who I was. Neither was my mother. Neither was *I*.

"Just listen to me," she said, "and remember I'm your best friend forever, okay? I always will be. Always, always, Gracie, no matter what!" Her eyes looked glassy and I started to cry without even knowing why. Anything that had her this upset was going to make a mess out of me, too.

"*Tell* me," I said.

"Ian was at my house like an hour ago."

"Ian?" What did Ian have to do with anything? "Is this more about the will?" I wasn't hurt that Noelle left more money to Jenny than to me. Jenny deserved it. I didn't.

"No, not the will. I thought that, too, but that wasn't it at all. I was upstairs while you and I were texting, and when I started to go downstairs for more juice, I heard them talking and… I don't remember what my mom was saying but it

made me stop and just listen in. They were talking about—"
Jenny hesitated "—I am so sorry to tell you this!"

"Tell me *what?*"

"They said how you're not really your mom's daughter.
How you were stolen from some other woman."

"What?" What was she saying? "Are you sure they were
talking about *me?*"

"Yes."

"That's… Why would they say that? It's ridiculous."

"I know. It sounds crazy, but they were talking about it
and I was totally shocked." She blew her nose again. "I just
stood there listening, trying to get what they meant. Your
mom doesn't know but they're going to tell her."

"Know *what?* How can they know something about me
that my own mother doesn't know?" I tried to laugh. "This
is like the most bizarre thing I've ever heard."

"I know, but—"

"Do you hear how stupid this sounds? You just said my
mother stole me, which is totally ridiculous, anyway, but if
she stole me, then how could she not know I was stolen?" I
wanted to throw something at Jenny. "Why are you screwing with my head?"

"I'm sorry! I know. But I can explain everything." She
opened the grocery bag and pulled out a big brown book
and a manila file folder. Her hands were shaking all over
the place. "I sat on the stairs until after Ian left and then I
went into the kitchen like I wanted more juice," she said.
"I think Mom was worried I'd overheard them, but I acted
like I just came downstairs right that minute and poured
some juice. I watched her put this book and things in the
drawer in the kitchen. You know by the desk she uses?"

"What's the book?" I sat down next to her on the bed.

"It's got notes from when Noelle delivered babies. I

looked over her notes from when you were born and it doesn't say anything weird that I could tell. But these things were with it." She opened the folder and took out a type-written sheet of paper. "This letter...part of a letter. Noelle wrote it." She handed it to me.

I could hardly believe what I was reading.

"This is *disgusting!*" I said, horrified. "I can't believe Noelle would do something like that."

"I know. Me neither, but—"

"Why would you think *I'm* the baby she took?"

"I don't understand for sure how they know it's you, but they do," Jenny said. "I think it's because of this. Because of the date here." She pulled two sheets of printer paper from the folder and showed me the top one. "See the URL at the bottom? This is from the website of the Missing Children's Bureau. It's just one line." She read it out loud in her raspy voice. "'Lily Ann Knightly was born August 29, 1994, and disappeared from a Wilmington, NC, hospital shortly after her birth.'"

I shook my head slowly. I was starting to feel nauseated. "Were there other...I mean, could it have been a different baby Noelle delivered? Why are they so sure it's me? Your birthday is a day closer to hers than mine." *Lily.* Could that really be my name?

"But Noelle had nothing to do with me being born."

Jenny put her arm around me. The truth was sinking in for both of us. We knew I looked nothing like my par-ents. I had their brown eyes, but so did half the kids in the country. Everyone always said I was quiet and smart like my father, but plenty of kids were quiet and smart. And I was nothing like my mother. Nothing.

"I can't believe this," I said quietly.

"I'm sorry," Jenny said. "I thought you had a right to know. I didn't know if they'd ever tell you."

I touched the sheet of printer paper. *Lily Ann Knightly. Lily.* "Who am I?" I asked.

Jenny pressed her cheek to my shoulder and her arm tightened around me. "You're Grace," she said. "My best friend, and don't you ever forget it."

My mind was miles away. "I always knew I didn't fit in. My mother... It's like she wishes I was someone else," I said. "That dead baby. That's who my mother was supposed to get as her daughter." I stood and waved my hands through the air. "Oh, my *God,* Jenny. A baby *died.* I hate Noelle. How could anyone do something like this?"

"If she never took you, you wouldn't be my friend, though, and I can't stand that thought."

It was true. I couldn't imagine my life without Jenny in it. But that felt like the only thing that was good about my life right then.

"When are they going to tell my mother?" That would be it, I thought. That would be the moment my mother cut me out of her heart. Right now, she had to love me and put up with me. *No wonder she's nothing like me,* my mother would think. How could she help but think that? How could she help but wonder about how different, how perfect, her real daughter would have been?

"I think Tuesday," Jenny said. "Don't tell her I told you, okay? My mother would kill me for snooping. I have to get these things back before she figures out I took them."

"What's the other paper?" I pointed to the two sheets of printer paper on her lap.

"It's just nothing." Jenny stuck both sheets back in the folder.

"Let me see," I said. Jenny was a terrible liar.

She hesitated, then reached into the folder and handed me another paper printed from the Missing Children's Bureau website.

Missing Children's Bureau director, Anna Chester Knightly, 44, has worked for MCB for ten years. Her infant daughter, Lily, disappeared from a Wilmington, North Carolina, hospital in 1994. She has one other daughter, Haley.

I couldn't speak. My mother? And a *sister.* "Where do they live?" I was finally able to ask. "Are they in Wilmington?"

"I don't think so. She's director of this Missing Children's place and I don't think that's here."

"She's been looking for me," I whispered. "All my life, she's been looking for me." I felt so much sympathy for her. Sympathy, and a longing so strong I felt it from the center of my heart to the ends of my fingers. "She probably thinks I'm dead."

Jenny took the paper from my hand and put it back in the folder. "Look, I've got to get home," she said. "I told my mother I was just going to the store for cough medicine. She'll be calling me any second."

"Leave the papers with me," I said.

"I can't. She'll notice they're gone."

"Please, Jenny. I need them."

"I can't." She started to put the folder back in the grocery bag, but I grabbed it from her and hugged it to my chest.

"Grace! I have to put them back!" she said.

"I'm keeping them. They're mine. They're about *me.*"

"Gracie. Please. She'll kill me." She grabbed for the folder but I turned around quickly, opened my dresser drawer and shut the file inside it.

"Grace!" She tried to get to the drawer but I held her away. "You can find the same stuff on that website," she said. "On that Missing Children's website."

I held my hands out to my sides to keep her from getting to the drawer. She was right; I could find the information on the site, but I wanted those sheets of paper. Suddenly I felt like I couldn't stand one more thing being taken away from me. "Let me keep them, Jenny," I pleaded. I felt tears running down my cheeks. "Let them be mine."

She stared at me a minute, then pulled me into a hug. "Make copies," she said into my hair. "Then give them back to me tomorrow." I wasn't sure which one of us was crying harder.

I sat in my room for an hour after Jenny left, the two sheets of paper on my lap. I'd stared at the words on them for a long time before it got too dark to see them any longer, and it was like I didn't have the energy to turn on the light. When my mother came home, she stopped in my room to tell me she'd picked up sandwiches for dinner. I turned on the light then because I wanted to see if she looked any different to me, but she didn't. She wasn't the one who had changed in the past couple of hours.

After my mother went downstairs again, I logged on to the internet. I found the website for the Missing Children's Bureau and followed the URL to the page about Anna Knightly. I caught my breath. A picture! Omigod, she looked so amazing. She had this open, beautiful face. You could tell so much from a picture. She looked gentle and full of love. She had green eyes, which had to be where my flecks of green came from. I didn't think she looked anything like me otherwise, though. My own mother—at least, the mother who raised me—looked more like me than Anna Knightly did. I tried to find myself in her face, holding my hand mirror in front of me so I could look back and forth from my reflection to her photograph. My real father, I thought. I must look more like him. I shivered, creeped out by the thought of having any other father than the one I'd grown up with. The one I would love forever, no matter what.

I read the one sentence over and over again. "Her infant daughter, Lily, disappeared." How did they tell her that her baby had vanished? I pictured this pretty, soft-looking woman going into the hospital nursery to take her daughter home, and all the nurses scrambling to look for the baby, their panic rising as they realized she was gone. *I* was gone. I still couldn't get it through my head that *Lily* was *me*. I could imagine how Anna Knightly felt when they told her. How she'd grieved for her. For *me*. I could have had a whole different life.

Missing children turned up dead. That's the way it always was on the news, and after all this time that had to be what Anna Knightly expected. She only knew I disappeared. She didn't know the rest of my story.

"I'm alive," I said to the picture on my monitor. "I'm right here."

Where did she live? Could I find a phone number for her somehow? Could I call her right now? Right this second? I wanted to tell her I was alive. She could die tomorrow and we never would have known each other.

There was a phone number for the Missing Children's Bureau and I wrote it down. There was an address, too, in Alexandria, Virginia, one state away. My mother—my biological mother—was only one puny state away.

★ ★ ★

I couldn't sleep. I kept picturing a map. Alexandria was in the northern part of Virginia, wasn't it? Near Washington? Washington was only like five hours away. I needed to meet Anna. I needed to find out who I really was. I could call her at the Missing Children's Bureau early in the morning, but it would be so much better to meet her in person. I sat up, totally wired. I had to meet her *now,* I thought, as soon as I possibly could. Life was short. Tomorrow Anna could get killed driving to work. It happened.

I grabbed my phone and speed-dialed Cleve's number and when he picked up—*he picked up!*—I burst into tears.

"Don't hang up. Don't hang up!" I said. "I have to talk to you. It's not about us. Don't worry. I just have to talk to you or I'll go crazy."

"Grace, it's nearly midnight." He sounded wide-awake. I heard people talking in the background. A girl laughing. "We can talk tomorrow, okay?" he asked.

"I just found out I was stolen from another woman when I was a baby!"

He was quiet. "What the hell are you talking about?"

I explained everything: Jenny overhearing the conversation between her mother and Ian. Noelle's letter to Anna Knightly. The stolen baby. The Missing Children's Bureau.

"I don't believe this," he said. "Are you making this up?"

"No," I said. "Talk to Jenny tomorrow if you don't believe me. They're going to tell my mother Tuesday. She already thinks I'm..." My voice broke, catching me off guard. "I've never really been the daughter she wanted. The other baby, the one who died, probably would have been just like her."

"Hold on a sec," Cleve said. I heard him moving around. A door opening, maybe. "I had to go out in the hall," he said after a minute. "My roommate's got company. Look, I don't know what's going on, but your mom loves you. Everyone has issues with their mother, Grace. I'd love to disown mine half the time. But she's my mother and she loves me and yours does, too."

"That's the difference. Suzanne *is* your mother. My mother *isn't*. I want to meet my real mother and tell her everything. I'm going there."

"Where?"

"Virginia. I'm going to go meet her."

"When? And how do you plan to get there?"

"I'll drive. Tomorrow."

He laughed. "Don't be so twelve years old, Grace."

His words stung. "You don't know how this feels," I said.

"Look, tomorrow you tell your mother what Jenny told you, and—"

"I'll get Jenny in trouble. She's not supposed to know any of this."

"Jenny'll get over it. You tell your mom. If what you're saying is true—and I doubt it—you and your mom need a lawyer. Ian's a lawyer, right? There's all kinds of legal stuff that'll need to be sorted out."

"Lawyers screw everything up," I said. My father had been a great lawyer, but he always slowed things down when it came to his clients' cases. I bet Ian was the same way. Daddy wanted everybody to take their time. Not rush into things. If he was alive, I wondered what he would do with this mess. "Oh, Cleve," I said, "my dad's not really my dad!"

"He's your dad and your mom's your mom. Even if this other lady had you, your parents are still your parents."

"I'm really freaked out, Cleve," I said, but my mind was moving away from our conversation. I walked over to my computer, sat down and clicked on Google Maps.

Cleve sighed again. "Look," he said, "promise me you'll tell your mother tomorrow and that you won't do anything stupid. I care about you, Grace," he said. "That'll never change. So, promise?"

"I promise," I said, but I was already typing in the address for the Missing Children's Bureau.

42

Anna

Washington, D.C.

"What do you think of this look, Dad?" Haley asked Bryan as he opened the curtain around her hospital bed. We'd gotten her settled into the room a few hours earlier and it was very late, but she only now seemed to be winding down from a steroid-induced high. She'd lifted the top of her tray table to check her reflection in the mirror and she ran her hand over the dark stubble of hair that had sprouted up this past week.

"Very cool." Bryan stood next to her bed, running his hand over the short, soft bristles. I knew how her hair felt beneath his palm. The tickle of it beneath my own hand could give me a false sense of security. I had to keep reminding myself that the little bit of stubble was simply the lull before the storm.

Tomorrow she'd receive another dose of her maintenance chemotherapy and that regimen would continue until a donor was found. Once we had a donor, the chemo and radiation she'd receive would destroy far more than her hair as it readied her body to receive the transplant. I refused to think a donor might never be found before the disease claimed her. Would not even go there. And tonight, I wanted her simply to enjoy her stubbly reflection in the mirror and our last few hours with Bryan. I'd be staying overnight with Haley, but he'd head back to his apartment shortly. Tomorrow he'd be on a plane for San Francisco, where he'd have the interview for the D.C. job. I wasn't happy to see him go. I'd taken care of Haley by myself for most of her life, so it wasn't that I needed his help, although his help had been wonderful. It was that I'd grown attached to him and so had Haley. We wanted him around.

"There's our girl!" Tom, Haley's favorite nurse, came into the room. "I have your nighty-night pill."

Haley took the little paper cup from his hand.

"I knew you were coming in tonight," Tom said while she swallowed the pill, "so I cut this out in case you wanted an extra." He handed Haley a copy of the article about the bone marrow drive that had appeared in the *Washington Post* on Friday. Haley'd been great with the journalist from the *Post* and even better with the reporter from WJLA. She'd talked about what she remembered from her first bout with leukemia. "I just thought all little kids had to be hooked up to killer drugs all the time," she said simply. "I didn't know any different." She talked about Lily in a way I never would have been able to. "My mom lost my sister," she said. "I don't want her to lose me, too." I cringed inside when she said that, hoping no one would think she was being disingenuous. I knew she meant every word and I was touched. So apparently were many others. The car dealership showroom filled with people the following day, all of them volunteering to have their cheeks swabbed.

Once Tom had left the room, Haley lowered the head of

her bed until she was lying nearly flat. "Okay," she said to Bryan, "you're coming back Wednesday?"

"Wednesday at four o'clock." He clicked off the bright light on her night table. I was at the foot of her bed, and I watched the movement of flesh and muscle beneath the back of his polo shirt. This week, I'd discovered it wasn't only certain celebrities who could leave me weak in the knees. If anyone had told me the man I'd held in contempt for so many years could have the same effect on me, I would have said they were crazy.

"What do you want me to bring back from San Francisco?" he asked Haley.

"Just you," she said, and I saw the wave of emotion pass over Bryan's features. Haley was so open with her feelings these days. She never wore the mask that so many of us hid behind. She left herself vulnerable, as though she realized there was no time to waste with pretense. We had no promise of tomorrow. None of us did. I was learning so much from my daughter.

"You're sweet," Bryan said to her. "But seriously. How about some Ghirardelli chocolate?"

She made a face. "That sounds good right now, but I probably won't feel like eating it by Wednesday."

"We can save it for when you do want it, then." He looked at his watch. "I'd better run."

"I'll walk you down," I said, then turned to Haley, who had curled up beneath the covers with Fred cuddled in her arms. "Are you okay for a little bit?"

She yawned, nodding. Bryan bent down to kiss her on the cheek and she wrapped one arm around his neck. "Don't forget about us," she said softly.

He stood, holding her hand between both of his. "No," he said. "Never."

We walked quietly to the elevator and rode down to the parking garage, which was nearly empty this late. I walked him all the way to his car. I didn't want to see him go. Maybe I felt some of Haley's trepidation. Some of that *Don't forget about us*. But I didn't think that was it. I wanted to be with him every moment that I could. I was going to let go of my own mask.

He unlocked his car door, then turned to me.

"Hurry back," I said.

He smiled, then pulled me into a long hug that brought memories flooding back to me. They were the good memories, the ones from when we were young and the future held nothing but promise.

"Hold on," he said, letting go of me. He opened the rear door, then climbed in and tugged me in after him. I laughed, practically falling next to him on the bench seat. He kissed me and we made out like the kids we once were, laughing at first at how ludicrous it seemed to be two forty-something people, fooling around in the backseat in a parking garage, but after a while, our laughter stopped and the car filled with our breathing, our touching and the sweet new beginning of a complicated love.

43

Grace

Wilmington, North Carolina

I was still awake at three in the morning, lying in bed, planning my next move. The more I thought about going to Alexandria, the more I knew I had to do it. I'd already printed the directions to the Missing Children's Bureau and it looked pretty easy. Almost a straight shot from Wilmington to Alexandria, though I couldn't picture myself actually *driving* that straight shot, and it was a longer drive than I'd thought. According to Google Maps, it would take five hours and fifty minutes to get there. Five hours and fifty minutes to find my biological mother. When I thought about it that way, it sounded like no time at all.

I'd have to leave as soon as the sun came up. My mother didn't have school tomorrow because of the holiday, but she never slept in. Getting up before she did would be hard. I'd set my phone alarm for six, but now I changed it to five. I should leave while it was still dark. If I left at five-thirty in the morning, I'd be there by lunchtime. My heart thumped at the thought of walking into the Missing Children's

Bureau and announcing my identity to the woman who was my mother.

What if she went out to lunch, though? One of those long business-type lunches like my father used to take? I picked up my phone from the night table again and pressed the display to see the time. Three-ten and I was wide-awake. I'd never *been* so awake. I felt like I'd drunk a bucket of coffee. If I left right now, I could be at the Missing Children's Bureau way before lunch. But it was so dark outside and I could still hear the rain thrumming against my window. I'd only driven a few times in the rain before I'd lost my nerve behind the wheel altogether.

"Do it," I said out loud.

I got up quickly and put on the same cropped pants and blue sweater I'd worn that day. I dumped my textbooks and notebooks out of my backpack onto my bed and replaced them with clean underwear, my toothbrush and toothpaste, and the folder Jenny'd left with me. I was moving fast, as if I was in a race. In a way, I was. I was trying to beat the part of me that thought my plan was not only stupid but dangerous. I hadn't driven since before my father died, and I'd never driven alone and never more than a couple of hours at a time. I grabbed the directions I'd printed out, lifted my backpack to my shoulder and quietly walked downstairs. I took the keys to the Honda from the key cupboard by the back door and left the house before I could change my mind.

I did okay driving for about an hour. I knew I was going way too slow, but it was hard to see. The rain made the road as shiny as a mirror and I kept picturing deer zipping out of the darkness in front of my car. I nearly had the road to myself, though, and that was both good and spooky.

Then all of a sudden, the rain got unbelievably heavy. *Heavy* wasn't even the right word to describe it. It fell in blinding waves against my car, pounding so hard on the roof that I couldn't hear the radio. The wipers were set to their fastest setting, but it was still impossible to see more than a few feet in front of me. I slowed down to forty miles an hour, then thirty, sticking really close to the shoulder. There were more cars on the road by then and none of those drivers seemed to be having any problem with the rain as they zipped past me. One of them honked at me, probably because I was driving so slowly. My hands were sweaty, but I kept them glued to the steering wheel and I was leaning forward like I could somehow see better if my face was closer to the windshield.

I'd just decided I'd better pull over and wait for the rain to ease up when it suddenly did. I sat back a little and let out my breath. I could hear the music on the radio again. I pressed harder on the gas and got my speed up to fifty-five, which was as fast as I was willing to go until the sun was up. So much for that five hours and fifty minutes.

It was light out by the time I crossed the border into Virginia, but it was still raining a little. I was going back and forth in my mind about whether I should call Jenny to tell her where I was when I had a horrible thought. I remembered changing the alarm on my phone to five o'clock. I could see the phone on my night table, but I had no memory of picking it up and putting it in my backpack. *Oh, my God.* I pressed the brake and swerved onto the shoulder of the road. A truck honked and I felt my car sway as it whizzed past me, way too close. I found the button for the emergency blinkers and put them on and then I started hunting for my phone in my backpack, the whole time knowing it wasn't there. How could I have been so stupid?

I was hours from home, on the highway, with no phone. I sat there paralyzed for a few minutes, glancing every once in a while at the floor of the car or the passenger seat as though a phone might magically appear. What could I do? I was two-thirds of the way there. I just had to keep going. Swallowing hard, I turned off my blinkers and waited for a long break between the cars. Then I pulled onto the road again.

A couple of hours later, I didn't know where I was, but I was good and stuck in traffic. People complained about rush-hour traffic in Wilmington, but they didn't know what they were talking about. I'd sit still for five minutes, then move about ten feet, then sit still again. There were gigantic trucks on both sides of me and I felt trapped and claustrophobic. They were so big that I could see beneath them to the cars in the other lanes. At least when I'd been driving through the rain and the darkness, I'd had no time to think about anything other than staying alive. Now I was tired and worn-out and the plan that had seemed so right at three in the morning was starting to feel idiotic.

I should have left a note for my mother, though I wasn't sure what I could have said. When she figured out I was gone, she'd probably think I went to Chapel Hill. It didn't matter. I was going to be in tons of trouble either way.

Suddenly I remembered something Daddy told me once when I was angry at my mother. "You know how Mom arranges orange slices on a plate for your soccer team and has activities planned for your birthday parties two months in advance?" he'd asked me. "That's the way she shows her love, Gracie." Why was I thinking about that now? I could hear his voice so clearly, like he was talking to me from the backseat of the car. *That's the way she shows her love, Gracie.*

She loved me. I never really doubted that. It would hurt

her to realize I wasn't hers and to find out that her own baby died. I pictured Emerson sitting her down to tell her the truth and I could see my mother's face crumple.

The traffic was starting to move now. I let the trucks pull away from me and I could see old buildings and smokestacks and cranes, and everything was a blur through my tears.

I clutched the steering wheel. "What are you doing?" I whispered to myself. *"What are you doing?"*

44

Tara

Grace was sleeping in, and I thought that was a good thing. She'd been so upset about Cleve the day before and I knew I hadn't handled the situation well. I'd had to put my foot down about the trip to Chapel Hill, of course, but could I have done it a different way? Some way that didn't shut down communication? *What* communication? We had none. Next week, I'd call the therapist we'd seen a couple of times after Sam died. Grace wouldn't talk to her, either, but maybe the woman could give me some ideas for a fresh start with my daughter. Grace and I needed a do-over.

I sat at the kitchen table and made out a grocery list, trying to focus on something less nerve-racking than the deteriorating relationship between Grace and myself. I left a note for her on the table, telling her I was going to the store, then walked through the mudroom to the garage.

In the garage, I stopped short. Sam's old Honda was gone. It gave me such a jolt. I had a flash of irrational hope that Sam was alive and on his way to work. That the past seven months had been a terrible dream. But I was too much of a realist to dwell in that fantasy for long. Either the car had been stolen or Grace had taken it. I didn't know which possibility seemed more unlikely.

I went back in the house and knocked on Grace's door, opening it when there was no answer. Her room was a mess as usual, her bed so heaped with junk that I had to move the books and clothing to prove to myself she was really gone. I felt no anger, only sheer unadulterated terror. My baby girl was driving, no doubt to Chapel Hill. It was raining and she was upset and not thinking clearly and she hadn't driven in seven months. She'd be driving on the highway with complicated on- and off-ramps and speeding cars and drivers hungover from the night before. Sam had been killed at the familiar Monkey Junction intersection. What chance did Grace have to make it to Chapel Hill alive?

I reached for the phone on Grace's desk, but stopped myself from dialing. I didn't want her to try to answer her cell phone while she was driving. Then I remembered Jenny's older friend was with her and that she was probably doing the driving. I let out my breath in relief. At least I could stop picturing Grace behind the wheel. I only wished I knew Jenny's friend and that she was trustworthy.

I dialed Grace's cell phone and jumped when I heard its distinctive ring coming from inches away on her night table. "Oh, no," I said, grabbing her phone. The display was lit up, our home number prominently displayed. She'd left without her phone? I hung up and sank onto her bed, trying to figure out what was going on. Grace never went anywhere without her phone.

I scrolled through the numbers on her phone and dialed Jenny's cell. It took a few rings before she picked up and I knew I'd awakened her.

"I thought about you all night," she said, her voice thick and hoarse. "You okay?"

She was obviously in on this grand adventure. "It's Tara, Jenny," I said.

There was a beat of silence. "Oh," she said. "Sorry. Why are you calling on Grace's phone?"

"I need the cell phone number for your friend who's with Grace," I said tersely. "I can't remember her name."

Jenny was quiet again. "I don't know what you mean," she said. "Isn't Grace there?"

"No. She left the house before I got up this morning, and I assume..." Could I be wrong? "She took the Honda and forgot her phone. I assume she's on her way to see Cleve. She told me yesterday she wanted to go and would have a friend of yours—an older girl—along as a supervising driver."

Jenny said nothing and I knew she was either hiding something or as much in the dark as I was.

"Jenny?" I asked. "Do you know where she is?"

"I'm totally confused," she said.

"Who's your older friend? Helen or...Elena!" I suddenly remembered. "Her name was Elena."

"I...I'm not sure what's going on."

I got to my feet. "Jenny!" I said, sharply now because panic was rising inside me. "What do you know? This is serious! Did she tell you she was going to Chapel Hill?"

"No!" Jenny said. "I honestly don't know where she is. Did you try calling her?"

"I told you, she forgot her phone. I'm going to call Cleve. If you hear anything from her or from Elena... Do you have a friend named Elena?"

She didn't answer.

"Jenny!"

"No," she admitted.

Damn it. "Call me if you hear anything," I said, then

hung up. I found Cleve's number on Grace's phone and dialed it, but my call was dumped into his voice mail. "Cleve, this is Tara," I said. "Call me the second you get this. I'm serious!" I gave him my number so he wouldn't have to dig it up.

I hung up the phone and looked at my watch. It was a little after ten. She must have taken off before I got up at seven. It was possible, though not likely, that she was in Chapel Hill by now.

Through her bedroom window, I could see the rain battering the leaves of the maple tree in our side yard and I shook my head. I couldn't picture her driving around the block. Imagining her driving in this rain was both impossible and horrifying.

Please, God, let her be safe!

Then I picked up her phone and tried Cleve's number again.

45

Grace

Alexandria, Virginia

I was on a highway called the Beltway and I'd never seen so many cars going so fast at one time. It was like being stuck in a parking lot that was moving at sixty-five miles an hour, and my leg muscles shook as I pressed on the gas trying to keep up. I was so glad to see the exit for Alexandria. My GPS gave me a few turns to make and I was suddenly in the middle of a busy road in a little town. I needed gas and, even worse, coffee. I spotted a gas station and pulled in. I bought twenty dollars worth of gas and a comb. The only one they had was made for men and it had teeth so close together I'd probably never be able to get it through my hair. I bought a cup of coffee that tasted really old and lukewarm, but I didn't care and I chugged it down right there in the disgusting gas station store.

When I pulled back onto the road, my GPS said I was only a mile from my destination. Then half a mile. Then four hundred feet, and I began to think it was leading me the wrong way. Wouldn't the Missing Children's Bureau be in a big office building? All during the drive, that's where I pictured meeting my mother. On the fourth or fifth floor of a big office building. But the buildings on this road were small and they looked more like little shops and town houses than offices.

I was stuck at a red light when I noticed a banner about a block in front of me. It hung high in the air above the street. Columbus Day Parade! Oh, no. Oh, no. I'd forgotten about it being a holiday. Would the Missing Children's Bureau be closed?

My GPS said, "Arriving at destination." I was certain it had screwed up, but the traffic wasn't moving and I had a chance to look at the building numbers and there it was—237. It was a little yellow town house in the middle of a string of other little town houses. It had to be wrong, yet I could see some kind of rectangular plaque hanging next to the door, although I couldn't read it from where I sat. I'd have to get closer.

I couldn't parallel park. I'd screwed it up every time I tried during my driver's training and there was no way I could do it with all these cars around me. I turned down a side street and drove a couple of blocks before I found two spaces together and was able to slip the car next to the curb. When I finally turned off the engine, I just sat there for a minute as what I'd done really hit me. *I just drove all the way from Wilmington to Alexandria,* I thought, and even though I was doing the craziest thing I'd ever done in my life, I felt proud of myself. Whatever happened next, I'd done something pretty amazing.

Now, though, came the really hard part.

I looked at my face in the rearview mirror. I looked terrible. I did my best to comb my hair, but it was impossible with that stupid comb.

Please be open, I thought as I got out of the car and started walking on the wet sidewalk toward the main street. I walked fast, my backpack over my shoulder, the folder inside it ready to tell the story.

The rectangular sign next to the door read Missing Children's Bureau, and I could see a light on inside. The door was unlocked and I pushed it open and walked into a small room filled with old-fashioned chairs and a love seat and a bay window overflowing with plants. There was a desk right in the middle of the room, but there was no sign of another human being and I wasn't sure what to do.

I heard a clinking noise coming from somewhere in the next room and a woman suddenly appeared in the doorway. She had really short gray hair, narrow little black-framed glasses and she was holding a stick of celery in her hand. Her eyebrows shot halfway up her forehead when she saw me.

"You startled me!" she said, then smiled. "May I help you?"

"I'm here to see Anna Knightly," I said.

"Oh, Ms. Knightly's with her daughter at Children's," she said, sitting down behind the desk.

I felt suddenly dizzy at hearing someone else talk about Anna Knightly like she really, truly existed. It had all started to feel like a fantasy to me. I had to balance myself with my hand on the edge of the desk.

"Are you all right, honey?" the woman asked me, and then her words sunk in. Her daughter. My *sister.* And wasn't I *at* the Missing Children's Bureau?

"Children's?" I asked. "Do you mean…isn't this the Missing Children's Bureau?"

"Yes." She looked confused. "Oh. No, no. She's at Children's *Hospital.* Did you—" she looked at me strangely, then checked her computer screen "—you didn't have an appointment with her, did you? I thought I reached everyone."

"No, but I need to see her." A hospital? My sister was sick? "I know something about a missing child," I said. "I need to talk to her about it." I didn't want to tell the woman who I was. What if she thought I was lying? What if she called the police?

"Oh, well, you can give me the information. Ms. Knightly doesn't generally deal directly with—"

"No, that's okay. I really need to talk to her. When will she be back?"

"She's taking some time off to be with her daughter. Would you like some coffee? A soda?"

The woman was worried about me now. I imagined how I looked after a sleepless night, my hair half-combed, my teeth unbrushed. I'd totally forgotten about the toothbrush in my backpack.

"No, thank you. I came a long way to see her, though." I felt my voice break. "How can I talk to her? Please. I really need to."

She looked at me like she was trying to decide what to do. "Give me your cell phone number and I can—"

"I don't have one." My voice cracked again and I knotted my hands together in front of me. "I forgot it when I left the house. Just tell me where the hospital is." I could tell right away that was a mistake.

The woman shook her head. "Now, look," she said. "Ms. Knightly is dealing with a serious private matter and you can't disturb her, all right?"

I'm a serious private matter, I thought. "Oh, I know," I said. "I wouldn't."

The woman handed me a small notepad. "Write down your name and a way she can reach you."

"There *is* no way. I forgot my phone."

She sighed. "Tell me what this is regarding, honey, so I can help you."

"It's private," I said.

She gave me one of those smiles that said she was getting annoyed. "Well, look." She leaned back in her chair. "I'll be here until five. I'm sure I'll speak with her sometime today. I'll ask her how you can get in touch with her, then you can stop back late this afternoon and I'll tell you what she says. But if you could give me some more information, it would be very helpful."

I thought about those prepaid phones you could buy. I'd never used one, but maybe I could get one of them and give the number to this woman and she could give it to Anna Knightly.

"Can I get your number?" I asked.

"Of course." She handed me a card from a little tray on her desk and I put it in my pocket.

"Thanks," I said, and turned to go.

"You'll come back later?" she asked, but I was already out the door, trying to figure out my next move.

I passed a bank on my way back to my car and used the ATM to get some money. I had forty dollars with me, but I'd need more for gas and maybe a prepaid phone if I could find one. My mind was moving in a different direction, though. When I got to my car, I turned on the GPS and did a search for hospitals. There were a bunch of them, but the only one that had to do with children was called Children's National Medical Center. Was that it? I liked the words *medical center* a lot better than I liked the word *hospital*.

It was in Washington. I plugged the address into the GPS. It was thirty-two minutes away. Yesterday, thirty-two minutes of driving would have sounded impossible to me.

Now it sounded almost as easy as taking my next breath. But...the woman *had* used the word *hospital*. I couldn't deny that, and I saw my father's torn-apart face. I quickly waved my hand in front of my eyes as if I could erase the vision that way. I'd go. I'd go into the lobby and ask someone to take a note to Anna Knightly. I'd just driven three hundred and eighty-two miles by myself on no sleep. I could handle a hospital lobby. I had to.

46

Emerson

Wilmington, North Carolina

The café was swamped. Even though it was a holiday, half the people in Wilmington seemed to have stopped by *Hot!* this morning. We'd run out of the raspberry-cream-cheese croissants I was becoming known for and Sandra and my waitress were having trouble keeping up. So I ignored my cell when it rang, not even taking the time to glance at the caller ID. Jenny was off from school, most likely lolling around the house, and I'd check my messages as soon as I had a break. But then the café phone rang and that I couldn't ignore. Offices often placed their lunch orders in the morning to be picked up later, but I didn't expect many of those calls on Columbus Day.

I grabbed the phone near the cash register. "Hot!" I said.

"Mom!" Jenny shouted in my ear, her voice raspy and frightened. "I have to tell you something."

"What?" I carried the phone into the kitchen, alarmed.

"Please don't kill me!" She sounded as though she'd set

the house on fire. "I think Grace is on her way to find that Anna Knightly lady."

I frowned, disbelieving. How could Grace—how could *Jenny*—possibly know about Anna Knightly? "What do you mean?"

"Tara called to say that Grace is gone. She took the car and Tara thinks she went to Chapel Hill, but I'm afraid—"

"Grace doesn't even drive." I felt so confused. I wanted to poke holes in whatever story Jenny was trying to tell me.

Sandra whisked by me with a tray of sandwiches and I stepped closer to the back door and out of the way.

"I called Cleve and he said he talked to Grace last night and she said she wanted to go to Virginia to find her mother."

"Wait!" I had to stop her. "How could she—or you, for that matter—possibly know about her...about Anna Knightly?"

Jenny didn't answer right away. "I heard you." She sounded tearful. "I wasn't trying to snoop, but I was coming downstairs when you and Ian were talking yesterday. And then I found that letter Noelle wrote. I went over to Grace's and told her everything."

I remembered the creaking sound from the stairs. *Oh, God.* I tried to imagine how devastated Grace had to have been. I pictured her reading Noelle's letter to Anna Knightly. "You should have come to *me* with this, not Grace!"

"I'm sorry," Jenny said. "But Grace had a right to know."

"She may have a right to know, but, Jenny! We hadn't even told Tara yet."

"I didn't think she'd, like, take off or anything," she said. "Cleve said he thought he'd talked her out of going, but she was gone this morning and she's not in Chapel Hill, at least not when I talked to him. So I think she's on her way to find that woman!" Her voice rose to a fever pitch again.

"I need to get off the phone," I said. "I'm going to Tara's to tell her what's going on."

"Grace is such a terrible driver," Jenny said. "If I thought she'd do something like this I never would have—"

"I know. I've got to get off."

I hung up the phone and grabbed Sandra to tell her I was sorry, but she was going to have to take over for the next couple of hours. She gave me a frantic look, but she could tell from my face that there was no point arguing with me. In my car, I tried to call Ian before starting the ignition but his voice mail picked up and I imagined he was deep in his golf game by now. I was going to be on my own with this.

Yet when I pulled up in front of Tara's house, I saw Jenny's car parked on the street, Jenny waiting for me on the sidewalk in the misty rain. She was hugging herself, shivering, her arms tight across her chest, and I knew I was not going to be on my own with this, after all.

47

Tara

I heard the car door slam and ran to the front window, hoping against hope I'd see Grace walking up the sidewalk. But it was Emerson and Jenny, and as I watched them nearly run up to my front door, all I could think about was that they had horrible news to give me. The scenario was completely different, yet I had that same sickening feeling as I had the day the cop showed up at my classroom door to tell me Sam was dead. I knew the second I saw that young guy in uniform that something terrible had happened. I had the same feeling now.

I pulled open the front door. *"What?"* I called as they neared the porch. I felt the blood leave my face and the two of them swirled in my vision.

"We think we know where Grace is," Emerson said as she stepped onto the porch.

"With Cleve?" I asked.

Emerson turned me to face the house. "We think she's okay, Tara. Let's sit down someplace, all right? We have a lot to explain to you."

"What are you talking about?" I allowed her to lead me

toward the family room. "Jenny, have you spoken to her? What do you mean, you *think* she's okay? Where is she?"

"We're *sure* she's okay," Emerson said more emphatically. She had her hand on my back and was guiding me toward the sofa. I sank into it. She and Jenny sat shoulder to shoulder on the love seat.

"Is she with Cleve?" I looked at Jenny, who shook her head, then lowered her eyes to her lap as though she couldn't bear to look at me, which did nothing to ease my mind.

"Listen to me, Tara," Emerson said. "The other day, I figured out the identity of the baby Noelle stole from the hospital. I think it was Grace."

I stared at her, not comprehending. "That's impossible. Grace was never in the hospital, you know that." I glanced at Jenny. She was still avoiding my eyes, but apparently she knew about Noelle and the baby.

Emerson leaned forward. "Honey, listen," she said. "I found more information on when Anna Knightly's baby disappeared. It was around the time Grace was born. Right around the end of August 1994."

"No," I said, confused. "You mean 1998, when she stopped being a midwife."

"It was 1994, and Grace was the only baby Noelle delivered around that time."

"But Grace was born September first." I knew I was stubbornly missing the gist of this conversation.

"I know it's confusing," Emerson said. "I know it's unbelievable. But I think Noelle delivered your baby, not Grace, and it was your baby she accidentally dropped. And then she went to the hospital and took Anna Knightly's baby and brought it back to your house and passed it...her...off as your baby. And that was Grace."

"That's insane," I said.

"There were no other babies Noelle delivered during that time," Emerson said. "No torn-out pages from the book or anything. I really think it was Grace, Tara. I'm so sorry."

I ran my hand through my hair, thinking, thinking. I remembered the night Grace was born. The realization that something was wrong. The moments when Noelle was debating whether to call an ambulance before she managed to turn Grace inside me. I remembered that long dark night and the deathlike sleep that had gripped me afterward.

"I held her, though," I said, frowning. "I nursed her right away." She'd felt so warm, almost hot, against my skin. I'd loved that warmth. I could still remember it. Then the dreamless sleep. But Sam…had he been asleep, too? Could we have slept long enough for my child to slip through Noelle's hands? Had we slept long enough for her to rush to the hospital and steal her replacement? As unbelievable as I'd found the whole idea before, now it seemed a hundred times more so.

"You're saying…the baby I gave birth to died?"

Emerson stood from the love seat and sat down next to me, her arm around me. "I'm so sorry," she said. "I—"

"How does Jenny know all of this?" I asked. Jenny still wouldn't look at me. She reminded me of Grace today, she was so quiet.

Emerson hesitated. "I talked to Ian about this yesterday, when I…connected the dots, and Jenny overheard."

"You told Ian? Before you told *me*?" I pulled away from her, suddenly angry. "I'm the last to know about my own child? How long have *you* known?"

"I figured it out the night before Suzanne's party," Emerson confessed.

"And you didn't tell me?" I felt like slapping her, I was

so furious. I stood. "How could you tell Ian and not me?" I asked. "How dare you do that?"

"I didn't know how…" Emerson shook her head. "I was afraid of hurting you."

I couldn't absorb it all. Just couldn't. "Where is *Grace?*" I asked. There was no room in my mind at that moment for the baby I'd lost. A child who didn't quite exist for me yet. There was only room for the child I loved with all my heart. "Where is she? Why is she—"

"She called Cleve last night after I told her," Jenny said hoarsely. "She was really upset and she told him she wanted to go to Virginia to try to find her…that woman. He tried to talk her out of it."

"You should *never* have talked to Grace about this!" I said.

"I know." Her eyes were bloodshot and she sank deeper into the love seat.

"Please, Tara," Emerson pleaded. "Jenny knows she screwed up."

"How would she know where to find Anna Knightly?" I paced between the sofa and the window.

"The Missing Children's place, I think," Jenny said. "In Alexandria."

Alexandria! I pictured Grace trying to make that long drive by herself in the rain, wondering who she was. Only a tremendous need could make my daughter get behind the wheel of a car for that long. A need I hadn't been able to fill. "Oh, my poor baby," I said. I remembered how quiet she'd been the night before in her bedroom. Had she known then? "She has to be so scared and confused," I said. I thought of how she'd feel when she realized she'd left her phone at home. I could hardly bear to imagine her reaction.

"I feel terrible," Emerson said.

"I don't care about *your* damn feelings right now, Emerson," I said. "All I care about is finding Grace. You had no right to keep this from me. Something that impacts Grace's safety. You've—" I turned my face away from them. "I'm so furious with both of you! If anything happens to her, I'll never forgive either of you." I started for the kitchen and the telephone. "Who do we call?" I asked the air. "How do we find her?"

48

Grace

Washington, D.C.

I stopped at another gas station, bought a cheapy prepaid cell phone and made a deal with myself. If I couldn't track down Anna Knightly at the Children's Medical Center in an hour, I'd call that woman at the Missing Children's Bureau and give her the number. One way or another, I was finding my mother today.

Finally, I saw a sign for the Children's National Medical Center. I drove into a big underground garage and it was worse than driving on the highway. Cars were pulling out in front me and honking behind me, but I finally managed to get into a space.

At the entrance to the lobby, there was a sign that said you needed to show your ID, so I pulled out my driver's license. The guard looked at it and, without even glancing at me, asked, "Where's your supervising adult?"

My hands were shaking and I wondered if I looked guilty. "My mother and sister are inside," I said.

He started yelling, "Hey! You!" at a guy somewhere

behind me, and he must have been more interested in the guy than me, because he just nodded at me to walk through the entrance. I walked fast. I knew I'd lucked out.

The lobby was big and open, and I thought if I were a kid coming here to see a doctor, I'd be comfortable. It was colorful and didn't feel at all like a hospital and nothing like the emergency room where they'd taken my father. But I wasn't a kid and I wasn't there to see a doctor. I wasn't one hundred percent sure *what* I was doing there. The lobby was filled with parents and children and doctors and nurses, everyone looking like they had someplace to go except me.

I spotted an information desk on one side of the lobby and walked up to the woman sitting behind it. She was African-American with gray hair and gray glasses and she smiled at me. I tried my best to look eighteen. I was afraid of getting kicked out.

"Hi," I said. "I have to get an important message to someone. She's the mother of a patient here. If I write a note can someone take it to her?"

"Patient's name?" the woman asked. In spite of her smile, she sounded a little annoyed.

"Haley..." Did Haley have the same last name as her mother? "Her mother's name is Anna Knightly. *K-N-I—*"

"I know how to spell it. Her daughter's in the East Wing. Room 416. Give me your note and I'll ask a volunteer to take it up when they have time. We're short. Might be a while." She held out her hand for the note I hadn't written yet.

"I have to write it," I said. "I'll be right back."

I found a flyer announcing a Fun Run for Children's! The other side was blank and I sat down on one of the benches and pulled a pen from my backpack.

Now what?

"Mrs. Knightly," I wrote. *"My name is Grace Vincent. Please come to the lobby. I have to talk to you. It's very important. I'll be by the information desk. I have very long hair and am sixteen."*

I folded the note and took it back to the woman, who acted like she'd never seen me before. "This is the note for the woman in Room 416 in the East Wing," I said.

She took it from me. "It'll be a while," she said again.

I went back to the bench. After about twenty minutes, a volunteer—an old man—went up to the information desk, picked up a vase of flowers and headed for the elevator. The woman behind the desk didn't even hand him my note.

There were signs everywhere, and one of them said East Wing with an arrow pointing down a hallway. *Don't be a chicken,* I told myself. I stood and walked down the hall to a bunch of elevators. I stood with a couple of doctors and a nurse and a woman with a little boy who leaned sleepily against her leg. The elevator came and we all got on. The nurse pushed the button for the fourth floor and I felt dizzy as we started going up. I hadn't eaten in forever.

The nurse and I got off on the fourth floor. She kept walking down the hall, but I just stood there, frozen. The carpet had huge geometric patterns on it that only made me dizzier. A sign pointed the way to the rooms. Room 416 was to my right, but I couldn't seem to move. I hadn't noticed the hospital smell in the lobby, but it was definitely up here on the fourth floor.

Don't think about Daddy. Just don't.

"Can I help you?" a woman asked. She was probably a nurse. She wore a stethoscope around her neck and the fabric of her medical jacket was covered with dogs. "You look lost," she said.

"No." I managed to smile. "I'm good." I started walking, pretending I knew exactly where I was going and why.

I reached 416 and stood near the open door. My heart was beating so fast I thought I might end up in the E.R. myself. There were people walking up the hallway toward me and I knew I couldn't just stand there forever. I got up my courage and peeked around the doorframe as though I needed to slowly, slowly see whoever was in the room.

They'd just been names before. Not real people. Suddenly, though, reality smacked me in the face. A nearly bald girl was sitting in a huge bed. A woman sat in a chair next to her bed and they were looking at something in the girl's lap. A book or magazine or something. The woman laughed. The girl smiled. In one single second, I felt the tenderness between the two of them. They were like a little clique that did not include me. All at once, I knew I didn't belong in that room. I belonged nowhere.

The woman glanced in my direction and our eyes locked, just for a second. I stepped quickly away from the door and pressed my back against the wall. My heart was going so fast it was more like a buzzing in my ears than a beating. I didn't know what to do.

From the corner of my eye, I saw the woman walk into the hallway.

"Hi," she said.

I took a step away from the wall and turned toward her. Her smile was beautiful.

"Hi," I said.

"Are you a friend of Haley's from the unit?" She looked puzzled.

"I'm your daughter," I said.

The woman's smile disappeared. She took a step away from me. "What do you mean?"

"I just found out," I said. "I live in Wilmington, North Carolina, and I found a letter...or some friends found a letter that this woman who was my mother's midwife wrote to you, only never mailed." I lowered my backpack from my shoulder and tried reaching into it for the folder but my hands were shaking so hard I couldn't get a grip on it and I gave up. "She—the midwife—was apologizing for stealing your baby from the hospital the night I was born."

The woman wasn't following me and I didn't blame her. She said nothing, a sharp line between her eyebrows. Her chest was rising and falling so fast I thought she might faint. I licked my lips and kept going. "She dropped my mother's—the woman who I thought was my mother—she dropped her baby and killed it."

I felt a knot tighten in my chest. It was all too much, and suddenly I missed my mother desperately. I wanted her to hold me. The mother who knew me. Not the stranger in front of me whose smile was totally gone, whose eyes told me she thought I was lying. Coming here had been a mistake. An impulsive crazy mistake and the smells of the hospital rushed over me like a wave in the ocean and I knew I was going to pass out. I leaned against the wall to keep from falling over. I was so far from home and my mother. It seemed like I'd have to cross half the universe to get back to her.

"Is this…has someone put you up to this?" the woman asked. "Is this some sort of cruel joke?"

I couldn't speak. My throat was thick and I'd never felt so alone and so lonely. I shook my head.

The woman took my arm. "Come with me," she said.

49

Tara

Wilmington, North Carolina

We stood in the kitchen, Emerson hunting on my laptop for the number of the Missing Children's Bureau while I held the phone, ready to dial. Jenny stood near the island, biting her lip. I wanted to yell at both of them to get the hell out of my house, but I needed their help to find Grace. I didn't look at them. I was holding on tight to my anger.

"Here's the number," Emerson said. "Oh, it's a hotline number, not the office number." She rattled it off and I dialed. I explained to the man who answered that I was trying to reach the bureau's Alexandria office. I was careful what I said, although Emerson kept trying to put words in my mouth. "Shut up!" I said to her finally, then I apologized to the man and somehow convinced him to give me the office number. When I called there, though, I was dumped to voice mail.

"I need to speak with Anna Knightly," I said. "Please have her—have *someone*—call me right away. This is extremely urgent." I left both my cell and home number.

Emerson was trying to reach Ian again, but I knew he was unreachable when he was on the golf course. "Maybe we should call the police," Emerson said after leaving another message for Ian. "They can be on the lookout for Grace's car. They could have someone go to the Missing Children's Bureau and wait for her to show up."

"I'm going up there," I said.

"You don't know where she is, though," Emerson said. "It's better to stay here."

"I'm going." I grabbed my purse and headed for the garage.

"I'll drive you." Emerson ran after me. "You're too upset to drive."

I spun around. "I don't want you near me!"

"You need me," Emerson said, "and Grace is going to need Jenny. We're driving you."

It was as if we were flying instead of driving. I sat in the passenger seat, clutching my phone on my lap, so filled with fear and anger and anxiety that my limbs trembled. Behind me in the backseat, Jenny kept apologizing. Emerson, too. But I tuned them out, and for a couple of hours I didn't speak at all except to leave my own message on Ian's voice mail, telling him where we were and what was going on. Emerson kept trying to get me to talk to her, but all I could think of was Grace, who had to be feeling alone and upset and scared. I *knew* that was how she felt. It might have been the first time since she was small that I knew her feelings without being near her. The first time in so long that I felt that invisible connection to her. My blood was in her blood. My heart in her heart. I didn't care what a DNA test might say. She was my daughter.

I didn't want to think about Anna Knightly. When I'd

been trying to figure out who had her child, I'd felt sympathy for her. She'd been a stranger to me. A name in a letter. I'd thought about what it would feel like to realize your baby was missing. Now I knew how it felt firsthand. Anna Knightly had another daughter, I thought. Let her be satisfied with that one.

I wished Grace were in the car with me right that instant. I'd hold her and tell her that no matter how poor a job I was doing at being her mother, I loved her. I'd do anything for her. Whether she wanted me to or not, I'd hold her so tight that no one would be able to pry her from my arms. Sometimes it was hard to express how much you loved someone. You said the words, but you could never quite capture the depth of it. You could never quite hold someone tightly enough. I wanted that chance with my daughter.

"Do either of you need to stop?" Emerson asked when the traffic slowed near Richmond.

"No," I answered for both of us. I didn't care if Jenny needed to stop. Jenny could burst for all I cared. "Just keep driving."

Two wildly opposing emotions were at war inside me. Hatred toward Noelle that was spilling over to Emerson and Jenny, regardless of how irrational that might have been. And love for my daughter. "Oh, Grace," I said out loud, although I hadn't meant to.

Emerson reached over to rest her hand on my forearm. "She'll be all right," she said. "It will be all right."

I turned my face away from her.

"It was my fault," Jenny said from behind me. There were tears in her voice and I wondered how long she'd been crying back there.

There was plenty of blame to go around. Emerson and Ian for keeping this from me. Jenny for stupidly taking what she'd learned to Grace. Myself, for not knowing how to mother my daughter. For not being the sort of mom she could turn to when she learned this devastating truth. She would have turned to Sam. I could blame Mattie Cafferty, who took my husband from me and left me to cope alone. And, of course, I could blame Noelle for her criminal, unconscionable act. And yet...if Noelle hadn't done what she did, I wouldn't have my Grace.

My Grace.

My phone rang and I lifted it to my ear. "This is Tara Vincent." My words spilled over one another.

"This is Elaine Meyers from the Missing Children's Bureau, returning your call."

"Yes! Thank you." I pressed my hand to my cheek. "This is very complicated but my sixteen-year-old daughter is probably going to show up there looking for Anna Knightly and I need—"

"Pretty girl? Long hair?"

"*Yes.* Is she there?"

"She was. But I explained to her that Ms. Knightly isn't here. She was quite upset. She said she had information about a missing child."

"Where did she go?"

"I have no idea. She wouldn't leave her name and she said she had no phone. I was concerned about her."

"Could she be...waiting around? Outside maybe?"

"No, I told her Anna's at Children's Hospital with her daughter and that she wouldn't be back for—"

"What do you mean 'with her daughter'?"

I felt Emerson's quick glance.

"Her daughter is very ill and Anna's at the hospital with her."

"Could she…could my daughter… She knows Anna Knightly's at Children's Hospital?"

"I did mention it. But I don't think—"

"Where is it. It's in D.C., isn't it?"

"On Michigan Avenue. But—"

Jenny was fast. She reached between my seat and Emerson's to show me the address for Children's Hospital on her iPhone.

"I've got it," I said to the woman. "Please call me back if you hear anything more from her." I hung up and turned to Jenny. "Can you get the directions?" I asked.

"Yes."

I tapped my phone against my lips, thinking. "She wouldn't go to a hospital, though," I said. "You know how she feels about hospitals. I can't imagine—"

"Should we call the police?" Emerson asked.

I shook my head. "Not yet," I said. "Not until we've exhausted every other way to reach her." I didn't want the police between my daughter and myself. I wanted *no one* between my daughter and myself.

50

Anna

Washington, D.C.

I'd dreamed of this moment many, many times, yet what was happening now was nothing like my dreams. In my dreams, I'd seen the girl. Sometimes she was a toddler. Sometimes nine or ten. Occasionally this age: sixteen. This perfect age that fit reality. Yet there was one thing in each of those dreams that was missing in the here and now, and that was the instant recognition that this was indeed my daughter. My Lily. The child I'd carried beneath my heart. Sitting in the small lounge with Grace—and she seemed more like a Grace than a Lily to me—listening to her speak in a voice so quiet I had to lean close to hear her, I studied her lovely, heart-shaped face. She showed me the letter, her hands trembling violently as she pulled it from her backpack. She told me about the suicide of the midwife.

I read the letter and was still filled with disbelief. I was being suckered into something. There'd been so much publicity around the bone marrow drive. Bryan and I had been too open about Lily's disappearance in our attempt to garner attention and sympathy for Haley's plight. We'd allowed Lily and our ordeal to be written about, talked about, embellished. Now someone had fabricated a letter, a girl, a story, all to mess with my mind. But why? Did someone think I had money? If so, they'd be wrong.

Where was the instinctive maternal bond I'd felt in my dreams? The girl looked nothing like me. Nothing like Haley or Bryan. Her eyes were large and brown, but the shape of them was off. *How dare you dissect this child?* I thought to myself. I felt her pulling back from me, shutting down, as if she was picking up on my ambivalence.

"When were you born?" I asked, determined to trip her up.

"September first, 1994."

"Oh, really?"

She dug her wallet out of her backpack, her hands only slightly less shaky than they'd been a few minutes earlier. She pulled out her driver's license and handed it to me. I stared at the date. *September 1, 1994.* It fit. It fit all too well. Could the license be a fake? I didn't know how to tell.

I looked at her again. I was afraid to let myself hope. So afraid. I'd been disappointed before. Maybe the girl *was* Lily, but I wasn't thinking, *Let's do a DNA test right this minute!* Instead, I was thinking about her bone marrow. My reaction horrified me, but I couldn't help what I felt. I wasn't ready to think of her as my daughter. Rather, I saw her as a commodity. A way to save the life of the daughter I knew for sure was mine.

"Do your parents know you're here?" I asked. If she was for real, someone would be worried about her.

"My father is dead," she said. "And, no. My mother—the woman who thinks she's my mother—doesn't know I'm here. She doesn't actually know anything about this yet. Her friend figured it out and hasn't told her."

Her story was growing so convoluted that I was beginning to think it must be true. No one could make this up.

"Where does your mother think you are?"

"I… Probably with my boyfriend in Chapel Hill. My ex-boyfriend."

"You need to call her right away and tell her where you are," I said.

"But she doesn't even *know* about this." She looked a little panicky. "She doesn't know I'm not her daughter."

"You still need to let her know where you are," I said.

The girl licked her lips. "All right," she said, though she made no move for her phone.

"Listen to me," I said. "This is extraordinarily strange in so many ways. I don't know you and you don't know me, and in a…if things were different, we would slowly get to know each other and find out if you're really my daughter, but right now, my daughter—" I almost said my *real* daughter "—Haley is very ill. She has leukemia. She's a wonderful girl and she needs a bone marrow transplant to give her a chance to live. It's her only chance. Only certain people can be donors and we haven't been able to find a match for her." My voice started to break; sometimes the emotion still caught me by surprise. "It's possible, just possible that a sister might be a match." I felt cruel. Whoever this girl in front of me was she had not asked for this. She hadn't bargained for it. But I didn't care. I wanted her tested. I needed to see if maybe, by some wild chance, she could be a match, whether she was Haley's sister or not.

Grace swallowed and I could see how scared she was. What I was doing felt wrong and yet I couldn't help myself. Haley was slowly dying.

"I'd like you to meet Haley, if you're both willing," I said. "Then you can decide if you want to be tested to see if you're a match. It's just a cheek swab. Doesn't hurt at all. Only if you want. Your mother would have to give permission." I sat back with a long sigh. The girl's hands were folded together on her lap in a tense knot. "I don't know what's going on here, Grace," I said, "but sometimes things happen for a reason and they're very hard for us to explain."

She lifted her chin at those words and I saw that they had meaning for her. "You believe that, don't you?" I said softly. "That things happen for a reason?"

She nodded. "I want to believe it," she said, though her eyes, which were *nothing* like Haley's, gave away her doubt. But her words, so tender and heartfelt, touched me and I softened toward her.

"I don't believe you're my daughter," I said. "It doesn't make sense. My newborn baby had hair that was darker than yours, just like Haley's. Like her father's. I bet your hair was very light when you were born."

"Brownish. It's really more brown than this." She touched her long, thick hair. "I get highlights put in it."

"I doubt it's as dark as my daughter's would be." I stood. "Do you need something to eat or drink?" I asked.

She shook her head. Hugged her arms. "I couldn't," she said.

"You're nervous?"

"I hate hospitals."

I cocked my head at her. "You're brave to come here, then," I said. "Let me talk to Haley first. You stay right here." I worried that I'd frightened her, that she might take off. I wished I had a long rope and could tether myself to her while I spoke to Haley. "Please promise me you'll stay right here," I said. "And call your mother to tell her where you are and what's going on. But please don't leave. You don't have to do the bone marrow thing. I just—"

"I won't leave," she said. "I came all this way. I won't leave."

"Where'd you go?" Haley asked when I walked back into her room.

"Well, Haley—" I stood at the end of her bed, leaning on the footboard "—something wild just happened."

"You're shaking."

I was. I was making her whole bed rattle. I straightened up and smiled at her. "Did you notice the girl who was in the hallway a minute before I left your room?"

She shook her head.

"Well, there was a girl there. A teenager. And she claims to be Lily."

Haley's eyes widened. "*Our* Lily?"

"That's what she says."

Her mouth fell open. "Our Lily?" she asked again, this time in a whisper.

"I don't know if she is or not, honey." I still wouldn't let myself feel hope. "I don't know what to make of it," I said. "She showed me a letter from a midwife…. Do you know what a midwife is?"

Haley shook her head.

"A woman who delivers babies. This one—the one who wrote the letter—delivered babies at home apparently. Anyway, I need to talk fast because I left the girl out—"

"Hurry, then!" She glanced toward the hallway. "Is she out there?"

"She's in a little room down the hall." At least, I hoped

that's where she was. I knew I'd scared her in half a dozen different ways.

I told Haley what I could remember from the letter and she stared at me, openmouthed.

"Holy shit," she said.

"Yes," I agreed. "Holy shit. The dates match up to when Lily disappeared, and this girl thinks she's Lily. She drove up here from Wilmington because she thinks I'm her mother."

"Is it her?" Haley asked.

"I remember Lily so well," I said. "I remember her like someone painted her in my brain, and I don't picture her growing up looking like this girl. And yet—"

"I want to meet her!"

"Are you sure? It's going to seem weird, Haley. And you don't know if she's your sister or not. You have to keep that in mind. Not get your hopes up."

"I definitely want to meet her. I've wanted to meet her my whole life."

"But she might not be—"

"I want her to be Lily so much!" she said.

I remembered when she was diagnosed with leukemia this time, she told me she wished I had Lily so I wouldn't be alone if she died. I'd been touched by her bravery. Her generosity. Yet I didn't want her to feel that way. Not at all.

I reached for her foot where it was covered by the blanket. "You know that no one can ever, ever take your place, right?" I asked.

"Let me meet her, Mom," she pleaded, shooing me away from her bed with her hands. "Go get her before she disappears again."

51

Grace

I folded my hands in my lap and sat very still. As freaked out as I was about what might happen next, it was my mother who kept popping into my mind. When would she have figured out I was gone? When would she figure out I wasn't in Chapel Hill? She would be so worried. She'd call Emerson then, maybe, and Emerson would tell her that I wasn't really her daughter. My chest hurt just thinking about it and I pressed my hands together hard. My mother would feel totally alone then. No husband. No daughter. She'd think about her real baby, the one who died, and wonder how amazing that baby would have turned out. Probably brilliant, like her dad, and a bubbly social butterfly like her mom. Nothing like the girl they'd ended up with.

But my mother loved me and, right then, I wanted to be with her. I wanted to be able to let her know I was okay, but that I needed to work something out on my own. I was afraid to call her, though. I was going to be in so much trouble.

This Anna woman was cold. I'd expected something totally different. I'd expected her eyes to light up with joy when she heard who I was. I'd expected her to pull me into her arms and be filled with the kind of instant love all mothers had for their children. There'd been none of that. She was suspicious of me and all she really cared about was her other daughter, Haley. I was falling through the cracks between two worlds. My real mother—Anna—had long ago given me up for dead and focused all her love on her other daughter, while the mother who raised me was by now probably grieving for the baby she'd lost.

Mom. Why did I always push her away? She was worried about me. I knew that. She'd be seriously freaking out right now.

I pulled the phone from my backpack and dialed her number. It rang a couple of times before she picked up.

"Hello?" she said, and I could tell with that one word that she was a mess.

"It's me," I said.

"Grace! Grace! Where are you? Are you okay? Where are you calling from? You left your phone—"

"I'm okay," I said. "I just wanted to let you know that. I have to do something and then I'll—"

"Are you at Children's Hospital?"

I didn't know what to say. How could she know that?

"I'm on my way there with Emerson and Jenny," she said. "Is that where you are? I love you, Grace. I love you so much. I've been so scared, honey."

"Mom. You don't have to come here. I'm—" I looked up to see Anna standing in the doorway. "I have to go," I said, and flipped the phone closed.

"Was that your mother?" Anna asked. "You spoke with her?"

I nodded. The phone rang and I dropped it into my backpack.

"You don't want to get that?" Anna asked.

I shook my head.

Anna smiled at me. She did have a really nice smile. "Haley would like to meet you, if you're willing," she said.

I stood. Anna put an arm around me as we walked into the hall. It felt like the arm of a stranger. She rested it lightly on my back, the way you'd guide someone you didn't know well from one room to another. My mother's voice echoed in my ears. *I love you, Grace. I love you so much.* I smiled a little to myself.

"My mother said she's coming here," I said.

"Oh, that's very good," Anna said. "We need to get some things straightened out, don't we? How far away is she?"

"She's in Wilmington...except she said she was already on her way, so I don't know how close she is. My best friend and her mother are with her." I pictured the three of them driving together.

"Here we are," Anna said. We were back at the door to Haley's room. "Come on in."

I followed her into the room and stood just inside the door.

"Haley, this is Grace," Anna said. "Grace, this is Haley."

Haley was sitting cross-legged on the bed and she was hooked up to a bunch of bags and poles and wires. She had very short brown hair that had either been shaved that way or was just growing in.

"Hi," I said.

"Wow, you are so not what I expected Lily to look like," she said.

I had the feeling I was disappointing both of them. I clutched my backpack to my chest. "Well, I didn't expect to have a sister, period." I tried to smile again, but seemed to have lost the ability.

"And you may *not* have a sister," Anna warned. "Grace's mom is on her way here, Haley, so we'll get some answers then. Right now I'm going to call your dad." She glanced at me. "Why don't you have a seat, Grace?" She pointed toward the couch across the room from Haley's bed. I walked over to it and sat down, still hugging my backpack. "I'll be back in a few minutes," Anna said, and then I was alone with Haley. My phone rang again and I pulled it from my backpack and turned the ringer off.

"Maybe that's your mother," Haley said.

"That's okay." I wasn't sure what to say to Haley. I felt sorry for her for being so sick. I knew she was a lot braver than I'd be, hooked up to all that stuff. "How do you feel?" I asked.

"Mom explained the whole thing about the midwife and all that drama," she said, like I hadn't asked her a question. Her eyes bored into me while she talked. "You look freezing."

I was shivering, though I didn't think it had anything to do with the temperature in the room. "I'm okay," I said.

"Look under this techno bed," Haley said. "Grab a blanket to wrap up in."

I got up and pulled a blanket from the shelf beneath her bed. It was pale blue and soft and I wrapped it around my shoulders.

"Do you really think you're my sister?" Haley asked.

"Did your mother tell you about the letter?" I reached into my backpack one more time and pulled out the letter. I handed it to her and watched her read it.

"Omigod," Haley said when she finished the letter. "This is totally crazy! It would be so cool if it's real, though. I mean, me and my mom have made it, like, our job to find Lily. I never expected her—*you*—to just pop up like this."

I took the letter back, folded it in half and slipped it into my backpack.

"What are your parents like?" Haley asked. "The people who raised you? Did you ever feel like you didn't belong?"

"All the time," I said, although it wasn't quite the truth, was it? I'd belonged to my father, just not my mom. "I never felt like 'oh, I'm adopted' or anything like that," I said. "But I don't get along with my mother at all."

"What about your father?"

"He died in a car accident in March. One of my mother's students—she's a teacher—killed him because she was texting while she was driving."

"Holy shit," Haley said. "That's so terrible!" A machine on one of the poles next to her bed started beeping and she turned off the sound with a push of a button, like it was no big deal. "I never really knew my father until now," she said. "I mean, I knew who he was and everything, but he left when I was little. When I got sick this time, he sort of showed up. I actually like him. I mean, I'm pissed at how he wasn't around for most of my life, even though he sent money and everything, but Mom says he was just really immature and he couldn't take it when I got sick so he just pulled out of the picture. First Lily disappeared and my mom was sick and all that was hard for him to handle, and then *I* got sick and it was too much for him, which totally screwed up my respect for him. I mean, my mom didn't have the luxury of walking out, right? But he's back now and he's trying to be a dad. He's doing this big drive to try to find bone marrow donors for me."

"He's my father, too," I said, still shivering beneath the blanket.

"If you're Lily, then, yeah," she said.

I thought of how that must feel to Haley. She finally got

a relationship going with her father and then this strange girl shows up to claim part of him. "I didn't ask for this," I said. "I'm not trying to step on your toes or anything. I just need to—"

"Hey, chill," Haley said. She was smiling. "If you're Lily, we want you, okay? We've prayed to find you. Or, at least, I have. My mom doesn't really pray, but I've been looking for you since I was a little kid."

"How old are you?" I asked.

"Almost thirteen."

I couldn't believe she was more than three years younger than me. She was pale and a little puffy and it was clear she was sick, but she seemed so together. So confident and sure of herself, like Jenny. I already felt in competition with her and I'd known her five minutes. "You're so...you're not like me at all," I said.

"What do you mean?"

"You're very...you seem more like my mother. I mean the mother who raised me. You're more like her than *I* am. You seem really positive and outgoing."

Haley shrugged. "I'm not always so positive," she said. "I can get majorly depressed. Like, I've been on antidepressants a million times. But I've got hope, with a capital *H*. That's my middle name. I mean my *actual* middle name is Hope. I've had leukemia before and went into remission. I think this time, though, hope's not going to be enough." She glanced up at one of the bags hanging from the pole next to her bed. "This disease sucks."

"I'm sorry," I said. "Your mother said a bone marrow transplant could help you."

"Only we can't find a donor. She's hoping that if you're Lily, you might be a match."

"I know," I said.

"My mom always hoped she'd find Lily," she said. "She looked for her everywhere. She never gave up looking for her. We went to Wilmington a bunch of times, just looking for someone who looked like me."

"I've been there the whole time," I said.

"What's your life been like?" Haley asked.

"My life's been…" I had to stop and think, the question catching me off guard. I thought of my house, always obsessively neat with the exception of my room. I thought of how Jenny and I redecorated our bedrooms during the summer, filling them with color and polka dots as we talked about Cleve and Devon and laughed our butts off. I thought of how Daddy and I would invent elaborate coffee drinks together. I remembered how people brought us food for weeks after he died. With an ache in my heart, I thought of how my mother always planned my birthday parties down to the color of the sprinkles on the cake. *That's the way she shows her love, Gracie.* I thought of growing up with Jenny and Emerson and Ted and even Noelle as my extended family. Of Wilmington and everything I loved about it, from the Spanish moss hanging on the live oaks to the Riverwalk to the little park in my neighborhood. And suddenly, I couldn't imagine my life without all of that. All of the good and the bad that made up my existence. It seemed so wrong to be glad that Noelle had stolen me, yet in that moment, I *was* glad.

How could I possibly explain all that to someone who didn't know all the people and places in my world? "My life's been, you know, the usual," I said weakly. "Some good and some bad."

"I hope you'll get tested," Haley said. "I wouldn't blame you if you didn't want to be, though. I mean, you just show up and meet your real family and they all grab you and go after your body parts." She laughed and I wrapped the blanket even more tightly around myself.

"Your mother said just a cheek swab or something like that," I said.

"Right. First it's only the cheek. Then if you match up with your cheek cells, they look at your blood. And then if that's a match, you have to have surgery to remove some of your bone marrow, but I don't think it's all that bad. Not as bad as what they'll put me through. They'll do chemo and radiation to kill off my whole immune system so I don't reject the bone marrow. But it's, like, my only chance."

I thought of my father and the way I'd felt when I learned he died—how it seemed like there should have been something I could do to bring him back to us, if only I could think of what it was. I thought of the email I'd mistakenly sent to Noelle that might have caused her to take her life. This time, maybe there *was* something I could do to save someone. Something hard and horrible, but good and right. It would mean needles and scalpels and probably staying in the hospital overnight. But maybe I could save a life. My *sister's* life.

The thing was, I wanted my mother with me before I'd let them touch me.

I wanted to hear my mother tell me that everything would be okay.

52

Anna

Oh, shit, I was afraid.

I sat near the hospital coffee shop and dialed Bryan's cell phone number with trepidation so deep and wide I felt as though it might drown me. Bryan had only recently found the courage to move back into our lives. He was only now finding his footing with the two of us. Now this. I was afraid he would run again. Maybe stay in California. I reminded myself that he was not the man he'd been back when Lily disappeared. Not the man he'd been when Haley first got sick. He'd grown up. He was solid. Or was I kidding myself? I worried that I was only imagining that he was the man I wanted him to be. An even greater worry right now was that I'd allow myself to believe the girl in Haley's room was truly Lily and then have those hopes dashed yet again. I'd taught Haley never to give up hope, yet I knew the truth: hope could lead you down the garden path.

I'd dared to leave Haley and Grace together for the time it would take to make this call. I had to talk to him before Grace's mother arrived. I just couldn't hold on to this revelation alone any longer.

"Hey," Bryan answered. "Everything okay?" Oh, the warmth in that voice! I was so afraid of losing that warmth. I was afraid that whatever Bryan and I had recaptured between us would be gone in a few moments' time.

"Yes," I said. Nothing was okay, of course, but I knew what he meant. He meant, *Nothing's changed for the worse with Haley, has it?* And nothing had.

"Something unbelievable's happened," I said.

"Uh, unbelievably good or unbelievably bad?"

"A girl showed up at the hospital today claiming to be Lily."

He said nothing and I wondered what the words meant to him. Was he as afraid of hope as I was?

"Who is she? What's her game? Do you think all the publicity—"

"I don't know." I cut him off. "She has this letter with her." I told him about the letter. About the date of birth on her driver's license. "I don't think anyone put her up to this," I said. "But something doesn't feel right about it. I can't put my finger on it. Her mother is on her way here from Wilmington. Apparently, the girl—her name is Grace—found all this out from a friend and took off without telling her mother. Her father is dead."

He was quiet, taking it all in. "Have you spoken to the mother?" he asked finally.

"Not yet. Bryan, the girl's willing to be tested to see if she's a match."

"Do you believe she's really Lily?"

"I don't know what to believe. I… Of course I want her to be but she doesn't look like I imagined Lily looking. She doesn't look like either of us and nothing like Haley. She's beautiful and seems like a nice kid, but—"

"Where is she now?"

"With Haley."

"You let her meet Haley?" His voice told me he didn't approve, but I felt confident I'd done the right thing.

You still don't really know your daughter, I wanted to say to him. "I explained it all to Haley. I told her my doubts. She wanted to meet her."

"Look, I'll get a flight back tonight," he said. "The interview went great today and I have one scheduled with a higher-up tomorrow morning, but I'll tell them I have a family emergency and need to—"

"No, don't," I said. "Stay there and do the interview. I can handle things here."

"You've been handling everything alone for ten years," he said. "I want to be there."

"All right," I said. "I'd better get back to the room. Call me when you know what time you're getting in."

I hung up the phone and walked back to Haley's room, a small smile on my lips. He was coming home.

53

Tara

I must have dialed Grace's number ten times from the car before she finally picked up.

"Stay on the phone with me!" I said to her. "Please. Just stay on until I get there."

"I don't have that many minutes, Mom. It's one of those prepaid phones. As soon as you get here, I need you to give them permission to get a test to see if I'm a match for this girl who's my sister. Do you…do you know about her? Haley? She has leukemia and needs a bone marrow transplant and they need to see if I'm a match."

I was horror-stricken. What were they doing to my daughter? I had never thought of her as so vulnerable, so in need of me, as I did at that moment.

"Grace." I kept my voice far calmer than I'd thought possible. We needed a lawyer. I wished Ian would check his damn voice mail. "Slow down, honey, please. I need to get there and talk to…the medical staff and everyone. You may feel as though you know these people but you don't. *We* don't. You are my daughter." I bit off each word. "Do you understand that? And you do not have my permission for anyone to lay a hand on you. When I get there, we'll sort everything out."

Emerson took her eyes from the road to glance at me. "What's going on?" she asked.

"She could die," Grace said, but I knew that voice. She was afraid. She wanted me to say no. To protect her. I knew my daughter better than I'd realized.

"I'll be there in… How close are we?" I asked Emerson.

"Very close," Emerson said. "Depending on this damn traffic."

"Minutes," I said to Grace. "I'll be there in minutes, honey."

"Mom? I don't know what to do."

My eyes brimmed with tears. "I'll take care of it, Grace. We'll work this out together."

I didn't want to let her off the phone but she was gone before I could say another word. I turned off my phone and looked at Emerson.

"My God," I said.

"What's happening?" Jenny leaned forward from the backseat.

"It sounds like Anna Knightly's daughter needs a bone marrow transplant and they want to test Grace to see if she's a match."

"You're kidding!" Emerson said. "These people sound heartless."

"You mean, Grace walks in and they see her as a bunch of cells instead of a person?" Jenny asked. "Oh, Mom, drive faster."

"No one's going to touch her without my permission, so don't worry about that," I said.

My phone rang and I saw Ian's cell number on the caller ID. "Ian!" I nearly shouted into the phone.

"Tara, I'm so sorry you found—"

"Look, I'm mad at you, but right now just help me, all right?"

"This Knightly woman," he said. "Don't talk to her, Tara. Just get Grace and go. Have Knightly's attorney contact me and we'll deal with it from there. I'm going to call some people I know at the police department in Wilmington. But for right now, you just want to make sure Grace is safe."

Get Grace and go. "Okay," I said.

"I'm sorry. I know you must be—"

"I don't want to tie up the line in case Grace calls me back," I said.

"Okay, we'll talk later."

I hung up the phone and wiped my hand across my forehead. I was perspiring. "He said just to get Grace and go," I said, as if that hadn't been my plan all along. I thought back to how Grace had sounded on the phone. "She has to be so scared," I said, then turned to Jenny. "What did I do wrong with her, Jenny?" My own vulnerability bubbled to the surface. "Why can't I ever seem to reach her?"

"It's just typical kids-not-getting-along-with-their-parents stuff," Jenny said kindly.

"No, it's not," I argued.

"Oh, it is!" Emerson insisted.

I kept my gaze on Jenny. "You and your mom have a better relationship than Grace and I do," I said. "I know that. I feel like I screwed it up somehow."

"I don't think you screwed anything up," Jenny said. "Grace is just deep. She just feels everything more than most people and it makes it hard to get close to her sometimes."

I still thought she was being kind. Sam had never had a problem getting close to her. I remembered Noelle's eulogy at Sam's memorial service. "Sam was a champion listener," Noelle had said. "That's what made him such a good lawyer. Such a good husband and father." Her voice had broken in the hushed church. "And such a good friend."

Such a good father, I thought now. He knew how to be still with Grace. Not like me. I always needed to be talking, moving, doing.

"There's a sign for the hospital." Emerson pointed ahead of us. "Once we get inside, do you want Jenny and me to come with you, or would it be better if we found the cafeteria and hung out there while you find Grace? Having us underfoot might just add to the confusion. What do you think?"

I would have loved to have Emerson with me for moral support, but I was only going to get Grace and go, as Ian had advised. We didn't need any big scene with all four of us. "You go to the cafeteria," I said, "but keep your cell on and I'll call if I need you, okay?"

The hospital came into view in front of us, a huge geometric collection of glass and metal. My daughter was in there. I couldn't believe she'd had the courage to set foot inside. To actually *drive* herself there. She was just deep, Jenny had said. Yes, she was. I wanted to know every millimeter of that depth. I wanted it not to be too late for us and I was so afraid it was.

54

Grace

Anna moved around Haley's hospital room, rearranging books and remote controls and tissue boxes and drinking glasses, and Haley chattered about a movie she'd seen and I kept looking at the doorway. We were all waiting for my mother to show up. It would change everything, having Mom here. She would take charge, and I realized how much I depended on that—on my mother taking charge of things.

The three of us were talking about the most unimportant things—my school and Old Town Alexandria and what Wilmington was like, as though I was just someone who'd dropped by for a visit, not their daughter or sister.

I jumped every time I saw someone in the hallway. Finally, there she was. My mother. She barely looked like herself, she was so pale and frazzled. I jumped up from the couch, the blanket falling from my shoulders, and ran into her arms.

"*Mom,*" I said, and suddenly everything I'd been through in the past twenty-four hours—Jenny showing me the letter, the horrible drive through the dark rain, the search for Anna Knightly—hit me all at once. My leg muscles felt like mush, and I knew I was only able to stand because my mother was holding me up.

"Sweetie," Mom said, her voice quiet in my ear. "My sweetheart. It's okay. I'm here."

I held on to her. "I'm sorry I left like that," I said.

"Doesn't matter," she said. Her eyes were wet. "None of that matters."

I could have stayed like that for the rest of my life, wrapped safely in her arms, but I could feel Anna behind me and Haley staring at us from her bed. I pulled away from my mother.

"This is my mom," I said to Anna.

My mother walked over to Anna, her hand outstretched. "I'm Tara Vincent," she said.

"Anna Knightly," Anna said. "And this is my daughter, Haley."

My mother looked at Haley. "Hi, Haley." She put her arm around my shoulders. "I've spoken with my attorney," she said to Anna. "He'll be in touch with you."

Anna tilted her head to the side and I knew she didn't like my mother's attitude. "Could we talk for a minute?" she asked. "Please? Mother to mother?"

"We can't just *leave*, Mom," I said. I knew she didn't get exactly what was happening. She didn't realize there was a life-or-death situation going on in that room.

My mother looked from me to Anna. "All right," she said, "but I want to talk to my daughter alone first."

Anna nodded. I could tell she was afraid my mother would take me away. I wanted to leave. I did. But I wouldn't. "There's a lounge at the end of the hall," Anna said. "It's usually empty. Go ahead."

My mother held my hand as if I were a little girl as we walked down the hall. As if I were *her* little girl.

If only I could be.

55

Tara

There was so much I wanted to say. I wanted to ask her a thousand questions about her fears and her confusion and to know everything she was thinking and feeling. I wanted her to know that she would always be my daughter, that I would never allow her to be taken from me and that her body was *hers*. She didn't have to offer a single one of her cells to see if she was a match for the stranger in the hospital bed.

But I said none of it as we sat on the two love seats in the tiny room. I asked her no questions. I felt Sam in the room with us, holding me back. He would have listened to her without prodding. Without picking her brain. He knew how to love our daughter.

"I love you," I said, and it turned out to be all I needed to say. She began to cry.

"I'm so sorry I just left like that," she said again. "It was so stupid."

"It doesn't matter," I said. "All that matters is that you're safe."

"I wish I never found out you're not my mother."

"We'll need a DNA test before I'll believe that," I said, "but a blood test will never change how I feel about you, Grace."

She wound the end of her hair around her finger. "I get so mad at you," she said. "I even hate you sometimes. And today I can't even remember why I ever felt that way. I wanted to go see Cleve and you said no and I got so angry and now that seems really stupid."

I nodded, just to let her know I was listening.

"Right now I'm not even thinking about Cleve," she said. "He's like the last thing on my mind." She let go of her hair and leaned toward me. "I don't know who I *am*, Mom."

I wanted to tell her who she was. She was the sensitive writer in the family, the quiet girl who had so much to say on paper. She was the apple of her father's eye and the thread that had always connected Sam and me, biology be damned. She was the beauty who, truth be told, looked like neither of us. She was the girl I wanted so much to get to know.

I struggled instead to find the most open-ended thing to say. The Sam thing to say. "You're still Grace," I said, and knew at once it had been exactly right. She wore a small frown as she stared at me, and I could nearly see the wheels turning in her mind.

"I don't want to lose Grace," she said. "Even though I spend so much time wishing I was…not me. Wishing I could be more like you."

She did? I had never once thought she wished she could be like me and I wanted to ask her why, but managed to keep my mouth shut.

"I always wished I could be more like Jenny. Everybody

loves Jenny. I never know what to say around people and I just… I'm so different. I'm weird."

No, you're not, I wanted to say. How could I let that comment go unchallenged? But she kept going before I had a chance to respond.

"But it's like all of a sudden I want to just be me, Mom," she said. "I don't want to be somebody else's daughter. Haley is nice. She's cool. But I suddenly feel like everybody wants me to save her life and—" She shook her head. "Please…can you make this all go away?"

I moved next to her on the love seat, my arms around her. "You and I share the same wish, Grace." I smoothed my hand down the length of her hair. How long since she'd let me do that? "I wish I could make this all go away, too, but I don't know that I can." I was the one who fixed things. Who controlled things. Never had anything felt so out of my control. "The one thing I can promise you is that I will slow this train down, okay?"

"She could die if I don't give her my blood marrow."

I nearly corrected her but let the mistake stand. She seemed so small in my arms, a child who didn't know *bone* marrow from *blood* marrow, and I would allow her to be that child for as many more hours as possible.

"Your baby died." Her cheek was on my shoulder, her breath against my throat.

At some point, I knew that phantom baby would work her way into my heart, but she wasn't there yet. "I'm not thinking about that baby," I said. "I'm thinking about you."

"Can I be with you when you talk to Anna? Please?"

It had been easy for Ian to tell me to get Grace and go. Easy for me to think of doing exactly that before I'd set foot in that hospital room, where "Anna Knightly" turned from a mere name to a woman. A mother.

I hugged Grace closer to me. I knew she was afraid that Anna would somehow convince me to turn her over without a fight. Why was it that on this day I understood my daughter so well? Had I known her all along?

"Yes," I said. "This is all about you and you can be with us."

56

Anna

The woman, Tara, wanted Grace to be with us as we sat in the little room. I thought it would be better to leave her out of the discussion. She could stay with Haley while Tara and I talked, but Tara and Grace were a unit. Two against one. *That's good,* I told myself. *That's the way it should be.* If Grace turned out to be my Lily, I wanted her to have had the sort of life where she was loved and protected. Yet Grace seemed so fragile that I wasn't sure she should be privy to our conversation. Still, it wasn't my call.

Grace looked more like Tara than she did like me, that was for sure, but frankly, she didn't look much like either of us. She and Tara sat side by side on the love seat, holding hands. Both of them probably had brown hair beneath the blond highlights and both of them had brown eyes, yet their features were dissimilar. I couldn't help but study them, comparing one nose to the other. The shape of their lips. The curve of their eyebrows.

I couldn't get past my lack of feeling for Grace except as a possible bone marrow donor for Haley, and that upset me.

I never expected to feel so flat at the prospect of seeing my lost daughter in front of me.

"I don't understand how all this happened," Tara said. "Were you living in Wilmington?"

"I've been asking myself the same question for the past couple of hours," I said. "And no, I was living here, but I was a pharmaceutical rep and I often traveled to Wilmington." I remembered back. I needed to figure this out for myself. "I was about thirty-five weeks pregnant with Lily on my last trip down there. Bryan, my husband, was stationed overseas at the time. While I was in Wilmington, I went into premature labor and delivered Lily down there. She was already six pounds three ounces and healthy. I was having trouble with my blood pressure, though, and a few hours after Lily was born, I had a stroke and slipped into a coma."

"Oh, my God," Tara said.

"They transported me to Duke," I said. "Bryan was still in Somalia, trying to get permission to come home, but of course I was out of it and had no idea what was happening. When Bryan got home, he stayed in a hotel near Duke. I guess it was a terrible time for him." It was something I rarely thought about, how incredibly difficult that period must have been for Bryan. "Our home was up here in Alexandria. Our newborn baby was in Wilmington. And I was in a coma in Durham. He called the hospital in Wilmington to ask about Lily, and they told him she wasn't there. That she must have been transferred with me. Bryan tried to reach the EMTs who transferred me, but no one had a record of a baby being moved with me. She—" I looked at Grace "—she had just vanished along with any record of her birth. Bryan didn't know the name of the doctor who delivered her. It was all a big mess. I was in a coma a little more than two weeks. I'd actually had very little damage from the stroke, thank God. My left side was weak. My vision and speech were a little off. My left hand is still not all that strong." I flexed my fingers. "My memory was worthless. I couldn't remember any doctors' names, either. The only thing I remembered was that I'd had a beautiful baby and I wanted her back."

"I'm sorry," Tara said, but I saw her tighten her hand around Grace's as if she had no intention of ever letting her go.

"When I was well enough to travel," I continued, "we went to Wilmington. Lily would have been about seven weeks old by then. We worried that someone thought Lily had been abandoned, which in a way she had been, and that they'd moved her to foster care, so we searched through the foster system."

"How terrible for you," Tara said, but she was still clutching Grace's hand hard.

"I saw the letter your midwife wrote to me," I said. "I… It's hard to take it all in. Did you have any idea?"

"None," Tara said. "Noelle died recently.…" She looked at Grace. "Did you tell her?"

Grace nodded.

"She committed suicide and my friend and I found the letter and we began searching for the 'Anna' Noelle was writing to. We finally figured out it was you, but we didn't know whose baby she…whose baby died. We never in a million years thought it was mine."

"Didn't you see your baby…I mean, wouldn't you know if your baby suddenly looked different?" I asked.

"It was the middle of the night when she was born and my labor had been very difficult. When Noelle brought her to me in the morning, I guess she'd already...made the substitution, because that baby was definitely Grace."

"I don't think much of your midwife," I said.

"She did a terrible thing," Tara said. "But it's hard for me to let it define who she was."

"Tell her about the babies program," Grace said softly.

"Would you like to tell her?" Tara asked. "You're more involved with it than I am."

"She started an organization to help babies...preemies and poor babies and sick babies," Grace said. "She won the Governor's Award for it, but she wouldn't accept it."

I couldn't look at her as she spoke. I was so afraid of attaching to her. Instead, I looked at Tara. "Maybe this is why," I said, sweeping my hand through the air to take in the three of us and our predicament. "Maybe she felt she didn't deserve any awards."

"Could be," Tara agreed. She put her arm around Grace. "I think we need a DNA test," she said. "And I think we'd both better lawyer up. I don't mean that in an adversarial way, but we—"

"I agree completely," I said. "We all need to know what we're dealing with. But I did explain to Grace earlier about Haley's need for a bone marrow donor. She's extremely ill. She's—" I shrugged, giving into the word "—she's *terminally* ill. And Grace agreed..."

"Grace didn't know what she was agreeing to, Anna," Tara said. "I'm sorry, but I have to put the brakes on right now, okay? Let's take things a little more slowly. I'll have my lawyer contact yours and see what timeline they recommend for the DNA test and then go from there."

I felt like jumping from my seat and barring the door. "In a normal world, that would make sense," I said. *No tears. Please no tears.* Tara was a cool customer and one thing I'd learned in my line of business was the need to stay calm. Still, I couldn't keep the tremor out of my voice. "Please understand, Tara. I don't know if Grace is Lily..." I looked at Grace. "I'm sorry to speak about you in the third person," I said. "I just don't know, but what if she is? And what if she's a match for Haley? And what if we find that out too late? We haven't been able to find a donor and a sibling has a one in four chance of being a good match."

Tara shook her head. "You're asking a lot of her," she said. "That decision will just have to wait."

"I want to do it," Grace said. She looked at her mother. "I have to."

"No, you don't, honey. You don't have to do anything."

"I want to," she repeated.

Please let her, I thought.

I saw Tara weaken. A lawyer would say to wait, I was sure of it, but this was different. This was two mothers. Two daughters.

"All right." Tara gave in. "If you're sure."

57

Emerson

Jenny's ice cream sundae had melted into a mocha-colored soup in her bowl and she pushed the soft liquid around with her spoon. My salad was practically untouched. We sat by the window in the cafeteria, surrounded by the chatter of doctors and nurses and visitors, but Jenny and I were in our own little bubble.

Maybe we should have gone with Tara to the girl's room. I told myself that giving them privacy had been for the best. It was going to be confusing enough as it was; adding two more people to the mix could only make it messier. But I'd been glad Tara hadn't wanted us with her. I didn't think I could stand to watch her go through it all. I felt so guilty. Guilty for not telling her the moment I suspected that Grace was Anna Knightly's child. Guilty that it was my daughter who hurt Grace with the truth. And I was tormented by the thought of how Tara felt at that moment.

I could imagine the conversation between Tara and Anna Knightly. Two mothers fighting over their daughter. Of course, Grace would always be Tara's. Anything else was unthinkable. Yet Anna's baby had been stolen from her.

How could she not demand at least a part of that child's life back?

Jenny pushed her bowl of ice cream soup away from her. "I am so sorry, Mom," she said once again. I'd lost track of how many times she'd apologized.

"Look," I said, moving my salad aside, "you screwed up by not telling me you overheard. I screwed up by not talking to Tara right away. But none of that would change the fact that Noelle did what she did and now everyone has to deal with the consequences. That's what you and I need to focus on. Helping Tara and Grace handle what's coming."

"I don't want her to move away and be part of some other family and live up here and—"

"I doubt any of that will happen," I said. "Grace is sixteen and she'll have a say in any decision. And you don't think Tara would say, 'Oh, here, she's yours,' do you?"

"What would you do if you were in Tara's place right now?" Jenny asked.

I blew out a breath and looked up at the ceiling. "I would give the other woman—Anna Knightly—I would give her my deepest sympathy, but I would do just what I hope Tara is doing. Get Grace out of here and let the lawyers handle everything." I was worried, though. Jenny and I had debated over getting something to eat because we thought Tara would call us within minutes. Now, nearly forty minutes had passed. What was taking so long?

"How would you feel in *Grace's* shoes right now?" I asked.

She gnawed on her lip for a moment. "I'd want to get to know the people," she said. "My other family. But I wouldn't want them to try to take me away from you and Dad. I absolutely wouldn't let them. And I'd feel sad that your baby died that way. That's so awful. Poor Tara."

"I know," I said. "It's unbearable to think about."

"I just can't stand how Grace must be feeling right now."

"I know exactly what you mean." I looked her in the eye. "They're really going to need our support, Jen," I said.

"I think we should have gone with Tara to the room," she said.

My daughter was braver than I was. "You want to be with Grace?" I asked.

Jenny nodded.

"All right." I got to my feet. "Let's go find them."

58

Grace

Mom was being her usual self, chatting up Haley and Anna as we waited on the couch in Haley's room for a nurse to come swab my cheek. Someone had brought in another chair so everyone could sit and I was still cold, even though I knew the temperature in the room was fine. I had the blue blanket wrapped around my shoulders again and it felt like armor. I didn't know what to hope for. If I was a match, I was afraid of what would happen to me next. If I wasn't a match, Haley could die. When I thought about it that way, I knew I had no choice.

My mother was just as nervous as I was. She was talking a mile a minute, which wasn't all that unusual, and within ten minutes she knew everything there was to know about the neighborhood where Haley and Anna lived in Virginia and what Haley liked in school and all that typical stuff. She was acting like the always-on Tara Vincent, but her eyes were darting between Haley and Anna and the open door of the room and she had moved her chair right next to mine and hadn't stopped touching me since she showed up at the hospital. I was glad of that. *I belong to her,* I wanted to say to

Anna. *I know I'm your baby and it wasn't fair someone ripped me off, but my mom raised me and I belong to her, okay?*

The whole time my mother was talking, Anna and Haley kept staring at me like I was a peach in the grocery store and they were trying to decide if they wanted to take me home with them or not. Finally, I couldn't take it anymore.

"Everyone please stop staring at me," I said. Mom moved closer to me on the sofa, but Anna and Haley just laughed.

"We can't help it," Anna said.

"I would so seriously like some of that hair," Haley said.

I wondered if I could give her some of it. Have it cut and donate it to the Locks of Love program so they could make it into a wig for her. Could you specify who you wanted to receive your hair?

While I was thinking about how I could donate my hair, Emerson and Jenny suddenly showed up in the doorway.

"Knock, knock," Emerson said. "We just wanted to see how Tara and Grace are doing."

Anna stood from her chair like someone had poked her with a stick, and Haley suddenly sat up straight in her bed.

"Holy shit," she said.

Then everything turned upside down.

59

Noelle

Wilmington, North Carolina
1994

She'd had taxing deliveries before, scary deliveries where a birth she'd expected to proceed without complications suddenly turned into something that made her pulse race. But Tara's delivery of Grace would forever remain one of the most frightening experiences of her professional life.

Tara had called early that morning to tell her that her contractions had started, so Noelle didn't take her morning cocktail of drugs for her back pain. Instead, she put pinches of turmeric between her cheek and gum and made a thermos of red clover tea, without much hope of relief. There was something to be said for herbal remedies in childbirth, but they were failing her when it came to her back. Her pain was worse than ever these days. The only thing that helped were the drugs, and she blessed the inventors of Percocet and Valium.

With each hour of Tara's long, grueling labor, Noelle's back seized harder until she occasionally had to mask her tears of pain, not wanting Tara or Sam to worry about her when they needed to be concentrating on themselves. Her own concentration was split between the task at hand and the pills she had in her purse. *Just one Percocet,* she thought to herself over and over again. *Just enough to take the edge off.* But she fought the need for the drugs and kept on going.

Around four in the afternoon, Emerson called to say that her water had broken and a neighbor was driving her to the hospital. Ted was in California at a Realtors' convention and she was facing labor alone. She cried on the phone, and Noelle felt torn in two.

"Ted's on his way to the airport," Emerson said. "He'll get the first flight out, but he has to change planes in Chicago. It's going to take him forever to get here."

"You're in excellent hands, honey," Noelle assured her. Without Ted or her two closest friends by her side, Emerson would suffer emotionally, but medically, she'd get good care and that was what mattered most right now. Everything had to go well for her. After the two lost babies, Noelle couldn't bear the thought of Emerson having anything less than the smooth delivery of her healthy baby girl.

She kept in touch with her by phone, comforting her and cheering her on as she labored. Once Tara gave birth and she was certain both mother and baby were stable, she'd talk to Tara and Sam about bringing in the postpartum doula she'd been working with for the past couple of years. Tara knew Clare Briggs and would be comfortable with her. Then, if Emerson was still in labor, Noelle could run over to the hospital to be with her.

Late that night, while Ted was stuck in Chicago and Tara was fighting fear and pain, Noelle called the hospital and learned that Emerson was having an emergency C-section. Oh, how she wanted to be there to hold her sister's hand!

She kept in touch with the hospital—she knew nearly every nurse in the unit—and she breathed a sigh of relief when Jenny was born and both the baby and Emerson were reported to be healthy and stable.

She poured apple juice for Tara, Sam and herself, and between Tara's contractions they toasted the birth of Jenny McGarrity Stiles. Sam alone knew her relationship to that baby. He squeezed her hand as she sat on the edge of their bed. Noelle couldn't wait to see her niece, but first she had a baby to deliver.

Midwifery was always physically taxing. The bending, leaning, twisting and supporting were part of the process, and for the first time Noelle wasn't sure she'd make it through. The red-hot torture in her lower back wouldn't let up and she once again toyed with the idea of taking one of her pills. *Just one.* She could almost hear them calling to her from her bag in the kitchen. She'd be more effective if she could move with less pain, she told herself, but she knew better. She knew the danger. This delivery was too risky. She was dealing now with posterior arrest: the baby was stuck and she knew her only option might be to transport Tara to the hospital for Pitocin to strengthen her contractions. Tara wept at the idea. "Your healthy baby's more important than a home birth," Noelle said, but she assured her they would try everything else she could think of first. She wanted to separate Tara's actual need for transport from her own longing to be in the hospital near Emerson and her baby, as well as her desire to have this delivery behind her so she could take something for her back. She and Sam worked together, physically supporting Tara, changing her position on the bed, walking her around the room, giving her tincture of cohosh and other herbs—in short, doing everything she could think of to help the little girl who was trying to be born.

With only one option left to her short of transport, Noelle attempted to manually rotate the baby. The delicate maneuvering seemed to take forever, though she knew it must have seemed far longer to Tara. Noelle wished she'd had an assistant—she needed four hands to manage the rotation. Maybe five. She let out an enormous sigh of relief when the baby finally turned into position, her fetal heart tones strong and reassuring. A short time later, the infant slipped into the world and Noelle wasn't sure which of the four of them in that hot, dark room was the most exhausted or the most relieved.

She was bathing the infant in the kitchen when Sam came into the room to watch. "She's all right now, isn't she?" he asked. "Tara?"

"She'll be fine," Noelle said, and she knew that when Tara had briefly lost consciousness after the delivery, he'd been afraid. She knew how much he loved Tara. She saw it every time she was in the same room with them, and she felt both happiness for the two of them—two people she loved—and a searing envy that had never eased up. Now they had a child to bind them together even more tightly. She was glad she was only a couple of months away from marrying Ian. For the first time in her life, she had someone to fantasize about the future with. Her longing for children, for an out-in-the-open family tied together by blood, would someday soon be a reality.

She sent Sam back into the bedroom to be with Tara while she finished examining the baby and calling Clare Briggs to come over. Then she wrapped the baby in warm receiving blankets, resting her carefully on a thick towel at the rear of the kitchen counter as she rummaged in her purse for her pill bottles. *Finally.* This delivery was over. Clare would be here in a few minutes. She could afford some relief now.

She carried the infant back into the bedroom and found Sam and Tara huddled together on the bed. Tara smiled tiredly and reached for her baby.

"We're going to name her Noelle," Sam said. She knew in that instant that he'd forgiven her for the night on the beach, but although she was touched by the gesture, she couldn't let it happen. It was so wrong. There were moments when her guilt from that night could still find her, and this was one of them.

"Oh, no, you're not," she said. "Promise me you won't saddle this baby with my name."

She must have sounded even more vehement than she felt, because they quickly backed off and she was relieved. She couldn't allow Tara, in her ignorance, to name her baby after her.

Clare arrived, bustling into the house with the self-confident attitude that always put new parents at ease. Noelle made sure everyone was as comfortable with one another as possible, then left for the hospital. She was beyond exhaustion, but she couldn't wait to check on Emerson and see her niece. This was a child who might actually look like her. Wouldn't that be something? She only hoped she wouldn't look *too* much like her. Not enough to bring attention to the fact.

She took another Percocet before leaving Sam and Tara's house. The past twenty-four hours had simply been too grueling for her back. By the time she was driving to the hospital, she felt the drugs soften the prickly edges of her pain. The muscles in her back loosened ever so slightly and her clenched jaw relaxed. She felt deliciously floaty as she walked from her car to the entrance of the women and new-born unit. The relief from pain combined with exhaustion and the excitement of being minutes from seeing Emerson's baby made her feel almost giddy.

She loved the unit at night when it was dimly lit and nearly silent. The unit was broken into pods of four rooms each. A small nurses' station designed for one or two nurses sat at the center of each pod.

Noelle found the correct pod for Emerson. Jill Kenney, a nurse Noelle had known for years, was bending over one of two clear plastic bassinets next to the counter, changing the diaper of a caramel-skinned baby. She looked like she'd had as long and hard a night as Noelle and she gave her a tired smile.

"Hey, Noelle," she said quietly. "I bet you're here to see the Stiles baby. I thought you'd scrub in for that one. The mom's your best friend, isn't she?"

"I had a home birth of another friend." Noelle returned the smile. "I'm going to ask them to time their babies a little better next time." Standing inside the doorway of the pod, she felt as though she were in a dream. It was a pleasant, welcome sensation. Her back seemed to be made of cotton, soft and yielding and, finally, pain-free.

"She named her Jenny." Jill straightened up from the bassinet and moved to the sink to wash her hands. "Not Jennifer. Jenny. I think that's cute."

Noelle walked toward the bassinets. "Who are these two?" she asked.

Jill sat down at the counter. She rubbed her temple with her fingers, her face pale against her short dark hair. "Well, this one's mom needed a break." She pointed to the darker-skinned infant.

"Do you feel all right?" Noelle asked.

"Actually, no." Jill frowned. "Migraine. Therese is going to relieve me soon and I'm going home. It's been wild tonight, too. It's always that way, isn't it?" She glanced at one of the monitors on the counter, then pressed a couple of buttons on her keyboard before looking up at Noelle again. "The time you don't feel well is the time all hell breaks loose."

"That seems to be the way it goes." Noelle looked at the second bassinet. "Why's this other babe out here?" she asked.

"Oh, that one's really tragic." Jill said. "Mom stroked out and is in a coma."

"*Damn.*" Noelle peered into the bassinet. The baby's wispy brown hair fringed her little pink knit hat. She was six and a half pounds, Noelle thought—she could judge a baby's weight by looks alone—and her color was excellent. Whatever had befallen her mother didn't seem to have had an adverse effect on her.

"They're getting ready to transfer her mother to Duke." Jill punched another few buttons on the keyboard. "I don't know if they've decided whether to move the baby with her or send her to the peds unit."

"Prognosis on the mom?" Noelle rested a hand against the counter. She felt a little unsteady on her feet and was looking forward to sitting down in Emerson's room.

Jill shook her head, then winced as though the motion had done nothing to help her migraine. "Doesn't look good right now," she said, "and the dad is deployed, do you believe it? Mom was four weeks early and traveling here on business, so there's no family. We'll call Ellen first thing in the morning unless they take the baby with the mother tonight."

"Good," Noelle said. Ellen was the social worker for the unit. "So which room is Emerson's?"

Jill pointed to the door behind her. "She's sleeping, but I was about to change the baby and give her a bottle. Would you like to?" She looked so hopeful, Noelle laughed.

"You really need to go home to a dark room, don't you?" She smiled with sympathy. She knew all about pain. Her own had eased up nicely. She loved the floaty sensation that now filled her head.

Jill looked at her watch. "Can't wait. Therese'll be here any second."

"I'll take care of the Stiles baby," Noelle said. She rested a hand on Jill's shoulder. "Hope you get out of here soon."

Emerson was sleeping soundly in the softly lit, quiet room. She looked beautiful and Noelle was filled with tenderness as she leaned over to kiss her forehead. "You finally have your baby, Em," she whispered. "Your little girl." She wished she could have been here for her. She hated that Emerson had felt alone and deserted at such a difficult time.

She set the bottle Jill had given her on the small table near the recliner. Then she scrubbed her hands at the sink and moved to the bassinet.

For a strange moment of déjà vu, she felt as though she'd already seen this baby. There was the little pink hat fringed by honey-brown wisps of hair. The delicate facial features. The six and a half beautiful pounds. It took her only a fraction of a second to realize it had been the baby at Jill's station she'd seen a moment ago, not this little one. Only a fraction of a second, but long enough to let her know she was more out of it than she'd thought.

"Hello, precious," she whispered, beginning to change the little diaper. The baby—Jenny—began to stir, a small frown on her face, a tiny whine coming from her throat. Noelle's eyes filled and she bit her lip to stop it from trembling.

When Jenny was clean and diapered, Noelle lifted her from the bassinet, then sat down in the recliner, the baby cradled in her arms. Jenny's eyes were starting to blink open and closed, the frown deepening between her barely-there eyebrows, and her tiny perfect lips parted in the way Noelle knew preceded a good howl of hunger. She teased the baby's lips with the nipple and felt a little surge of pride when Jenny started sucking without much prompting at all. The infant's hand rested against her own, each finger a tiny sculpture in perfection. Noelle bent low to kiss her forehead. She'd held hundreds of babies in her life, and for the first time she whispered the words *I love you* to one of them.

60

Anna

Washington, D.C.
2010

When the girl showed up in the doorway, I took her in with one glance and that was all that was necessary for my heart to lurch toward her. My body, though, stayed frozen in shock. I stood next to Haley's bed, one hand on her tray table, the other pressed to my chest. Tara moved toward the girl and her mother. She was speaking, words that may as well have been a foreign language. Making introductions that were no more than white noise. Haley grasped my hand where it rested on her table, pressing her fingertips into my wrist and I knew that, like me, she no longer saw Grace and Tara. She didn't see the other woman, either. All either of us could see was the girl.

The white noise of Tara's voice suddenly stopped and she was staring at us.

"Mom," Haley said. "*Say* something."

"What's going on?" Tara asked.

If Haley and I had seen this girl on the street on one of

our trips to Wilmington, we would have chased her for blocks, for miles, until we caught up with her. We'd been looking for her for so long. We would have known we'd found her, just as we knew that now.

"Did the midwife—" I had to clear my throat "—Noelle… Did she deliver you, too?" I asked the girl, although I already knew the answer. The woman in the doorway put an arm around her, tugging her close.

"No," she said. "Jenny was born in the hospital, delivered by an obstetrician."

She was lying. She had to be. My legs were rubbery, but I took two steps toward the night table and picked up the photograph of Haley with the Collier cousins in the Outer Banks. I held it with both hands as if it were very fragile and carried it toward the woman and girl in the doorway.

"This is my sister-in-law and her daughters," I said, holding it toward the woman. "Haley's cousins. Look at them."

I knew what they were seeing in the photograph. Four girls with round dark eyes. Nearly black hair and fair skin. Chins that receded ever so slightly. Noses a hairbreadth too wide to be beautiful. I stepped away from them, back to Haley's side, because I was afraid I would touch the girl. I would try to pull her into my arms. Right now, I had to settle for breathing the air she was in. *Finally,* I thought. *Finally.*

Tara and Grace moved next to the woman and Tara touched the frame where it shivered in her hand. "Oh, my God, Emerson," she said when she saw the picture. "How can this be?"

"Tara," the woman said, as if asking her friend to fix something that had moved entirely out of her control. "It *can't* be," she said. "It *isn't.*"

I watched all four of them stare at the photograph. I

watched as the truth sank in. I held Haley's hand, waiting for the moment I could take my other child, my firstborn daughter, into arms that had ached to hold her for sixteen years. In that girl's beautiful dark eyes, I saw confusion and fear and it broke my heart.

"Jenny," I said. "Is that your name? Did I get it right?" I hadn't really heard the introductions.

The girl slowly raised her gaze from the photograph. "Yes," she whispered.

"Don't be afraid," I said.

Grace looked at her mother. "I'm not…?"

It took Tara a moment to shake her head. "I don't think so." She touched the other woman's shoulder. "Em," she said, "is this possible? What do you remember?"

"I had her in the hospital," the woman said again. "It's impossible. It's ridiculous."

"When is your birthday?" I asked Jenny.

"August 31," she whispered.

My baby, I thought, my eyes filling. She'd lain alone in a hospital for two days with no mother to hold her. No mother to talk to her. She'd been all by herself until the midwife stole her away, quietly, taking all records of her existence with her, erasing her so that I'd never be able to find her again.

"You're my Lily, Jenny. I'm certain of it."

"Stop it!" the woman snapped at me, tugging Jenny close to her, and I knew I'd said too much, too fast, but I hadn't been able to help myself.

The girl pulled free of her mother and fled down the hallway. Grace took off after her. Tara grabbed the woman's arm to stop her from following them. "Let Grace," she said.

The woman looked terrified. "I don't understand what's going on!"

"She's Lily," Haley said. "She's so Lily."

Tara looked at me, her hands wrapped around the woman's forearm. "Let me talk to Emerson," she said.

I didn't want them to leave. I was afraid Lily would vanish once more into thin air. But what could I do?

"All right," I said. Emerson had already turned away, disappearing into the hallway, getting away from me as quickly as she could. "Please don't leave, though," I added, but they were gone and only Haley heard my words.

61

Noelle

Wilmington, North Carolina
1994

She awakened with a great start and couldn't immediately figure out where she was. The odd, dim lighting in the room disoriented her. She blinked hard, trying to focus. The small sink. The bassinet. She turned her head to the right and saw the bed where Emerson slept. She felt something hard against her thigh through her skirt and glanced down to see a bottle next to her on the seat of the recliner. She'd been feeding the baby. What was her name? Grace? They'd wanted to name her Noelle. No, this baby wasn't Grace. It was Emerson's child. Jennifer. Jenny. She had the vaguest memory of getting up to return the baby to the bassinet, but the bassinet was empty. She tried to think. Had Jill come in to take the baby from her arms? She drew in a long slow breath, worried she'd feel dizzy once she got to her feet. She pressed her hands on the seat of the chair to keep her balance, but as she started to stand, her glance fell to the floor at her feet and she saw the baby who had slipped from her tired arms down the silky fabric of her skirt.

She couldn't breathe. She bent over too quickly to reach for the infant and fell from the chair to the floor, landing hard on her hip. Grabbing the baby, she pulled her onto her lap but knew right away she was too late. Too impossibly late. The baby's head was at an unnatural angle, her lips already blue and lifeless.

Noelle stared at the infant, eyes wide, horror filling her chest. *You killed her, you killed her, you killed her!* Her hands trembled as she attempted to straighten the little head on the broken neck. She leaned over to try to breathe life into the purplish lips and tiny nose, where a trickle of blood had already crusted.

She pulled herself to her feet, one hand on the edge of the sink. She felt as though she was wailing, but the sound was caught inside her chest and couldn't come out. She picked up the baby and placed her in the bassinet, then stood stock-still, trying to clear her head. Trying to think.

The baby in the nurses' station. The twin to this one. The one with the dying mother. The missing father.

How would she get Jill away? Quietly, she crossed the room and opened the door to the nurses' station to find it empty. Jill wasn't there, but the baby was still in the bassinet. Brown hair. Six and a half pounds. No time to waste. No time to think.

Noelle lifted the infant into her arms. She grabbed the thin chart attached to the bassinet and slipped back into Emerson's room. Her hands shook wildly as she placed the motherless baby next to Emerson's child in the bassinet. Then she wrapped a flannel blanket around the lifeless infant, Emerson's little Jenny, and slipped her gently into her huge leather purse.

The wristbands! She reached into her purse and worked the band from the baby's wrist, then exchanged it for the one worn by the infant in the bassinet, but not before she noticed the name: *KNIGHTLY, baby girl*. She dropped that baby's record and wristband into her purse. She'd burn the records. She could already picture the fire in her fireplace.

She stole out of the hospital, passing a couple of nurses and one obstetrician she knew, but they barely acknowledged her as they raced down the hall. The unit was an uncalm place tonight. As uncalm as she felt inside. As uncalm as she would feel for the rest of her life.

It was three-thirty in the morning by the time she got home and by then she was operating on sheer adrenaline. Almost without thinking, she found the shovel in her shed. She selected the corner of her yard farthest from the house and, in the darkness, she dug and dug and dug, the earth soft from August rains. She made the hole deep and narrow. She wrapped the baby in her favorite skirt, because it was beautiful and because she needed to sacrifice something she loved. She lay flat on the ground and carefully lowered the baby deep into the ground, then she shoveled the earth over her, finally letting her tears come.

When she was finished she sat on the ground above the baby, above Emerson's Jenny, not moving even when a misty rain started to fall. She sat there until the sky began to lighten with strands of pink and lemon and lavender, like a bouquet of flowers for a baby girl. That was what she would do this morning, she thought. She'd go to the garden shop and ask them what plants would bloom into a lush blanket of pastel blossoms that even a stranger would not be able to look at without thinking, *This is a garden that's filled with love.*

62

Tara

Washington, D.C.
2010

We found Grace and Jenny in the little room at the end of the hall. They sat on the floor, leaning against one of the love seats and my daughter—*my* daughter, I was sure of it—had her arm around her best friend. They looked up when Emerson and I walked into the room.

"Mom," Jenny said. "Please tell me I'm not her daughter! Just because I look like those girls doesn't mean anything."

Emerson sank onto the love seat. Every trace of color had left her face. She smoothed her hand over Jenny's head, gently squeezing a fistful of her hair as if she could hold on to her that way. "I don't understand how you possibly could be her daughter," she said. "Noelle had nothing to do with your birth."

I saw the doubt in Emerson's eyes as she spoke. We'd both seen the picture of those girls. You could exchange Jenny for one of them in the photograph and no one would know the difference.

"The letter Noelle wrote to Anna," I said. "It didn't say where she was when she dropped the baby, did it?"

Emerson jerked her head toward me, a look of betrayal on her face. "Do you actually think Jenny could be the one?" she nearly barked at me. "Tell me how that could possibly have happened."

I sat down on the love seat opposite them, wondering how much to say. How to say it all without being cruel because what happened now seemed so clear in my mind. "Noelle was upset you were alone when you were in labor." I felt all their eyes on me. "Ted was trying to get a plane home and Noelle was with Sam and me, remember? But once Grace was born, she had a doula come over so she could go see you at the hospital."

"She never *came* to the hospital," Emerson argued.

I looked down at my lap, where I was twisting my wedding ring on my finger. "That's what she told us later," I said quietly. I lifted my gaze to Emerson again. "Of course, that's what she'd tell us—that she never made it there. That she was so tired, she just went home and went to sleep. Didn't that seem unbelievable at the time, Em? That she wouldn't come see you?"

Emerson looked away from me. In her hand, she still held a fistful of Jenny's hair.

"Mom." Jenny put her hands over her ears as though she could somehow block out what was happening. "I can't *stand* this!"

I felt such relief to know that Grace and I were free from the nightmare, yet I was now reliving the emotions of this long day again, reliving them through the friend I loved so much. *Tell Jenny she'll always be yours,* I thought, leaning forward, and Emerson seemed to get my unspoken message.

"I don't know what's going on, Jenny," she said. "We'll

figure it out. But I don't care who gave birth to you, your dad and I raised you and you're our daughter."

"Haley needs a bone marrow transplant," Grace said, unhelpfully. "I was going to get tested to see if I'm a match. They only need to swab your cheek."

"*Grace,*" I said more sharply than I'd meant to. "Give Jenny and Emerson a chance to figure out what's happening, honey. Remember how you felt a couple of hours ago?"

Grace looked contrite. "Right," she said. "Sorry." She had grown up today, I thought. Driven hundreds of miles alone. Walked into a hospital. Agreed to endure medical treatments to help a sister she didn't know. She wasn't the same girl she'd been the day before.

"I want to go home," Jenny said. "Don't make me go back to that room, Mom. Please just take me home."

Emerson looked at me. "I think we should leave," she said. "I need to talk to Ian."

I stood. "I'll go back and tell them we're leaving," I said. "I'll have to give them your contact information, Emerson, all right? And get theirs for you?"

Emerson shook her head. "I don't want them calling me," she said.

Of course not. "I'll just give them Ian's number."

She gave me a reluctant nod. I stood, then bent over to hug her and kiss the top of Jenny's head. "Love you, Jen," I said. "I'll be back in a minute."

I found Anna sitting on the edge of Haley's bed and it was clear they'd both been crying. I could imagine how they felt, suddenly so near the girl they'd feared they would never find, yet unable to touch or even talk to her.

Anna jumped to her feet and rushed over to me. "How is she?" she asked. "Is she okay?"

I nodded. "She and Emerson have a lot to think about," I said. "They're not sure...well, you can imagine how overwhelmed they are right now. I came to tell you that we're leaving and to—"

"No!" Haley wailed. "We need to talk to Lily!"

I shook my head. "I'm sorry, Haley," I said. "Jenny wants to go home and, right now, I think that's best. But Emerson will talk to her lawyer and he'll get in touch with you and your mother very soon. Tell me the best way for him to contact you."

Anna picked up a briefcase from the floor near the sofa. I could tell she was fighting tears as she pulled out a business card. She added some other phone numbers to the back of it and I wrote Ian's number on a slip of paper from my notepad.

"We don't want to hurt her. Lily. Jenny," Anna said, as she handed me the card. "We want to do this the right way. But Haley needs—"

"I know," I said. "Jenny's in shock right now. So is Emerson." I tried to smile. "So am I, actually."

"Us, too," Haley said. "Seriously."

As I turned to leave the room, Anna caught my arm. "Grace is beautiful," she said. "When I saw her, I thought, *What a beautiful girl,* but I felt nothing...here." She pressed her hand to her chest. "When I saw Jenny, though, I knew. Even if she didn't look exactly like Haley's cousins, I would have known. It was like a missing piece of my heart suddenly appeared in the doorway. Can you understand that?"

I nodded. The missing piece of my own heart was in the room at the end of the hall, and on this difficult day, I felt that piece slipping slowly, cautiously back into place.

63

Grace

Jenny and I rode in the backseat, while my mother drove. We'd had to leave Emerson's car in the parking garage at the hospital. We didn't have a choice. Only one of the four of us was in any shape to drive and that was my mom, and even she wasn't doing all that well.

Everything had reversed itself in the weirdest way. It was as if you had to do one of the worst things you could imagine, like walk barefoot across burning coals, and suddenly your best friend was going to do it for you. You know just how your friend feels because you felt the same way, and it hurts to watch your friend go through it all.

I'd thought before about how love could sneak up on you. One day when I was eleven years old, I suddenly realized I loved Jenny the same way I loved my mother and father. We'd been on the beach at Wrightsville, hanging out together in the sun and jumping in the waves, and I'd felt so happy. I looked over at Jenny and thought, *I love you,* just like that. It was a revelation, really. About a year later, Jenny said, "Love you," when we talked on the phone, the same way our mothers said those words to each other, and it was like there was suddenly more color in my life. Love came with some hurt, though. When Jenny broke her ankle two years ago, I sat with her on her porch steps while we waited for the ambulance, and it was as though my own ankle had been broken. That's how bad I felt.

Now, sitting in the back of the car with Jenny, I felt the same way again.

"What are they like?" Jenny asked me. "That girl and her mother? I didn't even get a look at them, really."

"They're nice," I reassured her, although a couple of hours earlier, I'd felt nothing for them. I thought of Anna's coolness. "It's hard to tell because I just, you know, popped into the room and said, 'Hi! I'm your daughter!' so they were obviously freaked. And you freaked them even more."

Emerson and my mother were talking quietly in the front seats. From where I sat, I could see a tissue wadded up in Emerson's fist. For the first hour of the drive, I'd heard words like *I refuse to believe it* and *This will kill Ted* and *Where is my baby?* They were whispered words I didn't want Jenny to hear, so I tried to talk over them. I heard Emerson speak to Ted on the phone, so quietly I couldn't understand what she said. How would she tell Ted their daughter was probably not their daughter, after all?

"So...tell me about this disease Haley has," Jenny said after a while.

"It's leukemia," I said. "I only talked to her for a little while, but she's cool." I felt a tiny bit of jealousy: if Jenny was really Anna's daughter, then she had a sister. "She seems really strong. She doesn't seem like she's going to die tomorrow or anything, but she could." I couldn't help myself. I knew my mother thought Jenny couldn't handle this, but she needed to know the truth. "She *is* going to die if she can't get a bone marrow transplant," I said.

"Now they'll want me to do it, won't they?" she said.

"You don't have to," I said. "But I think you should. A sibling has a one in four chance of being a match."

Emerson must have heard me. She turned in her seat. "Jenny, don't even think about this now, all right? We have no idea what's going on yet, really, and even if you turn out to be the baby Noelle took, you don't need to decide a *thing* right now. Not about being a part of their lives, and absolutely not about donating bone marrow." I didn't think I'd ever heard Emerson sound so firm. "You don't need to *ever* decide, if you don't want to," she added.

Jenny didn't say anything, but when Emerson had faced forward again, she turned to me. "What does it take," she asked. "Being a donor?"

"Cheek swab first," I said. "Then if you're a match with the cheek swab, they do a blood test. If you're a match after that, they have to take some of your bone marrow. I don't know exactly how they do it. If you need to do it, though, I'll go with you."

"You were going to do it?" she asked.

"That doesn't mean you have to."

"But you're such a wimp. And *you* were going to do it."

I was amazed by that myself. "She could die," I said with a shrug.

Jenny wrinkled her nose, then leaned forward and tapped Emerson on the shoulder. "Mom?" she said. "I need to find out if I'm a match for her. For Haley."

Emerson turned around again. She looked at Jenny. Then she looked at me. Her face was a pasty-white mess, smeared with mascara. "All right," she said. "We'll figure it out."

Jenny's phone rang and she checked the caller ID.

"It's Cleve." She looked at me. "I talked to him while we were driving to Washington and told him what was going on. Should I answer?"

I took the phone from her. "Hey," I said.

"Grace! You're with Jenny? Where are you? I've been worried about you! I've been going out of my freakin' mind, wondering what's going on."

I smiled. He'd been worried. Going out of his freakin' mind. "I'm fine," I said, "but it's too long to go into right now. I'll talk to you tomorrow?"

"Just tell me you're all right," he said.

"I'm good," I said.

Cleve wasn't a part of this. He'd never be able to understand everything that had happened. I was with the people who *did* understand: my mom and Emerson and Jenny. I felt like Cleve was from another part of my life that suddenly seemed so long ago, and I realized that, on this very long day when I thought I would turn into someone else, that was exactly what had happened.

64

Emerson

Topsail Island, North Carolina

I stood at the sliding glass door of the oceanfront cottage Ted, Jenny and I were renting. Midweek in October and not a soul on the beach for as far as I could see. We knew we'd practically have the island to ourselves. That's why we came.

Ted and Jenny and the dogs were out there somewhere, but I'd begged off with the excuse that I wanted to make lasagna for dinner. Really, though, I wanted the time alone. Time to think.

The DNA test results had come in the day before. I hadn't fallen apart as I'd expected, I guess because by the time we got the phone call, I'd known there was no other explanation for what had happened than the one Tara had offered. Ted called a Realtor he knew and booked this cottage and I called Hunter High to pull Jenny out of school for a few days. We needed the time together, just the three of us, before we'd allow anyone else—Anna Knightly and her family, to be specific—into our lives. Three days for Jenny, Ted and me to come to grips with this new reality.

For a couple of days after that miserable trip to Washington, I was filled with such a crazy quilt of emotions I could hardly stand it. One minute I'd be furious with Noelle, the next I'd be full of gratitude. One minute, I'd be racked with grief over the baby I'd lost without ever having the chance to see her or touch her, the next I'd be filled with a love for Jenny so pure and bottomless that I was drowning in it. Now, all those emotions had been erased by one simple question: What did our future hold? The only thing I knew for sure, the only thing I cared about, was that I needed to help Jenny find her way through that future. My own fears and losses and anger no longer mattered. All that mattered was Jenny.

I spotted the dogs first. Shadow and Blue bounded in and out of the shallow water, chasing each other across the sand with an energy they never displayed at home. Then I saw Ted and Jenny walking a distance behind the dogs. Ted made an expansive motion with his arms as though he was illustrating the enormity of the ocean. Or maybe, I thought, he was describing his love for Jenny. I'd never felt closer to Ted than I had in the past few days. We were on the same team. "You're our daughter," he said to Jenny with such force that no one could doubt that he meant it. "Do you think a DNA test can change that?"

As they came closer to the house, I watched Ted take Jenny's hand. They swung their arms back and forth between them like they were kids. Like nothing bad had happened or ever could happen. Like our lives hadn't taken as grim a turn as I'd thought. Watching them, I felt an unexpected surge of happiness.

I opened the sliding glass door and stepped out on the

deck. I waved to them and they waved back, and I couldn't wait for them to come into the cottage. Tonight we'd watch a movie after dinner. Maybe play a game. There'd be time later to make sense of our new and uncertain future. All I knew was that we'd be facing it together.

My husband.

Myself.

And my daughter.

EPILOGUE

Tara

The cleansing of Noelle's cottage is Emerson's idea, and I'm so glad she thought of it. I pull up in front of the house and take in the view. The cottage, now yellow with white trim and black shutters, is adorable. Two white rockers sit on the small porch and the yard is filled with azaleas ready to pop with color.

Suzanne is moving into the cottage next week. She knows nothing about the cleansing. She's never seemed the least bit concerned that Noelle killed herself in the house, but we're certain Noelle would have approved of what we're doing here today.

Emerson's car is in the driveway, and I park across the street. I've been inside the cottage a couple of times since its transformation. The kitchen and bathroom have been gutted and refurbished, the floors refinished, and the walls in every room painted in warm Tuscan colors, as Suzanne suggested. It took forever—Emerson had other things on her mind—but it's finished now and ready for Suzanne to give it a new life.

Emerson greets me in the kitchen. "You'll take the east corner," she says as she hands me a bowl containing a smoldering bundle of sage. A tendril of smoke rises into the air above it. She points toward the second bedroom near the rear of the house and instructs me what to do.

Tonight, after the cleansing of the house is complete, Grace and Jenny will begin moving the bags of donated baby items into the second bedroom with some help from Cleve, who's home on spring break. I can't go so far as to say that Grace is over Cleve. I swear I can sense her heart beating a little faster when he's around. But she started going out with a friend of Jenny's boyfriend, Devon, and she tells me he's "okay," which I think means she likes him quite a bit. Grace is never going to be an open book, like me. I've learned that the harder I dig, the more she withdraws. But if I wait, if I'm there for her the way Sam used to be without pushing or prodding, she eventually turns to me. Some days it feels like waiting for paint to dry. Every shared confidence, though, is precious. For an entire day, I was unsure who she was and how we fit together. Ironic that the day I feared I was no longer her mother was the day I learned how to mother her.

Jenny was not a match for Haley, but Haley was able to receive her transplant in January after a donor was found through the global database. Her recovery has been extremely difficult, filled with uncertainty, infections and one hospitalization after another. But she's at home now, at least for a while, and she and Jenny Skype every day. Every *minute,* according to Grace, who's a little jealous of the relationship forming between Jenny and her sister. Emerson has her own jealousy to contend with, but she's learning to share Jenny with Anna, as we all are, and she's trying hard to expand her vision of family to include Anna, Haley and Bryan.

Now Emerson stands on a stepladder to take out the batteries from the smoke detector. Then she lights her own bowl of sage from the candle burning on the counter. She blows it out to let it smolder. "I just hope we don't burn the place down," she says as she heads for the room that had been Noelle's bedroom.

In the second bedroom, I walk in a large circle, stopping to fill the corners with the aromatic smoke. At the windows, I look out at the garden, where daffodils and crocuses seem to have sprung up overnight. We don't know for sure and we never will, but we believe we understand the love Noelle had for her garden and the birdbath with its statue of the little girl. We thought back, remembering that she first planted the garden shortly after Emerson gave birth to her daughter. Noelle had never shown any interest in her yard before then, but she tended that garden with so much love. Almost the sort of love you'd lavish on a child. A niece, perhaps.

I believe that Sam knew. I believe that one day, when Noelle could no longer keep this final, most devastating secret to herself, she asked Sam to meet her someplace where none of us would bump into them. Someplace like Wrightsville Beach. Maybe she told him everything, client to attorney. She must have told him about the garden, prompting him to question me about it a short time later. *What's with Noelle's garden?* Out of the blue.

Through the bedroom window, I see Emerson walk toward the garden. I watch as she plucks a few dead leaves from the birdbath, then rests her hand on the head of the little bronze girl. I fill with love for her. I carry the bowl of sage into the bathroom and run a little water onto it, then rest it on the counter. I want to be with Emerson. In this year of changes, only one thing has been certain and solid, and that's the bond I have with my best friend. I walk outside to help her prepare the garden to welcome the spring.

★ ★ ★ ★ ★

READER'S GUIDE

1. Tara and Emerson have very different personalities, yet they've remained best friends for more than twenty years. What do you think drew them together initially? What keeps them together now?

2. Tara's mother had a history of psychiatric problems. How has this shaped Tara as a mother? As a widow?

3. Imagine yourself in Noelle's place when she learns that Emerson is her sister. Would you be able to keep that relationship to yourself for two decades? Do you think Noelle should have revealed the relationship to Emerson? Discuss the internal struggle you might have if you were in her position.

4. What was Sam's attraction to two women as different as Tara and Noelle? Why do you think he chose Tara over Noelle?

5. Emerson values being liked above being ambitious and successful. This is typically a feminine trait and one that can often get in the way of advancing in a career. Yet Emerson, with her new café, *Hot!*, has clearly found a path to professional success without sacrificing her values. Why do you think she's succeeded

at this endeavor? How do you feel about the sometimes conflicting values of "being nice" versus "being ambitious"?

6. Grace is a strong introvert, while her mother is passionately extroverted. How do these differing personality traits affect their relationship?

7. Tara has enormous guilt over her feelings toward her former favorite student, Mattie Cafferty. Discuss how her relationship with Mattie may have impacted her relationship with Grace prior to Sam's death.

8. Any major change often throws the structure of a comfortable family out of balance. Why do you think Grace had such a close relationship with her father? How did the family dynamic between Grace, Tara and Sam support that relationship? How did Sam's death alter that dynamic and what did that change mean for both Grace and Tara? Discuss the different ways in which Tara and Grace grieved for Sam and how those different styles of grieving created conflict and misunderstanding.

9. Anna has made the search for missing children her life's work and has involved Haley in that cause in both a professional and personal way. How do you think this has impacted the relationship between mother and daughter?

10. Bryan deserted Anna and Haley during the most vulnerable time of their lives. When he returns, they both need his support, but does Anna forgive him too

easily? How does her role as a mother or a woman feed into that forgiveness?

11. How are the three mother-daughter relationships (Tara and Grace; Emerson and Jenny; Anna and Haley) the same or different?

12. Discuss Noelle's choice to become a gestational surrogate. Why did she choose this particular path to atonement? Why do you think she had no children of her own?

13. Noelle lived not just one lie, but many. Discuss what it must be like to keep the most significant parts of your life a secret from your closest friends. When Ian learns about her surrogacy, he says "It must have been so lonely, being Noelle." Do you think Noelle was lonely and if so, were there ways that she compensated for that loneliness?

14. Imagine yourself in Emerson's place when she feels certain that Noelle substituted Grace for Tara's infant. How would you feel knowing such devastating information about your best friend? Would you handle it the way Emerson did or in some other way?

15. As the reader, you're unable to see the world through Grace's point of view until the final third of the story. Did that impact how you perceived Grace? Did being in her point of view change your feelings about her?

16. Tara learns that her missing daughter is not her biological daughter and at the same time realizes that her

biological daughter is dead. What does she learn about herself as a mother in those moments?

17. Anna's reaction to Grace's arrival at the hospital is conflicted and hesitant. Did this surprise you? Do you think some sort of maternal intuition came into play in this scene or was some other emotion at work? Discuss Anna's reaction to Grace's pronouncement that she is Anna's daughter.

18. Noelle is a powerful woman even from the grave. Every character in the story has been hurt by her in some way. Yet ultimately this is a story of forgiveness. Trace the complicated relationships Tara and Emerson had with Noelle. Why do you think they are able to make peace with Noelle's hurtful actions?

19. *The Midwife's Confession* is also a story about deep and abiding friendships between women. What would you say is the ultimate take-away message about friendship?

20. Who do you think grew the most over the course of the story and why? What do you think the future holds for Tara and Grace? Emerson and Jenny and Ted? Anna, Haley and Bryan?

ACKNOWLEDGMENTS

North Carolina offers so many unique areas in which to set a novel and I loved getting to know beautiful Wilmington better as I wrote *The Midwife's Confession*. Thank you to my North Carolina publicists, Tori Jones and Kim Hennes, for sharing their love of Wilmington with me as they carted me around town. You two are excellent tour guides! Thanks also to Beth Scarbrough, who attended UNC Wilmington at the same time as the Galloway Girls and who helped me paint a picture of their campus life.

As usual, the other six members of the Weymouth Seven helped me brainstorm this story in between games of Balderdash, chats with ghosts and work on their own novels. Thank you Mary Kay Andrews, Margaret Maron, Katy Munger, Sarah Shaber, Alexandra Sokoloff and Brenda Witchger. Two other author friends, Emilie Richards and Maureen Sherbondy, also contributed their ideas at various points in the story, as did my sister, Joann Scanlon, and my assistant, Denise Gibbs, and I'm grateful to all of them.

Thank you Tina Blackwell for the Native American legend on Spanish moss, which I shamelessly altered to suit my story. Thank you Kelly Williamson for giving me a peek into the life of a North Carolina high school student. Thank you Janina Campbell for sharing your poignant memories of your father as I shaped Grace's character. Eleanor Smith helped me map out Emerson's library research, and Phyllis Sabourin updated my recollection of maternity units and hospital nurseries, which have come a long way since my days as a hospital social worker.

The internet not only allows for impersonal factual research, but it also gives us an intimate look into the life journeys of real people through their public blogs. The research I did into Haley's leukemia put me in touch with many of these stories, and they touched me deeply. I was particularly moved by the experiences of Kay Howe of the Netherlands. Even when my research was complete, I continued reading the blog written by Kay's father as I rooted for that courageous ten-year-old girl whose zest for life inspired me every day. I was stunned and saddened when Kay lost her fight with leukemia, and she and her family will always have a place in my heart.

Thank you to my agent, Susan Ginsburg, who has to be the most positive person in the book business. I love your optimism! Special thanks to my editor, Miranda Indrigo, who's not only able to see the forest for the trees but who always helps me blaze the best trail through the undergrowth.

Finally, for reading every word of nearly every draft and offering his honest critique along with his support, for being my resident photographer and best friend, thank you John Pagliuca. Sorry there was no place to put that car chase you wanted. Maybe next time!

Award-winning author
DIANE CHAMBERLAIN

Joelle D'Angelo's best friend, Mara, is left with brain damage after she suffers an aneurysm giving birth to her son. Alone and grieving, Joelle turns to the only other person who understands her pain: her colleague—and Mara's husband—Liam. What starts out as comfort between friends gradually becomes something more, something undeniable.

Torn by guilt and the impossibility of her feelings for Liam, Joelle goes in search of help for Mara. She is led to a healer in Monterey, California, who is keeping her own shocking secrets. But Joelle soon discovers that while some love is doomed, some love is destined to survive anything.

The Shadow Wife
Available wherever books are sold.

MIRA®

www.MIRABooks.com

MDC2844TR

BESTSELLING AUTHOR
DIANE CHAMBERLAIN

Dr. Olivia Simon is on duty at North Carolina's
Outer Banks Hospital when a gunshot victim is brought in.
Midway through the effort to save the woman's life, Olivia
realizes who she is—Annie O'Neill. The woman Olivia's
husband, Paul, is in love with.

When Annie dies on the operating table,
she leaves behind three other victims.
Alec O'Neill, who thought he had the
perfect marriage. Paul, whose fixation
with Annie is unshakable. And Olivia,
who is desperate to understand the
woman who destroyed her marriage.

Now they are left with unanswered
questions about who Annie
really was. And about the secrets
she hid so well.

Keeper of the Light

Available wherever books are sold.

DIANE
CHAMBERLAIN

Maya and Rebecca Ward are
both accomplished physicians,
but that's where the sisters'
similarities end. Maya runs a
sedate medical practice with her
husband, Adam, while Rebecca
is a risk taker.

After a hurricane hits the
coast of North Carolina, Maya
reluctantly joins the relief effort
with Rebecca and Adam. When
Maya's helicopter crashes, there
appear to be no survivors.

Forced to accept that Maya
is gone, Rebecca and Adam
turn to one another—first for
comfort, then in passion—
unaware that, miles from
civilization, Maya is injured
and trapped with strangers
she can't trust. Maya must save
herself—while the life she knew
has changed forever.

The Lies We Told

*Available wherever
books are sold.*

A riveting novel by acclaimed author

DIANE CHAMBERLAIN

An unsolved murder.
A missing child.
A lifetime of deception.

In 1977 pregnant Genevieve Russell
disappeared. Twenty years later her
remains are discovered and
Timothy Gleason is charged with
murder. But there is no sign of
an unborn child.

CeeCee Wilkes knows how
Genevieve Russell died, because
she was there. Now Timothy Gleason
is facing the death penalty, and she
has to make a choice...tell the
truth and destroy her family,
or let an innocent man die
in order to protect a lifetime
of lies....

the SECRET LIFE of
CeeCee Wilkes

"Diane Chamberlain is
a marvelously gifted author!
Every book she writes is a real gem!"
—*Literary Times*

Available wherever books are sold.

MIRA®

DIANE CHAMBERLAIN

On her eleventh birthday, Daria Cato discovers an abandoned newborn baby on the beach beside her North Carolina home. The infant cannot be identified and is adopted by Daria's loving family. But her silent secrets continue to haunt Daria.

Now, twenty years later, Shelly has grown into an unusual, ethereal young woman whom Daria continues to protect. But when Rory Taylor, a friend from Daria's childhood and now a television producer, returns at Shelly's request to do a story about the circumstances surrounding her birth, closely guarded secrets and the sins of that long-ago summer begin to surface and a mystery nobody wants to face becomes exposed.

Summer's Child

Available wherever books are sold.

MIRA®